ONE STEP BEHIND

Henning Mankell is the prize-winning and inter-
nationally acclaimed author of the Inspector
Wallander Mysteries, now dominating bestseller
lists throughout Europe. He devotes much of his
time to working with Aids charities in Africa,
where he is also director of the Teatro Avenida in
Maputo.

Ebba Segerburg teaches English at Washington
University in St Louis, Missouri.

ALSO BY HENNING MANKELL

Fiction

Faceless Killers
The Dogs of Riga
The White Lioness
The Man Who Smiled
Sidetracked
The Fifth Woman
Firewall
The Return of the Dancing Master
Before the Frost
Chronicler of the Winds
Depths
Kennedy's Brain
The Eye of the Leopard

Non-fiction

I Die, but the Memory Lives On

Young Adult Fiction

A Bridge to the Stars
Shadows in the Twilight
When the Snow Fell
The Journey to the End of the World

HENNING MANKELL

One Step Behind

TRANSLATED FROM THE SWEDISH BY
Ebba Segerberg

VINTAGE BOOKS
London

Published by Vintage 2008

6 8 10 9 7

First published with the title *Steget Efter* by Ordfronts Förlag
Stockholm 1997

First published in Great Britain in 2002 by the Harvill Press

Vintage
Random House, 20 Vauxhall Bridge Road,
London SW1V 2SA

www.vintage-books.co.uk

Addresses for companies within The Random House Group Limited can
be found at: www.randomhouse.co.uk/offices.htm

The Random House Group Limited Reg. No. 954009

A CIP catalogue record for this book
is available from the British Library

ISBN 9780099526636

The Random House Group Limited supports The Forest
Stewardship Council (FSC), the leading international forest
certification organisation. All our titles that are printed on
Greenpeace approved FSC certified paper carry the FSC logo.
Our paper procurement policy can be found at
www.rbooks.co.uk/environment

Printed and bound in Great Britain by
CPI Cox & Wyman, Reading RG1 8EX

There are always many more disordered than ordered systems

FROM THE SECOND LAW OF THERMODYNAMICS

The Overture to *Rigoletto*

GIUSEPPE VERDI

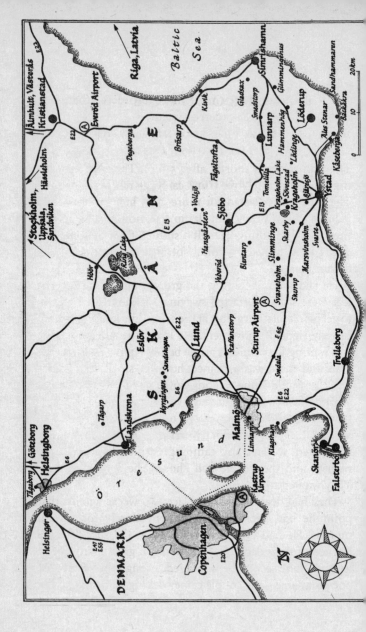

PROLOGUE

The rain stopped shortly after 5 p.m. The man crouching beside the thick tree trunk carefully removed his coat. The rain hadn't lasted for more than half an hour, and it hadn't been heavy, but damp had nonetheless seeped through his clothing. He felt a sudden flash of anger. He didn't want to catch a cold. Not now, not in the middle of summer.

He laid the raincoat on the ground and stood up. His legs were stiff. He started swaying back and forth gently to get his circulation going, at the same time looking around for any signs of movement. He knew that the people he was waiting for wouldn't arrive before 8 p.m. That was the plan. But there was a chance, however small, that someone else would come walking down one of the paths that snaked through the nature reserve. That was the only factor that lay beyond his control, the only thing he couldn't be sure of. Even so, he wasn't worried. It was Midsummer's Eve. There weren't any camping or picnic areas in the reserve, and the people had chosen the spot with care. They wanted to be alone.

They had decided on this place two weeks ago. At that point he had been following them closely for several months. He had even come to look at the spot after he learned of their decision. He had taken great pains not to let himself be seen as he wandered through the reserve. At one point an elderly couple came walking along one of the paths and he had hidden himself behind some trees until they passed.

Later, when he found the spot for their Midsummer festivities, he had immediately been struck by how ideal it was. It lay in a hollow with thick undergrowth all around. There were a few trees further up the hill. They couldn't have chosen a better spot – not for their purposes, nor his own.

The rain clouds were dispersing. The sun came out and it immediately became warmer. It had been a chilly June. Everyone had complained about the early summer in Skåne, and he had agreed. He always did. It's the only way to sidestep life's obstacles, he thought, to escape whatever crosses one's path. He had learned the art of agreeing.

He looked up at the sky. There would be no more rain. The spring and early summer had really been quite cold. But now, as evening approached on Midsummer's Eve, the sun came out at last. It will be a beautiful evening, he thought. As well as memorable.

The air smelt of wet grass. He heard the sound of flapping wings somewhere. To the left below the hill was a glimpse of the sea. He stood with his legs apart and spat out the wad of chewing tobacco that had started to dissolve in his mouth, then stamped it into the sand. He never left a single trace. He often thought that he should stop using tobacco. It was a bad habit, something that didn't suit him.

They had decided to meet in Hammar. That was the best place, since two of them were coming from Simrishamn and the others from Ystad. They would drive out to the nature reserve, park their cars, and walk to the spot they had chosen. They had not been able to agree upon anything for a long time. They had discussed various alternatives and sent the proposals back and forth. But when one of them finally suggested this place, the others had quickly assented, perhaps because they had run out of time. One of them took care of the food, while another went to Copenhagen and rented the clothes and wigs that were needed. Nothing would be left to chance. They even took the possibility of bad weather into account. At 2 p.m. on Midsummer's Eve, one of them put a big tarpaulin in his red duffel bag. He also included a roll of tape and some old aluminium tent pegs. If it rained, they would have shelter.

Everything was ready. There was only one thing that could not have been anticipated. One of them suddenly became ill. It was a young woman, the one who had perhaps been looking forward to the Midsummer's Eve plans most of all. She had met the others less than a year before. When she woke up that morning she had felt nauseated. At first she thought it was because she was nervous. But some hours later, when it was already midday, she had started vomiting and running a temperature. She still hoped it would pass. But when her lift arrived, she stood at the door on trembling legs and said that she was too ill to go.

Consequently, there were only three of them in Hammar shortly before 7.30 p.m on Midsummer's Eve. But they did not allow this to spoil the mood. They were experienced; they knew that these things happened. One could never guard against sudden illness.

They parked outside the nature reserve, took their baskets, and disappeared down one of the paths. One of them thought he heard an accordion in the distance. But otherwise there were just birds and the distant sound of the sea.

When they arrived at the selected spot they knew at once

that it had been the right choice. Here they would be undisturbed and free to await the dawn.

The sky was now completely free of clouds. The midsummer night would be clear and beautiful. They had made the plans for Midsummer's Eve at the beginning of February, when they had spoken of their longing for light summer nights. They had drunk large quantities of wine and quarrelled at length about the precise meaning of the word dusk. At what point did this particular moment between light and dark arrive? How could one really describe the landscape of twilight in words? How much could you actually still see when the light passed into this obscure state of transition, defined by a certain length of the shadows? They had not come to an agreement. The question of dusk had remained unsolved. But they had started planning their celebration that evening.

They arrived at the hollow and put down their baskets, then separated and changed behind some thick bushes. They wedged small make-up mirrors in the branches so they could check that their wigs were on straight.

None of them sensed the man who observed their careful preparations from a distance. Getting the wigs to sit straight turned out to be the easiest part. Putting on the corsets, padding and petticoats was more difficult, as was arranging the cravat and the ruffles, not to mention applying the thick layers of powder. They wanted every detail to be perfect. They were playing a game, but the game was in earnest.

At 8 p.m. they came out from behind their bushes and looked at each other. It was a breathtaking moment. Once more they had left their own time for another age. The age of Bellman, the bacchanalian 18th-century poet.

They drew closer and burst into laughter. But then they

4

regained their composure. They spread out a large table-cloth, unpacked their baskets and put on a tape with several renditions of the most famous songs from Bellman's work, *Fredman's Epistles*. Then the celebration began.

When winter comes, they said to each other, we will think back on this evening. They were creating yet another secret for themselves.

At midnight he had still not made up his mind. He knew he had plenty of time. They would be staying until dawn. Perhaps they would even stay and sleep all morning. He knew their plans down to the last detail. It gave him a feeling of unlimited power. Only he who had the upper hand would escape.

Just after 11 p.m., when he could tell that they were tipsy, he had carefully changed his position. He had picked out the starting point for his actions on his first visit. It was a dense thicket a bit higher up the hill. Here he had a full view of everything that was happening on the light-blue tablecloth. And he could approach them without being seen. From time to time they left the tablecloth in order to relieve themselves. He could see everything they did.

It was past midnight. Still he waited. He waited because he was hesitating. Something was wrong. There should have been four of them. One of them had not come. In his head he went through the possible reasons. There was no reason. Something unexpected must have happened. Had the girl changed her mind? Was she sick?

He listened to the music and the laughter. From time to time he imagined that he too sat down there on the light-blue tablecloth, a wineglass in his hand. Afterwards he would try on one of the wigs. Perhaps some of the clothes, too? There was so much he could do. There were no limits. He could not have had more power over them if he had been invisible.

He continued to wait. The laughter rose and fell. Somewhere above his head a night bird swooped by.

It was 3.10 a.m. He couldn't wait any longer. The moment was at hand, the hour he alone had appointed. He could barely remember the last time he had worn a watch. The hours and minutes ticked continuously within him. He had an inner clock that was always on time.

Down by the light-blue tablecloth everything was still. They lay with their arms wrapped around one another, listening to the music. He didn't know if they were sleeping, but they were lost in the moment, and did not sense that he was right behind them.

He picked up the revolver with the silencer that had been lying on his raincoat. He looked around quickly, then made his way stealthily to the tree located directly behind the group, and paused for a few seconds. No one had noticed anything. He looked around one last time. But there was no one else there. They were alone.

He stepped out and shot each of them once in the head. He couldn't help it that blood splattered onto the white wigs. It was over so quickly that he barely had time to register what he was doing. But now they lay dead at his feet, still wrapped around each other, just like a few seconds before.

He turned off the tape recorder that had been playing and listened. The birds were chirping. Once again he looked around. Of course there was no one there. He put his gun away and spread a napkin out on the cloth. He never left a trace.

He sat down on the napkin and looked at those who

had recently been laughing and who now were dead. The idyll hasn't been affected, he thought. The only difference is that we are now four. As the plan had been all along.

He poured himself a glass of red wine. He didn't really drink, but now he simply couldn't resist. Then he tried on one of the wigs. He ate a little of the food. He wasn't particularly hungry.

At 3.30 a.m. he got up. He still had much to do. The nature reserve was frequented by early risers. In the unlikely event that someone left the path and found their way into the hollow, they must not find any traces. At least not yet.

The last thing he did before he left the spot was look through their bags and clothes. He found what he was looking for. All three had been carrying their passports. Now he put them into his coat pocket. Later that day he would burn them.

He looked around one last time. He took a little camera out of his pocket and took a picture.

Only one. It was like looking at a painting of a picnic from the 18th century, except that someone had spilled blood on this painting.

It was the morning after Midsummer's Eve. Saturday, June 22. It was going to be a beautiful day. Summer had come to Skåne at last.

Part One

CHAPTER ONE

On Wednesday, 7 August 1996, Kurt Wallander came close to being killed in a traffic accident just east of Ystad. It happened early in the morning, shortly after 6 a.m. He had just driven through Nybrostrand on his way out to Österlen. Suddenly he had seen a truck looming in front of his Peugeot. He heard the truck's horn blaring as he wrenched the steering wheel to one side.

Afterwards he had pulled off the road. That was when the fear set in. His heart pounded in his chest. He felt nauseated and dizzy, and he thought he was about to faint. He kept his hands tightly clenched on the wheel. As he calmed down he realised what had happened. He had fallen asleep at the wheel. Nodded off just long enough for his old car to begin to drift into the opposite lane. One second longer and he would have been dead, crushed by the heavy truck.

The realisation made him feel suddenly empty. The only thing he could think of was the time, a few years earlier, when he had almost hit an elk outside Tingsryd. But then it had been dark and foggy. This time he had nodded off at the wheel.

The fatigue. He didn't understand it. It had come over him without warning, shortly before the start of his holiday at the beginning of June. This year he had taken his holiday early, but the whole holiday had been lost to rain. It was only when he returned to work shortly after

Midsummer that the warm and sunny weather had come to Skåne. The tiredness had been there all along. He fell asleep whenever he sat down. Even after a long night's undisturbed sleep, he had to force himself out of bed. Often when he was in the car he found himself needing to pull over to take a short nap.

His daughter Linda had asked him about his lack of energy during the week that they had spent sightseeing together in Gotland. It was on one of the last days, when they had stayed in an inn in Burgsvik. They had spent the day exploring the southern tip of Gotland, and had eaten dinner at a pizzeria before returning to the inn. The evening was particularly beautiful.

She had asked him point-blank about the fatigue. He had studied her face in the glow of the kerosene lamp and realised that her question had been thought out in advance, but he shrugged it off. There was nothing wrong with him. Surely the fact that he used part of his holiday to catch up on lost sleep was to be expected. Linda didn't ask any more questions. But he knew that she hadn't believed him.

Now he realised that he couldn't ignore it any longer. The fatigue wasn't natural. Something was wrong. He tried to think if he had other symptoms that could signal an illness. But apart from the fact that he sometimes woke in the middle of the night with leg cramps, he hadn't been able to think of anything. He knew how close to death he had been. He couldn't put it off any longer. He would make an appointment with the doctor that day.

He started the engine, rolling down the windows as he drove on. Although it was already August, the heat of summer showed no sign of easing. Wallander was on his way to his father's house in Löderup. No matter how many times he went down this road, he still found it hard to adjust to the fact that his father wouldn't be sitting there in his studio, wreathed in the ever-present smell of turpentine, before the easel on which he painted pictures with a recurring and unchanging subject: a landscape, with or without a grouse in the foreground, the sun hanging from invisible threads above the trees.

It had been close to two years now since Gertrud had called him at the police station in Ystad to tell him that his father was lying dead on the studio floor. He could still recall with photographic clarity his drive out to Löderup, unable to believe it could be true. But when he had seen Gertrud in the yard, he had known he could not deny it any longer. He had known what awaited him.

The two years had gone by quickly. As often as he could, but not often enough, he visited Gertrud, who still lived in his father's house. A year went by before they began to clean up the studio in earnest. They found a total of 32 finished paintings. One night in December of 1995, they sat down at Gertrud's kitchen table and made a list of the people who would receive these last paintings. Wallander kept two for himself, one with a grouse, the other without. Linda would get one, as would Mona, his ex-wife. Surprisingly, and to Wallander's disappointment, his sister Kristina hadn't wanted one. Gertrud already had several, and so they had 28 paintings to give away. After some hesitation, Wallander sent one to a detective in Kristianstad with whom he had sporadic contact. But after giving away 23 paintings, including one to each of Gertrud's relatives, there were five paintings remaining.

Wallander wondered what he should do with them. He knew that he would never be able to make himself burn them. Technically they belonged to Gertrud, but she had said that he and Kristina should have them. She had come into their father's life so late.

Wallander passed the turn-off to Kåseberga. He would be there soon. He thought about the task that lay before him. One evening in May, he and Gertrud had taken a long walk along the tractor paths that wound their way along the edges of the linseed fields. She had told him that she no longer wanted to live there. It was starting to get too lonely.

"I don't want to live there so long that he starts to haunt me," she had said.

Instinctively, he knew what she meant. He would probably have reacted the same way. They walked between the fields and she asked for his help in selling the house. There was no hurry; it could wait until the summer's end, but she wanted to move out before the autumn. Her sister was recently widowed and lived outside the town of Rynge, and she wanted to move there.

Now the time had come. Wallander had taken the day off. At 9 a.m. an estate agent would come out from Ystad, and together they would settle on a reasonable selling price. Before that, Wallander and Gertrud would go through the last few boxes of his father's belongings. They had finished packing the week before. Martinsson, one of his colleagues, came out with a trailer and they made several trips to the dump outside Hedeskoga. Wallander experienced a growing sense of unease. It seemed to him that the remnants of a person's life inevitably ended up at the nearest dump.

All that was left of his father now – aside from the memories – were some photographs, five paintings, and a few boxes of old letters and papers. Nothing more. His life was over and completely accounted for.

Wallander turned down the road leading to his father's house. He caught a glimpse of Gertrud waiting in the yard. To his surprise he saw that she was wearing the same dress she had worn at their wedding. He immediately felt a lump in his throat. For Gertrud, this was a moment of solemnity. She was leaving her home.

They drank coffee in the kitchen, where the doors to the cupboards stood ajar, revealing empty shelves. Gertrud's sister was coming to collect her today. Wallander would keep one key and give the other to the estate agent. Together they leafed through the contents of the two boxes. Among the old letters Wallander was surprised to find a pair of children's shoes that he seemed to remember from his childhood. Had his father saved them all these years?

He carried the boxes out to the car. When he closed the car door, he saw Gertrud on the steps. She smiled.

"There are five paintings left. You haven't forgotten about them, have you?"

Wallander shook his head. He walked towards his father's studio. The door was open. Although they had cleaned it, the smell of turpentine remained. The pot that his father had used for making his endless cups of coffee stood on the stove.

This may be the last time I am here, he thought. But unlike Gertrud, I haven't dressed up. I'm in my baggy old clothes. And if I hadn't been lucky I could be dead, like my father. Linda would have had to drive to the dump with what was left after me. And among my stuff she would find two paintings, one with a grouse painted in the foreground.

The place scared him. His father was still in there in the dark studio. The paintings were leaning against one wall. He carried them to the car. Then he laid them in the boot and spread a blanket over them. Gertrud remained on the steps.

"Is there anything else?" she asked.

Wallander shook his head. "There's nothing else," he answered. "Nothing."

At 9 a.m. the estate agent's car swung into the yard, and a man got out from behind the wheel. To his surprise, Wallander realised that he recognised him. His name was Robert Åkerblom. A few years earlier his wife had been brutally murdered and her body dumped in an old well. It had been one of the most difficult and grisly murder investigations that Wallander had ever been involved in.

He frowned. He had decided to contact a large estate agent with offices all over Sweden. Åkerblom's business did not belong to them, if it even still existed. Wallander thought he had heard that it had shut down shortly after Louise Åkerblom's murder.

He went out onto the steps. Robert Åkerblom looked exactly as Wallander remembered him. At their first meeting in Wallander's office he had wept. The man's worry and grief for his wife had been genuine. Wallander recalled that they had been active in a non-Lutheran church. He thought they were Methodists.

They shook hands. "We meet again," Robert Åkerblom said.

His voice sounded familiar. For a second Wallander felt confused. What was the right thing to say? But Robert Åkerblom beat him to it.

"I grieve for her as much now as I did then," he said slowly. "But it's even harder for the girls."

Wallander remembered the two girls. They had been so young then. They had been unable to fully understand what had happened.

"It must be hard," Wallander said. For a moment he was afraid that the events of the last meeting would repeat themselves; that Robert Åkerblom would start crying. But that didn't happen.

"I tried to keep the business going," Åkerblom said, "but I didn't have the energy. When I got the offer to join the firm of a competitor, I took it. I've never regretted it. I don't have the long nights of going over the books any more. I've been able to spend more time with the girls."

Gertrud joined them and they went through the house together. Åkerblom made notes and took some photographs. Afterwards they had a cup of coffee in the kitchen. The price that Åkerblom came up with seemed low to Wallander at first, but then he realised that it was three times what his father had paid for the place.

Åkerblom left a little after 11 a.m. Wallander thought he should stay until Gertrud's sister came to get her, but she seemed to sense his thoughts and told him she didn't mind being left alone.

"It's a beautiful day," she said. "Summer has come at last, even though it's almost over. I'll sit in the garden."

"I'll stay if you like. I'm off work today."

Gertrud shook her head. "Come and see me in Rynge," she said. "But wait a couple of weeks. I have to get settled in."

Wallander got in his car and drove back to Ystad. He was going straight home to make an appointment with his doctor. Then he would sign up to use the laundry and clean his flat. Since he wasn't in a hurry, he chose the longer way home. He liked driving, just looking at the landscape and letting his mind wander. He had just passed Valleberga when the phone rang. It was Martinsson. Wallander pulled over.

"I've been trying to get hold of you," Martinsson said. "Of course no one mentioned that you were off work today. And do you know that your answerphone is broken?"

Wallander knew the machine sometimes jammed. He also immediately knew that something had happened. Although he had been a policeman for a long time, the feeling was always the same. His stomach tensed up. He held his breath.

"I'm calling you from Hansson's office," Martinsson said. "Astrid Hillström's mother is here to see me."

"Who?"

"Astrid Hillström. One of the missing young people. Her mother."

Now Wallander knew who he meant.

"What does she want?"

"She's very upset. Her daughter sent her a postcard from Vienna."

Wallander frowned. "Isn't it good news that she's finally written?"

"She claims her daughter didn't write the postcard. She's upset that we're not doing anything."

"How can we do anything when a crime doesn't seem to have been committed, when all the evidence indicates that they left of their own accord?"

Martinsson paused for a moment before answering. "I don't know what it is," he said. "But I have a feeling that there's something to what she's saying. Maybe."

Wallander immediately grew more attentive. Over the years he had learned to take Martinsson's hunches seriously. More often than not, they were proved right.

"Do you want me to come in?"

"No, but I think you, me, and Svedberg should talk this over tomorrow morning."

"What time?"

"How about 8 a.m.? I'll tell Svedberg."

Wallander sat for a moment when the conversation was over, watching a tractor out on a field. He thought about what Martinsson had said. He had also met Astrid Hillström's mother on several occasions. He went over the events again in his mind. A few days after Midsummer's Eve some young people were reported missing. It happened right after he had returned from his rainy holiday. He had reviewed the case together with a couple of his colleagues. From the outset he had doubted that a crime had been committed and, as it turned out, a postcard arrived from Hamburg three days later, with a picture of the central railway station on the front. Wallander could recall its message word for word. *We are travelling around Europe. We may be gone until the middle of August.*

Today it was Wednesday, 7 August. They would be home soon. Now another postcard written by Astrid Hillström came from Vienna. The first card was signed by all three of them. Their parents recognised the signatures. Astrid Hillström's mother hesitated, but she allowed herself to be convinced by the others.

Wallander glanced in his rear-view mirror and drove out onto the main road. Perhaps Martinsson was right about his misgivings.

Wallander parked on Mariagatan and carried the boxes and five paintings up to his flat. Then he sat down by the phone. At his regular doctor's office he only reached an answerphone message telling him that the doctor wouldn't be back from holiday until August 12th. Wallander wondered if he should wait until then, but he couldn't shake the thought of how close to death he had come that morning. He called another doctor and made an appointment for 11 a.m. the following morning. He signed up to do his laundry, then started cleaning his flat. He was already completely exhausted after doing the bedroom. He ran the vacuum cleaner back and forth a few times over the living room floor, then put it away. He carried the boxes and paintings into the room that Linda used on her sporadic visits. He drank three glasses of water in the kitchen, wondering about his thirst and the fatigue. What was causing them?

It was already midday, and he realised he was hungry. A quick look in the refrigerator told him there wasn't much there. He put on his coat and went out. It was a nice day. As he walked to the centre of town, he looked at the properties for sale in the windows of three separate real estate offices, and realised that the price Robert Åkerblom had suggested was fair. They could hardly get more than 300,000 kronor for the house in Löderup.

He stopped at a takeaway restaurant, ate a hamburger and drank two bottles of mineral water. Then he went into a shoe shop where he knew the owner, and used the lavatory. When he came back out onto the street, he felt unsure of what to do next. He should have used his day off to do his shopping. He had no food in the house, but he didn't have the energy to go back for the car and drive to a supermarket.

Just past Hamngatan, he crossed the train tracks and turned down Spanienfararegatan. When he arrived down at the waterfront, he strolled along the pier and looked at the sailing boats, wondering what it would be like to sail. It was something he had never experienced. He realised he needed to pee again, and used the lavatories at the harbour café, drank another bottle of mineral water, and sat down on a bench outside the red coast guard building.

The last time he had been here it had been winter, the night Baiba left. It was already dark as he drove her to Sturup Airport, and the wind made whirls of snow dance in the headlights. They hadn't said a word. After he had watched her disappear past the checkpoint, he had returned to Ystad and sat on this bench. The wind had been very cold and he was freezing, but he sat here and realised that everything was over. He wouldn't see Baiba again. Their breakup was final.

She came to Ystad in December of 1994. His father had recently died and he had just finished one of the most challenging investigations of his career. But that autumn he had also, for the first time in many years, been making plans for the future. He decided to leave Mariagatan, move to the country, and get a dog. He had even visited a kennel and looked at Labrador puppies. He was going to make a fresh start. And above all, he wanted Baiba to come and live with him. She visited him over Christmas and Wallander could tell that she and Linda got along well. Then, on New Year's Eve 1995, the last few days before she was due to return to Riga, they talked seriously about the future. Maybe she would move to Sweden permanently as early as next summer. They looked at houses together. They looked at a house on a subdivision of an old farm outside Svenstorp several times. But then, one evening in March, when Wallander was already in bed, she called from Riga and told him she was having doubts. She didn't want to get married, didn't want to move to Sweden – at least not yet. He thought he would be able to get her to change her mind, but the conversation ended with an unpleasant quarrel, their first, after which they didn't speak for more than a month. Finally, Wallander called her and they decided he would go to Riga that summer. They spent two weeks by the sea in a run-down old house that she had borrowed from one of her colleagues at the university.

They took long walks on the beach and Wallander made a point of waiting for her to broach the question of the future. But when she finally did, she was vague and noncommittal. Not now, not yet. Why couldn't things stay as they were?

When Wallander returned to Sweden, he felt dejected and unsure of where things stood. The autumn went by without another meeting. They had talked about it, made plans, and considered various alternatives, but nothing had eventuated. Wallander became jealous. Was there another man in Riga? Someone he didn't know anything about? On several occasions he called her in the middle of the night and although she insisted that she was alone, he had the distinct feeling that there was someone with her.

Baiba had come to Ystad for Christmas that year. Linda had been with them on Christmas Eve before leaving for Scotland with friends. And it was then, a couple of days into the new year, that Baiba had told him she could never move to Sweden. She had gone back and forth in her mind for a long time. But now she knew. She didn't want to lose her position at the university. What could she do in Sweden, especially in Ystad? She could perhaps become an interpreter, but what else? Wallander tried in vain to persuade her to change her mind. Without saying so explicitly, they knew it was over. After four years there was no longer any road leading into the future. Wallander spent the rest of that winter evening on the frozen bench, feeling more abandoned than ever before. But then another feeling had crept over him. Relief. At least he now knew where things stood.

A motorboat sped out of the harbour. Wallander got up. He needed to find a lavatory again.

They called each other from time to time, but gradually that had stopped too. Now they hadn't been in touch for over six months. One day when he and Linda were walking around Visby she had asked if things with Baiba were finally over.

"Yes," he replied. "It's over."

She had waited for him to continue.

"I don't think either of us really wanted to break it off," he had told her. "But it was inevitable."

When he got home, he lay down on the sofa to read the paper but fell asleep almost immediately. An hour later he woke up with a start in the middle of a dream. He had been in Rome with his father. Rydberg had also been with them, and some small, dwarf-like creatures who insisted on pinching their legs.

I'm dreaming about the dead, he thought. What does that mean? I dream about my father almost every night and he's dead. So is Rydberg, my old colleague and friend, the one who taught me everything I can claim to know. And he's been gone for almost five years.

He went out to the balcony. It was still warm and calm. Clouds were starting to pile up on the horizon. Suddenly it struck him how terribly lonely he was. Apart from Linda, who lived in Stockholm and whom he saw only occasionally, he had almost no friends. The people he spent time with were people from work. And he never saw them socially.

He went into the bathroom and washed his face. He looked in the mirror and saw that he had a tan, but the tiredness still shone through. His left eye was bloodshot. His hairline had receded further. He stepped on the scales, and noted that he weighed a couple of kilos less than he had at the start of the summer, but it was still too much.

The phone rang. It was Gertrud.

"I just wanted to let you know that I made it safely to Rynge. Everything went well."

"I've been thinking about you," Wallander told her. "I should have stayed there with you."

"I think I needed to be alone with all my memories. But things will be fine here. My sister and I get along well. We always have."

"I'll be out to see you in a week or so."

After he had hung up the phone rang again immediately. This time it was his colleague Ann-Britt Höglund.

"I just wanted to hear how it went," she said.

"How what went?"

"Weren't you supposed to meet with an estate agent today to discuss selling your father's house?"

Wallander recalled that he had mentioned it to her the day before.

"It went pretty well," he said. "You can buy it for 300,000 kronor if you like."

"I never even got to see it," she replied.

"It feels quite strange," he told her. "The house is so empty now. Getrud has moved and someone else will buy it. It'll probably be used as a summer house. Other people will live in it and not know anything about my father."

"All houses have ghosts," she said. "Except the newest ones."

"The smell of turpentine will linger for a while," Wallander said. "But when that's gone there will be nothing left of the people who once lived there."

"That's so sad."

"It's just the way it is. I'll see you tomorrow. Thanks for calling."

Wallander went to the kitchen and drank some water. Ann-Britt was a very thoughtful person. She remembered things. He would never have thought to do the same if the situation had been reversed.

It was already 7 p.m. He fried some Falu sausage and potatoes and ate in front of the TV. He flipped through the channels, but nothing seemed interesting. Afterwards he took his cup of coffee and went out onto the balcony. As soon as the sun went down, it grew cooler, and he went back in again.

He spent the rest of the evening going through the things he had brought back from Löderup earlier that day. At the bottom of one of the boxes there was a brown envelope. When he opened it he found a couple of old, faded photographs. He couldn't recall ever having seen them before. He was in one of them, aged four or five, perched on the hood of a big American car. His father was standing beside him so he wouldn't fall off.

Wallander took the photograph into the kitchen and got a magnifying glass from one of the kitchen drawers.

We're smiling, he thought. I'm looking straight into the camera and beaming with pride. I've been allowed to sit on one of the art dealer's cars, one of the men who used to buy my father's paintings for outrageous prices. My father is also smiling, but he's looking at me.

Wallander sat with the snapshot for a long time. It spoke to him from a distant and unreachable past. Once upon a time he and his father had been very close, but all that had changed when he decided to become a policeman. In the last few years of his father's life, they had slowly been

25

retracing their steps back to the closeness that had been lost.

But we never made it this far, Wallander thought. Not all the way back to the smile I had as I sat on the hood of this gleaming Buick. We almost got there in Rome, but it still wasn't like this.

Wallander tacked the photo to his kitchen door. Then he went back out onto the balcony. The clouds had come closer. He sat down in front of the TV and watched the end of an old movie.

At midnight he went to bed. He had a meeting with Svedberg and Martinsson the next day, and he had to go to the doctor. He lay awake in the darkness for a long time. Two years ago he had thought about moving from the flat on Mariagatan. He had dreamed of getting a dog, of living with Baiba. But nothing had come of it. No Baiba, no house, no dog. Everything had stayed the same.

Something's got to happen, he thought. Something that makes it possible for me to start thinking about the future again.

It was almost 3 a.m. before he finally fell asleep.

CHAPTER TWO

The clouds started clearing during the early hours of the morning. Wallander was already awake at 6 a.m. He had been dreaming about his father again. Fragmented and unconnected images had flickered through his subconscious. In the dream he had been both a child and an adult. There had been no coherent story. Recalling the dream was like trying to follow a ship into fog.

He got up, showered, and drank some coffee. When he walked out onto the street he noticed that the warmth of summer still lingered and that it was unusually calm. He drove to the police station. It was not yet 7 a.m., and the corridors were empty. He got another cup of coffee and went into his office. For once his desk was virtually free of folders and he wondered when he'd last had so little to do. During the past few years Wallander had seen his workload increase in proportion to the diminishing resources of the police force. Investigations were rushed or ignored altogether. Often a preliminary report resulted in a suspected crime going uninvestigated. Wallander knew that this would not be the case if only they had more time, if only there were more of them.

Did crime pay? That age-old question was still open to debate. Even those who felt that crime now had the upper hand were hard-pressed to pinpoint the moment when the tables had turned. Wallander was convinced that the criminal element had a stronger hold in Sweden than ever before. Criminals engaged in sophisticated financial dealings seemed to live in a safe haven, and the judicial system seemed to have capitulated completely.

Wallander often discussed these problems with his colleagues. He noticed that civilian fears at these developments were growing. Gertrud talked about it. The neighbours he ran into in the laundry talked about it. Wallander knew their fears were justified. But he didn't see any signs of preventive measures being taken. On the contrary, the reduction of numbers within the police force and judicial personnel continued. He took off his coat, opened the window, and looked out at the old water tower.

During the last few years, vigilante groups had been on the rise in Sweden, groups like The Civilian Guard. Wallander had long feared this development. When the justice system started to break down, the lynching mentality of the mob took over. Taking justice into one's own hands came to seem normal.

As he stood there at the window, he wondered how many illegal weapons were floating around Sweden. And he wondered what the figures would be in a couple of years.

He sat down at his desk. His door was slightly ajar and he heard voices out in the corridor, and a woman's laugh. Wallander smiled. That was their chief of police, Lisa Holgersson. She had replaced Björk a few years ago. Many of Wallander's colleagues had resisted the idea of a woman in such a high position, but Wallander gained respect for her early on.

The phone rang. It was Ebba, the receptionist.

"Did it go well?" she asked.

Wallander realised she meant yesterday. "The house isn't sold yet, of course," he said. "But I'm sure it will go well."

"I'm calling to see if you have time to talk to some visitors at 10.30 this morning."

"Visitors at this time of year?"

"It's a group of retired marine officers who meet in Skåne every August. They have some sort of society. I think they call themselves 'The Sea Bears'."

Wallander thought about his doctor's appointment. "I think you'll have to ask someone else this time," he answered. "I'm going to be out between 10.30 and midday."

"Then I'll ask Ann-Britt. These old sea captains might enjoy talking to a woman police officer."

"Or else they'll think just the opposite," Wallander said.

By 8 a.m. Wallander had not managed to do anything more than rock back and forth in his chair and look out the window. Tiredness gnawed at his body, and he was worried about what the doctor would find. Were the fatigue and cramps signs of a serious illness?

He got up out of his chair and walked to one of the conference rooms. Martinsson was already there, looking clean-cut and tanned. Wallander thought about the time, two years earlier, when Martinsson had come very close to giving up his career. His daughter had been attacked in the playground because her father was a policeman. But he had stuck it out. To Wallander he would always be the young man who had just joined the force, despite the fact that he had worked in Ystad longer than most of them.

They sat down and talked about the weather. After five minutes Martinsson said, "Where the hell is Svedberg?"

His question was justified, since Svedberg was known for his punctuality.

"Did you talk to him?"

"He had already gone when I tried to reach him. But I left a message on his answerphone."

Wallander nodded in the direction of the telephone that stood on the table.

"You should probably give him another call."

Martinsson dialled the number.

"Where are you?" he asked. "We're waiting for you."

He put the receiver down. "I'm just getting the machine."

"He must be on his way," Wallander said. "Let's start without him."

Martinsson leafed through a stack of papers. Then he pushed a postcard over to Wallander. It was an aerial shot of central Vienna.

"This is the card that the Hillström family found in their letter box on Tuesday, 6 August. As you can see, Astrid Hillström says that they're thinking of staying a little longer than they had originally planned. But everything is fine and they all send their regards. She asks her mother to call around and tell everyone that they're well."

Wallander read the card. The handwriting reminded him of Linda's. It was the same round lettering. He put it back.

"Eva Hillström came here, you said."

"She literally burst into my office. We knew she was the nervous type, but this was something else. She's clearly terrified and convinced that she's right."

"What's she so sure of?"

"That something's happened to them. That her daughter didn't write that postcard."

Wallander thought for a moment. "Is it the handwriting? The signature?"

"It resembles Astrid Hillström's writing. But her mother claims it's a very easy style to copy, as is her signature. She's right about that."

Wallander pulled over a notebook and a pen. In less

than a minute he had perfected Astrid Hillström's hand-writing and signature.

"Eva Hillström is anxious about her daughter's welfare and turns to the police. That's understandable. But if it isn't the handwriting or the signature that's worrying her, then what is it?"

"She couldn't say."

"But you did ask her."

"I asked her about everything. Was there something about the choice of words? Or was there something in the way she put it? She didn't know. But she was certain that her daughter hadn't written the card."

Wallander made a face and shook his head. "It must have been something."

They looked at each other.

"Do you remember what you said to me yesterday?" Wallander asked. "That you were starting to get worried yourself?"

Martinsson nodded. "Something doesn't add up," he said. "I just can't put my finger on it."

"Let's put the question another way," Wallander said. "If they haven't left on this unplanned holiday, then what's happened? And who's writing these cards? We know that their cars and their passports are missing."

"I'm obviously mistaken," Martinsson answered. "I was probably influenced by Eva Hillström's anxiety."

"Parents always worry about their children," Wallander said. "If you only knew how many times I've wondered what Linda was up to. Especially when you get postcards from strange places all around the world."

"So what do we do?" Martinsson asked.

"We continue to keep the situation under surveillance," Wallander said. "But let's go over the facts from the beginning, just to make sure we haven't missed anything."

Martinsson summarised the events in his unfailingly clear fashion. Ann-Britt Höglund had once asked Wallander if he realised that Martinsson had learned how to make presentations by observing him. Wallander had scoffed at this, but Höglund had stood her ground. Wallander still didn't know if it was true.

The chain of events was simple enough. Three people, all between the ages of 20 and 23, decided to celebrate Midsummer's Eve together. One of them, Martin Boge, lived in Simrishamn, while the other two, Lena Norman and Astrid Hillström, came from the western part of Ystad. They were old friends and spent a lot of time together. Their parents were all wealthy. Lena Norman was studying at Lund University while the other two had temporary jobs. None of them had ever had any problems with the law or with drugs. Astrid Hillström and Martin Boge still lived at home; Lena Norman lived in halls of residence in Lund. They didn't tell anyone where they were planning to hold their Midsummer's Eve party. Their parents had talked to one another and to their friends but no one seemed to know anything. This was not unusual, since they were often secretive and never divulged their plans to outsiders. At the time of their disappearance, they had two cars at their disposal: a Volvo and a Toyota. These cars disappeared at the same time as their owners, on the afternoon of 21 June. After that no one had seen them again. The first postcard was sent on 26 June from Hamburg, stating their intention to travel through Europe. A couple of weeks later, Astrid Hillström had sent a second postcard from Paris in which she explained that they were on their way south. And now she had apparently sent a third postcard.

Martinsson stopped talking.

Wallander reflected on what he had said. "What could possibly have gone wrong?" he asked.

"I have no idea."

"Is there any indication of anything out of the ordinary in relation to their disappearance?"

"Not really."

Wallander leaned back in his chair. "The only thing we have is Eva Hillström's anxiety," he said. "A worried mother."

"She claims her daughter didn't write the cards."

Wallander nodded. "Does she want us to file a missing persons report?"

"No. She wanted us to do something. That was how she put it: 'You have to do something.'"

"What can we really do other than file the report? We've alerted Customs."

They fell silent. It was already 8.45 a.m. Wallander looked questioningly at Martinsson.

"Svedberg?"

Martinsson picked up the receiver and dialled Svedberg's number, then hung up.

"The answerphone again."

Wallander pushed the postcard back across the table to Martinsson. "I don't think we're going to get much further," he said. "But I think I'll have a talk with Eva Hillström. Then we'll evaluate what action to take from here. But we have no grounds for declaring this a missing persons case, at least not yet."

Martinsson wrote her number on a piece of paper. "She's an accountant."

"And the father?"

"They're divorced. I think he called once, just after Midsummer."

Wallander got up while Martinsson collected the

33

papers. They left the conference room together.

"Maybe Svedberg did the same thing I did and took a day off without us being told about it."

"He's already been on holiday," Martinsson said emphatically. "He hasn't got any holidays left."

Wallander looked at him with surprise. "How do you know that?"

"I asked him if he could switch one of his weeks with me. But he couldn't because for once he wanted an unbroken chunk of time."

"I don't think he's ever done that before," Wallander said.

They parted outside Martinsson's office and Wallander went to his office. He sat down at his desk and dialled the first phone number Martinsson had given him. Eva Hillström answered the phone. They agreed that she should come by the police station later that afternoon.

"Has anything happened?" she asked.

"No," Wallander answered. "I just think I should talk to you as well."

He hung up and was about to go and get a cup of coffee when Höglund appeared at his door. Although she had just returned from a holiday, she was as pale as ever. Wallander thought her pallor came from within. She still hadn't recovered from a serious gunshot wound of two years earlier. She was healed physically, but Wallander doubted how well she was emotionally. Sometimes he felt that she was still afraid. It didn't surprise him. Almost every day, he thought about the time that he had been stabbed. And that had happened more than 20 years ago.

"Is this a good time?"

Wallander gestured to the chair opposite his desk, and she sat down.

"Have you seen Svedberg?" he asked.

She shook her head.

"He was supposed to come to a meeting with me and Martinsson, but he didn't show up."

"He's not one to miss a meeting."

"You're right. But he did today."

"Have you called him at home? Is he sick?"

"Martinsson left several messages on his answerphone. And besides, Svedberg is never sick."

They contemplated Svedberg's absence for a while.

"What was it you wanted to talk to me about?" Wallander asked finally.

"Do you remember those Baltic car smugglers?"

"How could I forget? I worked on that miserable case for two years before we got them. At least the ones in Sweden."

"Well, it seems as though it's started up again."

"Even with the leaders in jail?"

"It looks like others have stepped in to fill their shoes. Only this time they aren't working out of Gothenburg. Their tracks point towards Lycksele, among other places."

Wallander was surprised. "Lapland?"

"With today's technology you can operate from virtually anywhere."

Wallander shook his head, but he knew that Höglund was right. Organised criminals always made use of the latest technology.

"I don't have the energy to start again," he said. "No more car smuggling for me."

"I'll take it on. Lisa asked me to. I think she realises how tired you are of stolen cars. But I'd like you to outline the situation for me, as well as give me a couple of pointers."

Wallander nodded. They set a time for the next day, then went and got some coffee and sat down by an open window in the canteen.

"How was your holiday?" he asked.

Her eyes suddenly filled with tears. Wallander went to say something but she stopped him with a gesture.

"It wasn't so great," she said when she had regained her composure. "But I don't want to talk about it."

She picked up her cup of coffee and got up quickly. Wallander watched her leave. He remained seated, thinking about her reaction.

We don't know very much, he thought. They don't know much about me and I don't know much about them. We work together, maybe over the course of an entire career, and what do we learn about each other? Nothing.

He looked down at his watch. He had plenty of time, but he decided to set off walking down to Kapellgatan, where the doctor's office was. He was filled with dread.

The doctor was young. He was called Göransson and came from somewhere up north. Wallander told him about his symptoms: the fatigue, the thirst, the increased urination. He also mentioned his leg cramps.

The doctor's diagnosis was swift, and surprised him.

"It sounds like too much sugar," he said.

"Sugar?"

"Diabetes."

For a split second Wallander was paralysed. The thought had never occurred to him.

"You look like you weigh a little too much," the doctor said. "We'll find out if that's the case. But I want to start off by listening to your heart. Do you know if you have high blood pressure?"

Wallander shook his head. Then he took off his shirt and lay down on the table.

His pulse was normal, but his blood pressure was too high. 170 over 105. He got on the scale: 92 kilos. The doctor sent him for a urinalysis and a blood test. The nurse smiled at him. Wallander thought she looked like his sister Kristina. After she had finished, he went back in to see the doctor.

"Normally you should have a blood-sugar level of between 2.5 and 6.4," Göransson said. "Yours is 15.3. That's much too high."

Wallander started to feel sick.

"This explains your fatigue," Göransson continued. "It explains your thirst and the leg cramps. It also explains why you need to urinate so often."

"Is there medication for this?" Wallander asked.

"First we'll try to control it by changing your diet," Göransson said. "We also have to reduce your blood pressure. Do you exercise frequently?"

"No."

"Then you'll have to start right away. Diet and exercise. If that doesn't help we'll have to go a step further. With this blood-sugar level you're wearing down your whole system."

I'm diabetic, Wallander thought. At that moment it struck him as something shameful.

Göransson seemed to sense his dismay. "This is something we can control," he said. "You won't die from it. At least not yet."

They took more blood tests, and Wallander was given dietary guidelines, and was told to come back on Monday morning.

He left the surgery at 11.30 a.m. He walked over to the cemetery and sat down on a bench. He still couldn't grasp what the doctor had told him. He found his glasses and started reading the meal plans.

He got back to the police station at 12.30. There were some phone messages for him, but nothing that couldn't wait. He bumped into Hansson in the corridor.

"Has Svedberg turned up?" Wallander asked.

"Why, isn't he in?"

Wallander didn't elaborate. Eva Hillström was supposed to come in shortly after 1 p.m. He knocked on Martinsson's half-open door, but the room was empty. The thin folder from their meeting that day was lying on the desk. Wallander took it and went into his office. He quickly leafed through the few papers there were and stared at the three postcards, but he was having trouble concentrating. He kept thinking about what the doctor had told him.

Finally Ebba called him from the reception desk and told him that Eva Hillström had arrived. Wallander walked out to meet her. A group of older, jovial men were on their way out. Wallander guessed they were the retired marine officers who had come for a tour.

Eva Hillström was tall and thin. Her expression was guarded. From the first time he met her, Wallander formed the impression that she was the kind of person who always expected the worst. He shook her hand and asked her to follow him to his office. On the way he asked her if she wanted a cup of coffee.

"I don't drink coffee," she said. "My stomach can't take it."

She sat down in the visitor's chair without taking her eyes off him.

She thinks I have news for her, Wallander thought. And she expects the news to be bad.

He sat down at his desk. "You spoke with my colleague yesterday," he said. "You brought by a postcard you received a couple of days earlier, signed by your daughter and sent from Vienna. But you claim it wasn't written by her. Is that correct?"

"Yes." Her answer was forceful.

"Martinsson said you couldn't explain why you felt this way."

"That's right, I can't."

Wallander took out the postcards and laid them in front of her.

"You said that your daughter's handwriting and signature are easy to forge."

"Try for yourself."

"I've already done that. And I agree with you; her handwriting isn't very hard to copy."

"Then why do you have to ask?"

Wallander looked at her for a moment. She was just as tense as Martinsson had described.

"I'm asking these questions in order to confirm certain statements," he said. "It's sometimes necessary."

She nodded impatiently.

"We have no real reason to believe that someone other than Astrid wrote these cards," Wallander said. "Can you think of anything else that makes you doubt their authenticity?"

"No, but I know I'm right."

"Right about what?"

"That she didn't write this card, or any of the others."

Suddenly, she stood up and started to scream at him. Wallander was completely unprepared for the violence of her reaction. She was leaning over his desk, and she grabbed his arms and shook him, screaming the whole time.

"Why don't you do anything? Something must have happened!"

Wallander freed himself from her grasp with some difficulty and stood up.

"I think you'd better calm down," he said.

But Eva Hillström kept screaming. Wallander wondered what people walking by his door were thinking. He went around his desk, grabbed her firmly by the shoulders, pushed her down in the chair and and held her there. Her outburst stopped as abruptly as it had begun. Wallander slowly loosened his grip and returned to his chair. Eva Hillström stared down at the floor. Wallander waited, thoroughly shaken. There was something about her reaction, something about her conviction, that was contagious.

"What is it that you think has happened?" he asked after a little while.

She shook her head. "I don't know."

"There is nothing to indicate an accident or anything else."

She looked at Wallander.

"Astrid and her friends have gone on trips before," he said. "Although perhaps not for as long as this one. They had cars, money, passports. My colleagues have gone over this before. What's more, they're of an age when you're inclined to act on impulse without having made prior plans. I have a daughter myself who is a couple of years older than Astrid. I know how it is."

"I just know," she said. "I know I tend to worry. But this time there's something that doesn't feel right."

"The other parents don't seem quite as worried as you do. What about Martin Boge's and Lena Norman's parents?"

"I don't understand them."

"We take your concern seriously," he said. "That's our job. I promise to review this case one more time."

His words seemed to reassure her momentarily, but then the anxiety returned. Her face was open and vulnerable. Wallander felt sorry for her.

The conversation was over. She got up, and he followed her out to the reception area.

"I'm sorry I lost control," she said.

"It's natural to be worried," Wallander said.

She shook his hand quickly, then disappeared through the glass doors.

Wallander went back to his room. Martinsson stuck his head out the door of his office and looked at him with curiosity.

"What were you doing in there?"

"She's genuinely frightened," Wallander said. "We have to acknowledge that; but I don't know what to do about it." Wallander looked thoughtfully at Martinsson. "I'd like to do a thorough review of this case tomorrow with everyone who has the time. We have to decide if we should declare them missing or not. Something about this whole thing worries me."

Martinsson nodded. "Have you seen Svedberg?" he asked.

"He still hasn't been in touch?"

"No. Just the same old answerphone message."

Wallander grimaced. "That's not like him."

"I'll try him again."

Wallander continued to his room. He closed the door and called Ebba. "No calls for the next half hour," he said. "Anything from Svedberg, by the way?"

"Should there be?"

"I was just wondering."

Wallander put his legs up on the desk. He was tired and his mouth was dry. On an impulse, he grabbed his coat and left the room.

"I'm going out," he told Ebba. "I'll be back in an hour or two."

It was still warm and calm. Wallander went down to the central library on Surbrunnsvägen. With some effort he found his way to the medical section. Soon he found what he was looking for: a book about diabetes. He sat down at a table, put his glasses on, and started reading. After an hour and a half he thought he had a better idea of what diabetes entailed. He realised he only had himself to blame. The foods he ate, his lack of exercise, and his on-and-off dieting had all contributed to the disease. He put the book back on the shelf. A sense of failure and disgust came over him. He knew there was no way out. He had to do something about his lifestyle.

It was already 4.20 p.m. when he returned to the police station. There was a note on his desk from Martinsson saying that he still hadn't managed to get in touch with Svedberg.

Once more Wallander read through the summary of events regarding the disappearance of the three young people. He scrutinised the three postcards. The feeling that there was something he was overlooking returned. He still couldn't pin it down. What was there he wasn't seeing?

He felt his anxiety increase and could almost see Eva Hillström in front of him. Suddenly the gravity of the situation struck him. It was very simple. She knew her daughter hadn't written that card. How she knew this was irrelevant. She was sure and that was enough. Wallander got up and stopped in front of the window. Something had happened to them. The question now was what.

CHAPTER THREE

That evening Wallander tried to start his new regime. All he had for dinner was some bouillon soup and a salad. He was concentrating so hard on making sure that only the right things found their way onto his plate that he forgot he had signed up for the laundry, and by the time he remembered it was too late.

He tried to convince himself that what had happened could be viewed as something positive. An elevated blood-sugar level was not a death sentence; he had been given a warning. If he wanted to stay healthy, he would have to take some simple precautions. Nothing drastic, but he would have to make significant changes.

When he was done eating, he still felt hungry, and ate another tomato. Then, still sitting at the kitchen table, he tried to make a meal plan for the coming days from his dietary guidelines. He also decided to walk to work from now on. On the weekends he would drive to the beach and take long walks. He remembered that he and Hansson once talked about playing badminton. Perhaps that could still be arranged.

At 9 p.m. he got up from the kitchen table and went out onto the balcony. The wind was blowing softly from the south, but it was still warm. The dog days were here.

Wallander watched some teenagers walking past on the street below. It was hard to concentrate on his meal plans and recommended weight chart. Thoughts of Eva

Hillström and her anxiety kept returning to him. Her outburst had shaken him. The fear she felt at her daughter's disappearance was plain to see, and it was genuine.

Sometimes parents don't know their children, he thought. But sometimes a parent knows her child better than anyone else, and something tells me that this is the case with Eva Hillström and her daughter.

He went back into the flat and left the door to the balcony open. He had the feeling that he was overlooking something that would indicate how they should proceed; something that would lead them to a well-founded, investigative hypothesis, and to determine whether Eva Hillström's concerns were justified.

He went out into the kitchen and made some coffee, wiping the table clean while he waited for the water to boil. The phone rang. It was Linda. She was calling from the restaurant where she worked, which surprised him since he thought it was open only during the day.

"The owner changed the hours," she said in answer to his question, "and I make more money working in the evenings. I have to make a living."

He could hear voices and the rattle of pots and pans in the background. He had no idea what Linda's plans for her future were. For a time she wanted to become a furniture upholsterer, then she changed her mind and started exploring the world of theatre. Then that plan also came to an end.

She seemed to read his thoughts. "I'm not going to be a waitress all my life," she said. "But I'm saving some money right now and next winter I'm going to travel."

"Where to?"

"I don't know yet."

It wasn't the right time to discuss this in detail, so he

mentioned that Gertrud had moved and that her grandfather's house was on the market.

"I wish we had kept it," she said. "I wish I had the money
to buy it."

Wallander understood. Linda had been close to her
grandfather. There were even times when seeing them
together had made him jealous.

"I have to go now," she said. "I just wanted to hear how
you were."

"Everything is fine," Wallander replied. "I went to the
doctor today. He didn't find anything wrong with me."

"Didn't he even tell you to lose weight?"

"Apart from that, he said that everything was fine."

"That doctor was too nice. Are you still as tired as you
were on holiday?"

She sees right through me, Wallander thought helplessly. And why don't I tell her the truth, that I'm becoming a diabetic, that I may already be one? Why am I behaving
as if it were something shameful?

"I'm not tired," he said. "That week on Gotland was an
exception."

"If you say so," she said. "I've got to go now. If you want
to reach me here in the evenings you'll have to call a new
number."

He quickly memorised it. Then the conversation was
over.

Wallander took his coffee with him into the living room
and turned on the TV. He turned the sound down, then
jotted down the phone number she had given him on the
corner of a newspaper. He wrote sloppily. No one else would
have been able to read the number. It was at that moment
that he realised what was bothering him. He pushed his
coffee cup away and looked at his watch. It was 9.15 p.m.

He wondered briefly if he should call Martinsson, and wait until the following day before making up his mind. He went into the kitchen, got out the phone book, and sat down at the kitchen table.

There were four families called Norman in Ystad, but Wallander remembered seeing the address among Martinsson's papers. Lena Norman and her mother lived on Käringgatan, north of the hospital. Her father was called Bertil Norman and had the title "CEO" next to his name. Wallander knew that he owned a company that supplied heating systems for pre-fabricated houses.

He dialled the number and a woman answered. Wallander introduced himself, trying to sound as friendly as possible. He didn't want to worry her. He knew how unnerving it was to be called by the police, especially after hours.

"Am I speaking to Lena Norman's mother?"

"This is Lillemor Norman."

Wallander recognised the name.

"This conversation could really have waited until tomorrow," he said. "But there is something I need to know and unfortunately policemen work all hours of the day and night."

She did not seem particularly concerned. "How can I help you? Or would you like to speak with my husband? I can get him for you. He's just helping Lena's brother with his maths homework."

Her answer surprised him. He hadn't realised that schools still had anything called homework.

"That won't be necessary," he said. "What I want is a sample of Lena's handwriting. Do you have any letters from her?"

"Well, apart from the postcards, we haven't received anything. I thought the police knew that."

"I mean an old letter."

"Why do you need it?"

"It's just routine procedure. We need to compare some handwriting samples, that's all. It's not particularly important."

"Do policemen really bother calling people at night about such unimportant matters?"

Eva Hillström is afraid, Wallander thought. Lillemor Norman, on the other hand, is suspicious.

"Do you think you can help me?"

"I have a number of letters from Lena."

"One is enough. About half a page."

"I'll find one. Will someone be by to pick it up?"

"I'll come myself. Expect me in about 20 minutes."

Wallander went back to the phone book. In Simrishamn he found only one entry for the name "Boge", an accountant. Wallander dialled the number and waited impatiently. He was just about to hang up when someone answered.

"Klas Boge."

The voice that answered sounded young. Wallander assumed it was Martin Boge's brother. He told him who he was.

"Are your parents home?"

"No, I'm alone. They're at a golf dinner."

Wallander wasn't sure he should continue. But the boy seemed reasonably mature.

"Has your brother Martin ever written a letter to you? Anything you might have saved?"

"Not this summer."

"Earlier, perhaps?"

The boy thought for a moment. "I have a letter he wrote to me from the United States last year."

"Was it handwritten?"

47

"Yes."

Wallander calculated how long it would take him to drive to Simrishamn. Perhaps he should wait until the next morning.

"Why do you want one of his letters?"

"I just need a sample of his handwriting."

"Well, I could fax it over to you if you're in a hurry."

The boy was a fast thinker. Wallander gave him the number of one of the faxes at the police station.

"I'd like you to mention this matter to your parents," he said.

"I'm planning to be asleep when they get back."

"Could you tell them about it tomorrow?"

"Martin's letter was addressed to me."

"It would be best if you mentioned it anyway," Wallander said patiently.

"Martin and the others will be back soon," the boy said. "I don't know why that Hillström lady is so worried. She calls us every day."

"But your parents aren't worried?"

"I think they're relieved that Martin's gone. At least Dad is."

Somewhat surprised, Wallander waited to see if the boy would go on, but he didn't.

"Thanks for your help," he said finally.

"It's like a game," the boy said.

"A game?"

"They pretend they're in a different time. They like to dress up, like children do, even though they're grown up."

"I'm not sure that I follow," Wallander said.

"They're playing roles, like you would in the theatre. But it's for real. They might have gone to Europe to find something that doesn't really exist."

"So that was what they normally did? Play? But I'm not sure I would call a Midsummer's Eve celebration a game. It's just the same eating and dancing as at any other party."

"And drinking," the boy said. "But if you put on costumes, that makes it something else, doesn't it?"

"Is that what they did?"

"Yes, but I don't know more. It was secret. Martin never said much about it."

Wallander didn't completely follow what the boy was saying. He looked down at his watch. Lillemor Norman would be expecting him shortly.

"Thanks for your help," he said, bringing the conversation to an end. "And don't forget to tell your parents that I called and what I asked for."

"Maybe," the boy replied.

Three different reactions, Wallander thought. Eva Hillström is afraid. Lillemor Norman is suspicious. Martin Boge's parents are relieved he's gone, and his brother in turn seems to prefer it when their parents are gone. He picked up his coat and left. On the way out, he reserved a new time at the laundry for Friday.

Although it wasn't far to Käringgatan, he took the car. The new exercise regimen would have to wait. He turned onto Käringgatan from Bellevuevägen, and stopped outside a white two-storey house. The front door opened as he was opening the gate, and he recognised Lillemor Norman. In contrast to Eva Hillström, she looked robust. He thought about the photographs in Martinsson's file and realised that Lena Norman and her mother looked alike.

The woman was holding a white envelope.

"I'm sorry to bother you," Wallander said.

"My husband will have a few words with Lena when she

comes back. It's completely irresponsible of them to go away like this without a word."

"They're adults and can do as they please," Wallander said. "But of course it's both irritating and worrying."

He took the letter and promised to return it. Then he drove to the police station and went to the room where the officer on duty was manning the phones. He was taking a call as Wallander stepped into the room, but pointed to one of the fax machines. Klas Boge had faxed his brother's letter as promised. Wallander went to his office and turned on the desk lamp. He laid the two letters and the postcards next to each other, then angled the light and put on his glasses.

He leaned back in his chair. His hunch was correct. Both Martin Boge and Lena Norman had irregular, spiky handwriting. If someone had wanted to forge any one of the three's handwriting, the choice would have been clear: Astrid Hillström. Wallander felt profoundly disturbed by this, but his mind kept working methodically. What did this mean? It was nothing, really. It didn't supply an answer to why someone would want to write postcards in their names, and who would have had access to their handwriting. Nonetheless, he couldn't shake off his concern.

We have to go through this thoroughly, he thought. If something has happened, they've been missing for almost two months.

He got himself a cup of coffee. It was 10.15 p.m. He read through the description of events one more time but found nothing new. Some good friends had celebrated Midsummer's Eve together, then left for a trip. They sent a few postcards. And that was all.

Wallander shuffled the letters together and put them in the folder along with the postcards. There was nothing more he could do tonight. Tomorrow he would talk to Martinsson and the others, go through this Midsummer's Eve case one last time, and then decide if they would proceed with a missing persons investigation.

Wallander turned off the light and left the room. In the corridor he realised that Ann-Britt Höglund's light was on. The door was slightly ajar, and he pushed it open gently. She was staring down at her desk but there were no papers in front of her. Wallander hesitated. She almost never stayed this late at the station. She had children to take care of, and her husband travelled often with his job and was rarely at home. He recalled her emotional behaviour in the canteen. And now here she was staring down at an empty desk. She probably wanted to be left alone. But it was also possible that she wanted to talk to somebody.

She can always ask me to leave, Wallander thought.

He knocked on the door, waited for her answer, and stepped inside.

"I saw your light," he said. "You aren't normally here so late, not unless something has happened."

She looked back at him without answering.

"If you want to be left alone, just say the word."

"No," she replied. "I don't really want to be left alone. Why are you here yourself? Is something going on?"

Wallander sat down in her visitor's chair. He felt like a big, lumbering animal.

"It's the young people who went missing at Midsummer."

"Has anything turned up?"

"Not really. There was just something I wanted to double-check. But I think that we'll need to do a thorough reexamination of the case. Eva Hillström is seriously concerned."

"But what could really have happened to them?"

"That's the question."

"Are we going to declare them missing?"

Wallander threw his arms out. "I don't know. We'll have to decide tomorrow."

The room was dark except for the circle of light projected onto the floor by the desk lamp.

"How long have you been a policeman?" she asked suddenly.

"A long time. Too long, maybe. But I'm a policeman through and through. That's not going to change, at least until I retire."

She looked at him for a long time before asking her next question. "How do you keep going?"

"I don't know."

"Don't you ever run out of steam?"

"Sometimes. Why do you ask?"

"I'm thinking of what I said in the canteen earlier. I told you I'd had a bad summer and that's true. My husband and I are having problems. He's never at home. It can take us a week to get back to normal after his trips, and then he just has to leave again. This summer we started talking about a separation. That's never an easy thing, especially when you have children."

"I know," Wallander said.

"At the same time I've started questioning my work. I read in the paper that some of our colleagues in Malmö were arrested for racketeering. I turn on the television and learn that senior members of the force are involved in the world of organised crime. I see all this and I realise it's happening more and more. Eventually it leads me to wonder what I'm doing. Or, to put it another way, I wonder how I'm going to last another 30 years."

"It's all coming apart at the seams," Wallander agreed.

"It's been going on for a long time. Corruption in the justice system is nothing new and there have always been police officers willing to cross the line. It's worse now, of course, and that's why it's even more important that people like you keep going."

"What about you?"

"That applies to me too."

"But how do you do it?"

Her questions were full of anger. He recognised a part of himself in her. How many times had he sat staring into his own desk, unable to find a reason to continue?

"I try to tell myself that things would be even worse without me," he said. "It's a consolation at times. A small one, but if I can't think of any other I take it."

She shook her head. "What's happening to our country?"

Wallander waited for her to continue, but she didn't. A truck rattled past on the street outside.

"Do you remember that violent attack last spring?" Wallander asked.

"The one in Svarte?"

"Two boys, both 14 years old, attack a third boy who is only 12. There's no provocation, no reason behind it. When he's lying there unconscious they start stomping on his chest. Finally he's not just unconscious, he's dead. I don't think it ever hit me so clearly before. People have always had fights, but they would stop when the other person was down. You can call it what you like. Fair play. Something you take for granted. But that's not the way it is any more, because these boys never learned it. It's as if a whole generation has been abandoned by their parents. Or as if not caring has become the norm. You have to rethink what it means to be a police officer because the parameters have changed. The experience you've acquired after years and years of grinding work doesn't apply any more."

He stopped. They heard voices from the corridor. Some of the officers on night duty were talking about a drunk driver. Then everything went quiet again.

"How have you been these past few years?" he asked her.

"You mean since I was shot?"

He nodded.

"I dream about it," she said. "I dream that I die or that the bullet hits me in the head. I think that's almost worse."

"It's easy to lose your nerve," Wallander said.

She got up. "The day I get seriously scared I'll quit," she said. "But I'm not quite there yet. Thanks for stopping by. I'm used to dealing with my problems on my own, but tonight I needed someone to talk to."

"It takes some strength to admit that."

She put her coat on and smiled her pale smile. Wallander wondered how well she was sleeping, but he didn't ask her.

"Can we talk about the car smugglers tomorrow?" she asked.

"How about in the afternoon? Don't forget we have to talk about these young people in the morning."

She looked at him closely.

"Are you really worried?"

"Eva Hillström is, and I can't disregard that."

They walked out together. She rejected his offer of a ride home.

"I need to walk," she said. "And it's so warm. What an August it's been!"

"We're in the dog days," he said. "Whatever that saying means."

They said goodbye. Wallander drove home. He drank a cup of tea and leafed through the Ystad daily paper, then

54

went to bed. He left the window slightly open since it was so warm, and fell asleep at once.

A violent pain woke him up with a start. His left calf muscle was locked in a spasm. He lowered his leg onto the floor and flexed it. The pain disappeared. He lay down again carefully, afraid that the cramp would return. The alarm clock on the bedside table read 1.30 a.m. He had been dreaming about his father again, in a disjointed way. They walked around the streets of a city that Wallander didn't recognise. They were looking for someone. Who, he never found out.

The curtain in front of the window moved slowly. He thought about Linda's mother, Mona. He had been married to her for a long time. Now she was living a new life with another man who played golf and probably did not have elevated blood-sugar levels.

His thoughts kept wandering. All at once he saw himself walking along Skagen's endless beaches with Baiba. Then she was gone.

Suddenly he was wide awake. He sat up in bed. He didn't know where the thought came from; it simply appeared among the others and fought its way to the front: Svedberg.

The fact that he hadn't called in sick didn't make sense. Not only was he never sick, if something had happened he would have let them know. He should have thought of it before. If Svedberg hadn't been in contact, it could only mean one thing: something was preventing him from communicating with them.

Wallander felt himself getting worried. Of course it was just his imagination. After all, what could have happened to Svedberg? But the feeling of unease was strong. Wallander looked at the clock again, then went out into the kitchen, searched for Svedberg's number, and dialled it. After a few rings the machine picked up. Wallander hung up. Now he was sure that something was wrong. He put on his clothes and went down to the car. The wind had picked up but it was still warm. It took him only a few minutes to drive to the main square. He parked the car and walked towards Lilla Norregatan where Svedberg lived. The lights were on inside his flat. Wallander felt relieved, but only for a few seconds. Then the worry returned even more strongly. Why didn't Svedberg pick up the phone if he was at home? Wallander tried the door to the building. It was locked. He didn't know the security code, but the crack between the front doors was wide enough. Wallander took out a pocketknife and looked around. Then he slipped the thickest blade between the doors and pushed. They opened.

Svedberg lived on the fourth floor. Wallander was out of breath by the time he made it up the stairs. He pressed his ear against the door but heard nothing. Then he opened the letter slot. Nothing. He rang the bell, the sound echoing inside the flat. He rang three times, then pounded on the door. Still nothing.

Wallander tried to gather his thoughts. He felt a strong urge not to be alone. He groped for his mobile phone but realised it was still on the kitchen table at home. He went down the stairs and pushed a small stone between the two front doors. Then he hurried out to one of the telephone booths on the main square, and dialled Martinsson's number.

"I'm sorry to have to wake you up," Wallander said when Martinsson answered, "but I need your help."

"What is it?"

"Did you ever get hold of Svedberg?"

"No."

"Then something must have happened."

Martinsson didn't reply, but Wallander sensed that he was now fully awake.

"I'm waiting for you outside his block of flats on Lilla Norregatan," Wallander said.

"Ten minutes," Martinsson said. "At the most."

Wallander went to his car and unlocked the boot. He had some tools wrapped up in a dirty plastic bag. He took out a crowbar, then returned to Svedberg's building.

After less than ten minutes Martinsson drove up. Wallander saw that he was wearing his pyjama top under his jacket.

"What do you think has happened?"

"I don't know."

They walked upstairs together. Wallander nodded to Martinsson to ring the doorbell. Still no one answered. They looked at each other.

"Maybe he keeps some spare keys in his office."

Wallander shook his head.

"It'll take us too long," he said.

Martinsson took a step back. He knew what would be next. Wallander wedged the crowbar into the door, and forced it open.

CHAPTER FOUR

The night of 8 August 1996 became one of the longest of Kurt Wallander's life. When he staggered out from the flat building on Lilla Norregatan at dawn, he still hadn't managed to rid himself of the feeling that he was caught up in an incomprehensible nightmare.

But everything he had seen during that long night had been real, and this reality was horrifying. He had witnessed the remains of a bloody and brutal drama many times in the course of his career, but never had it touched him as closely as now.

When he forced open the door to Svedberg's flat he still didn't know what lay in store for him. Yet from the moment he wedged the crowbar in the door he had feared the worst, and his fears had been confirmed.

They walked silently through the hall as if they were about to enter enemy territory. Martinsson stayed close behind. Lights were shining further down the hall. For a brief moment they stood there without making a sound. Wallander heard Martinsson's anxious breathing behind him. In the doorway to the living room, he jerked back so violently that he collided with Martinsson, who then bent forward to look at what Wallander had seen.

Wallander would never forget the sound Martinsson made, the way he whimpered like a child in front of the inexplicable thing before him on the floor.

It was Svedberg. One of his legs was hanging over the

broken arm of a chair that had been knocked over. The torso was strangely twisted, as if Svedberg had no spine.

Wallander stood in the doorway, frozen with horror. There was no doubt in his mind about what he was seeing. The man he had worked with for so many years was dead. He no longer existed. He would never again sit in his usual place at the table in one of the conference rooms, scratching his bald spot with the end of a pencil.

Svedberg didn't have a bald spot any more. Half of his head was blown away.

A short distance from the body lay a double-barrelled shotgun. Blood was spattered several metres up the white wall behind the overturned chair. A confused thought went through Wallander's mind: now Svedberg will never be troubled by his phobia for bees again.

"What happened?" Martinsson said in an unsteady voice. Wallander realised that Martinsson was close to tears. He was a long way from such a reaction. He couldn't cry over something he didn't yet fully comprehend. And he really didn't comprehend the scene in front of him. Svedberg couldn't be dead. He was a 40-year-old police officer who would be in his usual chair again tomorrow when they had one of their regular team meetings. Svedberg with his bald spot, his fear of bees, who used the police station's sauna on his own every Friday night. It simply couldn't be Svedberg who lay there. It was someone else who looked just like him.

Wallander glanced instinctively at his watch. It was 2.09 a.m. They stood in the doorway for a few more seconds, then walked back out into the hall. Wallander turned on the light. He saw that Martinsson was shaking. He wondered what he looked like himself.

"Tell them to put all units on red alert."

There was a phone on a table in the hall, but no

answerphone. Martinsson nodded and was about to pick up the receiver when Wallander stopped him.

"Wait," he said. "We need time to think."

But what was there really to think about? Maybe he was hoping for a miracle, that Svedberg would suddenly appear behind them and that nothing they had seen would turn out to be real.

"Do you know Lisa Holgersson's number?" he asked. He knew from experience that Martinsson had a good head for addresses and numbers. There used to be two with this particular gift: Martinsson and Svedberg. Now only one was left.

Martinsson recited the number, stammering. Wallander dialled and Lisa Holgersson picked up on the second ring. Her phone must be right beside her bed, he thought.

"This is Wallander. I'm sorry to wake you up."

She seemed awake at once.

"You should come down here right away," he said. "I'm in Svedberg's flat on Lilla Norregatan. Martinsson is also here. Svedberg is dead."

He heard her groan. "What happened?"

"I don't know. He's been shot."

"That's terrible. Is it murder?"

Wallander thought about the shotgun on the floor.

"I don't know," he said. "Murder or suicide, I don't know which."

"Have you been in touch with Nyberg?"

"I wanted to call you first."

"I'll be right over, I just have to get dressed."

"We'll contact Nyberg in the meantime."

Wallander handed the phone to Martinsson. "Start with Nyberg," he said.

The living room was accessible from two directions. While Martinsson used the phone, Wallander walked out through the kitchen. A kitchen drawer lay on the floor. The door to a cupboard was ajar. Papers and receipts lay strewn all over the room.

Wallander made a mental note of everything he saw. He could hear Martinsson explaining to Nyberg, the head of forensics in Ystad, what had happened. Wallander kept walking. He looked carefully where he was going before putting his feet down. He came to Svedberg's bedroom. All three drawers in a chest of drawers were pulled out. The bed was unmade and the blanket lay on the ground. With a feeling of boundless sorrow he noted that Svedberg had slept in flowery sheets. His bed was a meadow of wildflowers. Wallander kept going, arriving at a little study between the bedroom and living room. There were some bookcases and a desk. Svedberg was a neat person. His desk at the police station was kept meticulously free of clutter. But here his books had been pulled from their shelves, and the contents of the desk lay on the floor. There was paper everywhere.

Wallander entered the living room again, this time from the other side. Now he was closer to the shotgun, with Svedberg's twisted body at the far end. He stood completely still and took in the whole scene, every detail, everything that had been frozen and left behind as a marker of the drama that had taken place. The questions raced through his mind. Had someone heard the shot or shots? The scene suggested that a burglary had taken place. But when did it happen? And what else happened here?

Martinsson appeared in the doorway on the other side of the living room.

"They're on their way," he said.

Wallander slowly retraced his steps. When he was back in the kitchen he heard the bark of a German shepherd and then Martinsson's agitated voice. He hurried out to the hall and bumped into a dog patrol. Some people in bathrobes were huddled in the background. The patrol officer with the dog was called Edmundsson and had recently moved to Ystad.

"We received a call about a possible burglary," he said uncertainly when he saw Wallander. "At the flat of someone called Svedberg."

Wallander realised that Edmundsson had no idea which Svedberg the caller had been talking about.

"Good. There has been an incident here. By the way, it's Officer Svedberg's flat.".

Edmundsson went pale. "I didn't know."

"How could you? But you can go back to the station. Back-up is on its way."

Edmundsson looked inquiringly at him. "What's happened?"

"Svedberg is dead," Wallander answered. "That's all we know."

He immediately regretted having said even that much. The neighbours were listening. Someone could take it into their heads to call the press. What Wallander wanted least of all was to have reporters hanging about. A policeman dying in mysterious circumstances was always news.

As Edmundsson disappeared down the stairs, Wallander thought fuzzily that he didn't know what the dog was called.

"Can you take care of the neighbours?" he said to Martinsson. "If nothing else, they must have heard the shots. Maybe we can establish a time of death."

"Was there more than one shot?"

"I don't know, but someone must have heard something."

The front door slammed below them and they heard approaching footsteps. Martinsson started rounding up the sleepy and anxious people and herded them into the flat next door. Lisa Holgersson came rushing up the stairs.

"I want you to prepare yourself," Wallander said.

"Is it that bad?"

"Svedberg was shot in the head with a shotgun at close range."

She made a face, then steeled herself. Wallander followed her into the hall and pointed to the living room. She went up to the doorway then quickly turned away and swayed as if she were about to faint. Wallander took her by the arm and helped her into the kitchen. She sank down on a blue kitchen chair, and looked up at Wallander with wide eyes.

"Who did this?" she asked.

"I don't know."

Wallander took a glass and gave her some water.

"Svedberg was away yesterday," he said. "Without telling anyone."

"That's unusual," said Holgersson.

"Very unusual. I woke up in the middle of the night with a feeling that things weren't quite right, so I drove over."

"So you don't think it happened yesterday?"

"No. Martinsson is talking to the neighbours to see if anyone heard anything unusual, which they probably did. A shotgun is loud. But we'll have to wait for the autopsy report."

Wallander heard his factual statement echo inside his head. He felt nauseated.

"I know he wasn't married," said Holgersson. "Did he have any family?"

Wallander thought back. He knew that Svedberg's mother had died a couple of years earlier. He didn't know anything about his father. The only relative Wallander knew about for sure was one he had met a few years earlier during a murder investigation.

"He has a cousin called Ylva Brink. She's an obstetric nurse. I can't think of anyone else."

They heard Nyberg's voice out in the hall.

"I'll stay here for a few minutes," said Holgersson.

Wallander went out to talk to Nyberg, who was kicking off his shoes.

"What the hell happened here?"

Nyberg was a brilliant forensic specialist, but he was moody and could be hard to work with. He seemed not to have understood that this emergency concerned a colleague. A dead colleague. Maybe Martinsson had forgotten to tell him.

"Do you know where you are?" Wallander asked carefully.

Nyberg shot him an angry look.

"Some flat on Lilla Norregatan," he answered. "But Martinsson was unusually muddled on the phone. What's going on?"

Wallander looked at him steadily. Nyberg noticed his demeanour and became quiet.

"It's Svedberg," Wallander said. "He's dead. It looks like he's been murdered."

"You mean Kalle?" Nyberg said incredulously.

Wallander nodded and felt a lump in his throat. Nyberg was one of the few who called Svedberg by his first name. His name was actually Karl Evert. Nyberg used his nickname, Kalle.

"He's in there," Wallander said. "Shot in the face with a shotgun."

Nyberg grimaced.

"I don't have to tell you what that looks like," Wallander said.

"No," Nyberg said. "You don't have to do that."

Nyberg went in. He turned away like the others when

he reached the doorway. Wallander waited briefly, to give Nyberg a moment to comprehend what he saw in front of him. Then he walked over.

"I already have a question for you," he said. "One of the most important. As you see, the gun is at least two metres away from the body. My question is, could it have ended up over there if Svedberg committed suicide?"

Nyberg thought about it, then shook his head. "No," he said. "That's impossible. A shotgun aimed by himself wouldn't be thrown that far."

For a moment Wallander felt strangely relieved. Svedberg didn't kill himself, he thought.

People were beginning to congregate in the hall. The doctor arrived, as did Hansson. A technician was unpacking his bag.

"Please listen, everybody," Wallander said. "The person lying in there is your colleague, Officer Svedberg. He's dead, probably murdered. I want to prepare you for the fact that it's a terrible sight. We knew him and we grieve for him. He was our friend as well as our colleague and that makes our job much harder."

Wallander stopped. He felt he should say more but couldn't think of anything. He lacked the words. He returned to the kitchen while Nyberg and his assistants got to work. Holgersson was still sitting at the table.

"I have to call his cousin," she said. "If she's the closest living relative."

"I can do it," Wallander said. "After all, I already know her."

"Give me an overview of the events. What happened here?"

"I'll need Martinsson for that. I'll get him."

Wallander went out onto the stairs. The door to the next flat was slightly ajar. He knocked and went in. Martinsson was in the living room with four people. One of them was fully dressed, the others were still in their dressing gowns. There were two women and two men. He signalled for Martinsson to come with him.

"Please remain here for now," he told the others.

They went into the kitchen. Martinsson was very pale.

"Let's start from the beginning," Wallander said. "When was the last time anyone saw Svedberg?"

"I don't know if I was the last one," Martinsson said. "But I caught a glimpse of him in the canteen on Wednesday morning at around 11 a.m."

"How did he seem?"

"Since I didn't think about it, I suppose he must have been like he always was."

"You called me that afternoon. We decided to have a meeting on Thursday morning."

"I went into Svedberg's office straight after our conversation, but he wasn't there. At the front desk they told me he'd gone home for the day."

"What time did he leave?"

"I didn't ask."

"What did you do then?"

"I called him at home and left a message about the meeting. Then I called back a couple of times but I didn't get an answer."

Wallander thought hard. "Sometime on Wednesday, Svedberg leaves the police station. Everything seems normal. On Thursday he doesn't show up, which is unusual, regardless of whether he heard your message. Svedberg never stayed away without letting someone know."

"That means it could have happened as early as Wednesday," Lisa Holgersson said.

Wallander nodded. At what point does the normal suddenly become the abnormal? he thought. That's the moment we have to find.

Another thought struck him – Martinsson's remark about his own answerphone not working.

"Wait here a minute," he said and left the kitchen.

He walked into Svedberg's study. His answerphone was on the desk. Wallander went into the living room where Nyberg was kneeling beside the shotgun, and took him back into the study.

"I'd like to listen to the answerphone, but I don't want to destroy any clues."

"We can get the tape to return to the same place," Nyberg said. He was wearing plastic gloves. Wallander nodded and Nyberg pressed the play button. There were three messages from Martinsson. Each time he stated the time of day. There were no other messages.

"I'd also like to hear Svedberg's greeting," Wallander said.

Nyberg pressed another button.

Wallander flinched when he heard Svedberg's voice. Nyberg also seemed upset by it.

I'm not here, but please leave a message. That was all.

Wallander went back into the kitchen. "Your messages are still on the machine," he said. "But we can't tell if anyone listened to them or not."

The room was quiet. Everyone was thinking about what Wallander had said.

"What do the neighbours say?" he asked.

"No one heard anything," Martinsson answered. "It's quite strange. No one heard a shot and almost everyone was at home."

Wallander frowned. "It's not possible that no one heard anything."

"I'll keep talking to them."

Martinsson left. A police officer came into the kitchen.

"There's a reporter outside," he said.

Goddamn it, Wallander thought. Someone had already contacted the press. He looked at Holgersson.

"We have to notify his relatives first," she said.

"We can't put it off any longer than midday," Wallander said.

He turned to the waiting police officer. "No comment right now," he said. "But we'll issue a statement later this morning."

"At 11 a.m.," Holgersson said.

The officer disappeared. Nyberg shouted at someone in the living room. Then everything was quiet again. Nyberg had a bad temper but his outbursts were always brief. Wallander went out into the study and picked up a phone book off the floor. He looked up Ylva Brink's number at the kitchen table and looked questioningly at Holgersson.

"You make the call," she said.

Nothing was as difficult as notifying a relative of a sudden death. Whenever possible, Wallander tried to make sure he was accompanied by a police minister. Although he had gone through this many times, he never became accustomed to it. And even if Ylva Brink was only Svedberg's cousin, it would be hard enough. He heard the first ring and noticed himself start to tense up.

Her answerphone came on with a message saying that she was working the night shift at the hospital. Wallander put the receiver back down. He suddenly remembered visiting her at the hospital with Svedberg two years ago. And now Svedberg was dead. He still couldn't comprehend it.

"She's at the hospital," he said. "I'll have to go and see her in person."

"It really can't wait," Lisa Holgersson said. "Svedberg might have had other relatives that we don't know about."

Wallander nodded. She was right.

"Do you want me to come with you?" she asked.

"That's not necessary."

It occurred to Wallander that he would have liked to have Ann-Britt Höglund with him, and then he realised that no one had contacted her.

She should be here working on this with the others, he thought.

Holgersson got up and left the kitchen. Wallander sat down in her chair and dialled Höglund's number. A man's sleepy voice came on the line.

"I need to speak to Ann-Britt. This is Wallander."

"Who?"

"Kurt. From the police."

The man was still sleepy but now he sounded angry as well.

"What the hell is going on?"

"Isn't this Ann-Britt Höglund's number?"

"There's no bitch by that name around here," the man grunted and slammed down the phone. Wallander could almost feel the impact. He had dialled the wrong number. He tried again slowly and Höglund picked up after the second ring, as quickly as Holgersson had.

"It's Kurt."

She didn't sound particularly sleepy. Maybe she had been awake? Maybe her problems were keeping her awake. Now she'll have one more to add to the list, Wallander thought.

"What's happened?"

"Svedberg has been killed, probably murdered."

"That can't be true."

"Unfortunately it is. It happened in his home, the flat on Lilla Norregatan."

"I know where it is."

"Can you come down here?"

"I'm on my way."

Wallander hung up and remained at the kitchen table. One of the technicians looked in, but Wallander waved him away. He needed to think, if only for a minute. There was something strange about all this, he realised. Something that didn't add up. The crime technician came back into the kitchen.

"Nyberg wants to talk to you."

Wallander got up and went out into the living room, where the discomfort and distress of the people at work was palpable. Svedberg hadn't been a colourful personality, but he was well liked. And now he was dead.

The doctor was kneeling by the body. Now and then a flash went off in the room. Nyberg was making notes. He came over to Wallander, who stopped in the doorway.

"Did Svedberg have any weapons?"

"You mean the shotgun?"

"Yes."

"I don't know, but I can't imagine he did."

"It's just strange that the killer would leave his weapon behind."

Wallander nodded. That had been one of his first thoughts.

"Have you noticed anything else strange around here?" he asked.

Nyberg narrowed his eyes. "Isn't everything about a colleague having his head blown off strange?"

"You know what I mean."

But Wallander didn't wait for an answer. He turned and walked away, bumping into Martinsson in the hall.

"How did it go? Have you established a time?"

"No one heard anything, and if I'm right in my calculations there has been someone in the building continuously since Monday. Either on this level or in the flat below."

"And no one heard anything? That's impossible."

"There was a retired high school teacher who seemed a little hard of hearing, but the others were fine."

Wallander didn't understand it. Someone must have heard the shot or shots.

"You'll have to keep working on this," he said. "I have to drop by the hospital. Do you remember Svedberg's cousin, Ylva Brink? The midwife?"

Martinsson nodded.

"She's probably his nearest relative."

"Didn't he have an aunt somewhere in Västergötland?"

"I'll ask Ylva."

Wallander went down the stairs. He needed to get some air. A reporter was waiting outside the front door. Wallander recognised him as a reporter from Ystad's daily paper.

"What's going on? All units called out in the middle of the night to the home of a police officer by the name of Karl Evert Svedberg."

"I can't tell you anything," Wallander said. "We're issuing a statement to the press at 11 a.m."

"You can't say anything or you won't?"

"I really can't."

The reporter, whose name was Wickberg, nodded.

"That means someone's dead, and you can't say anything until the next of kin has been notified. Am I right?"

"If that were the case I could have picked up the phone."

Wickberg smiled in a firm but not unfriendly way.

"That's not how it's done. You get hold of a police minister first, if one's available. So Svedberg's dead?"

Wallander was too tired to get angry.

"Whatever you want to guess or think is your business," he said. "We'll release information at 11 a.m. Before then I won't say another word."

"Where are you going?"

"I need to get some air."

He walked along Lilla Norregatan and continued a few blocks, then looked back. Wickberg was not following him. Wallander turned right onto Sladdergatan, then left onto Stora Norregatan. He was thirsty and had to take a leak. There were no cars around. He walked up to a building and relieved himself. Then he kept going.

Something's wrong, he thought. Something about this whole thing is completely odd. He couldn't think of what it was, but the feeling became stronger. There was a gnawing pain in his stomach. Why had Svedberg been shot? What was it about the terrible image of the man with his head blown off that didn't add up?

Wallander arrived at the hospital, walked around to the emergency entrance, and rang the bell. He took the elevator to the maternity ward, a rush of images of him and Svedberg on their way to talk to Ylva Brink flitting through his mind. But this time there was no Svedberg. It was as if he had never existed.

Suddenly he caught sight of Ylva Brink through the double glass doors. She met his gaze, and he saw that it took her a couple of seconds to remember who he was. She walked over to the doors and let him in. At that moment he saw that she realised something was wrong.

CHAPTER FIVE

They sat down in the office. It was 3 a.m. Wallander told her the facts. Svedberg was dead. He had been killed with a shotgun. Who the killer was, why it had happened and when, remained unanswered. He avoided giving her too much detail of the crime scene.

When he finished, one of the nurses on the night shift came in to ask Ylva Brink a question.

"Can it wait?" Wallander said. "I've just notified her of a death in the family."

The nurse was about to leave when Wallander asked if he could have a glass of water. He was so dry that his tongue was sticking to the roof of his mouth.

"We're all in shock," Wallander said after the nurse left. "It's completely incomprehensible."

Ylva Brink didn't say anything. She was very pale but had not lost her composure. The nurse returned with the glass of water.

"Let me know if I can do anything else," she said.

"We're fine right now," Wallander answered.

He emptied his glass, but it didn't quench his thirst.

"I just can't get it into my head," she said. "I don't understand."

"I can't either," Wallander said. "It'll be a while before that happens, if ever."

He found a pencil in his coat pocket, but as usual he didn't have a notebook handy. There was a wastepaper basket next to the chair. He took out a piece of paper on which someone had doodled stick figures, smoothed it out, and took a magazine from the table to lean on.

"I have to ask you some questions," he said. "Who were his next of kin? I must admit you're the only one I can think of."

"His parents are gone and he had no siblings. Besides me there's only one cousin. I'm a cousin on his father's side and he has a cousin on his mother's side as well. His name is Sture Björklund."

Wallander noted down the name.

"Does he live here in Ystad?"

"He lives on a farm outside of Hedeskoga."

"So he's a farmer?"

"He's a professor at Copenhagen University."

Wallander was surprised. "I can't recall Svedberg ever mentioning him."

"They hardly ever saw each other. If you're asking which relatives Svedberg had any contact with, then the answer is just me."

"He'll still have to be notified," Wallander said. "As you can understand, this will be making a lot of headlines. A police officer who dies a violent death is big news."

She looked at him carefully. "A violent death? What do you mean by that?"

"That he was murdered."

"Well, what else could it have been?"

"That was going to be my next question for you," Wallander said. "Could it have been suicide?"

"Isn't it always a possibility? Under the right circumstances?"

"Yes."

"Can't you tell by looking at the body if he's been murdered or if he's committed suicide?"

"Yes, we'll probably be able to, but certain questions are a matter of routine."

She thought for a while before answering.

"I've considered it myself during a particularly difficult time. God only knows all that I've been through. But it's never occurred to me that Karl would do anything like that."

"Because he had no reason to?"

"He wasn't what I would call an unhappy person."

"When did you last hear from him?"

"He phoned me last Sunday."

"How did he seem?"

"He sounded perfectly normal."

"Why did he call?"

"We talk to each other once a week. If he didn't get in touch, I did, and vice versa. Sometimes he came over and had dinner, other times I went over to his place. As you may remember, my husband isn't home very often. He works on an oil tanker. Our children are grown up."

"Svedberg could cook?"

"Why wouldn't he be able to?"

"I've never imagined him in a kitchen."

"He cooked very well, particularly fish."

Wallander went back a little. "So he called you last Sunday. That was 4 August. And everything seemed fine?"

"Yes."

"What did you talk about?"

"This and that. I remember him telling me how tired he was. He said he was completely overworked."

Wallander looked at her intently. "Did he really say that he was overworked?"

"Yes."

"But he had just taken his holiday."

"I remember it very clearly."

Wallander thought hard before asking his next question. "Do you know what he did on his holiday?"

"I don't know if you know this, but he didn't like to leave Ystad. He usually stayed home. He might have taken a short trip to Poland."

"But what did he do at home? Did he stay in the flat?"

"He had various interests."

"Such as?"

She shook her head. "You must know as well as I do. He had two big passions: amateur astronomy and Native American history."

"I knew about the Indians, and how he sometimes went to Falsterbo to do some bird-watching. But the astronomy is new to me."

"He had a very expensive telescope."

Wallander couldn't remember seeing one in the flat.

"Where did he keep it?"

"In his study."

"So that's what he did on his holidays? Looked at stars and read about Indians?"

"I think so. But this summer was a little unusual."

"In what way?"

"We usually see a lot of each other over the summer, more so than during the rest of the year. But this year he had no time. He turned down several invitations to dinner."

"Did he say why?"

She hesitated before answering. "It was as if he didn't have the time."

Wallander sensed that he was nearing a crucial point.

"He didn't say why?"

"No."

"That must have puzzled you."

"Not really."

"Did you notice a change in his behaviour? Did something seem to be bothering him?"

"He was just the same as always. The only thing was that he seemed to be pressed for time."

"When did you first notice this?"

She thought about it. "Shortly after Midsummer, right about the time he took his holiday."

The nurse reappeared in the doorway. Ylva Brink got up.

"I'll be right back," she said.

Wallander looked for a washroom. He drank two more glasses of water and relieved himself. When he came back to the office Ylva was waiting for him.

"I think I'll go now," he told her. "Other questions can wait."

"I can call Sture, if you like. We have to make the funeral arrangements."

"Try to call in the next couple of hours," Wallander said. "We'll be issuing a statement to the press at 11 a.m."

"It still feels unreal," she said.

Her eyes had filled with tears. Wallander had trouble keeping his own eyes from welling up. They sat quietly, both fighting back their tears. Wallander tried to concentrate on the clock hanging on the wall, counting the seconds as they ticked by.

"I have one last question," he said after a while. "Svedberg was a bachelor. I never heard mention of a woman in his life."

"I don't think there ever was one," she answered.

"You don't think that something like that could have happened this summer?"

"You mean that he met a woman?"

"Yes."

"And that was why he was overworked?"

Wallander realised it seemed absurd. "These are questions I have to ask," he repeated. "Otherwise we won't get anywhere."

She followed him to the glass doors.

"You have to catch the person who did this," she said and gripped Wallander's arm tightly.

"You have my word," Wallander said. "Svedberg was one of us. We won't stop until we've caught whoever killed him."

They shook hands.

"Do you know if he used to keep large sums of money in the flat?"

She looked at him with disbelief. "Where would he have got large sums of money? He always complained about how little he earned."

"He was right about that."

"Do you know how much a midwife makes?"

"No."

"I'd better not tell you. You could say we wouldn't be comparing who makes more but who makes even less."

When Wallander left the hospital he drew a deep breath. Birds were chirping. It was barely 4 a.m. There was only a faint trace of wind and it was still warm. He started walking slowly back to Lilla Norregatan. One question seemed more important than the others. Why had Svedberg felt overworked when he had just been on holiday? Could it have something to do with his murder?

Wallander stopped in his tracks on the narrow footpath. In his mind he went back to the moment when he had stood in the doorway of the living room and first witnessed the devastation. Martinsson had been right behind him. He had seen a dead man and a shotgun. But almost at once he was struck by the feeling that something wasn't quite right. Could he make out what it was? He tried again without success.

Patience, he thought. I'm tired. It's been a long night and it's not over yet.

He started walking again, wondering when he would have time to sleep and think about his diet. Then he stopped again. A question suddenly came to him.

What if I die as suddenly as Svedberg? Who will miss me? What will people say? That I was a good policeman? But who will miss me as a person? Ann-Britt? Maybe even Martinsson?

A pigeon flew by close to his head. We don't know anything about each other, he thought. What did I really think of Svedberg? Do I actually miss him? Can you miss a person you didn't know?

He started walking again, but he knew these questions would follow him.

Going into Svedberg's flat again was like walking back into a nightmare. Gone was all feeling of summer, sun, and birdsong. Inside, beneath the harsh beams of the spotlights, there was only death.

Lisa Holgersson had returned to the police station. Wallander beckoned Höglund and Martinsson to follow him into the kitchen. He stopped himself at the last moment from asking them if had seen Svedberg. They sat down around the kitchen table, grey-faced. Wallander wondered what his own face looked like.

"How is it going?" he asked.

"Can it be anything other than a burglary?" Höglund asked.

"It could be a lot of other things," Wallander answered. "Revenge, a lunatic, two lunatics, three lunatics. We don't know, and as long as we don't know we have to work with what we can see."

"And one other thing," Martinsson said slowly.

Wallander nodded, sensing what Martinsson was about to say.

"The fact that Svedberg was a policeman," Martinsson said.

"Have you found any clues?" Wallander asked. "How is Nyberg's work going? What's in the medical report?"

They both rifled through the notes they had made. Höglund finished first.

"Both barrels of the shotgun were fired," she read. "The pathologist and Nyberg are sure that the shots came in quick succession. The shots were fired directly at Svedberg's head at close range."

Her voice shook. She took a deep breath and continued. "It isn't possible to determine whether or not Svedberg was sitting in the chair when the shots were fired, nor what the exact distance was. From the arrangement of the furniture and the size of the room it cannot have been more than four metres, but it could have been much closer."

Martinsson got up and mumbled something, then disappeared into the bathroom. They waited. He returned after a few minutes.

"I should have quit two years ago," he said.

"We're needed now more than ever," Wallander said sharply, but he understood Martinsson only too well.

"Svedberg was fully dressed," Höglund continued. "That means he wasn't forced out of bed, but we still have no time frame."

Wallander looked at Martinsson.

"I've been over this point again and again," he said. "But none of the neighbours heard anything."

"What about noise from the street?" Wallander asked.

"I don't think it would cover the sound of a shotgun going off. Twice."

"So we have no way of pinpointing the time of the crime. We know that Svedberg was dressed, which may allow us to eliminate the very late hours of the night. I've always been under the impression that Svedberg went to bed early."

Martinsson agreed.

"How did the killer enter the flat? Do we know that?"

"The door shows no signs of a forced entry."

"But remember how easy it was for us to get in," Wallander said.

"Why did he leave his weapon behind? Was it panic?"

They had no answers to Martinsson's question. Wallander looked at his colleagues, who were tired and depressed.

"I'll tell you what I think," he said. "For what it's worth. As soon as I came into the flat I had the feeling that something was odd. What it was I don't know. There's been a murder that suggests a burglary. But if it isn't a burglary, then what? Revenge? Or is it possible to imagine that someone came here not to steal anything but rather to find something?"

He got up, picked up a glass from the kitchen counter, and poured himself some more water.

"I've talked to Ylva Brink at the hospital," he said. "Svedberg had almost no family. He had two cousins, one of whom is Ylva. They seem to have been in close contact. She mentioned one thing that I found odd. When she talked with Svedberg last Sunday he complained of being

81

overworked. But he had just returned from holiday. It doesn't make any sense."

Höglund and Martinsson waited for him to continue.

"I don't know if it means anything," Wallander said. "But we need to know why."

"Was it something to do with Svedberg's investigation?" Höglund asked.

"The young people who went missing?" Martinsson said.

"There must have been something else as well," Wallander said, "since that wasn't a formal investigation. Anyway, he went on holiday just a few days after the parents first notified us."

No one could come up with an answer.

"One of you will have to find out what he was working on," Wallander said.

"Do you think he had a secret of some kind?" Martinsson asked carefully.

"Doesn't everybody have one?"

"So is that what we're looking for? Svedberg's secret?"

"We're looking for the person who killed him. That's all."

They decided to meet again at the station at 8 a.m. Martinsson immediately returned to the flat next door to continue his interviews with the neighbours. Höglund lingered. Wallander looked at her tired and ravaged face.

"Were you awake when I called?"

He regretted the question as soon as it came out. He had no business asking whether or not she had been up. But she didn't seem to mind.

"Yes," she said. "I was wide awake."

"You came down here so quickly that I assume your husband must be at home with the children."

"When you called, we were in the middle of an argument. Just a stupid little argument, the kind you have when you don't have the energy for the big ones any more."

They sat quietly. Now and then they heard Nyberg's voice.

"I just don't understand it," she said. "Who would want to hurt Svedberg?"

"Who was closest to him?" Wallander said.

She looked surprised. "I thought it was you."

"No, I didn't know him that well."

"But he looked up to you."

"I have trouble imagining that."

"You didn't see it, but I did. Maybe the others noticed it as well. He always took your side, even when you were wrong."

"That still doesn't answer our question," Wallander said, and asked it again. "Who was closest to him?"

"No one was close to him."

"Well, we have to get close to him now. Now that he's dead."

Nyberg came into the kitchen, a cup of coffee in his hand. Wallander knew that he always had a thermos ready in case he was called out in the middle of the night.

"How's it going?" Wallander asked.

"It looks like a burglary," Nyberg said. "What we don't know is why the killer left his gun."

"We don't have a time of death," Wallander said.

"That's up to the pathologist."

"I still want to hear your opinion."

"I don't like to make guesses."

"I know, but you have a certain experience in these matters. I promise I won't hold you to it."

Nyberg rubbed his hand over his unshaven chin. His eyes were bloodshot.

"Maybe 24 hours," he said. "I doubt it's less than that."

They let his words sink in. That means Wednesday night or early Thursday, Wallander thought. Nyberg yawned and left the kitchen.

"You should go home now," Wallander said to Höglund. "We have to be ready to organise the investigation at 8 a.m."

The clock on the wall read 5.15 a.m. She put on her coat and left. Wallander stayed in the kitchen. A pile of bills lay on the window sill. He leafed through them. We have to start somewhere, he thought. Next he went in to Nyberg and asked for a pair of rubber gloves. He returned to the kitchen and looked slowly around. He went through the cupboards and drawers methodically and noted that Svedberg kept his kitchen as neat as his office at work.

He left the kitchen and went into the study. Where was the telescope? He sat down in the desk chair and looked around. Nyberg came by and said they were ready to take Svedberg's body away. Did he want to see it again? Wallander shook his head. The image of Svedberg with half his head blown off was forever fixed in his mind. It was an image that didn't spare a single gruesome detail.

He let his gaze continue to wander around the room. The answerphone was on the desk, as well as a pencil holder, some old tin soldiers, and a pocket calendar. Wallander picked up the latter and leafed through it month by month. On 11 January, at 9.30 a.m., Svedberg had had a dentist's appointment. 7 March was Ylva Brink's birthday. On 18 April Svedberg had written the name "Adamsson". The name was also jotted down on 5 and 12 May. In June and July there were no notes at all.

Svedberg had taken his holiday. Afterwards he complained that he was completely overworked. Wallander kept turning the pages, more slowly now, but there were no more notes. The last days of Svedberg's life were a complete blank. 18 October was Sture Björklund's birthday, and the name Adamsson appeared again on 14 December. That was all. Wallander put the pocket calendar back in its place, and leaned back in the chair, which was very comfortable. He felt tired and thirsty. He closed his eyes, wondering who Adamsson was.

Then he leaned forward and picked up the business cards that were tucked into a corner of the brown desk pad. There was a card from *Boman's Second Hand Book Shop* in Gothenburg, and the Audi specialist in Malmö. Svedberg had been a loyal customer and had always driven an Audi, the same way that Wallander always traded in his Peugeot for another Peugeot. Wallander put the desk pad back and looked through a packet of letters and postcards. Most of the letters were more than ten years old, and almost all of them were from Svedberg's mother.

He put them back and looked at a couple of the post-cards. To his surprise he found one that he had sent from Skagen. *The beaches here are amazing*, it said. Wallander sat looking at the card for a while.

That had been three years ago. He had taken an extended medical leave, doubting that he would ever return to active duty. He had spent part of that time wandering along Skagen's wintery and abandoned beaches. He didn't remember writing the postcard. His memories from that period in his life were few.

Eventually he had returned to Ystad and started work-ing again. He remembered Svedberg on his first day back at work. Björk had just welcomed Wallander, and the conference room grew quiet. None of them had expected him to return. The person who finally broke the silence

85

was Svedberg. Wallander could still remember exactly what he said.

"Thank God you finally came back, because I really don't think we could've made it another day without you."

Wallander held on to the memory and tried to see Svedberg clearly. He was the quiet type, but someone who could often ease an uncomfortable situation. He was a good policeman, not outstanding in any way, but good. Stubborn and conscientious. He didn't have a lot of imagination and he wasn't a particularly accomplished writer. His reports were often poorly written, and they irritated the prosecutors. But he had been an important part of the team.

Wallander got up and went into Svedberg's bedroom. There was no sign of the telescope. He sat down on the bed and picked up a book off the bedside table. It was called *A History of the Sioux Indians* and was written in English. Svedberg didn't speak very good English, but perhaps he was better at reading it.

Wallander flipped through the book absentmindedly and found himself staring at a remarkable picture of Sitting Bull. Then he got up and went into the bathroom. He opened a mirrored cabinet and found nothing that surprised him. His own bathroom cabinet was exactly the same.

Now only the living room remained. He would have preferred to skip it, but knew he couldn't. He went into the kitchen and drank a glass of water. It was close to 6 a.m. and he was very tired.

Finally he went out into the living room. Nyberg had put on knee-guards and was crawling around the black leather sofa that stood against a wall. The chair was still overturned and no one had moved the shotgun. The only thing that had been moved was Svedberg's body.

Wallander looked around the room and tried to imagine the events that had taken place. What had happened right before the fatal moment, before the gun went off? But he couldn't see anything. The feeling that he was ignoring something important came over him again. He stood completely still and tried to coax the thought to the surface, but he got nothing.

Nyberg came up to him and they looked at each other.

"Do you understand this?" Wallander asked.

"No," Nyberg answered. "It's strangely like a painting."

Wallander looked closely at him. "What do you mean 'a painting'?"

Nyberg blew his nose and carefully refolded his handkerchief.

"Everything is such a mess," he said. "Chairs have been overturned, drawers pulled out, papers and china thrown all over the place. It's almost as if it's too messy."

Wallander knew what he meant, although he had not yet followed this thought to its conclusion.

"You mean it looks arranged."

"Of course it's only a thought at this point. I don't have anything to back it up with."

"What exactly gave you this feeling?"

Nyberg pointed to a little porcelain rooster that lay on the ground.

"It seems plausible to assume that it came from that shelf over there," he said, and pointed it out to Wallander. "Where else could it have come from? But if it fell because someone was pulling out the drawers and going through them, why would it have landed all the way over here?"

Wallander nodded.

"There's probably a completely rational explanation," Nyberg said. "But if so, you'll have to tell me what it is."

Wallander didn't say anything. He stayed in the living room for a few more minutes, then left the flat. When he came out on the street it was already morning. A police car stood parked outside the building, but there were no onlookers. Wallander assumed that the police officers had been instructed not to give out any information.

He stood completely still and drew a couple of deep breaths. It was going to be a beautiful, late summer's day. Only now was he starting to sense the overwhelming nature of his sorrow, which stemmed as much from genuine affection as from the reminder of his own mortality. Death had come close this time. It was not like when his father had died. This frightened him.

It was 6.25 a.m. on Friday, 9 August. Wallander walked slowly to his car. A cement mixer started up in the distance.

Ten minutes later he walked through the doors of the police station.

CHAPTER SIX

They gathered in the conference room shortly after 8 a.m. and held an impromptu memorial service. Lisa Holgersson lit a candle at the place where Svedberg normally sat. All those at the station that morning were gathered in the room, filling it with a palpable sense of shock and sadness. Holgersson said only a few words, fighting to keep her composure. Everyone in the room prayed for her not to break down. It would make the situation unbearable. After she had spoken, they stood for a minute's silence. Uneasy images floated through Wallander's mind. He was already having trouble picturing Svedberg's face. He had experienced the same thing when his father died, and earlier with Rydberg.

Although one can certainly remember the dead, it's as if they never existed, he thought.

The impromptu service came to an end, people started to leave. Apart from the members of the investigative team, Holgersson was the only one to stay behind. They sat down at the table. The flame of the candle flickered when Martinsson closed one of the windows. Wallander looked questioningly at Holgersson, but she shook her head. It was his turn to speak.

"We're all tired," he began. "We're upset and sad and confused. What we've always feared the most has finally occurred. Normally we try to solve crimes, even violent crimes, that do not affect people from our own world. This time it's happened in our midst, but we still have to try to approach it as if it were a regular case."

He paused and looked around. No one spoke.

"Let's go over the facts," Wallander said. "Then we can begin to plot our strategy. We know very little. Svedberg was shot sometime between Wednesday afternoon and Thursday evening. It happened in his flat, which shows no signs of forced entry. We can assume that the shotgun lying on the floor was the murder weapon. The flat looks like it was burgled, which may indicate that Svedberg was confronted by an armed assailant. We don't know if this was the case; it is simply a possibility. We cannot disregard other scenarios. We have to keep our search as broad as possible. We also cannot disregard the fact that Svedberg was a policeman. This may or may not be significant. We have no exact time of death yet, and a perplexing fact is that none of the neighbours heard any shots. We therefore have to wait for the autopsy report."

He poured himself a glass of water and emptied it before continuing.

"This is what we know. The only thing to add is that Svedberg did not turn up for work on Thursday. We all appreciate how unusual this is. He gave no reason for his absence, and the only rational assumption is that there was something preventing him from coming in. We know what that means."

Nyberg interrupted him with a gesture.

"I'm not a pathologist," he said, "but I doubt that Svedberg died as early as Wednesday."

"Then we have to deal with the question of what could have prevented Svedberg from coming to work yesterday," Wallander said. "Why didn't he call in? When was he killed?"

Wallander described his conversation with Ylva Brink. "Apart from telling me about the only other relative that Svedberg was in touch with, she said something that stuck in my mind. She said that in the last few weeks Svedberg complained about feeling overworked. But he had just returned from holiday. It doesn't make any sense, particularly if you know that he didn't tend to take strenuous trips on his holiday."

"Did he ever leave Ystad?" Martinsson asked.

"Not very often. He made a day-trip to Bornholm or occasionally took the ferry to Poland. Ylva Brink confirmed this. But he seems mostly to have spent time on his two hobbies, which were Native American history and amateur astronomy. Ylva Brink told me that he owned an expensive telescope, but we haven't found it yet."

"I thought he went bird-watching," said Hansson, who had been silent until now.

"Sometimes, but apparently not so often," Wallander said. "I think we should assume that Ylva Brink knew him quite well, and according to her it was stars and Indians that mattered."

He looked around. "Why was he overworked? What does that mean? It may not be important at all, but I can't help thinking that it is."

"I looked over what he was working on before our meeting," Höglund said. "Just before he went on holiday, he spoke to all the parents of the young people who are missing."

"Which young people?" Holgersson asked, surprised. Wallander explained and Höglund continued.

"The last two days before he went on holiday, he visited the Norman, Boge, and Hillström families, one after the other. But I can't find any notes from those visits even though I searched thoroughly."

Wallander and Martinsson looked at each other.

"That can't be right," Wallander said. "All three of us had a thorough meeting with those families. We had never talked about pursuing them for further questioning, since there was no indication of a crime."

"Well, it looks like he went and saw them anyway," Höglund said. "He's noted the exact times of his visits in his calendar."

Wallander thought for a moment. "That would mean that Svedberg was pursuing this on his own without telling us about it."

"That's not like him," Martinsson said.

"No," Wallander agreed. "It's as strange as him staying home from work without notifying anyone."

"We can easily verify this information," Höglund said.

"Please do," Wallander said. "And find out what questions Svedberg was asking."

"This whole situation is absurd," Martinsson said. "We've been trying to meet with Svedberg with regard to these young people since Wednesday and now he's gone and here we are still talking about them."

"Have there been any new developments?" Holgersson asked.

"Nothing apart from the fact that one of the mothers has become extremely anxious. Her daughter sent her another postcard."

"Isn't that good news?"

"According to her, the handwriting was faked."

"Who would do that?" Hansson asked. "Who the hell forges postcards? Cheques I understand. But postcards?"

"I think we should keep the two cases separate for

now," Wallander said. "Let's work out how to tackle the investigation of Svedberg's killer or killers."

"Nothing indicates that there was more than one," Nyberg said.

"Can you be sure that there wasn't?"

"No."

Wallander let his palms fall flat onto the table. "We can't be sure about anything right now," he said. "We have to cast a wide net. In a couple of hours we're going to release the news of Svedberg's death, and then we'll really have to move."

"This will take top priority, of course," Holgersson said. "Everything else can wait."

"The press conference," Wallander said. "Let's take care of that right now."

"A police officer has been murdered," Holgersson said. "We'll tell them exactly what happened. Do we have any leads?"

"No." Wallander's answer was firm.

"Then that's what we'll say."

"How detailed should we get?"

"He was shot at close range. We have the murder weapon. Is there any reason to withhold that information?"

"Not really," Wallander said, and he looked around the table. No one had any objections.

Holgersson got up. "I'd like you to be there," she said. "Maybe all of you should be there. After all, a colleague and friend has been killed."

They decided to meet 15 minutes before the press conference.

Holgersson left. The candle went out when the door closed. Höglund lit it again. They went through what they knew one more time and divided up the work at hand.

They were returning to work mode. They were just about to stop when Martinsson raised one more issue.

"We should probably decide now if the young people should be left aside for now or not."

Wallander felt unsure. But he knew it was up to him.

"We'll put it aside for now," he said. "At least for the next few days. Then we'll revisit it, unless of course Svedberg was asking some extraordinary questions."

It was 9.15 a.m. Wallander got a cup of coffee and went into his office. He got out a pad of paper and wrote a single word at the top of the first page: *Svedberg*. Underneath it he drew a cross that he immediately scratched out. He didn't get any further. He had been meaning to write down all the thoughts that had come to him during the night. But he put down the pen and walked to the window. The August morning was sunny and warm. The thought that there was something not quite right about this case returned. Nyberg felt there was something arranged about the murder scene. If so, then why, and by whom?

He looked for Sture Björklund's number in the phone book and dialled it. The phone rang several times.

"Please accept my condolences," Wallander said, when the man answered.

Sture Björklund's voice sounded strained and distant.

"Likewise. You probably knew my cousin better than I did. Ylva called me at 6 a.m. this morning to tell me what had happened."

"Unfortunately this will make headlines in the papers," Wallander said.

"I know. As it happens it's the second murder case in our family."

"Really?"

"Yes, in 1847, or more precisely on 12 April 1847, a man who was Karl Evert's great-great-great-great-uncle was killed with an axe somewhere on the outskirts of Eslöv. The murderer was a soldier by the name of Brun, who had been given a dishonourable discharge from the army for a number of reasons. The murder was simply a matter of money. Our ancestor was a cattle man and fairly wealthy."

"What happened?" Wallander asked, trying to hide his impatience.

"The police, which I guess consisted of a sheriff and his assistant, made heroic efforts and arrested Brun on his way to Denmark a few days later. He was sentenced to death and executed. When Oscar I became king he took on the business of processing death sentences blocked by his predecessor, Charles XV. As many as 14 prisoners were executed as soon as he came to power. Brun was beheaded, somewhere in the vicinity of Malmö."

"What a strange story."

"I did some research into our ancestry a couple of years ago. Of course the case of Brun and the murder in Eslöv was already known."

"If it's all right with you, I'd like to come out to see you as soon as possible."

Sture Björklund immediately put up his guard.

"What about?"

"We're trying to clarify our picture of Karl Evert." It felt unnatural to use his first name.

"I didn't know him very well, though, and I have to go to Copenhagen this afternoon."

"This is urgent and it won't take much time."

The man was quiet at the other end of the line. Wallander waited.

"What time?"

"Around 2 p.m.?"

"I'll call Copenhagen and let them know I won't be in today."

Sture Björklund gave Wallander directions. His house didn't seem hard to find.

After the phone conversation, Wallander spent a half hour writing out a summary of the case. He was still searching for the thought he had had when he first saw Svedberg lying on the floor – the thought that something wasn't quite right, the same idea that had also struck Nyberg. Wallander realised that it could simply be a reaction to the unbearable and incomprehensible experience of seeing a colleague dead. But he still tried to explore what might have caused it.

A little after 10 a.m. he went to get another cup of coffee. A number of people were gathered in the canteen. There was a general atmosphere of shock and dismay. Wallander lingered for a while, talking to some traffic officers. Then he walked back to his office and called Nyberg on his mobile phone.

"Where are you?" Wallander asked.

"Where do you think?" he replied sourly. "I'm still in Svedberg's flat."

"You haven't seen a telescope, by any chance?"

"No."

"Anything else?"

"We have a number of prints on the shotgun. We'll be able to get complete copies of at least two or three of them."

"Then we'll hope he's already in the database. Is that it?"

"Yes."

"I'm on my way to question Svedberg's other cousin,

who lives outside Hedeskoga. After that I'll be back to do a more thorough search of the flat."

"We'll be done by then. I'm also planning to attend the press conference."

Wallander couldn't remember Nyberg ever coming to a meeting that involved the press before. Maybe it was Nyberg's way of expressing how upset he was. Wallander was suddenly moved.

"Have you found any keys?" he asked after a moment.

"There are some car keys and a key to the basement storage area."

"Nothing in the attic?"

"There don't seem to be storage areas in the attic, only in the basement. You'll get the keys from me at the press conference."

Wallander hung up and went to Martinsson's office.

"Where's Svedberg's car?" he asked. "The Audi."

Martinsson didn't know. They asked Hansson, who didn't know either. Höglund wasn't in her office.

Martinsson looked at his watch.

"It's got to be in a car park close to the flat," he said. "I think I have time to check before 11 a.m."

Wallander went back to his office. He saw that people had started to send flowers. Ebba looked like she had been crying, but Wallander didn't say anything to her. He hurried past her as fast as he could.

The press conference started on time. Afterwards Wallander remembered thinking that Lisa Holgersson conducted the proceedings with dignity. He told her that no one could have done a better job. She was wearing her uniform and standing in front of a table with two bouquets of roses. Her speech was clear and to the point. She told the press the known facts, and her voice did not fail her this time. A respected colleague, Karl Evert Svedberg, had been found murdered in his flat. The exact time of death and the motive were not yet known, but there were indications that Svedberg was attacked by an armed burglar. The police did not have any leads. She concluded by describing Svedberg's career and his character. Wallander thought her description of Svedberg was very good, not exaggerated in any way. Wallander answered the few questions that were asked. Nyberg described the murder weapon as a Lambert Baron shotgun.

It was all over in half an hour. Afterwards, Holgersson was interviewed by the *Sydnytt* newspaper, while Wallander spoke to some reporters from the evening papers. It was only when they asked him to pose outside the block of flats on Lilla Norregatan that he let his impatience show.

At midday Holgersson asked the members of the investigative team to a simple lunch at her home. Wallander and Holgersson spoke about some of their memories of Svedberg. Wallander was the only one who had heard Svedberg explain why he had decided to become a police officer.

"He was afraid of the dark," Wallander said. "That's what he said. The fear had been with him since his earliest childhood, and he had never been able to understand it or overcome it. He became a police officer because he thought it would be a way to fight this fear, but it never left him."

A little before 1.30 p.m. they returned to the station. Wallander drove back with Martinsson.

"She handled that very well," Martinsson said.

"Lisa's good at her job," Wallander answered. "But you knew that already, didn't you?"

Martinsson didn't answer.

Wallander suddenly remembered something. "Did you find the Audi?"

"There's a private car park at the back of the building. It was there. I looked it over."

"Did you see a telescope in the boot?"

"There was only a spare tyre and a pair of boots. And a can of insecticide in the glove compartment."

"August is the month for bees," Wallander said glumly.

They went their separate ways when they arrived at the station. Wallander had got a bunch of keys from Nyberg at the lunch, but before he returned to the flat he drove to Hedeskoga. Sture Björklund's directions were very clear, Wallander thought, as he turned into a little farmhouse that lay just outside the town. There was a fountain in front of the house, and the large lawn had plaster statues dotted all over it. Wallander saw to his surprise that they all looked like devils, all with terrifying, gaping jaws. He wondered briefly what he would have expected a professor of sociology to have in his garden, but his thoughts were interrupted by a man wearing boots, a worn leather coat, and a torn straw hat. He was very tall and thin. Through the tear in the hat Wallander could see one similarity between Svedberg and his cousin: they were both bald.

Wallander was thrown for a moment. He hadn't expected Professor Björklund to look like this. His face was sunburnt, and had a couple of days' worth of stubble. Wallander wondered whether professors in Copenhagen really appeared unshaven at their lectures. But then he reminded himself that the semester had not yet started and that Björklund probably had other business across the strait.

"I hope this isn't too much of an inconvenience," Wallander said.

Sture Björklund threw his head back and laughed. Wallander noted a certain amount of derision in his laughter.

"There's a woman I meet in Copenhagen every Friday," Sture Björklund said. "I suppose you would call her a mistress. Do policemen in the Swedish countryside have mistresses?"

"Hardly," Wallander said.

"It's an ingenious solution to the problems of coexistence," Björklund said. "Each time may be the last. There's no co-dependence, no late-night discussions that might get out of hand and lead to things like furniture buying or pretending that one takes the idea of marriage seriously."

This man in the straw hat with the shrill laugh was starting to get on Wallander's nerves.

"Well, murder is something to take seriously," he said.

Sture Björklund nodded and took off the hat, as if he felt compelled to show a sign of something resembling mourning.

"Let's go in," he said.

The house was not like anything Wallander had ever seen before. From the outside it looked like a typical Scanian farmhouse. But the world that Wallander entered was completely unexpected. There were no walls left on the inside of the house – it was simply one big room that stretched all the way to the rafters. Here and there were little tower-like structures with spiral staircases made out of wrought iron and wood. There was almost no furniture and the walls were bare. One of the walls at the end of the house was entirely taken up by a large aquarium. Sture Björklund led him to a huge wooden table flanked by a church pew and a wooden stool.

"I've always thought that chairs should be hard,"

Björklund said. "Uncomfortable chairs force you to finish what you have to do more quickly, whether it's eating, thinking, or talking to a policeman."

Wallander sat down in the pew. It really was very uncomfortable.

"If my notes are correct, you're a professor at Copenhagen University," he said.

"I teach sociology, but I try to keep my course load down to an absolute minimum. My own research is what interests me, and I can do that from home."

"This is probably not relevant, but what is it you do your research on?"

"Man's relationship to monsters."

Wallander wondered if Sture Björklund was joking. He waited for him to continue.

"Monsters in the Middle Ages were not the same as they were in the 18th century. My ideas are not the same as those of future generations will be. It's a complicated and fascinating world: hell, the home of all terror, is constantly changing. Above all, this kind of work gives me a chance to make extra money, a factor which is not insignificant."

"In what way?"

"I work as a consultant for American film companies that make horror movies. Without boasting, I think I can claim to be one of the most sought-after consultants in the world when it comes to commercial terror. There's some Japanese man in Hawaii, but other than that it's just me."

Just as Wallander was starting to wonder if the man sitting across from him on the little stool was insane, he handed him a drawing that had been lying on the table.

"I've interviewed seven-year-olds in Ystad about monsters. I've tried to incorporate their ideas into my own work and have come up with this figure. The Americans love him. He's going to get the starring role in a cartoon series aimed at frightening seven- and eight-year-olds."

Wallander looked at the picture. It was extremely unpleasant. He put it down.

"What do you think, Inspector?"

"You can call me Kurt."

"What do you think?"

"It's unpleasant."

"We live in an unpleasant world."

He laid the straw hat on the table and Wallander smelt a strong odour of sweat.

"I've just decided to cancel my telephone service," he said. "Five years ago I got rid of the TV. Now I'm getting rid of the phone."

"Isn't that a little impractical?"

Björklund looked at him seriously. "I'm going to exercise my right to decide when I want to have contact with the outside world. I'll keep the computer, of course. But the phone is going."

Wallander nodded and took the opportunity to change the subject.

"Your cousin, Karl Evert Svedberg, has been killed. Apart from Ylva Brink, you are the only remaining relative. When was the last time you saw him?"

"About three weeks ago."

"Can you be more precise?"

"Friday, 19 July, at 4.30 p.m."

The answer came so quickly that Wallander was surprised. "How can you remember the time of day so well?"

"We had decided to meet at that time. I was going to Scotland to see some friends, and Kalle was going to house-sit, like he always did. That was really the only time we saw each other, when I was going away and when I came back."

"What was involved in house-sitting?"

"He lived here."

The answer came as a surprise to Wallander, but he had no reason to doubt Björklund.

"This happened regularly?"

"For the last ten years at least. It was a wonderful arrangement."

Wallander thought for a moment. "When did you come back?"

"27 July. Kalle picked me up at the airport and drove me home. We chatted for a bit and then he went back to Ystad."

"Did you have the feeling that he was overworked?"

Björklund threw his head back and laughed his shrill laugh again.

"I take it you meant that as a joke, but isn't it disrespectful to joke about the dead?"

"I meant the question seriously."

Björklund smiled. "I suppose we can all seem a bit overworked if we indulge in passionate relationships with women, can't we?"

Wallander stared at Björklund.

"What do you mean?"

"Kalle met his woman here while I was gone. That was part of the arrangement. They lived here whenever I went to Scotland or anywhere else."

Wallander gasped.

"You seem surprised," Björklund said.

"Was it always the same woman? What was her name?"

"Louise."

"What was her last name?"

"I don't know. I never met her. Kalle was quite secretive about her, or perhaps one should say 'discreet.'"

Wallander was caught completely by surprise. He had never heard of Svedberg having any relationship with a woman, let alone a long-term one.

"What else do you know about her?" he asked.

"Nothing."

"But Kalle must have said something?"

"Never. And I never asked. Our family is not one for idle curiosity."

Wallander had nothing more to ask. What he needed now was time to digest this latest piece of information. He got up, and Björklund raised his eyebrows.

"Was that it?"

"For now. But you'll hear from me again."

Björklund followed him out. It was warm and there was almost no breeze.

"Do you have any idea who might have killed him?" Wallander asked when they reached his car.

"Wasn't there a break-in? Who knows what criminal is lurking just around the corner?"

They shook hands and Wallander got into the car. He had just started the engine when Björklund leaned down to the window.

"There's just one more thing," he said. "Louise changed her hair colour pretty often."

"How do you know?"

"The hairs left in the bathroom. One year it was red, then black, then blond. It was always different."

"But you think it was the same woman?"

"I actually think Kalle was very much in love with her."

Wallander nodded. Then he drove away. It was 3 p.m.

One thing was certain, Wallander thought. Svedberg, our friend and colleague, may have been dead for just a couple of days, but we already know more about him than when he was alive.

At 3.10 p.m., Wallander parked his car in the town square and walked up to Lilla Norregatan. Without knowing why, he quickened his step. Something about this had suddenly become a matter of urgency.

CHAPTER SEVEN

Wallander went down into the basement. The steep stairs gave him the feeling that he was on his way to something far deeper than a normal basement; that he was journeying to the underworld. He arrived at a blue steel door, found the right key among the ones Nyberg had given him, and unlocked it. It was dark inside and the air smelt dank and musty. He took out the torch he had brought with him from the car and let the beam travel over the walls until he found the light switch. It was placed unusually low, as if for very small people. He walked into a narrow corridor with storage areas behind grilles on both sides. It occurred to him that Swedish basement storage lockers were not unlike rough prison cells, except that they didn't contain prisoners, but instead guarded old sofas, skis, and piles of suitcases. Svedberg's storage locker was all the way at the end of the corridor. The wire netting was reinforced with steel bars. A padlock hung around two of the bars. Svedberg must have reinforced this himself, Wallander thought. Is there something in there that he couldn't risk losing?

Wallander put on a pair of rubber gloves, opened the lock carefully, then turned on the light in the storage area and looked around. It was full of the things one would expect, and it took him only about an hour to go through everything there. He found nothing unusual. Finally, he straightened up and looked around again, looking for something that should have been there but wasn't, like the expensive telescope. He left the basement and locked it up.

He came back up into daylight. Since he was thirsty, he walked over to a café on the south side of the main square and drank some mineral water and a cup of coffee. He fought an inner battle over buying a Danish pastry. He knew he shouldn't but did it anyway.

Less than half an hour later he was back at the door of Svedberg's flat. It was deathly silent inside. Wallander held his breath before going in. The usual police tape was plastered across the door. He unpeeled the tape from the lock, got out the key, and let himself in. Immediately he heard the cement mixer from the street. He walked into the living room, cast an involuntary glance at the spot where Svedberg had lain, and walked over to the window. The rumble of the cement mixer seemed magnified among the buildings. Construction materials were being unloaded from a large truck. A thought suddenly came to Wallander. He left the flat and walked down to the street. An older man who had taken his shirt off was spraying water into the mixer. The man nodded at Wallander and seemed to know immediately that he was a police officer.

"It's terrible what happened," he yelled above the sound of the mixer.

"I need to speak to you," Wallander yelled back.

The man called out to a younger worker who was smoking in the shade. He came over and grabbed the hose. They went around the corner, where it was quieter.

"Do you know what has happened?" Wallander asked him.

"Some policeman by the name of Svedberg was shot."

"That's right. What I want you to tell me is how long

you've been working here. It looks like you're just getting started."

"We started on Monday. We're rebuilding the entryway to the building."

"When did you start using the mixer?"

The man thought about it. "It must have been on Tuesday," he said. "At around 11 a.m."

"Has it been on since then?"

"Pretty much continuously from 7 a.m. until 5 p.m. Sometimes even a little longer."

"Has it been in the same spot the whole time?"

"Yes."

"So you've had a clear view of everyone coming and going from the building."

The man suddenly realised the importance of Wallander's question and became very serious.

"Of course you don't know the people who live here," Wallander said. "But you've probably seen a number of people more than once."

"I don't know what that policeman looked like, if that's what you're asking."

Wallander hadn't thought of this.

"I'll get someone to come down and show you a photograph," he said. "What's your name?"

"Nils Linnman, like the man who does those nature programmes."

Wallander was of course familiar with Nils Linnman, the Swedish television personality.

"Have you noticed anything unusual during the time you've been working here?" Wallander asked while he desperately searched for something to write on.

"How do you mean?"

"Someone who may have seemed very nervous, or as if

they were in a hurry. Sometimes you notice things that just don't seem quite right."

Linnman thought it over and Wallander waited. He needed to pee again.

"No," Linnman said finally. "I can't think of anything. But Robban may have seen something."

"Robban?"

"The young guy who took over for me. But I doubt it. I think the only thing on his mind is his motorbike."

"We'd better ask him," Wallander said. "And if you think of anything later, please call me right away."

For once Wallander had a card with him, which Linnman tucked into the front pocket of his baggy overalls.

"I'll get Robban."

The ensuing conversation with Robban was very brief. His full name was Robert Tärnberg and he had heard only vague mention of someone being killed in the building. He had not noticed anything unusual. Wallander suspected he wouldn't even have noticed an elephant walking across the street, so he didn't bother giving him his card. He returned to the flat. At least he now had a satisfactory answer for why no one had heard the shots.

He went out into the kitchen and called the station. Höglund was the only one available. Wallander asked her to come down with a photo of Svedberg to show to the construction workers.

"We already have officers down there going door to door," she said.

"But they seem to have overlooked the workers."

Wallander walked out into the hall, then stopped and tried to rid himself of all extraneous thoughts. Many years ago, when Wallander had just moved to Ystad from Malmö,

Rydberg had given him the following advice: slowly peel away all the extraneous layers. There are tracks and marks left at every crime scene, like shadows of the event itself. That's what you have to find.

Wallander opened the front door and immediately noticed at least one detail that wasn't right. In a basket under the hall mirror there was a stack of newspapers, all copies of the local paper, *Ystad Allehanda*, which Svedberg subscribed to. But there was no copy on the floor under the post slot, although at least one should have been there.

Maybe even two or three by now. Someone had moved them. He walked into the kitchen and saw that the Wednesday and Thursday editions lay on the counter. Friday's edition lay on the kitchen table.

Wallander called Nyberg's mobile phone. He answered right away. Wallander started by telling him about the cement mixer. Nyberg sounded doubtful.

"Sound travels inwards," he said. "People on the street would be unable to hear shots from inside if the cement mixer had been on, but inside the building it would be a different story. Sound travels differently in buildings. I read about it somewhere."

"Maybe we should do some test shots," Wallander said. "With and without the cement mixer on and without telling the neighbours about it beforehand."

Nyberg agreed.

"But what I'm really calling about is the paper," Wallander said. "*Ystad Allehanda*."

"I put it on the kitchen table," Nyberg said. "But some-one else is responsible for the ones lying on the counter."

"We should test them for prints," Wallander said. "We don't know who might have put them there."

Nyberg was silent for a moment. "You're right," he said. "How the hell could I have missed it?"

"I won't touch them," Wallander told him.

"How long are you going to be there?"

"Two or three hours at least."

"I'll come down."

Wallander pulled out one of the kitchen drawers and found a couple of pens and a pad of paper where he remembered seeing them before. He wrote down Nils Linnman's and Robert Tärnberg's names and noted that someone should talk to the newspaper delivery person. Then he returned to the hall. Traces and shadows, Rydberg had told him. He held his breath while he let his gaze travel over the room. The leather coat Svedberg wore both winter and summer hung by the door. Wallander searched the pockets and found his wallet.

Nyberg has been sloppy, he thought.

He returned with it to the kitchen and emptied the contents onto the table. There was 847 kronor, a cash card, a card for petrol, and some personal identification cards. *Detective Inspector Svedberg*, he read. He compared the police ID and the driver's licence. The photo on the driver's licence was the older. Svedberg stared glumly into the lens. It looked like it had been taken in the summertime; the top of Svedberg's head was sunburned.

Louise should have told you to wear a hat, Wallander thought. Louise. Only two people claimed she existed. Svedberg and his cousin, the monster maker. But he had never seen her, only strands of her hair. Wallander made a face. It didn't make sense.

He picked up the phone and called Ylva Brink at the hospital. He was told she would be in that evening. Wallander looked up her home phone number and got her machine.

He went back to the contents of the wallet. The photo on the police ID was recent. Svedberg's face was a little fuller but just as glum. Wallander looked through the rest of the contents and found some stamps. That was all. He got out a plastic bag and dumped everything into it. Then he went out into the hall for the third time. Peel everything away, find the traces, Rydberg had said.

Wallander went into the bathroom and relieved himself. He thought about what Sture Björklund had said about the different coloured hairs. The only thing that Wallander knew about the woman in Svedberg's life was that she dyed her hair. He went out into the living room and stood beside the overturned chair. Then he changed his mind. You're proceeding too quickly, Rydberg would have told him. Traces of a crime need to be coaxed out, not rushed.

He returned to the kitchen and called Ylva Brink again. This time she answered.

"I hope I'm not disturbing you," he said. "I know you work all night."

"I can't sleep anyway," she said.

"A lot of questions have come up and I need to ask you some of them right away."

Wallander told her about his talk with Sture Björklund and Björklund's claim that Svedberg had a woman called Louise.

"He never told me any of this," she said when Wallander had finished.

He sensed that the information disturbed her.

"Who never told you? Kalle or Sture?"

"Neither one."

"Let's start with Sture. What kind of relationship do you two have? Are you surprised that he never told you about this?"

"I just can't believe it."

"But why would he lie?"

"I don't know."

Wallander realised that the conversation needed to be continued in person. He looked at the time. It was 5.40 p.m. He needed another hour in the flat.

"It's probably best if we meet," he suggested. "I'm free after 7 p.m. tonight."

"How about at the station? That's close to the hospital, and I could come by on my way to work."

Wallander hung up and returned to the living room. He approached the broken and overturned chair, looked around the room, trying to imagine the actions that had taken place. Svedberg had been shot straight on. Nyberg had mentioned the possibility that the buckshot had entered slightly from below, suggesting that the killer held the shotgun at hip or chest level. The bloodstain on the wall confirmed this upward trajectory. Svedberg must have then fallen to the left, most probably taking the chair down with him, at which point one of its arms broke. But had he been about to sit down, or get up?

Wallander realised the importance of this at once. If Svedberg had been sitting in the chair he must have known his killer. If a burglar had surprised him, he would hardly have sat down or remained sitting.

Wallander went over to the spot where the shotgun had been found. He turned around and looked at the room from his new vantage point. This may not have been the point from which the shot was fired, but it would have been close. He kept still and tried to coax the shadows from their hiding places. The feeling that something about the case was very strange grew stronger. Had Svedberg come in from the hall and surprised a burglar? If this was the case, he would have been in the way. This would also have been true if Svedberg had entered from the bedroom. It was reasonable to assume that a burglar would not have had the shotgun at the ready. Svedberg would no doubt have tried to attack him. He may have been afraid of the dark, but he was certainly not afraid to take action when necessary.

The cement mixer was suddenly turned off. Wallander listened. The sound of traffic was not very loud.

There is another alternative, he thought. The person who entered the flat was someone Svedberg knew. He knew him so well that it would not have worried him to see the shotgun. Then something happened, Svedberg was killed, and the unknown assailant turned the flat inside out looking for something.

Perhaps he simply tried to make it look like a burglary. Wallander thought about the telescope again. It was missing, but who could say if anything else was gone? Maybe Ylva Brink would know the answer.

Wallander went up to the window and looked down at the street. Nils Linnman was locking up a work shed. Robert Tärnberg must already have gone. He had heard the roar of a motorbike being started up a couple of minutes ago.

The doorbell rang. Wallander jumped. He opened the door, and Ann-Britt Höglund came in.

"The construction workers have gone home," Wallander said. "You're too late."

"I showed them Svedberg's picture," she said. "No one saw him, or at least they don't remember it."

They sat down in the kitchen and Wallander told her about his meeting with Sture Björklund. She listened attentively.

"If he's right then that changes our picture of Svedberg quite dramatically," she said when Wallander had finished.

"Why did he keep her a secret for so long?" Wallander asked.

"Maybe she was married."

"An illicit affair? Do you think they met only at Björklund's house? That doesn't seem feasible. They only had access to it a couple of times a year. She can't have come to this flat without anyone ever seeing her."

"Whatever the case, we have to find her," Höglund answered.

"There's something else I've been thinking about," Wallander said slowly. "If he kept her a secret, what else might he have hidden from us?"

He could see she was following his train of thought.

"You don't think it's a burglary."

"I doubt it. A telescope is missing, and Ylva Brink may be able to tell us if anything else is gone, but it doesn't add up. There's no coherence to the scene of the crime."

"We've checked his bank accounts," Höglund said. "At least the ones we've managed to find. There's nothing of note, no outlandish deposits or debts. He has a loan of 25,000 kronor for his car. The bank said that Svedberg always managed his affairs conscientiously."

"One shouldn't speak ill of the dead," Wallander said, "but to tell the truth I thought he was downright miserly."

"How do you mean?"

"We'd always share the tab when we went out, but I'd always leave the tip."

Höglund slowly shook her head. "It's funny how differently we can see people. I never thought of him like that."

Wallander told her about the cement mixer. He had just finished when they both heard a key turning in the lock. They were both struck by the same fleeting sense of dread until they heard Nyberg clearing his throat.

"Those damn newspapers," he said. "I don't know how I could have overlooked them."

He put them into a plastic bag and sealed it.

"When can we find out about prints?" Wallander asked.

"Monday at the earliest."

"What about the autopsy report?"

"Hansson's in charge," Höglund said. "But it should be done pretty quickly."

Wallander asked Nyberg to sit down, then recounted the story of Louise one more time.

"That sounds completely implausible," Nyberg said. "Was there a more confirmed bachelor than Svedberg? What about his lone sauna stints on Friday evenings?"

"It's even more implausible that a professor at Copenhagen University is lying to us," Wallander said. "We have to assume he's telling the truth."

"What if Svedberg simply invented her? If I understood you correctly, no one actually saw her."

Wallander thought about this. Could Louise be a figment of Svedberg's imagination?

"What about the hairs in Björklund's bathtub? They're clearly not an invention."

"Why would anyone invent a story like that about himself?" Nyberg asked.

"Because he's lonely," Höglund answered. "People can go to great lengths to invent the companionship missing from their lives."

"Have you found any hairs in the bathroom?" Wallander asked.

"No," Nyberg answered. "But I'll go and have another look."

Wallander got up. "Come with me for a minute," he said.

They went into the living room and Wallander walked them through the various thoughts that had come to him.

"I'm trying to come up with a provisional starting point for this case," he said. "If this is a burglary, there are many issues that need clearing up. How did the killer enter? Why was he carrying a shotgun? At what point did Svedberg appear? What besides the telescope has been stolen? And why was Svedberg shot? There's no sign of a struggle. There's a mess in almost every room, but I doubt they chased each other around the flat. I can't get the various pieces to fit together, and so I ask myself, what happens if we push the burglary hypothesis aside for a moment? What do we see then? Is it a matter of revenge? Insanity? Since there's a woman in the picture, we can entertain the idea of jealousy. But would a woman shoot Svedberg in the face? I doubt it. What other possibilities are there?"

No one spoke. This silence confirmed Wallander's impression that there was no obvious logic to this case, no simple way to categorise it as a burglary, crime of passion, or something else. There was no apparent reason for Svedberg's murder.

"Can I leave now?" Nyberg said finally. "I still have some reports to finish tonight."

"We're going to have another meeting tomorrow morning."

"What time?"

"We'll aim for 9 a.m."

Nyberg left the other two in the living room.

"I've tried to see an unfolding drama," Wallander said. "What do you see?"

He knew that Höglund could be sharp-sighted, and there was nothing wrong with her analytical skills.

"What if we start with the state of the flat?"

"Yes, what then?"

"There are three possible explanations for the mess. A nervous or hurried burglar, a person looking for something, which of course could also apply to a burglar although he wouldn't know what he was looking for. The third possibility is a person bent on destruction for its own sake. Vandalism."

Wallander followed her train of thought closely.

"There's a fourth possibility," he said. "A person who acts out of uncontrollable rage."

They looked at each other, and each knew what the other was thinking. Occasionally Svedberg would become so angry that he lost all self-control. His rage seemed to come out of the blue. Once he had almost destroyed his office.

"Svedberg could have done this himself," Wallander said. "It's not totally out of the realm of possibility. We know it's happened before. It leads us to a very important question."

"Why?"

"Exactly. Why?"

"I was there when Svedberg trashed his office, but I never understood why he did it," Höglund said.

"It was when Björk was chief of police. He accused Svedberg of stealing confiscated material."

"What kind of material?"

"Some valuable Lithuanian icons, among other things," Wallander answered. "It was loot from a big racketeering case."

"So Svedberg was accused of stealing?"

"No – incompetence and sloppy police work. But, of course, the suspicion was implicit."

"What came of it?"

"Svedberg felt humiliated and smashed everything in his office."

"Did the icons ever turn up?" she asked.

"No, but no one was ever able to prove anything. The racketeers were prosecuted successfully anyway."

"But Svedberg felt humiliated?"

"Yes."

"Unfortunately it doesn't help us. Svedberg trashes his own flat, but then what?"

"We don't know," Wallander said.

They left the living room.

"Did you ever hear of Svedberg receiving threats?" Wallander asked her when they had reached the hall.

"No."

"Has anyone else received any?"

"You know how it is – strange letters and calls are par for the course," she said. "But naturally there would be a record of it."

"Why don't you go through everything that's come in lately," Wallander said. "I'd also like you to talk to whoever delivers the newspapers."

Höglund wrote his requests in her notebook. Wallander opened the front door.

"At least it wasn't Svedberg's gun," she said. "He had no registered weapons."

"That's good to know."

She started walking down the stairs and Wallander returned to the kitchen. He drank a glass of water and thought that he should eat something soon. He was tired. He sat down with his head against the wall and fell asleep.

He was surrounded by snowy mountains that sparkled in the strong sun. His skis looked like the ones he had seen down in Svedberg's basement. He was going faster and faster and he was heading straight down towards a thick layer of fog. Suddenly a ravine opened up in front of him.

He woke up with a start. He looked at the kitchen clock and saw that he had been asleep for eleven minutes.

He sat still and listened to the silence. Then the phone rang. It was Martinsson.

"I thought that's where you were."

"Has anything happened?"

"Eva Hillström has been to see me again."

"What did she want?"

"She said she was going to go to the papers if we don't do something."

Wallander thought for a moment before answering. "I think I may have been misguided this morning," he said. "I'd been meaning to talk about it tomorrow morning anyway."

"What about?"

"Naturally our first priority is Svedberg. But we can't shelve the case of the missing young people. Somehow we have to find the time to do both."

"How are we going to do that?"

"I don't know. But it's not the first time we've had so much work to do."

"I promised Mrs Hillström I would call her after speaking with you."

"Good. Try to calm her down. We're going to move on it."

"Are you coming by?"

"I'm on my way. I'm going to see Ylva Brink."

"Do you think we'll solve Svedberg's murder?"

Wallander sensed Martinsson's concern.

"Yes," he said. "Of course we will. But I have a feeling it'll be complicated."

He hung up. Some pigeons flew by the window and a thought suddenly came to Wallander.

Höglund had said that the murder weapon was not registered in Svedberg's name. The reasonable conclusion to make was that Svedberg had no weapons. But reality was rarely reasonable. Weren't there countless unregistered guns floating around Swedish society? It was a constant source of concern for the police. Couldn't a police officer in fact also possibly be in possession of an unregistered weapon? What would that mean? What if the murder weapon did belong to Svedberg? Wallander felt his sense of urgency return. He got up quickly and left the flat.

CHAPTER EIGHT

István Kecskeméti had come to Sweden exactly 40 years earlier, part of that stream of Hungarian immigrants who were forced to leave their country after the failed revolution. He had been 14 years old when he came to Sweden with his parents and his three younger siblings. His father was an engineer who at the end of the 1920s had visited the Separator factories outside of Stockholm. That's where he was hoping to find work. But they never got further than Trelleborg. On the way down the steep stairs of the ferry terminal, he suffered a stroke. His second encounter with Swedish soil was when his body smacked into the wet asphalt. He was buried in the graveyard in Trelleborg, the family stayed in Skåne, and now István was 54 years old. He had long been the owner and manager of one of the many pizzerias dotting the length of Ystad's Hamngatan.

Wallander had heard István's story a long time ago. Wallander ate there from time to time, and if there weren't many customers around, István would happily sit down and talk. It was 6.30 p.m. when Wallander walked in, with half an hour to spare before meeting Ylva Brink. There were no other customers, just as Wallander had expected. From the kitchen came the sound of a radio and of someone banging a meat cleaver. István was just finishing a phone call by the bar, and waved to Wallander as he sat down at a table in the corner. He came over with a serious expression.

"Is it true what I've heard? That a policeman is dead?"

"Unfortunately yes," Wallander answered. "Karl Evert Svedberg. Did you meet him?"

"I don't think he ever came in," István said. "Do you want a beer? It's on the house." Wallander shook his head.

"I'd like to have something that's quick," he said. "And appropriate for someone with high blood-sugar levels."

István looked at him with concern.

"Have you become diabetic?"

"No. But my sugar level is too high."

"Then you are a diabetic."

"Well, perhaps temporarily. I'm in a bit of a hurry right now."

"How about a small steak, sautéed in a little oil, and a green salad?"

"That sounds good."

István left and Wallander wondered why he reacted as if diabetes was something to be ashamed of. Maybe it wasn't so strange. He hated the fact that he was overweight. He wanted to pretend the problem wasn't there.

As usual he ate much too fast. He drank a cup of coffee while István was tending to a group of Polish tourists. Wallander was happy to avoid having to answer questions about Svedberg's murder. He paid his bill and left.

He got to the police station just after 7 p.m. Ylva Brink had not yet arrived. He went straight to Martinsson's office. Hansson was also there.

"How is it going?" he asked.

"There are almost no leads from the public, which is a little unusual."

"Anything from Lund?"

"Not yet," Hansson said. "We'll have to wait until Monday."

"We need to establish the time of death," Wallander said. "As soon as we get that, we'll have a starting point."

"I've checked the files," Martinsson said. "Neither the murder nor the burglary matches any previous case."

"We don't know it was a burglary," Wallander said.

"What else could it have been?"

"I don't know. I have to go and see Ylva Brink now. I'll see you two tomorrow at 9 a.m."

He went to his office and found a note on his desk from Lisa Holgersson, who wanted to speak to him as soon as possible. Wallander tried to call her but she had left. Wallander decided to call her at home later that evening.

A few minutes later Ylva Brink arrived. Wallander asked her if she wanted some coffee but she said no. He decided to use a tape recorder for this interview. Normally he found it distracting, as if a third party were eavesdropping on the person he was interviewing, but he wanted to have access to this conversation word for word. He asked Ylva Brink if she had any objections, but she didn't.

"It's not like it's an interrogation," he said. "It's just that I want to remember what we talk about. This machine is better at that than I am."

He pushed the record button and the tape started turning. It was 7.19 p.m.

"Friday, 9 August, 1996," Wallander stated. "Interview with Ylva Brink in connection with Inspector Karl Evert Svedberg's death by manslaughter or homicide."

"Well, what other possibilities are there?" she asked.

"Police language is full of these redundant expressions," Wallander said. He too had thought that it sounded stilted.

"It's been a few hours," he began. "You've had some time to think. You've probably been asking yourself why it happened. A murder often seems senseless to everyone except the murderer."

"I still can't quite believe it's true. I talked to my husband several hours ago – it's possible to place satellite calls to the boat. He thought I was crazy. But when I heard the words come out of my mouth, the reality hit me."

"I would have liked to be able to wait before pressing you to talk about it. But we can't wait. We have to catch the killer as soon as possible. He has a head start and it's getting bigger all the time."

She seemed to be steeling herself for his first real question.

"This woman Louise," Wallander said. "Apparently Karl Evert had been meeting her for years. Did you ever see her?"

"No."

"Did you ever hear him talk about her?"

"No."

"What was your first reaction when I told you about her?"

"I didn't think it was true."

"What do you think now?"

"That it's true, but still completely incomprehensible."

"You and Karl Evert must have talked at some point about why he had never married. What did he say?"

"That he was a confirmed bachelor and happy that way."

"Was there anything unusual about the way he said this?"

"How do you mean?"

"Did he seem nervous? Could you tell if he was lying?"

"He was completely convincing."

Wallander detected a note of hesitation in her voice.

"I have the feeling you might just have thought of something."

She didn't answer immediately. The tape recorder was whirring in the background.

"Occasionally I wondered if he was different . . ."

"You mean, if he was gay?"

"Yes."

"Why did that occur to you?"

"Isn't it a natural reaction?"

Wallander recalled that he himself had sometimes been conscious of this possibility.

"Yes, of course it is."

"It came up in conversation once. He was invited over for Christmas dinner, quite a few years ago. We were discussing whether or not a person that we both knew was homosexual. I remember very clearly how vehemently disgusted he was."

"By the friend's supposed homosexuality?"

"By homosexuality in general. It was very unpleasant. I had always considered him a tolerant person."

"What happened after that?"

"Nothing. We never spoke of it again."

Wallander thought for a moment. "How do you think we could go about finding this Louise?"

"I have no idea."

"Since he never left Ystad, she must live here or in the near vicinity."

"I suppose so."

She looked at her watch.

"When do you have to be at work?" Wallander asked.

"In half an hour. I don't like to be late."

"Just like Karl Evert. He was always very punctual."

"Yes, he was. What's that saying? Someone you could set your watch by."

"What kind of a person was he, really?"

"You've already asked me that."

"Well, I'm asking you again."

"He was nice."

"How do you mean?"

"Nice. A nice person. I don't know how else to put it. He was a nice person who could sometimes fly into a rage, although that didn't happen very often. He was a little shy. Dutiful. Some people probably thought him boring. He might have seemed a bit aloof and slow, but he was intelligent."

Wallander thought her description of Svedberg was accurate and close to something he might have said if their roles had been reversed.

"Who was his best friend?"

Her answer shocked him.

"I thought you were."

"Me?"

"He always said so. 'Kurt Wallander is the best friend I have.'"

Wallander was dumbstruck. For him Svedberg had always been a colleague. They never saw each other outside of work. He hadn't become a friend in the way that Rydberg had been, and that Höglund was slowly becoming.

"That comes as quite a surprise," he said finally. "I didn't think of him in that way."

"But he may have considered you his best friend, regardless of what you thought."

"Of course."

Wallander suddenly realised how lonely Svedberg must have been. His definition of friendship had been grounded on the lowest common denominator, an absence of animosity. He stared into the tape recorder, then forced himself to continue.

"Did he have any other friends or people he spent a lot of time with?"

"He was in contact with a society for the study of Native American culture. I think it was called 'Indian Science'. But their activities were mainly conducted by correspondence."

"Anything else?"

"Sometimes he mentioned a retired bank director who lives in town. They shared an interest in astronomy."

"What was his name?"

She thought for a moment. "Sundelius. Bror Sundelius. I never met him myself."

Wallander made a note of the name.

"Anyone else you can think of ?"

"Just me and my husband."

Wallander changed the subject.

"Do you recall anything unusual during his last weeks? Was he anxious, or did he seem distracted?"

"He didn't say anything except that he felt overworked."

"But he didn't say why?"

"No."

Wallander realised he had forgotten to ask her something. "Did it surprise you that he said he was overworked?"

"No, not at all."

"So he usually mentioned how he was feeling?"

"I should have thought of this before," she said. "There's one more thing I would add to my description of him – that he was a hypochondriac. The smallest little ache would worry him enormously. And he was terrified of germs."

Wallander could see him, the way he was always running to the bathroom to wash his hands. He always avoided people with colds. She looked at the clock again. Time was running out.

"Did he own any weapons?"

"Not that I know of."

"Is there anything else you would like to tell me, anything that seems important?"

"I'm going to miss him. Maybe he wasn't such an extraordinary person, but he was the most honourable person I knew. I'm going to miss him."

Wallander turned off the tape recorder and followed her out. For a moment she seemed helpless.

"What am I going to do about the funeral?" she asked. "Sture thinks the dead should be scattered to the wind without priests and rites. But I don't know what his own thoughts were."

"He didn't leave a will?"

"Not that I know of. I'm sure he would have told me."

"Did he have a safe-deposit box at the bank?"

"No."

"Would you have known about it?"

"Yes."

"The police will attend the funeral, of course," Wallander said. "I'll ask Lisa Holgersson to be in touch."

Ylva Brink went out through the front glass doors. Wallander returned to his office. Yet another name had cropped up: Bror Sundelius. As Wallander looked him up in the phone book, he thought about the conversation with Ylva Brink. What had she really told him that he hadn't already known? That Louise was a well-kept secret. A well-guarded secret, Wallander thought.

He made some notes to himself. Why would you keep a woman secret for so long? Ylva Brink had told him about Svedberg's strong aversion to homosexuality, and about his hypochondria. She had also said he met with a retired bank director from time to time to study the night sky. Wallander laid down his pen and leaned back in his chair.

For the most part, his picture of Svedberg remained the same. The only revelation was this woman, Louise. And nothing seemed to point to an explanation of his death. He felt that he suddenly saw the whole drama clearly in front of him. Svedberg had failed to show up for work because he was already dead. He had caught a burglar by surprise who shot him on the spot, then fled with the telescope in his arms. The crime was unpremeditated, banal and horrifying. There was no other possible explanation.

It was 8.10 p.m. Wallander called Lisa Holgersson at home. She wanted to talk about the funeral and he told her to contact Ylva Brink. Then he told her what they had learned over the course of the afternoon. He also told her that he was starting to lean towards the violent-and-heavily-drugged-burglar theory.

"The national chief of police has called me," she said. "He wanted to express his condolences and his concern."

"In that order?"

"Yes, thank God."

Wallander told her he had arranged a meeting the next morning at 9 a.m., and promised to keep her abreast of any developments. After he'd hung up, Wallander dialled the number for Sundelius, but there was no answer or even an answerphone.

Once he put the phone down again he felt somewhat at a loss. Where should he go from here? He felt a growing impatience, but knew he had to wait for the autopsy report and the forensic evidence to come in.

He started to replay the conversation with Ylva Brink and thought about the last thing she had said, that Svedberg was honourable. There was a knock at the door and Martinsson entered.

"There's a bunch of impatient reporters at the door," he said. Wallander made a face.

"We don't have anything new to tell them."

"I think they'll make do with something old, just as long as they get something."

"Can't you send them away for now? Promise them a press conference as soon as we feel we have something to report."

"Have you forgotten the orders that came from on high instructing us to get along smoothly with the press?" Martinsson said, his voice heavy with irony.

Wallander hadn't forgotten. The national chief of police had recently issued directives to improve relations between the various police districts and local media. Reporters were now to be welcomed and treated with kid gloves.

Wallander got up heavily. "I'll talk to them," he said.

It took him 20 minutes to convince the reporters that he had no new information to give them. He almost lost his temper towards the end, when they continued to regard his claim with suspicion. But he managed to control himself and the reporters finally left. He got a cup of coffee from the canteen and went back to his office. He called Sundelius once more without success.

The phone rang. More reporters, Wallander thought despondently. But it was Sten Widén.

"Where are you?" Widén asked. "I realise you have a lot going on and you have my condolences, but I've been waiting here for a while now."

Wallander swore under his breath. He had completely forgotten his promise to visit Sten Widén at his horse ranch near the castle ruins at Stjärnsund. They had been friends since childhood and shared a passion for opera. As adults, they had started to grow apart. Wallander became a police officer and Sten Widén took over the ranch from his father, where he raised racehorses. A couple of years ago they had started seeing each other again, and they had made plans for this evening. It had totally slipped his mind.

"I should have called you," Wallander said. "I completely forgot."

"They announced it over the radio. Was your colleague murdered or was it manslaughter?"

"We don't know, it's too early to tell. But the last 24 hours have been horrific."

"We can get together some other time."

Wallander made up his mind. "Give me half an hour."

"Don't feel pressured."

"I don't; I need to get away for a while."

Wallander left the station, went to the flat and picked up his mobile phone, then took the E65 out of town. He saw the castle ruins and slowed down to turn into Widén's ranch. Apart from the neighing of a horse, all was quiet.

Widén came out to greet him. Wallander was used to seeing him in dirty work clothes, but now he was wearing a white shirt and his hair was combed back. As they shook hands Wallander smelt alcohol on his breath. He knew that Widén drank too much, but he had never said anything to him. Somehow it never came up.

"What a beautiful evening," Widén said. "Summer finally arrived in August. Or is it the other way around? August finally arrived with summer. Who really arrives with whom?"

Wallander felt a twinge of jealousy. This was what he had dreamed of, living out in the countryside with a dog and maybe even Baiba. But nothing had come of it.

"How's business?" he asked.

"Not so good. The eighties were the golden decade. Everyone seemed to have plenty of money then. Now they don't. People spend most of their time praying they won't lose their jobs."

"Isn't it just the wealthy who buy racehorses? I didn't think they had to worry about unemployment."

"They're still around," Widén agreed. "But there don't seem to be as many of them as before."

They walked down towards the stables. A girl wearing riding gear appeared around the corner with a horse.

"That's Sofia. She's the only one left. I had to get rid of everyone else," Widén said.

Wallander remembered hearing something a couple of years ago about Widén sleeping with one of the girls working on the ranch. What had her name been? Jenny?

Widén exchanged some words with the girl and Wallander caught the name of the horse, Black Triangle. The outlandish names still surprised him.

They went into the stables.

"This is Dreamgirl Express," Widén said, showing him another horse. "Right now she supports me almost all by herself. Owners complain about the upkeep being expensive, and my accountant keeps calling earlier and earlier in the morning. I really don't know how much longer I can get by."

Wallander stroked the horse's muzzle carefully.

"You've always managed before," he said.

Widén shook his head.

"Right now it doesn't look good," he said. "But I can probably get a good price for the place and then I'll take off."

"Where will you go?"

"I'm just going to pack my bags, get a good night's sleep, and decide in the morning."

They left the stables and walked up to the main house. Wallander remembered it being a huge mess, but surprisingly everything was very neatly arranged this time.

"A couple of months ago I realised that cleaning could be therapeutic," Widén said in answer to Wallander's obvious surprise.

"That doesn't work for me. God knows I've tried."

Widén gestured for him to sit at the table, where he had set out glasses and a couple of bottles. Wallander hesitated, then nodded and sat down. His doctor wouldn't like it but right now he didn't have the energy to abstain.

"Do you remember that time we went to Germany to hear Wagner?" Widén said, much later in the evening. "It's 25 years ago now. I found some photos the other day. Do you want to see them?"

"Sure."

"I treat them like valuables," Widén said. "I've put them in my secret compartment."

Wallander watched as Widén removed part of the wooden panelling next to the window and took out a metal box that had been jammed into the space underneath. The pictures were in the box. Widén held them out to Wallander, who took them, marvelling at what he saw.

One of the pictures was taken at a roadside rest area outside Lübeck. Wallander had a bottle of beer in his hand and was bellowing at the photographer.

"We had a great time," Widén said. "Maybe more fun than we've ever had since."

Wallander poured some more whisky into his glass. Widén was right. They had never had as much fun after that.

Close to 1 a.m., they called a company in Skurup and

ordered a taxi. Widén agreed to drive his car in the next day. Wallander already had a headache and felt sick to his stomach. He was very, very tired.

"We should go back to Germany sometime," Widén said as they were waiting for the cab.

"No, we shouldn't go back," Wallander said. "We should take a new trip. Not that I have any property I can sell."

The car came and Wallander got into the back seat, leaned back, and fell asleep immediately.

Just as they passed the turn-off to Rydsgård something pulled him up to the surface again. At first he didn't know what it was. Something had flickered through his mind in the dream he'd been having. But then he remembered what it was: Widén had removed a piece of the wood panelling.

Wallander's mind became crystal clear at once. Svedberg had kept the woman in his life a secret for years. But when Wallander had searched his desk he hadn't found anything except some old letters from his parents. Svedberg must have a secret compartment, Wallander thought. Just like Sten Widén.

He leaned forward to the driver and changed the destination from Mariagatan to the town square. A little after 1.30 a.m. he got out of the cab. He still had the keys to Svedberg's flat in his pocket. He remembered seeing some aspirin in Svedberg's medicine cabinet. He unlocked the front door of the flat, held his breath, and listened. Then he poured himself a glass of water and took the aspirin.

Some drunken teenagers walked by on the street below, and then the silence returned. He put the glass down and started looking for Svedberg's secret compartment. By 2.45 a.m. he had found it. A corner of the plastic flooring under the chest of drawers in the bedroom could be peeled away from the concrete base. Wallander repositioned the bedside lamp so that light fell on the exposed area. There was a brown envelope stuffed in the space under the mat. It wasn't sealed. He took it out into the kitchen and opened it.

Like Widén, Svedberg treated his photographs as valuables. There were two pictures inside the envelope. One was a studio portrait of a woman's face. The other photograph was a snapshot of a group of young people who sat in the shadow of a tree and raised their wineglasses towards an unknown photographer.

The scene was idyllic. There was only one thing that struck Wallander as odd. The young people were dressed in elaborate, old-fashioned costumes, as if the party had taken place in a bygone era.

Wallander put on his glasses. His stomach started to ache. He recalled having seen a magnifying glass in one of Svedberg's drawers, and he got it out and studied the photograph more closely. There was something familiar about these young people, especially the girl who sat on the extreme right. Then he suddenly knew who it was. He had seen another picture of her recently, one in which she was not dressed up. The girl on the far right was Astrid Hillström.

Wallander slowly lowered the photograph. Somewhere a clock struck 3 a.m.

CHAPTER NINE

By 6 a.m. on Saturday, 10 August, Wallander couldn't stand it any longer. He had spent most of the remaining night pacing back and forth in his flat, too anxious to sleep. The two pictures he had found at Svedberg's place lay on the kitchen table. They had been burning a hole in his pocket ever since he'd made his way home through the deserted town. It wasn't until he took off his coat that he realised it must have been raining slightly outside.

The photographs in Svedberg's secret compartment were a crucial find. What convinced him of this he couldn't say, but the free-floating anxiety he had felt since the beginning of this case had now escalated into full-blown fear. A case that hadn't even been a case, three young people who were travelling around Europe somewhere, now appeared in the middle of one of the most serious murder investigations the Ystad police had ever undertaken – the killing of one of their own. During the hours after Wallander's discovery, his thoughts were muddled and contradictory. But he knew that this was a crucial breakthrough.

What was it the photographs told him? The picture of Louise was in black-and-white, the snapshot in colour. There was no date printed on the back of either. Did that mean they weren't developed in commercial laboratories? Or were there local businesses that didn't use automatic dating systems? The sizes of the photographs were standard. He tried to decide if the pictures were taken by an amateur or not, since he knew that pictures developed in private darkrooms often did not dry to a uniform finish. But he lacked the expertise to answer his questions.

Next he asked himself what feelings the two photographs evoked. What did they say about the photographer? He was not yet willing to assume that they were taken by the same person. Had Svedberg taken the picture of Louise? Her gaze was impenetrable. The picture of the young people was also hard to pin down. He did not see a conscious sense of composition. The dominating principle appeared to be the inclusion of everyone in the frame. Someone had picked up a camera, told everyone to look over, and pushed the button. Maybe there was a whole series of pictures from this festive occasion. But where were they?

The sheer implausibility of the connection worried him. They already knew that Svedberg had started investigating the disappearance of the young people only a few days before he had gone on holiday.

Why would he have done that? And why would he have done it in secret? Where did the photograph of the young revellers come from? Where was it taken? And then this picture of the woman. It couldn't be anyone but Louise. Wallander studied it for a long time as he sat at the kitchen table. The woman was in her 40s, perhaps a couple of years younger than Svedberg. If they had met 10 years earlier, she might have been 30 and he 35. That seemed pretty reasonable. The woman had straight, dark hair in a style Wallander knew was called a page boy cut. Because it was a black-and-white photograph, he couldn't tell what colour her eyes were. She had a thin nose and face, and her lips were pressed together in the hint of a smile. It was a Mona Lisa smile, but the woman had no glimmer of a smile in her eyes. Wallander thought the picture had been retouched, or else she was heavily made up. There was something veiled about the photograph, something he couldn't place. The woman's face was evasive. It had been captured by the camera but was still not there somehow.

These photographs have been kept in a vacuum, Wallander thought. They lack fingerprints, like two unread books.

He managed to hold out until 6 a.m. and then he called Martinsson, who was an early riser. He answered almost at once.

"I hope I didn't wake you."

"If you call me at 10 p.m. you'd be in danger of doing that. But not at 6 a.m. I was about to go out and work in the garden."

Wallander came right to the point. He told him about the photographs. Martinsson listened without asking any questions.

"I want to meet with everyone as soon as possible," Wallander said when he finished. "Not at 9 a.m. At 7 a.m."

"Have you talked to anyone else?"

"No, you're the first."

"Who do you want?"

"Everyone, including Nyberg."

"Then you'll have to call him yourself – he's so moody in the mornings. I can't deal with angry people until after I've had my morning coffee."

Martinsson volunteered to call Hansson and Höglund, leaving the others to Wallander. He started with Nyberg, who was as sleepy and ill-tempered as expected.

"We're meeting at 7 a.m., not 9 a.m.," Wallander said.

"Has anything happened, or are you just doing this for the hell of it?"

"If you ever find you've been called to an investigative meeting just for the hell of it, you should contact your union representative."

He regretted that last comment to Nyberg. He went out to the kitchen and put on some water for a cup of coffee. Then he called Lisa Holgersson, who promised to be there. Wallander took the coffee with him out onto the balcony, where the thermometer indicated that it would be another warm day. There was the sudden clatter from something being pushed through the post slot in the front door.

It was his car keys. And after a night like that, he thought. Sten is amazing. He was weighed down with fatigue. With self-disgust, he suddenly imagined little white icebergs of sugar floating around in his veins.

He left the flat just after 6.30 a.m., and bumped into the person who delivered the newspapers, an older man named Stefansson who had bicycle clips around his trouser legs.

"Sorry I'm late today," he apologised. "There was something wrong with the presses this morning."

"Do you deliver papers at Lilla Norregatan as well?" Wallander asked.

Stefansson understood him at once. "You mean to the policeman who was killed?"

"Yes."

"A lady by the name of Selma works there. She's the oldest delivery person around. I think she started in 1947. What's that, nearly 50 years?"

"What's her last name?"

"Nylander."

Stefansson handed Wallander the paper.

"There's something about you in there," he said.

"Put it in my slot," Wallander said. "I won't have time to read it."

Wallander knew he could make it on time if he walked, but he took the car anyway. The start of his new life would have to be pushed back another day.

He ran into Höglund in the car park. "The person who delivers papers to Svedberg's building is called Selma Nylander," he told her. "Have you talked to her?"

"No, it turns out she doesn't have a phone."

Wallander thought about Sture Björklund's decision to throw out his telephone. Was it becoming a general trend? They went into the conference room. Wallander made himself a cup of coffee, and stood out in the corridor for a while trying to think how to organise the meeting. He was normally very well prepared, but this time couldn't think of anything except putting the photographs on the table and seeing what people had to say.

He closed the door behind him and sat in his usual spot. Svedberg's chair was still empty. Wallander took the pictures out of his coat pocket and told them briefly how he had found them. He omitted the fact that the thought had come to him while he lay in a drunken stupor in the back of a taxi. Since being stopped for driving under the influence by some of his colleagues six years ago, he never mentioned drinking alcohol.

The photographs lay in front of him. Hansson set up the projector.

"I'd like to point out that the girl to the far right in this picture is Astrid Hillström, one of the young people who has been missing since Midsummer."

He put both pictures into the projector. There was silence around the table. Wallander took the opportunity to study the pictures more closely himself as he waited, but couldn't pick out any additional details. He had used the magnifying glass carefully during those early hours.

Martinsson finally broke the silence. "You have to hand it to Svedberg," he said. "She's beautiful. Does anyone recognise her? Ystad isn't a big city."

No one had seen her before, nor any of the young people. It was, however, clear to everyone in the room that the girl to the far right was Astrid Hillström. The picture of her on file resembled this one closely, except for the clothes.

"Is it a masquerade?" Chief Holgersson asked. "What period is it meant to be?"

"The 17th century," Hansson said confidently.

Wallander looked at him with surprise. "How do you know that?"

"Maybe it's more like the 18th century," he said, changing his mind.

"I think it's the 16th century," Höglund said. "King Gustav I Vasa's time. They dressed in the same billowing sleeves and leggings."

"Are you sure?" Wallander asked.

"Of course I'm not sure. I'm just telling you what I think."

"Let's steer clear of educated guesses for a moment. The most important thing here is not how they're dressed up. It will eventually be important to figure out why they were dressed up, but even that can wait."

He looked around at everyone before continuing. "We have a picture of a woman in her 40s and a picture of a group of young people dressed up in some kind of costume. One of these young people is Astrid Hillström, who has been missing since Midsummer, although she's most probably travelling around Europe with two of her friends. This is what we know. I found these pictures hidden in the flat of our colleague Svedberg, who has been murdered. The way we need to begin our investigation is by determining what happened on Midsummer's Eve. That's where we start."

It took them three hours to go through the available material. Most of the time was spent formulating new questions and deciding who would do what. After two hours they took a short break and everyone except Chief Holgersson had coffee. Then they kept going. The team was starting to come together. At 10.15 a.m. Wallander felt they couldn't get any further.

Holgersson had been quiet for a long time, as she often was during their investigative work. Wallander knew she had great respect for their abilities. But now she raised her hand slightly.

"What do you really think has happened to them?" she asked. "If there's been any kind of an accident you would think it would have been discovered by now."

"I don't know," Wallander said. "The very supposition that something has happened to them leads us to conclude that their signatures on the postcards were forged. Why?"

"To cover up a crime," Nyberg suggested.

The room became quiet. Wallander looked at Nyberg and nodded slowly.

"And not just any crime," he said. "People who go missing either stay that way or turn up. There's only one possible explanation for these postcards having been forged, and that is that someone is trying to hide the fact that these three people – Boge, Norman and Hillström – are dead."

"That tells us another thing," Höglund said. "The person who sent these postcards knows what happened to them."

"Not just that," Wallander said. "It's the person who killed them, a person who can forge their signatures and handwriting, and who knows where they live."

It was as if Wallander needed time to get to his final conclusion. "If our supposition is correct," he said, "then we have to assume that these three were the victims of a calculating and well-organised murderer."

His words were followed by a long silence. Wallander already knew what he wanted to say next but wondered if anyone would jump in. Outside in the hall someone laughed loudly. Nyberg blew his nose. Hansson was staring off into space and Martinsson drummed his fingers on the table. Höglund and Holgersson were looking at Wallander.

My two allies, he thought.

"We are forced into the realm of speculation at this point," he said. "One line of reasoning will be particularly unpleasant and unimaginable, but we cannot overlook the part that Svedberg may have played in these events. We know he kept a photograph of Astrid Hillström and her friends hidden in his flat. We know that he conducted his investigations into their disappearance in secret. We don't know what drove him to do these things, but the three of them are still missing and he has been killed. It may have been a burglary of some kind, it may have been the case that someone was looking for something, perhaps for this very picture. But we cannot definitively rule out the possibility that Svedberg himself may have been involved in some way."

Hansson dropped his pen on the table. "You can't mean that!" he said, visibly upset. "One of our colleagues is brutally murdered, we're trying to find his killer, and you're suggesting that he was involved in an even greater crime."

"We have to consider it as a possibility," Wallander said.

"You're right," Nyberg interrupted. "However unappealing

it is. Since the Belgian case I've had the feeling that anything is possible."

Nyberg was right. The macabre string of child murders in Belgium had been linked in unsavoury ways to both the police and politicians. These links were still tenuous, but no one doubted that many dramatic revelations were to come.

Wallander nodded for Nyberg to continue.

"What I'm wondering is how Louise fits into the picture."

"We don't know," Wallander said. "We have to try to proceed in as open-minded a fashion as possible and try to answer all our questions, including who this woman is."

A certain gloom fell over the group as they divided up the tasks and accepted that they would now be working around the clock. Holgersson would see about bringing in extra personnel. They finished a little after 10.30 a.m. Wallander signalled to Höglund to remain behind. When they were alone, he gestured for her to close the door.

"Tell me what your thinking is on this," he said when she had sat down.

"Naturally some thoughts are so repulsive that you try to block them out."

"Of course. Svedberg was our friend. Now we have reason to speculate that he may have been a criminal."

"Do you really think so?"

"No, but I have to consider even what seems impossible, if that makes any sense."

"Then what do you think happened?"

"That's what I want you to tell me."

"Well, a connection has now been established between Svedberg and those three young people."

"No, that's not true. A connection has been established between Svedberg and Astrid Hillström."

She nodded.

"What else do you see?" he asked.

"That Svedberg was someone other than we thought."

Wallander pounced on this. "And how did we think he was?"

She thought a moment before answering. "That he was open, trustworthy."

"But in reality he turned out to be secretive and untrustworthy, is that what you mean?"

"Not exactly, but something like that."

"One of his secrets involved a woman, who may have been called Louise. We know what she looks like."

Wallander got up, turned on the projector, and slipped the picture back into the machine.

"I have the strange feeling that there's something wrong with this face. But I can't think what it is."

Höglund hesitated, but Wallander sensed that his statement didn't surprise her.

"There's something odd about her hair," she said finally. "Although I can't put my finger on it."

"We have to find her," Wallander said. "And we will."

He put the second photograph in the projector and looked at Höglund. Again she answered hesitantly.

"I'm quite convinced that they're wearing clothes from the 16th century. I have a book at home about fashion through the ages. But I could be wrong."

"What else do you see?"

"Young people who seem happy. Excited and drunk."

Wallander suddenly thought of the pictures that Sten Widén showed him from their trip to Germany, especially the drunken one of himself with the beer bottle in his hand. There was a similarity in the expressions on their faces.

"What else do you see?"

"The boy, the second from the left, is yelling something to the photographer."

"They're sitting on a blanket with food spread out, and they're dressed up. What does that mean?"

"A masquerade of some sort. A party."

"Let's assume it's a summer event of some kind," Wallander said.

"The whole picture gives the impression of warm weather. It could very well be a Midsummer's Eve party, but it can't have been taken this summer, since Norman isn't in the picture."

"And Astrid Hillström seems a little younger."

Wallander agreed. "I thought that too. The picture could be a couple of years old."

"There's nothing threatening in the photograph," she said. "At that age, they're as happy as they can be. Life seems endless, the sorrows few."

"I have such a strange feeling about this," Wallander said. "I've never been at the beginning of an investigation like this one. Svedberg is the centre, of course, but the compass needle keeps swinging back and forth. We can't see where we should go."

They left the room. Höglund took the envelope with the two photographs to give to Nyberg so he could check them for fingerprints. First she would make some copies of both. Wallander went to the lavatory and then drank almost a litre of water in the canteen.

Everyone set to work on their assigned tasks. Wallander's job was to talk to Eva Hillström and Sture Björklund again. He sat down in his office and reached for the phone. He was going to start with Hillström, but he decided against phoning her first. Höglund knocked on his door and handed him some photocopies of the pictures. The picture of the young people had been enlarged so that their faces appeared as clearly as possible.

It was around midday when Wallander left the station. He heard someone say that it was about 23°C. He took off his jacket before getting into the car.

Eva Hillström lived on Körlingsväg, which was just outside Ystad's eastern border. He parked the car outside the gate and looked at the house. It was a large, turn-of-the-century villa, with a beautifully maintained garden. He walked up to the front door and rang the bell. Eva Hillström opened the door and jumped when she saw who it was.

"Nothing's happened," Wallander said quickly, anxious to stop her from imagining the worst. "I just have some more questions."

She let him into a big hall that smelled strongly of disinfectant. She was barefoot and wearing a tracksuit. Her eyes darted anxiously around the room.

"I hope I'm not intruding," Wallander said.

She mumbled something unintelligible and he followed her into a spacious living room. The art and furniture gave the impression of being valuable. There was certainly nothing wrong with the Hillströms' finances. He sat down obediently on the sofa that she indicated to him.

"Can I get you anything?" she asked.

Wallander shook his head. He was thirsty but didn't want to ask for a glass of water. She was sitting on the very edge of her seat, and Wallander had the strange impression that she was a runner at the start of a race, waiting for the gun to go off. He took out his photocopies, and handed her the picture of Louise. She looked at it briefly and then up at him.

"Who is this?"

"You don't recognise her?"

"Does she have anything to do with Astrid?"

Her attitude was hostile and Wallander forced himself to sound very firm.

"It is sometimes necessary for us to ask routine questions," he said. "I just showed you a picture, and my question is, do you know who it is?"

"Who is she?"

"Just answer the question."

"I've never seen her before."

"Then we don't have to say anything more about it."

She was about to ask him something else when Wallander gave her the other picture. She looked at it quickly, then got up out of her chair and left the room, as if the starting gun had just gone off. She came back after about a minute and handed Wallander a photograph.

"Photocopies are never as good as the original," she said in response to his puzzled face.

Wallander looked down at the photo. It was the same as the photocopy, the same picture he had found in Svedberg's flat. He felt a step closer to something important.

"Tell me about this photograph," he said. "When was it taken? Who are the other people in it?"

"I don't know exactly where it is," she said. "Somewhere around Österlen, I think. Maybe at Brösarp's hill. Astrid gave it to me."

"When was it taken?"

"Last summer, in July. It was Magnus's birthday."

"Magnus?"

She pointed to the boy who was shouting at the unknown photographer. Wallander pulled out the notebook he had for once remembered to bring.

"What's his full name?"

"Magnus Holmgren. He lives in Trelleborg."

"Who are the rest?"

Wallander took down their names and where they lived. Suddenly he remembered something else.

"Who took the picture?" he asked.

"Astrid's camera had a self-timing mechanism."

"So she took it?"

"I just told you the camera had a self-timer!"

Wallander moved on.

"This is a birthday party for Magnus, but why are they dressed up?"

"That was something they did. I can't see anything strange about it."

"I don't either, I just have to ask these questions."

She lit a cigarette. Wallander felt she was on the verge of breaking down again.

"So Astrid has a lot of friends," he said.

"Not that many," Eva Hillström said. "But good ones."

She took up the photo again and pointed to the other girl.

"Isa wasn't with them this year at Midsummer," she said. "Unfortunately she fell ill."

It took a moment for her words to sink in. Then Wallander understood.

"You mean that this other girl was supposed to have been with them?"

"She fell ill."

"And so it was just the three of them? And they went ahead with the party and then took off together for a trip to Europe?"

"Yes."

Wallander looked down at his notes.

"What's her full name?"

"Isa Edengren. Her father is a businessman. They live in Skårby."

"What has she said about the trip?"

"That nothing had been decided in advance. But she's sure they've gone. They always took their passports with them on these occasions."

"Have they sent her any postcards?"

"No."

"Doesn't she think that's strange?"

"Yes."

Eva Hillström put out her cigarette.

"Something's happened," she said. "I don't know what it is, but Isa's wrong. They haven't left. They're still here."

Wallander saw that there were tears in her eyes.

"Why won't anyone listen to me?" she asked. "Only one person listened, but now he's gone too."

Wallander held his breath.

"Only one person has listened to you," he said. "Is that correct?"

"Yes."

"Do you mean the police officer who visited you at the end of June?"

She looked at him with surprise. "He came many times," she said. "Not just then. During July he came every week, and a couple of times this week as well."

"Do you mean Officer Svedberg?"

"Why did he have to die?" she said. "He was the only one who listened, the only one who was as worried as I was."

Wallander was silent. Suddenly he had nothing to say.

CHAPTER TEN

The breeze was so gentle that sometimes he didn't feel it at all. He counted how often he actually felt the wind on his face, just to make the time go a little faster. He was going to add this to his list of pleasures in life, the joys of the happy person. He had remained hidden behind a large tree for several hours. The fact that he was so early gave him a feeling of satisfaction.

It was still a warm evening. When he had woken that morning, he had known that the time had come to go public. He couldn't wait any longer. He had slept for exactly eight hours, like he normally did. Somewhere in his subconscious the decision had been made. He was going to recreate the events that had occurred 50 days ago.

He got up around 5 a.m., again like always, making no exception to his routine although this was his day off. After drinking a cup of the tea that he ordered directly from Shanghai, he rolled away the red carpet in the living room and did his morning exercises. After 20 minutes he measured his heart rate, wrote it down in a notebook, and took a shower. At 6.15 a.m. he sat down to work. This morning he was making his way through a large report from the department of labour that examined possible solutions to the problem of unemployment. He marked some passages with a pen, occasionally also commenting on them, but nothing really struck him as new.

He put down his pen and thought about the anonymous

people who had put this meaningless report together. They are in no danger of becoming unemployed, he thought. They are never to be granted the joy of being able to see straight through daily existence to what actually mattered, the things that gave life meaning.

He read until 10 a.m., and then dressed and went shopping. He made lunch and rested for a while until around 2 p.m. He had soundproofed his bedroom. It was very expensive but worth every penny. No sounds from the street ever intruded. The windows were gone. A soundless air conditioning unit provided him with air. On one side of the room he had a large picture of the world, on which he could follow the progression of sunlight around the globe. This room was the centre of his world. Here he could think clearly about what had happened and what was going to happen. He never had to think about who he was or if he was right. Right about there being no justice in the world.

They had been at a conference in the Jämtland mountains. The director of the engineering firm he worked for had suddenly appeared in his doorway and ordered him to go. Someone had fallen sick. Naturally he agreed, although he had already made plans for that weekend. He said yes because he wanted to please his boss. The conference was on something to do with new digital technology. It was spearheaded by an older man who had invented the mechanical cash registers that were manufactured in Åtvidaberg. He talked about the new era, and everyone stared down at their notebooks. On one of the last evenings, they had all decided to go to the sauna. He didn't really like being naked in front of other men, so he waited for them in the bar. He didn't know exactly how to act. Afterwards they joined him and sat drinking for a long time. Someone started telling a story about good ways to fire employees. All of the men except for him were in important positions at their companies. They told one story after another and finally looked at him. But he had never fired anyone. It never even occurred to him that he would one day be fired. He had studied hard, could do his job, had paid off his student loans, and had learned how to agree with people. Afterwards, after the catastrophe was a fact, he suddenly remembered one of the stories. A small, unpleasantly plump man from a factory in Torshälla told them about how he had once summoned an old worker and said, "I don't know how we could have managed without you here all these years." "It was great," the fat man said, laughing. "The old guy was so proud and happy that he wasn't on guard. Then it was easy. I just said, 'But we'll just have to try, starting tomorrow.'" So the old man was fired. He often thought about that story. If it had been possible he would have gone to Torshälla and killed the person who had fired the old man like that, and had the gall to show off about it afterwards.

He left his flat around 3 p.m. He drove eastwards until he reached a car park in Nybrostrand, where he waited until there were no other people around. Then he quickly switched to another car he had parked there and drove away.

When he arrived at the nature reserve he saw that he was in luck. There were no other cars around, which meant he didn't have to bother with the fake number plates. It was already 4 p.m. and a Saturday, and so he doubted that anyone else would turn up that evening. He had spent three Saturdays watching the entrance to the nature reserve and had noted the pattern of visitors. Almost no one came in the evening. The few who did always left by 8 p.m. He took his tools out of the boot. He had also packed a few sandwiches and a thermos of tea. He looked around, listened, then disappeared down one of the trails.

When the time was right, he started making his way towards the place. He immediately saw that no one had been there. In the space between the two trees that was the only natural opening into the clearing, he had hung a thin thread. He knelt down to examine it and saw that it was untouched. Then he got out his collapsible shovel and started digging. He went about his task calmly and methodically. The last thing he wanted to do was break out in a sweat, which would increase the risk of his catching a cold. He paused after every eighth shovelful and listened for noises. It took 20 minutes to remove the layer of sod and reach the tarpaulin. Before lifting it aside he smeared some menthol ointment under his nostrils and put on a mask. The three plastic bags were lying undisturbed in the ground. There was no unpleasant odour, which meant they hadn't leaked. He lifted up one of the bags and threw it over his shoulder. His workouts had made him strong. It only took him 10 minutes to carry all three bags to their original location. Then he filled the hole, replaced the layer of sod, and stamped the ground on top until it was flat, pausing from time to time to listen out for sounds.

Next he went to the tree where he had placed the three bags. He unpacked the tablecloth, glasses, and the remains of the rotting food that he had stored in his refrigerator. Then he took the bodies out of the bags. Their wigs were a little yellowed and the bloodstains had taken on a greyish tinge. He put the bodies in their places, breaking and cracking what was necessary so that everything looked like it had when he had taken the picture on Midsummer's Eve. His last touch was to pour a little wine into one of the glasses. He listened. Everything was still.

He folded the bags under his arm, stuffed them into a sack, and left. He had already removed his mask and wiped away the menthol. He didn't see a single person on his way back to the car. He drove to Nybrostrand, changed cars again, and made it back to Ystad before 10 p.m. He didn't drive straight home but continued in the direction of Trelleborg. He pulled over at a spot where he could drive down towards the water without being observed. He put two of the big bags inside the third, weighted them down with pieces of steel pipe that he had procured for this purpose, and threw them into the water. They sank immediately.

He returned home, burned his mask, and threw his shoes into the rubbish. He put the menthol ointment in the bathroom cabinet. Then he took a shower and rubbed his body with disinfectant.

Later, he had some tea. When he looked into the tea container, he realised he would soon have to order more. He wrote it down on the noticeboard he kept in the kitchen. He watched a programme about the homeless on TV. No one said anything he didn't already know.

Around midnight he sat down at the kitchen table with a stack of letters in front of him. It was time for him to start thinking of the future. He opened the first letter carefully and started to read.

Shortly before 1.30 p.m. on Saturday, 10 August, Wallander left the Hillströms' villa on Körlingsväg. He decided to drive straight to Skårby, where Isa Edengren, the girl whom Eva Hillström claimed should have been with the others on Midsummer's Eve, lived. Wallander had asked Hillström why she hadn't told him about this earlier, but inside he felt a growing sense of guilt over the fact that he had taken so long to realise that something might be seriously wrong.

He stopped at a café by the bus station and ordered a sandwich and a cup of coffee. He realised too late that he should have ordered his sandwich without butter. Now he was forced to try and scrape it off with his knife. A man at the next table was watching him, and Wallander guessed that he had recognised him from the papers. Probably this would lead to rumours about how the police frittered their time away scraping butter off sandwiches instead of searching for their colleague's killer. Wallander sighed. He had never been able to get used to the rumour mill.

He finished his coffee, went to the lavatory, and left the café. He chose to follow the smaller road that went through Bjäresjö. Just as he left the main road his mobile phone rang. It was Höglund.

"I just spoke to Lena Norman's parents," she said. "I think I've found out something important."

Wallander held the phone more closely to his ear.

"There was supposed to be a fourth person at that Midsummer party," she said.

"I know. I'm on my way to her house right now."

"Isa Edengren?"

"Yes, Eva Hillström picked her out from Svedberg's picture. It turns out that she had the original. Astrid took it last summer with the self-timer on her camera."

"It feels like Svedberg is always one step ahead of us," she said.

"We'll catch up with him soon," Wallander said. "Anything else?"

"Some people have called in with leads, but nothing looks promising."

"Do me a favour and give Ylva Brink a call," Wallander said. "Ask her how big Svedberg's telescope was, and if it was heavy. I can't figure out where it's gone."

"Have we already ruled out the possibility of a burglary?"

"We haven't ruled anything out yet, but if someone made off with a telescope, you would think they would've been seen."

"Do you want me to do it right away, or can it wait? I'm on my way to see one of the boys from the photograph who lives in Trelleborg."

"It can wait. Who's going to talk to the other one?"

"Martinsson and Hansson are going together. I gave them his name. Right now they're in Simrishamn with the Boge family."

Wallander nodded with satisfaction. "I'm glad we're getting hold of everyone today," he said. "I think we'll know a lot more about the case by this evening."

They hung up and Wallander continued to Skårby. He followed the directions Eva Hillström had given him. She had told him that Isa Edengren's father had a big piece of property with several full-time landscapers working on it. A private road lined with big trees led up to a two-storey house. A BMW was parked in front. Wallander got out of his car and rang the bell. No one answered. He banged on the door and rang the bell again. It was 2 p.m. He was sweating. He rang the bell once more, then walked around to the back of the house. The garden was large and old-fashioned, with a variety of well-pruned fruit trees. There was a pool and a set of sun loungers that Wallander thought looked expensive. At the bottom of the garden there was a glassed-in gazebo, surrounded and almost completely hidden by bushes and overhanging branches. Wallander walked towards it. The green door was slightly ajar. He knocked but there was no answer. He pushed the door open. The curtains in the windows were pulled shut and it took a while for his eyes to adjust to the dim light.

He saw that there was a person inside. Someone was sleeping on a divan. He could see black hair sticking up over a blanket, but the person's back was turned towards him. Wallander closed the door and knocked again. Still no answer. Wallander walked in and flicked on the light switch. Light flooded the room. He grabbed the sleeper by the shoulder and gave a couple of shakes. When there was still no reaction Wallander knew that something was wrong. He turned the person over and saw that it was Isa Edengren. He spoke to her, and shook her again. Her breathing was slow and laboured. He shook her hard and sat her up but she didn't show any signs of waking. After fumbling in his pocket for his mobile phone, he remembered he had left it on the car seat after talking to Höglund. He ran back to the car and made an emergency call to the hospital on his way back to the gazebo, giving careful directions to the house.

"I think it's either a suicide attempt or serious illness," he said. "What do I do?"

"Make sure she doesn't stop breathing," he was told. "You're a police officer, you should be familiar with the procedure."

The ambulance arrived after 15 minutes. Wallander had managed to get hold of Höglund, who had not yet left for Trelleborg, and asked her to meet the ambulance when it arrived at the hospital. He was going to stay in Skårby for a while. After the ambulance left, he tried the doors of the main house, but they were locked. Then he heard an approaching car. A man wearing rubber boots and over-alls got out of a little Fiat.

"I saw the ambulance," he said.

Wallander saw the look of worry in his eyes. After telling him who he was, Wallander said that Isa Edengren was ill. That was all he could say for the moment.

"Where are her parents?" he asked.

"Away."

The answer seemed deliberately vague.

"Can you be more specific? We'll have to notify them."

"They may be in Spain," the man said. "But they could also be in France. They own houses in both countries."

Wallander thought about the locked doors.

"Does Isa live here even when they're away?"

The man shook his head.

"What do you mean by that?"

"It's really none of my business," the man said and started backing towards his car.

"You've already made it your business," Wallander said firmly. "What's your name?"

"Erik Lundberg."

"Do you live close by?"

Lundberg pointed to a farm that lay south of where they were.

"Now I want you to answer my question: did Isa live here while her parents were away?"

"No, she wasn't allowed to."

"What do you mean by that?"

"She had to sleep in the gazebo."

"Why wasn't she allowed in the main house?"

"There had been trouble in the past. Some parties where things had either been broken or stolen."

"How do you know this?"

The answer came as a surprise.

"They don't treat her very well," Lundberg said. "Last winter when it was ten degrees below zero, they went away and locked up the house. But there's no heating in the gazebo. She came down to our place completely frozen and told us about it. Not me directly, that is, but my wife."

"Then we'll go back to your place," Wallander said. "I'd like to hear what she told your wife."

He asked Lundberg to go ahead of him. Wallander wanted to check the gazebo before he left. He found no trace of sleeping pills or letter, and nothing else of consequence. He looked around one more time then headed back to the car. His phone rang.

"She's just been admitted," Höglund said.

"What are the doctors saying?"

"Not very much for now."

She promised to call as soon as she heard anything. Wallander relieved himself next to the car before he went down to Lundberg's farm. A wary dog met him on the front porch. Lundberg came out and chased it away, and invited Wallander into a cosy kitchen. Lundberg's wife was making coffee. Her name was Barbro and she spoke in a Gothenburg dialect.

"How is she?"

"My colleague will let me know as soon as she hears anything."

"Did she try to kill herself?"

"It's too soon to know," Wallander said. "But I wasn't able to wake her up."

He sat down at the table and put the phone beside him.

"I take it she's attempted suicide before, since you immediately assumed that was the case," he said.

"It's a suicidal family," Lundberg said with distaste.

Then he stopped talking, as if he regretted his remark.

Barbro Lundberg put the coffee pot on the table. "Isa's brother passed away two years ago," she said. "He was only 19 years old. Isa and Jörgen were only one year apart."

"How did he do it?"

"In the bathtub," Lundberg said. "He wrote a note to his parents telling them to go to hell. Then he plugged a toaster into the wall and dropped it in the water."

Wallander felt sick to his stomach. He had a vague recollection of the incident. It came to him that Svedberg had been the one in charge of the investigation. A newspaper lay on an old sofa under the window. Wallander caught sight of a photo of Svedberg on the front page. He reached out for it and showed them the photograph.

"You may have heard about the policeman who was killed," he said. He got his answer before he even asked the question.

"He was here about a month ago."

"Did he come to see you or the Edengrens?"

"First to see them. Then he came here, just like you did."

"Were her parents gone that time as well?"

"No."

"So he met Isa's parents?"

"We don't know exactly who he spoke to," Lundberg said. "But her parents weren't gone then."

"Why did he come down here? What did he ask you about?"

Barbro Lundberg sat down at the table.

"He asked us about the parties they had when Isa's parents were gone, before they started locking her out," she said.

"That was the only thing that interested him," Lundberg said.

Wallander grew more attentive. He realised that this might give him an insight into the way Svedberg had spent his summer.

"I want both of you to try to remember exactly what he said."

"A month is a long time," she said.

"But you sat here at the kitchen table?"

"Yes."

"And you had coffee?"

Barbro Lundberg smiled. "He liked my bundt cake."

Wallander proceeded carefully. "It must have been right after Midsummer."

The couple exchanged looks. Wallander saw that they were trying to help each other remember.

"It must have been right at the beginning of July. I'm sure of it," she said.

"So he came here at the end of June. First to see the Edengrens and then to see you."

"Isa came with him. But she was sick with some kind of stomach bug."

"Did Isa stay here the whole time?"

"No, she only came down with him to show him the way. Then she left."

"And he asked you about the parties?"

"Yes."

"What exactly did he ask?"

"If we knew the people who used to come. But of course we didn't."

"Why do you say 'of course'?"

"They were just young people who came in cars and then left the same way."

"What else did he ask?"

"If any of these parties were masquerades," Lundberg said.

"Did he use that word?"

"Yes."

His wife shook her head. "No, he didn't. He just asked if the people who attended the parties used to dress up."

"Did they?"

They both looked at Wallander with surprise.

"How on earth would we know?" Lundberg asked. "We weren't there, and we don't go around peeking through the curtains."

"But didn't you see something?"

"The parties were sometimes in the autumn, and it was usually dark. We couldn't see how people were dressed."

Wallander sat quietly and thought for a moment. "Did he ask anything else?"

"No. He sat for a while scratching his forehead with his pen. He was only here for about half an hour. Then he left."

Wallander's mobile phone rang. It was Höglund.

"They're pumping her stomach."

"So it was a suicide attempt?"

"I don't think people can ingest this many sleeping pills by accident."

"Are the doctors saying anything at this stage?"

"The fact that she's unconscious suggests she may already be poisoned."

"Will she make it?"

"I haven't heard anything to the contrary."

"Then why don't you go on to Trelleborg?"

"That's what I was thinking. I'll see you later back at the station."

They hung up, and the couple looked at Wallander with anxious eyes.

"She'll make it," he said. "But I will need to contact her parents."

"We have a couple of phone numbers," Lundberg said, and got up.

"They wanted us to call if anything happened to the house," his wife explained. "They didn't say anything about this kind of situation."

"You mean what to do if anything happened to Isa?"

She nodded. Lundberg gave Wallander a piece of paper with the phone numbers.

"Can we visit her in the hospital?" Barbro Lundberg asked.

"I'm sure you can," Wallander answered. "But I think it would be best if you waited until tomorrow."

Erik Lundberg saw him out.

"Do you have any keys to the house?" Wallander asked.

"They would never entrust them to us," the man said.

Wallander said goodbye, returned to the Edengren house, and walked over to the gazebo. He searched it again thoroughly for about half an hour, unsure as to what exactly he was looking for. He ended up sitting on Isa's bed.

Something's repeating itself, he thought. Svedberg came to talk to the girl who didn't make it to the Midsummer celebration and did not go missing. Svedberg asked about parties, and about young people dressing up in costumes. Now Isa Edengren has tried to kill herself and Svedberg has been murdered.

Wallander got up and left the gazebo. He was worried. He wasn't finding anything reliable to point him in the right direction. There seemed to be clues pointing in many directions, but none of them seemed to lead anywhere. He got into his car and headed back to Ystad.

His next aim was to have another talk with Sture

Björklund. It was almost 4 p.m. when he pulled into Björklund's yard. He knocked on the door and waited, but no one answered. Björklund had probably gone to Copenhagen, or else he was in Hollywood discussing his latest ideas for a monster. Wallander banged hard on the door but didn't wait for anyone to open it. Instead he walked around to the back. The garden was neglected. Some half-rotting pieces of furniture were scattered in the long grass. Wallander peered in through one of the windows of the house, then continued down to a little shed. Wallander felt the door. It was unlocked. He opened it wide and pushed a piece of wood underneath it to keep it in place. It was a mess inside. He was about to leave when his attention was caught by a tarpaulin folded over something in the corner. There seemed to be some kind of equipment under it. He carefully pulled off part of the cover. It was a machine all right; or more precisely, an instrument. Wallander had never seen one like it before, but he still knew immediately what it was. A telescope.

CHAPTER ELEVEN

When Wallander walked back outside he noticed the wind had picked up. He turned his back to it and tried to collect his thoughts. How many people owned telescopes? Not many. The telescope had to be Svedberg's. He couldn't think of any other possible explanation. That brought up other questions: why hadn't Sture Björklund said anything?

Did he have something to hide, or didn't he know that the telescope was on his property? Could Sture Björklund have killed his own cousin? He doubted it.

He returned to his car and made some calls, but neither Martinsson nor Hansson was in his office. He asked the officer on duty to send a car out to Hedeskoga.

"What's happened?" he asked.

"I need some people to keep this place under surveillance," Wallander said. "For now you can simply say that it has to do with Svedberg's case."

"Do we know who shot him?"

"No. This is a routine matter."

Wallander asked for an unmarked car and described the intersection where he would meet it. When Wallander reached the intersection the car was already waiting for him. He explained to the patrol officers where they should wait, and that they should call him as soon as Sture Björklund turned up, then he started back to Ystad. He was very hungry and his mouth was dry. He stopped at a takeaway restaurant on Malmövägen and ordered a hamburger. While he was waiting for his food, he drank some soda water. After eating much too quickly he bought himself a litre of mineral water. He needed time to think, but knew he would inevitably be disturbed if he returned to the station, so he drove out of town and parked outside the Saltsjöbaden hotel. The wind was quite strong now but he walked on until he found a sheltered spot. For some reason there was an old toboggan there and he sat down on it and shut his eyes.

There has to be a point of entry into this mess, he thought. A point of connection that I am overlooking. He went through everything that had happened so far as carefully and clearly as he could, but despite his efforts, the facts remained as muddled and obscure as before.

What would Rydberg have done? When Rydberg had been alive, Wallander had always been able to ask him for advice. They would take a walk on the beach or sit in the station late into the night discussing the facts of a case until they arrived at something important. But Rydberg was gone now. Wallander strained to hear his voice in his head, but there was nothing there.

Sometimes he thought Ann-Britt Höglund was on her way to becoming his new partner. She listened as well as Rydberg and didn't hesitate to change track if she felt it could help them break through a new wall.

In time it may work out, he thought. Ann-Britt is a good police officer. But it takes time.

He got up heavily and started walking back to the car. There's only one thing that really sets this investigation apart, he thought. People dressed up in costume. Svedberg wanted to know about parties where people dressed up in costume. We have a photograph of people at a party dressed up in costume. There are people in costume at every turn.

Wallander knew it would be a long night. As soon as everyone had returned from their assignments, they would hunker down in the conference room. He went into his office, hung up his coat, and called the hospital. After being transferred a couple of times he finally reached a doctor who told him that Isa Edengren was in a stable condition and was expected to make a full recovery. He knew this doctor, having met him at least a couple of times before.

"Tell me something I know you aren't allowed to say," Wallander said. "Was it a cry for help or was she really trying to end it all?"

"I'm told you were the one who found her, is that right?" the doctor said.

"That's right."

"Then let me put it this way," he said. "It was lucky you found her when you did."

Wallander understood. He was about to hang up when another question came to him.

"Has anyone been to see her?"

"She's not allowed visitors yet."

"I understand. But has anyone asked to see her?"

"I'll find out for you."

While Wallander waited, he hunted out the piece of paper with Isa's parents' telephone numbers that Lundberg had given him. The doctor returned.

"No one has been here and no one has called," he said. "Who is going to get in touch with her parents?"

"We'll take care of that."

Wallander hung up and tried dialling the first number without knowing whether he was calling France or Spain. He counted 15 rings, then hung up and tried the other number. This time a woman answered almost immediately.

Wallander introduced himself and she said she was Berit Edengren. Wallander told her what had happened. She listened without interrupting. Wallander thought about her son Jörgen, Isa's brother. He tried to keep his details to a minimum, but it was a suicide attempt and he couldn't cover that up.

She sounded calm when she replied. "I'll tell my husband," she said. "We'll have to talk about whether we should return home immediately."

She loves her daughter, Wallander reminded himself, but he couldn't help feeling angry at her response. "I hope you understand that it could have ended badly."

"Thankfully it didn't."

Wallander gave her the number of the hospital and the name of the doctor. He decided against asking any questions about Svedberg yet. What he did ask was for information about the Midsummer's Eve celebration that Isa was to have attended.

"Isa doesn't tell us very much," she answered. "I didn't know anything about a Midsummer's Eve party."

"Would she have told her father?"

"I doubt it."

"Martin Boge, Lena Norman, and Astrid Hillström," Wallander recited. "Do you recognise these names?"

"They're friends of Isa's," she said.

"But Isa hadn't told you about any special plans for Midsummer?"

"No."

"This is a very important question and I need you to think carefully. Could she have mentioned a place where they were to meet?"

"There's nothing wrong with my memory. I know she didn't say anything to us."

"Do you know if she had any fancy dress costumes at home?"

"Is this really important?"

"Yes. Please answer the question."

"I don't go through her cupboards."

"Is there a spare key to the house?"

"We keep a spare hidden key in a drainpipe on the right wing. Isa doesn't know about it."

"And she won't find out about it in the next couple of days."

Wallander had only one more question for her. "Did Isa say anything about going on a trip after Midsummer?"

"No."

"Would she have told you if she was thinking about it?"

"Only if she had needed the money, which she always did."

Wallander had trouble controlling his temper.

"You'll hear from us again," he said.

He slammed down the phone, realising as he did so that he still didn't know whether they were in France or Spain.

He went out to the canteen and got a cup of coffee. On his way back to his office he remembered that he had one more call to make. He found the phone number and dialled it. This time someone answered.

"Bror Sundelius?"

"Speaking."

Wallander introduced himself and was about to explain why he was calling when Sundelius interrupted him.

"I've been waiting for the police to give me a call. It seems to me you've taken a long time."

He was an elderly man with a direct way of speaking.

"I've already called a couple of times and got no answer. Why did you think we would be in touch?"

Sundelius answered without hesitation. "Karl Evert did not have many close friends. I was one of the few. That's why I assumed that you would contact me."

"What do you think we wanted to talk to you about?"

"You should know that better than I do."

True, Wallander thought. At least he isn't going senile.

"I'd like to meet with you," Wallander said. "Here or at your place, preferably tomorrow morning."

"I used to go to work every day. Now I climb the walls," Sundelius said. "I have an endless amount of time that simply goes to waste. You can come tomorrow any time after 4.30 a.m. I live on Vädergränd. My legs aren't so good. How old are you, Inspector?"

"I'll be 50 soon."

"Then your legs are better than mine. At your age it's important to keep moving. Otherwise you'll develop heart problems or diabetes."

Wallander listened to him with surprise.

"Are you still there, Inspector?"

"Yes," said Wallander. "I'm here. How about 9 a.m.?"

They crowded into the conference room at 7.30 p.m. Lisa Holgersson had arrived early with the chief prosecutor filling in for Per Åkeson, who was in Uganda. Åkeson had taken a leave of absence and was working for the International Refugee Commission. He had been gone almost eight months and sent Wallander letters every now and then, describing his daily life, and the dramatic ways in which the new environment and work were changing him. Wallander missed him, even though they had never been close. He also sometimes felt a stab of envy when he thought about the decision Åkeson had made. Would he ever be anything other than a policeman? He would soon turn 50. The chances of starting something new were shrinking rapidly.

The acting chief prosecutor, Thurnberg, had come down from Örebro. Wallander had not had a lot to do with him up until now, as Thurnberg had only started in Ystad in the middle of May. He was a couple of years younger than Wallander, fit and quick-witted. Wallander had not yet decided what he thought about him. On a previous encounter, he had appeared rather arrogant.

Wallander knocked on the table with his pencil and looked around the room. Svedberg's chair was still empty. He wondered when someone was going to start using it. Wallander began by telling them about his find at Björklund's house, since he was expecting him to be back from Copenhagen later that evening.

"Before this meeting we were talking about something else that strikes us as odd," Martinsson said. "There are no diaries. I've asked the others, but none of the three seem to have kept a diary or a pocket calendar."

"There are no letters either," Hansson said.

"These people seem to have erased all traces of themselves," Höglund said.

"Is that the case with the others, too? The ones who were in Svedberg's photograph?"

"Yes," Martinsson said. "But we should probably probe further."

Martinsson flipped through his notes and was about to add something when there was a knock on the door. An officer came in and nodded in Wallander's direction.

"Björklund has just got home."

Wallander got up. "I'll go out there alone. It won't be an arrest, after all. We'll continue when I get back."

Nyberg got up as well. "I should probably have a look at the telescope right away," he said.

They drove out to Hedeskoga in Nyberg's car. The unmarked police car was still parked at the intersection. Wallander got out and spoke to the officer behind the wheel.

"He arrived about 20 minutes ago in a Mazda."

"Then you can go back," Wallander said.

"You don't want us to stay?"

"It won't be necessary."

Wallander got back in the car and they pulled up outside the house.

"He's home," he said to Nyberg. "No doubt about that."

Music was coming from an open window. It had a Latin beat. Wallander rang the bell and the music was turned down. Björklund opened the door wearing only a pair of shorts.

"I have a couple of questions that couldn't wait," Wallander said.

Björklund seemed to think for a moment, then smiled. "Now I understand," he said.

"What do you understand?"

"Why that car was parked up by the turn-off."

Wallander nodded. "I was looking for you earlier today. My questions can't wait."

Björklund let them in and Wallander introduced Nyberg.

"Once upon a time I also thought about becoming a forensic technician," Björklund said. "The idea of dedicating my life to interpreting evidence was appealing to me."

"It's not as exciting as you'd think," Nyberg replied.

Björklund looked mildly astonished.

"I wasn't talking about adventure," he said. "I was talking about being a person who follows traces."

They stopped in the entrance to the big room. Wallander noted Nyberg's amazement at Björklund's menage.

"I'm going to get right to the point," he said. "You have a small shed to the east of the house. There's an instrument in there hidden under a piece of tarpaulin. I think it's a telescope, and I want to determine whether or not it came from Svedberg's flat."

Björklund balked. "A telescope? In my shed?"

"Yes."

Björklund instinctively took a step back. "Who's been snooping around out here?"

"I told you that I came looking for you earlier today. The door to your shed was open and I went in. I found the telescope."

"Is that legal? Are the police allowed to enter other people's homes at will?"

"If you have an opinion to the contrary, feel free to make a report to the ombudsman."

Björklund looked at him with animosity. "I think I will," he said.

"For God's sake," Nyberg interrupted angrily. "Let's just get this cleared up."

"So you claim to have no knowledge of a telescope on your property."

"That's right."

"Do you realise that doesn't sound very believable?"

"I don't care what it sounds like. As far as I'm concerned, there's no telescope anywhere on my property."

"We'll soon determine whether that's the case," Wallander said. "If you refuse to cooperate I'll leave Nyberg here and get a search warrant from the chief prosecutor. You should have no doubts about that."

Björklund was still hostile. "Am I accused of a crime?"

"For now I simply want an answer to my question."

"I've already given you one."

"So you deny knowledge of the telescope? Could Svedberg have put it there without your knowledge?"

"Why would he have done that?"

"I'm simply asking if it's possible, that's all."

"Of course he could have done it while I was away over the summer. I never check what's in the shed."

Wallander sensed that Björklund was telling the truth, and experienced this as a relief.

"Shall we go and look?"

Björklund nodded and slipped on some clogs. His upper body was still bare.

When they had arrived at the shed and turned on the light, Wallander pulled the others back and turned to Björklund.

"Does anything in here look different?"

"Like what?"

"It's your shed. You should know."

Björklund looked around and shrugged. "It looks like it normally does."

Wallander directed them into the corner and lifted the tarpaulin. Björklund's surprise seemed genuine.

"I have no idea how that got there," he said.

Nyberg crouched down to have a better look, directing a strong torch beam at it.

"I don't think we need to speculate further about who it belongs to," he said, pointing to something.

Wallander looked more closely and saw a small metal plate with Svedberg's name on it. Björklund no longer seemed angry.

"I don't understand," he said. "Why would Karl Evert hide his telescope here?"

"Let's go back inside and leave Nyberg to his work," Wallander said.

As they walked back to the house, Björklund asked if he wanted some coffee. Wallander said no. He seated himself for a second time on the uncomfortable pew.

"Do you have any idea how long it could have been there?"

Björklund now seemed to be trying to give thorough answers.

"I don't have a good memory for rooms," he said. "My memory for objects is even worse. I don't think I could come up with any kind of a time frame for you."

Something seemed to occur to him. Wallander waited.

"Is it possible that someone else put it there?" Björklund asked.

"If so, it would probably have been someone who knew you two were related."

Wallander saw that something was troubling Björklund.

"What are you thinking about?"

"I don't know if this means anything," he said doubtfully. "But I had the feeling once that someone had been here."

"How did you get this feeling?"

"I don't know. It was just a feeling."

"Something must have set it off."

"That's what I'm trying to remember."

Wallander kept waiting. Björklund seemed lost in thought.

"It was a couple of weeks ago," he said. "I had been in Copenhagen and returned in the afternoon. It had been raining. As I walked across the yard something made me stop. At first I didn't know what it was, but then I saw that someone had moved one of the sculptures."

"One of the monsters?"

"They're copies of the medieval gargoyles from the cathedral in Rouen."

"I thought you had a poor memory for objects."

"That doesn't apply to my sculptures. Not when someone has changed their position. I was certain that someone had been in the yard while I was gone."

"And it wasn't Svedberg."

"No. He never came out here unless we had arranged it."

"You can't be sure of that, though."

"No, but I feel sure. I knew him, and he knew me."

Wallander nodded, encouraging him to continue.

"A stranger had been here."

"You didn't have anyone looking after the place when you were gone on short trips?"

"No one comes here except the postman."

Björklund sounded convinced and Wallander had no reason to doubt him.

"A stranger, then," he repeated. "And you think this person is the one who might have put the telescope in your shed?"

"I know it sounds unreasonable."

"Can you tell me the exact date when this happened?"

Björklund went and got a little pocket calendar and leafed through to a particular day.

"I was away on 14 and 15 July."

Wallander made a note of it. Nyberg came in, his mobile phone in hand.

"I've called for some equipment," he said. "I'd like to finish working on the telescope tonight. Why don't you take my car back and I'll have a squad car pick me up when I'm finished?"

Nyberg disappeared again. Wallander got up, and Björklund followed him to the door.

"You must have had time to think about what's happened," Wallander said to him.

"I don't understand why anyone would want to kill my cousin. I can't imagine a more meaningless act."

"No," Wallander agreed. "But these are the questions we have to answer: who would have wanted to kill him, and why?"

They parted in the yard. The gargoyles looked somewhat plaintive in the weak light from the house. Wallander returned to Ystad in Nyberg's car. Nothing had been resolved.

The meeting back at the station lasted almost until midnight. Everyone was tired, but Wallander didn't want to let them go.

"There's really just one thing we can do," he said. "We have to declare Boge, Norman and Hillström officially missing. We need to get them back home as soon as possible."

Everyone in the room agreed with him. Holgersson and Martinsson would see that it was done the next morning.

"It seems that all of these young people have been up to something," he said. "But we haven't been able to get them to tell us what it is. You've all said that you feel there's something they're not saying, that they have a secret. Is that right?"

"Yes," said Höglund. "There's something they're not letting us in on."

"But they don't seem particularly concerned, either," Martinsson said. "They're convinced that Boge, Norman and Hillström are travelling."

"I hope they're right," Hansson said. "I'm starting to feel worried."

"So am I," Wallander said. He threw his pen down. "What the hell was Svedberg up to? That's what we have to figure out. And who in God's name is Louise?"

"We've checked all of our photographic records," Martinsson said.

"That's not enough," Wallander said. "We'll have to publish the picture in the papers. We have a murder to solve. Not that she's a suspect. At least not yet."

"Women don't tend to shoot their victims in the face with a shotgun," Höglund said.

No one had anything further to say. They agreed to continue the following day. Wallander would start by visiting Sundelius. He walked out of the station with Martinsson.

"We have to get them home," he said again. "We'll talk to Isa Edengren, and we'll bring in the ones that you've already visited once. We'll get them to tell us what they know."

They walked to their cars. Wallander was extremely tired. The last thing he thought about before falling asleep was that Nyberg was still out in Björklund's shed.

A steady rain fell over Ystad at dawn. Then the clouds blew away. Sunday was going to be a warm and sunny day.

CHAPTER TWELVE

Rosmarie Leman and her husband Mats often drove out to parks and nature reserves to take their Sunday walk, depending on the weather and season. This morning, Sunday, 11 August, they had talked about driving up to Fyledalen but settled on the Hagestad nature reserve instead. The deciding factor was that they hadn't been there for a long time, not since the middle of June.

They were early risers and left Ystad a little after 7 a.m. As usual they were planning to be gone the whole day. They put two rucksacks in the boot. These contained everything they might possibly need, even raincoats. Although it looked like it was going to be a fine day, you could never be sure. They lived a well-organised life. She was a teacher, he an engineer. They never left anything to chance.

They parked at the reserve shortly before 8 a.m., had a cup of coffee, then put on their rucksacks and started walking. At 8.15 a.m. they looked around for a nice place to have breakfast. They heard some dogs barking at a distance but had not yet seen any other people. It was warm and there was no breeze. When they found a good spot they spread out a blanket and sat down to eat. On Sundays they discussed the things they didn't have time for during the week. Today it was buying a new car. The one they had was getting old, but could they really afford a new one? After talking for a while, they decided they would wait another month or so. When they had finished eating, Rosmarie Leman stretched out on the blanket and fell asleep. Mats Leman intended to do the same, but first he had to relieve himself. He took some toilet paper with him and walked to the other side of the path and headed down the slope towards an area surrounded by thick bushes. Before squatting down, he looked around carefully but saw no one.

This is the best part of Sunday, he thought when he had finished. To lie down next to Rosmarie and doze for half an hour. As he had this thought, he noticed something in the bushes. He didn't know what it was, but there was some colour that contrasted with the green foliage. Normally he was not particularly curious, but he couldn't help walking closer and parting the branches for a better look. What he saw he would never forget as long as he lived.

Rosmarie was woken by his screams. At first she didn't know what it was, then she realised to her horror that it was her husband's voice calling for help. She had just managed to stand up when he came running towards her. She couldn't know what had happened or what he had seen, but his face was completely ashen. He made it to her side by the blanket and tried to tell her something.

Then he fainted.

The police station in Ystad took the call at 9.05 a.m. The caller was so hysterical that he was difficult to understand. Finally, however, the policeman taking the call pieced together that the caller's name was Mats Leman and he claimed to have found some dead bodies in Hagestad's nature reserve. Although his account was disjointed, the policeman on duty realised that it was serious. He took down the caller's mobile-phone number and told him to stay where he was. Then he went into Martinsson's office, since he had seen him come in just a few minutes before. The policeman stood in the doorway and told him about the call. There was one detail in particular that made Martinsson's stomach knot up.

"Did he say three?" he asked. "Three dead bodies?"

"That's what he said."

Martinsson got up. "I'll check it out right now," he said. "Have you seen Wallander?"

"No."

Martinsson remembered that Wallander was going to see someone this morning, someone named Sundberg – or was it Sundström? He called Wallander's mobile.

Wallander had walked to Vädergränd from his flat on Mariagatan, stopped in front of a beautiful house that he had admired many times, and rang the bell. Sundelius opened the door, dressed in a neatly pressed suit. They had just sat down in the living room when the phone rang. Wallander saw Sundelius's disapproving look as he pulled it out of his pocket with a quick apology.

He listened to what Martinsson had to say. He asked the same question as Martinsson.

"Did he say three? Three people?"

"It hasn't been confirmed, but that's what he thought he saw."

Wallander felt as though a weight was starting to press against his head.

"You realise what this might mean," he said.

"Yes," Martinsson answered. "We have to hope he was hallucinating."

"Did he give that impression?"

"Not according to the officer who took the call."

Wallander looked at a clock hanging on Sundelius's wall. It was 9.09 a.m.

"Come by and pick me up. I'm at number seven, Vädergränd," he said.

"Should we have full back up?"

"No, let's check it ourselves first."

Martinsson was on his way. Wallander got to his feet. "Unfortunately our conversation will have to wait," he said.

Sundelius said he understood. "I take it there's been an accident of some kind?"

"Yes," Wallander said. "A traffic accident. Unfortunately, there's no way of knowing when something like this will come up. I'll be in touch about visiting you again."

Sundelius walked him to the door. Martinsson pulled up and Wallander jumped in. He reached out and placed the flashing police light on the roof. When they arrived at the nature reserve, a woman ran out to meet them. Wallander could see a man sitting on a rock with his head in his hands. Wallander got out of the car. The woman was distraught and kept pointing and shouting something. Wallander took her by the shoulders and told her to calm down. The man remained where he was. When Wallander and Martinsson walked over to him he looked up. Wallander crouched down beside him.

"What happened?" he asked.

The man pointed into the nature reserve. "They're in there," he mumbled. "They're dead. They've been dead for a long time."

Wallander looked at Martinsson. Then he turned back to the man.

"You said that there were three of them."

"I think so."

One question remained, perhaps the worst one. "Could you tell how old they were?"

The man shook his head. "I don't know."

"I know it must have been a terrible sight," Wallander said. "But you have to lead us to the spot."

"I'm never going back there," he said. "Never."

"I know where it is."

It was the woman. She came up behind her husband and put her arm around him.

"But you never saw them yourself?"

"Our rucksacks and blanket are still up there. I know where it is."

Wallander got up. "Let's go," he said.

She led them into the reserve. The air was very still, and Wallander thought he could hear the faint sound of the sea. He wondered if the sound was simply the jumble of anxious thoughts inside his own head. They walked quickly and Wallander had trouble keeping up with the other two. Sweat ran down his chest. He needed to pee. A rabbit dashed across their path. Wallander couldn't imagine what they were about to find, but he knew that it would not be like anything he had seen before. Dead people are no more alike than the living, he thought. Nothing is ever repeated or the same, just like this anxiety. He recognised the knot in his stomach. It was still as if he were experiencing it for the first time.

The woman slowed down. They were getting closer. When they arrived at the blanket, she turned around and pointed down a slope on the other side of the path. Her hand shook. Until this moment Martinsson had been in front, but now Wallander took the lead. Rosmarie Leman waited by the rucksacks.

Wallander looked down the hillside. There was nothing but bushes below them. He started down the slope with Martinsson close behind. They arrived where the bushes started, and looked around.

"Do you think she might be wrong about the spot?" Martinsson asked. His voice was low, as though he were afraid someone would overhear them.

Wallander didn't answer. Something else had caught his attention. At first he didn't know what it was and then it struck him. A bad smell. He looked at Martinsson, who hadn't caught a whiff of it yet. Wallander started pushing his way through the bushes. He didn't see anything, just some trees up ahead. The smell disappeared, then returned more strongly.

"What's that?" Martinsson asked.

As soon as he had said it he realised what the answer was. Wallander proceeded slowly with Martinsson close behind. Then he stopped suddenly and saw Martinsson flinch. There was something behind the bushes to the left. The smell became stronger.

Martinsson and Wallander looked at each other, and each put a hand over his nose and mouth. A feeling of nausea washed over Wallander. He tried to take some deep breaths through his mouth while he kept his nose shut.

"Wait here," he told Martinsson. His voice quavered.

He forced himself forward and parted the branches. Three young people lay entwined on a blue linen cloth. They had been shot in the head. And they were in an advanced state of decomposition. Wallander shut his eyes and sat down.

After a moment he got up and returned to the place where he had left Martinsson, and pushed him along in front of him as if someone were following them. He stopped only when they were up on the path again.

"I've never seen anything so fucking horrible," Wallander stammered.

"Is it – "

"It has to be."

They stood there in silence. Wallander would later remember that a bird sang in a nearby tree. Everything was like a strange nightmare, and yet at the same time an excruciating reality. Wallander used all his inner resources to force himself to start thinking like a policeman again, to start practising his profession. He got out his phone and called the station. After about a minute he got Höglund on the line.

"It's me, Kurt."

"Shouldn't you be visiting that retired bank manager this morning?"

"We've found them. All three of them. They're dead."

He heard her catch her breath. "You mean Boge and the others?"

"Yes."

"They're dead?"

"Shot."

"Oh my God."

"Listen to me. Here's what we have to do. This is a red alert. I want everybody out here. We're at Hagestad nature reserve. I'll put Martinsson at the turn-off to guide people down here. We need Lisa immediately. And we'll need extra help to keep the area cordoned off from the public."

"Who's going to call the parents?"

Wallander felt a degree of anguish and panic he had never experienced before. Of course the parents had to be notified; they had to identify their children's bodies. But he just couldn't do it.

"They've been dead for a long time," he said. "Do you understand? They may have been dead as long as a month."

She understood.

"I'll have to talk to Lisa about it," he said. "But we can't let the parents see this."

There was nothing else to say. Wallander was left staring down at the phone after they had hung up.

"You'd better get down to the turn-off," he told Martinsson.

Martinsson inclined his head in Rosmarie Leman's direction. "What do we do with her?"

"Get the important facts. Time, address, etcetera. Then send them home. Tell them not to talk to anyone about it until they hear otherwise."

"Are we allowed to do that?"

Wallander stared at Martinsson. "Right now we're allowed to do whatever the hell we want."

Martinsson and Leman left, and Wallander was alone. The bird kept singing. A couple of metres away, hidden behind thick bushes, three young people lay dead. How alone can a person possibly feel, he wondered. He sat down on a rock by the path. The bird flew away.

We didn't get them home, he thought. They never left for Europe. They were here the whole time and they were dead. Maybe even since Midsummer. Eva Hillström was right all along. Someone else wrote those postcards. They were here the whole time, in the same spot where they celebrated their Midsummer feast.

He thought about Isa Edengren. Did she realise what had happened? Was that why she had tried to commit suicide? Did she realise the others were dead, just as she would have been if she'd been with them that night?

There were already things that didn't make sense. Why had no one discovered the bodies for a whole month? Even if the spot was out of the way, someone would have come across it, or smelled them. Wallander didn't understand it, but he also couldn't quite bear to keep thinking about it. Who could possibly have wanted to kill three young people dressed up in costume and celebrating Midsummer together? It was an act of insanity. And somewhere in the network of connections to this act there was another dead body. Svedberg. How had he been involved in all this?

Wallander felt an increasing sense of helplessness. Although he had only gazed at the scene for a few seconds, he had not been able to mistake the bullet holes in their foreheads. The murderer knew what he was aiming at. And Svedberg had been the best shot in the force.

A breeze tossed the trees from time to time. In between the small gusts, all was calm. Svedberg was the best shot. Wallander forced himself to think this through. Could Svedberg possibly have been the one? What was there that spoke against this possibility? For that matter, were there any clear alternatives to choose from?

He got up and started walking to and fro along the path. He wished he could have called Rydberg on the phone. But Rydberg was dead, as dead as these three young people. As he moved along the path he had a sudden impulse to run away from it all. He didn't think he could handle the pressure any more. Someone else would have to take over: Martinsson or Hansson. He was burnt out. And he had developed diabetes. He was on a downward spiral.

Finally he heard people approaching. There were sounds of cars in the distance and branches breaking somewhere down the path. Then they were there, gathering around him. He would have to take charge and tell them what to do. He had known many of them for as long as 15 years. Lisa Holgersson was pale. Wallander wondered what he looked like himself.

"They're down there," he said and pointed to the bushes. "They've been shot. Although they haven't been identified yet, I'm sure they're the three missing young people, the ones we assumed, or hoped, were travelling through Europe. Now we know that isn't the case."

He paused before continuing. "I want to prepare you for the fact that the bodies may have been lying here since Midsummer. You all know what that means. There is every reason to put on a mask."

He looked at Holgersson. Did she want to see them? She nodded. Wallander led the way. The only sounds were rustling leaves and small branches breaking underfoot. When the smell of the bodies came wafting over them, someone groaned. Holgersson grabbed Wallander's arm. Wallander knew it was easier to deal with a macabre scene like this in a group rather than alone. Only one of the younger police officers had to turn away and vomit.

"We can't let their parents see this," Holgersson said with a shaky voice. "It's horrible."

Wallander turned to the doctor who had accompanied them. He was also very pale.

"The investigation has to be as quick as possible," Wallander said. "We need to take the bodies back and get them fixed up as soon as possible before the parents have to identify them."

The doctor shook his head. "I'm not touching this," he said simply. "I'm calling Lund."

He went off to the side and made a call on Martinsson's phone.

"We need to be clear about one thing," Wallander said to Holgersson. "We already have a dead police officer on our hands. Now we have three more murder victims. That means four murders to solve, and it's going to be huge when it gets out. There will be enormous pressure on us to catch the killer. We also have to be prepared for rumours of a connection between the two events. You understand where that may lead."

"The suspicion that Svedberg was the killer?"

"Yes."

"Do you think he did it?"

Her question came so quickly that he was taken by surprise. "I don't know," Wallander said slowly. "There are no indications that Svedberg had a motive. Somewhere there's a connection, yes. But we don't know what it is."

"How much should we say at this point?"

"I don't actually think it matters. We've never been able to protect ourselves from idle speculation."

Höglund was listening to their conversation. He noticed that she was shaking.

"There's one more thing to keep in mind," she said. "Eva Hillström is going to accuse us of not moving on this soon enough."

"She may be right about that," Wallander said. "It may be something we'll have to acknowledge. I'll bear responsibility for it."

"Why you?" Holgersson asked.

"Someone has to," Wallander said simply. "It doesn't matter who it is."

Nyberg gave them all rubber gloves, and they started working. There were specific routines to be followed, tasks that had to be done in a certain order. Wallander walked over to Nyberg, who was instructing someone with a camera.

"I want everything on video," Wallander said. "Both close-up and from far away."

"Will do."

"Try to get someone whose hand won't shake."

"It's always easier to look at death through the lens," Nyberg said. "But we'll use a tripod just in case."

Wallander gathered his team together: Martinsson, Hansson and Höglund. He started looking around for Svedberg but stopped himself.

"They're dressed up," Hansson said. "And they're wearing wigs."

"It's the 18th century," Höglund said. "This time I'm sure."

"So it happened on Midsummer's Eve," Martinsson said. "That's two months ago."

"We don't know that," Wallander broke in. "We don't even know that this is where the crime took place."

He knew how ridiculous it sounded, but it was strange that no one had discovered them for so long. Wallander started walking around the blue linen cloth. He tried to see what had happened. He slowly let his mind pull back from everything else.

They were here to have a party. There were supposed to be four of them but one had fallen ill. They carried food, drink and a tape recorder with them in two big baskets.

Wallander interrupted himself and went over to Hansson, who was talking on the phone. Wallander waited until he was done.

"The cars," he said. "Where are the cars that we assumed were somewhere in Europe? They must have got here somehow."

Hansson promised to look into it. Wallander resumed his slow circling of the tablecloth where the dead lay. They set their things out, they ate and drank. Wallander crouched down. There was an empty bottle of wine in one of the baskets, two more in the grass. Three empty bottles altogether.

When death came for you, you had already emptied three

bottles. That means you were drunk. Wallander got up thoughtfully. Nyberg came up behind him.

"I'd like to know if any wine ran out into the grass or if we can determine if they drank it all."

Nyberg pointed to a stain on the blue cloth.

"Some of it spilled right there. It's not blood, if that's what you're thinking."

Wallander kept going. You ate and drank and became intoxicated. You had a tape recorder, you were listening to music. Someone entered this scene and killed you when you were resting on the blue cloth with your arms around each other. One of you, Astrid Hillström, may in fact have been asleep. It was probably already morning, maybe early dawn.

Wallander paused.

His eyes fell on a wineglass near one of the baskets. He knelt down to examine it and waved a photographer over to get a close-up. The glass was leaning against the basket but there was a little pebble supporting it underneath. Wallander looked around. He lifted the edge of the cloth carefully but didn't see any stones or rocks anywhere. He tried to think what it meant. When Nyberg walked by he stopped him.

"There's a pebble propping up that wineglass. If you see any others like it please let me know."

Nyberg made a note of it. Wallander continued his rounds. Then he pulled back a bit and surveyed the scene from more of a distance.

You spread your feast out at the foot of a tree. You chose a private place where no one would see you. Wallander pushed his way through the bushes and stood on the other side of the tree.

He must have come from somewhere. There are no signs

of panic. You were resting on the cloth, and one of you was already asleep. But the other two were perhaps still awake.

Wallander went back and studied the corpses for a long time. Something wasn't right. Then he realised what it was. The picture in front of him wasn't real. It had been arranged.

CHAPTER THIRTEEN

As dusk approached on Sunday, 11 August, and police spot-lights gave an unearthly glow to the scene, Wallander did something unexpected. He left. The only person he spoke to was Höglund. He needed to borrow her car since his own was still parked at Mariagatan. He told her to get in touch with him on his mobile phone if he was needed. He didn't tell her where he was going. She returned to the crime scene, where there were no longer any bodies. They had been carried out around 4 p.m. Once the bodies had been removed, Wallander felt consumed by fatigue and nausea. He forced himself to put in a couple more hours; then he felt the need to leave the scene. When he asked Höglund for her car keys, he knew where he was going. He wasn't simply going away. However tired and depressed he got, he rarely functioned without a clear plan. He drove off almost in a hurry. There was something he wanted to see, a mirror he wanted to hold up in front of himself.

Wallander pulled up outside Svedberg's building on Lilla Norregatan. The cement mixer was still there, and Svedberg's keys were in his pocket. The air inside the flat was stale. He went into the kitchen and opened the window. Then he drank a glass of water and reminded himself that he had an appointment with Dr Göransson the next morn-ing. He knew he was going to miss it. He hadn't managed to improve his habits at all since receiving the diagnosis. He still ate as poorly, and had taken no exercise. At this point even his own health would have to be put on hold.

The streetlamps cast a faint light into the living room. Wallander stood completely still in the twilight. He had left the crime scene because he needed some perspective on what had happened. But there was also a thought that had occurred to him earlier and that he wanted time to consider. They had all talked about the connections between the crimes and the hideous possibility that Svedberg was involved. But suddenly it occurred to Wallander that they were ignoring the most likely scenario. Svedberg had been conducting his own investigation without telling anyone what he was doing. It looked like he spent most of his holiday investigating the disappearance of these three young people. Of course, this could mean that he had something to hide. But it could also be that he had stumbled upon the truth. He might have had grounds to doubt that Boge, Norman and Hillström were travelling around Europe. He might have believed that something was wrong, and he might have crossed someone's path, only to end up murdered himself. Wallander knew that this did not explain why Svedberg hadn't told his colleagues what he was doing, but he may have had a good reason.

The events of the day slowly passed through his mind. Only an hour or so after they had discovered the bodies, Wallander had come to the conclusion that there was something wrong with the scene. He discovered what it was when the pathologist told him he was certain that the time of death was not as long ago as 50 days. This suggested two possibilities: either the shots were fired later than Midsummer, or else the bodies had been stored somewhere in the meantime, where they would have been better preserved. They couldn't conclude that the place where the bodies were found was necessarily the same place as the location of the crime.

For Wallander and the team, it didn't seem possible that someone had killed the three people where they were found, moved them to an unknown location for storage, then returned them to their original place. Hansson had suggested that they really did go on their European holiday, but that they returned earlier than anticipated. Wallander acknowledged this as a possibility, however unlikely. But he didn't write anything off yet. He made his observations, listened to anyone who had anything to say, and felt he was being forced deeper and deeper into an endless fog.

The warm August day had seemed never-ending. They took refuge in the structure of police routines and made their thorough examination of the scene. Wallander watched his colleagues, downcast and horrified, do what was expected of them. He watched them and wondered if every one of them was wishing that he or she had become anything but a police officer. People left as soon as they got the chance. Some camping chairs and tables were placed along the path where they could drink cups of coffee that got colder each time the thermoses were opened. Wallander didn't see anyone eat anything all day.

It was Nyberg's tenacity that was the most impressive of all. He rummaged around the half-rotten, stinking food remains with sullen determination. He directed the photographer and the policeman doing the videotaping, sealed countless objects in plastic bags, and made detailed maps of the crime scene. Wallander sensed the hatred Nyberg felt for the person who had caused the mess he was now forced to root around in. He knew that no one else was capable of Nyberg's thoroughness. At one point Wallander had realised that Martinsson was exhausted. He took him aside and ordered him to go home, or at the very least to go down to the forensic technicians' van and sleep for a while. But Martinsson simply shook his head and continued his work on the area closest to the cloth. Some dog patrols from Ystad arrived. Edmundsson was there with his dog, Kall. The dogs had picked up a couple of different scents. One of them had found human excrement behind one of the bushes. In other places there were beer cans and pieces of paper. Everything was duly noted on Nyberg's maps. In one particular spot, under a tree a little distance away, Kall indicated a find but after a careful search they were still unable to locate any human object. Wallander returned to the spot behind this tree several times that day. He discovered that it was one of the most sheltered locations from which to observe the place where the Midsummer celebrations had taken place. He felt a cold grip around his stomach. Had the murderer stood in this very place? What had he seen?

Shortly after midday, Nyberg told Wallander to take a look at the tape recorder that lay on its side by the cloth. They found a number of unmarked cassette tapes in one of the baskets. Everyone stopped talking when Wallander turned on the tape recorder. A dusky male voice they all recognised came on: the singer Fred Åkerström interpreting a ballad from the collection *Fredman's Epistles*. Wallander looked at Höglund. She had been right. This was a celebration set in the 18th century, the age of that eternally popular poet Bellman.

Wallander got up and went into Svedberg's study. First he looked around for a minute, then he sat down at the desk. He let images from the investigation come to him. There were the three postcards that Eva Hillström had doubted from the very beginning. Wallander hadn't believed her; no one had. It had been inconceivable that someone would send fake postcards. But now they had found her daughter dead, they knew that the postcards had been sent by someone else. Someone had travelled all over Europe, to Hamburg, Paris and Vienna for this. Why? Even if the three young people were not killed on Midsummer's Eve, there was no doubt that they were killed before the last postcard came from Vienna. But what was the reason for this false trail?

Wallander stared blankly out into the dimly lit room.

I'm afraid, he thought. I've never believed in pure evil. There are no evil people, no one with brutality in their genes. There are evil circumstances and environments, not evil per se. But here I sense the actions of a truly darkened mind.

Wallander reached for Svedberg's pocket calendar and went through it again. There was the recurring name, "Adamsson". Could this be the surname of the woman in the photograph whom Sture Björklund told them was called Louise? Louise Adamsson. He went back to the kitchen and looked in the phone book. There was no Louise Adamsson listed. She could be married, of course, and have a different surname. He made a mental note to ask Martinsson to find out what Svedberg had done on the days marked "Adamsson" in his calendar.

He turned out the light and went to the living room. Here someone had walked across the floor with a shotgun in his hand. It had been aimed and fired at Svedberg's head, then thrown to the floor and left behind. Wallander tried to think whether this marked the beginning or end of a series of events. Or was it part of something even larger? He almost didn't have the energy to follow this last thought to its conclusion. Was there really someone out there who was going to continue the senseless killing? He didn't know. Nothing gave him the mental foothold he was looking for. He walked over to the place where the shotgun had been found and tried to see where Svedberg must have been sitting. The cement mixer would have been rumbling on the street. Two shots, Svedberg thrown to the ground – probably dead before he even hit the floor. Wallander didn't hear any argument or raised voices, only the dry shots from the gun. He changed his position and walked over to the chair that lay on the ground.

You let in a person you know, someone you are not afraid of. Or else someone enters who has his own key. Perhaps someone picks the lock. There are no marks on the door; he didn't use a crowbar. We'll assume it's a he. He has a shotgun, or else you keep an unregistered shotgun in the flat. A shotgun that is loaded, and that the person you have let in knows about. There are so many questions, but in the end it comes down to a who and a why. Only one who. And one lone why.

He went back to the kitchen and called the hospital. Luckily, the doctor he had spoken to before was in.

"Isa Edengren is doing well. She'll be released tomorrow or the day after."

"Has she said anything?"

"Not really. But I think she's happy you found her."

"Does she know it was me?"

"Shouldn't we have told her that?"

"What was her reaction?"

"I don't think I understand your question."

"How did she react when she was told that a policeman had come looking for her?"

"I don't know."

"I need to talk to her as soon as possible."

"Tomorrow will be fine."

"I'd rather talk to her tonight. I need to talk to you, too."

"It sounds rather urgent."

"It is."

"I'm actually on my way out. It would be more convenient to talk tomorrow."

"I wish it were that unimportant," Wallander said. "But I have to ask you to stay. I'll be there in ten minutes."

"Has something happened?"

"Yes. Something I don't think you could possibly imagine."

Wallander drank a glass of water and left the flat. It was still warm outside, with only a faint breeze.

When he arrived at the ward where Isa Edengren was being kept, the doctor was waiting for him. They went into an empty office and Wallander closed the door. On the way over he had decided to level with the doctor completely. He told him what they had found out in the nature reserve, that three young people had been murdered, and that Isa Edengren was meant to have been with them. The only detail he left out was the fact that they had been dressed up. The doctor listened in disbelief.

"I thought about going into pathology," he said afterwards. "But hearing this I'm glad I decided against it."

"You're right. It was a terrible sight."

The doctor got up. "I take it you want to see her now."

"Just one more thing. Naturally I'd like you not to mention this to anyone."

"Doctors have to take an oath."

"So do police officers. But information seems to have a way of getting out anyway."

They stopped outside Isa's door.

"I'll just make sure she's awake."

Wallander waited. He didn't like hospitals. He wanted to leave as soon as possible. He remembered what Dr Göransson said about checking his blood-sugar levels. It was apparently a very simple test. The doctor came back out.

"She's awake."

"One more thing," Wallander said. "This will sound strange, but can you check my blood-sugar level?"

The doctor looked at him with astonishment.

"Why?"

"I have an appointment with one of your colleagues tomorrow morning that I won't be able to attend. But I was going to have it checked."

"Are you diabetic?"

"No. My blood-sugar level is too high."

"Then you're diabetic."

"I just want to know if you can measure it or not. I don't have my insurance card with me but maybe you could make an exception in my case."

A nurse walked by and the doctor stopped her.

"Could you check this man's blood-sugar level? He's going to speak with Edengren afterwards."

"Of course."

The nurse's name tag said "Brundin". Wallander thanked the doctor for his help and followed the nurse. She pricked his finger and squeezed a drop of blood onto a strip of tape in a machine that looked like a Walkman.

"It's very high – 15.5," she said.

"It's way too high," Wallander said. "That's all I wanted to know."

She looked closely at him, but in a friendly way.

"You're a little on the heavy side," she said.

Wallander nodded. He felt suddenly ashamed of himself, like a naughty child.

He went back to Isa Edengren's room. He had expected her to be lying in bed, but she was curled up in an armchair with a blanket drawn tightly around her. The only light in the room came from the bedside lamp. As he came closer he saw something like fear in her eyes. He put out his hand and introduced himself, then sat down on a stool next to her.

She doesn't know what's happened, he thought. That three of her closest friends are dead. Or does she suspect it already? Has she been waiting for this discovery? Is that why she couldn't take it any longer?

He pulled his stool around so he was facing her. Her eyes never left him. When he had first walked into the room she had reminded him of Linda. Linda had also tried to commit suicide, at the age of 15. Wallander later realised it was part of the series of events that had led Mona to leave him. He had never really understood it, even though he and Linda talked about it years later. There was something there that he would never quite grasp. He wondered if he would be able to understand why this girl had tried to take her life.

"I'm the one who found you," he said. "I know you know that already. But you don't know why I came out to Skårby. You don't know why I walked around the back of the locked house and kept looking for you until I found you in the gazebo where you were sleeping."

He paused so she could speak, but she remained silent, watching him.

"You were supposed to have celebrated Midsummer with your friends Martin, Lena and Astrid," he continued. "But you fell ill. You had some kind of stomach bug and stayed at home. Isn't that right?"

No reaction. Wallander was suddenly unsure of how to proceed. How could he tell her what had happened? On the other hand it would be in all the papers tomorrow. She would suffer a great shock in either case.

I wish Ann-Britt were here, he thought. She would be better at this than I am.

"Astrid's mother received some postcards," he said. "They were signed by all three, or just by Astrid, and sent from Hamburg, Paris and Vienna. Had the four of you talked about going away after Midsummer?"

She finally began to answer his questions, but her voice was so low that Wallander had trouble hearing her.

"No, we hadn't decided anything," she whispered.

Wallander felt a lump in his throat. Her voice sounded as if it might break at any moment. He thought about what she was going to hear, that a simple virus had saved her life. Wallander wanted to call the doctor he had spoken to before and ask him what he should do. How would he tell her? He put it off for now.

"Tell me about the Midsummer party," he said.

"Why should I?"

He wondered how such a fragile voice could sound so determined. But she wasn't hostile. Her answers would depend on his questions.

"Because I'd like to know. Because Astrid's mother is worried."

"It was just a party."

"But you were going to dress up like 18th-century courtiers."

She couldn't know how he knew. He was taking a risk in asking the question, but she might be impossible to talk to after she found out what had happened to her friends.

"We did that sometimes."

"Why?"

"It made things different."

"To leave your own age and enter another?"

"Yes."

"Was it always the 18th century?"

There was an undertone of disdain in her answer. "We never repeated ourselves."

"Why not?"

She didn't reply, and Wallander immediately knew he had hit an important point. He tried to approach it from another direction.

"Is it possible to know how people dressed in the 12th century?"

"Yes, but we never entered that age."

"How did you choose an era?"

She didn't answer that either, and Wallander was starting to discern a pattern in the questions she wouldn't answer.

"Tell me what happened that Midsummer's Eve."

"I was sick."

"It must have come on suddenly."

"Diarrhoea usually does."

"What happened?"

"Martin came to get me and I told him I couldn't come."

"How did he react?"

"Like he was supposed to."

"How?"

"By asking me if it was true. Like he was supposed to."

Wallander didn't understand her answer. "What do you mean?"

"You're supposed to tell the truth. If you don't, they kick you out."

Wallander thought for a moment. "You took your

friendship seriously, then. No one was allowed to lie. One untruth meant expulsion?"

She looked genuinely puzzled. "What would friendship be otherwise?"

He nodded. "Of course friendship is always based on mutual trust."

"What else is there?"

"I don't know," Wallander said. "Love, perhaps."

She pulled the blanket up under her chin.

"How did you feel when you realised that they had left to travel around Europe without you?"

She looked at him for a long time before answering. "I've already answered that question."

It took Wallander a moment before he made the connection. "Are you referring to the police officer who visited you earlier this summer?"

"Who else would I be referring to?"

"Do you remember when he came to see you?"

"On 1 or 2 July."

"What else did he ask you?"

She leaned in towards Wallander so suddenly that he pulled back involuntarily.

"I know he's dead. He was called Svedberg. Have you come here to tell me about him?"

"Not exactly, but I'd like to hear more about your conversation with him."

"There's nothing more to tell."

Wallander frowned. "What do you mean? He must have asked you something else."

"He didn't. I have it on tape."

"You recorded your conversation with Svedberg?"

"In secret, yes. I do that a lot."

"And that's what you did when Svedberg came to see you?"

"Yes."

"Where is that tape now?"

"In the gazebo, where you found me. There's a blue angel on the outside of the tape."

"A blue angel?"

"I make the wrappers myself."

Wallander nodded. "Do you mind if I have someone get the tape for me?"

"Why would I mind?"

Wallander called the station and instructed the policeman on duty to send a squad car to the house to get the tape. He also told them to get the Walkman he had seen on the bedside table.

"A blue angel?" the policeman asked.

"Yes, a blue angel on the wrapper. Tell them to hurry."

It took them exactly 29 minutes. While he was waiting, Isa spent more than 15 minutes in the bathroom. When she came back Wallander realised she had washed her hair. It occurred to him that perhaps he should have worried that she was making a second attempt on her life.

An officer came into the room and gave him the tape recorder and tape. Isa nodded in recognition. She took the Walkman and fast-forwarded to the place she was looking for.

"Here," she said and handed the headphones to Wallander.

Svedberg's voice came at him full-strength. He flinched as if he had been struck. He heard Svedberg clear his throat and ask a question. Her answer disappeared in the surrounding noise. He rewound the tape and listened again. He had heard correctly.

Svedberg had asked a similar question. But Isa was wrong – it wasn't the same question. Wallander had asked, "How did you feel when you realised that they had left to travel around Europe without you?"

The way Svedberg phrased his question dramatically altered its meaning: "Do you really think they have gone on a trip to Europe?"

Wallander listened to it a third time. Isa's reply couldn't be heard. He took off the headphones.

Svedberg knew, he thought. By 1 or 2 July, Svedberg had known they weren't travelling around Europe.

CHAPTER FOURTEEN

They continued their conversation, although Wallander was finding it hard to concentrate. By 9 p.m. he didn't think he could hold off telling her the truth any longer. He excused himself by saying he was going to get a cup of coffee. In the hall he called Martinsson, who said that most of the officers were starting to return to Ystad. Soon only the forensic technicians and the security guards would be left. Nyberg and his team would work through the night. Wallander told him where he was and asked to speak to Höglund. She came to the phone, and he told her that he needed her help.

"Isa Edengren has to be notified of the deaths. I don't know how she's going to react."

"Well, at least she's already in the hospital. What do you think could happen to her?"

Her answer seemed unusually cold to Wallander until he realised that she was distancing herself from the situation. Nothing could be worse than the way she had spent this long August day.

"I'd still appreciate it if you could come over," he said. "That way at least I don't have to do this alone. She has just tried to commit suicide."

After they hung up, he looked for the nurse who had checked his blood-sugar levels and got the name and home number of the doctor he had spoken to. He also asked her what her impression of Isa Edengren was.

"Many people who try to commit suicide are very strong," she said. "There are always exceptions to the rule, but it's my impression that Isa Edengren is one such person."

He asked where he could get some coffee and she directed him to a vending machine in the foyer. Wallander called the doctor at home. A child's voice answered the phone, then he got a woman, and finally the doctor.

"I haven't been thinking clearly," Wallander said. "We have to tell her what happened right away, or she'll hear it herself tomorrow morning. Then we may not be able to intervene. I don't know how she's going to react."

The doctor said he would come in. Wallander set off in search of the vending machine, but when he found it he realised that he had no change in his pockets. An elderly man pushing a walking frame came by. When Wallander carefully asked him if he had any change, the old man simply shook his head.

"I'm going to die soon," he said. "In about three weeks or so. What do I need money for?"

He kept going, seemingly in high spirits. Wallander was left with a note in his outstretched hand. When he did find some change, he pushed the wrong button and ended up with cream in his coffee, which he almost never had.

When he returned to the ward, Höglund had arrived. She was pale and had dark circles under her eyes. They hadn't found any significant leads, she told him, and he could hear how tired she was.

We're all tired, he thought. Exhausted, before we've even begun to penetrate this nightmare we're in.

He told her about his conversation with Isa Edengren, and she listened with surprise when he mentioned the recording of Svedberg's voice. He told her his conclusion:

that Svedberg knew, or at least strongly suspected, that the three missing people hadn't set off on a trip.

"How on earth could he have known that," she asked, "unless he was extremely close to what happened?"

"The situation seems clearer to me now," Wallander said. "He is somehow very close to the events, but he doesn't know everything. If he did he would have no reason to be asking these questions."

"That would suggest that Svedberg wasn't the one who killed them," she said. "Not that any of us really thought so."

"It passed through my mind," Wallander said. "I'll admit it. Now the picture has changed. I'm prepared to go a step further and say that Svedberg knew only a couple of days after Midsummer that something was wrong. But what was it that he feared?"

"That they were dead?"

"Not necessarily. He's in the same situation we were in before we found them. But where does his fear or suspicion come from?"

"He knows something we don't?"

"Something makes him suspicious. Perhaps it is only a vague feeling, we'll never know. But he doesn't share these suspicions. He keeps them to himself, conducts a thorough investigation during his holiday."

"So we have to ask ourselves what he knew."

"That's what we're looking for, nothing else."

"But that won't explain why he was shot."

"Nor does it explain why he didn't tell us what he was doing."

She frowned. "Why do you keep something hidden?"

"Because there's information you don't want to get out. Or you don't want to be discovered," he answered. "We may find a link."

"I've thought the same thing. There may very well be a link between Svedberg and the young people. Someone else."

"Louise?"

"Maybe."

They heard a door slam at the end of the corridor and the doctor came walking towards them. It was time. Isa Edengren was still sitting in the chair when Wallander went back in.

"There's one last thing I have to talk to you about," he said, sitting down next to her. "I'm afraid it will be difficult for you to hear. That's why I'd like your doctor to be here while I tell you. And one of my colleagues, Ann-Britt Höglund."

He saw that she was getting scared. But there was no way out now. The others joined them, and Wallander told her the facts. Her three friends had been found, but they were dead. Someone had killed them.

"We wanted to tell you now," he finished. "So you don't read about it in the papers tomorrow."

She didn't react.

"I know this is hard for you," he said. "But I have to ask you if you have any idea who might have done this."

"No."

Her voice was weak but clear.

"Did anyone else know about your plans that night?"

"No outsider is ever told."

It occurred to Wallander that she sounded like she was reciting a rule. Perhaps she was.

"No one knew except you?"

"No one."

"You weren't there since you got sick. But you knew where they were going to be?"

"In the nature reserve."

"And you knew they were going to dress up?"

"Yes."

"Why was it so secret?"

She didn't answer. I've trespassed onto secret territory again, Wallander thought. She refuses to answer when I go too far. But he knew she was right. No one had known about their plans. He had no further questions.

"We're leaving," he said. "Please be in touch if you think of anything else. The people around here know how to get hold of me. I also want you to know that I spoke to your mother."

She jerked her head back. "Why? What has she got to do with this?"

Her voice was suddenly shrill, making Wallander feel uncomfortable.

"I had to tell her," he said. "When I found you, you were unconscious. It's my duty to notify the next of kin."

She seemed about to say more, but then she stopped herself, and started to cry. The doctor indicated that it was time for Wallander and Höglund to leave. When they were out in the corridor again and the door shut behind them, Wallander noticed that he was dripping with sweat.

"Every time it gets worse," he said. "Soon I won't be able to get through this any more."

They arrived back at the station around 10.30 p.m. Wallander was surprised to see that there were no reporters outside. He'd thought the news about the murders would already have been leaked. Wallander hung up his coat and went to the canteen. Tired police officers sat silently over their cups of coffee and the remains of takeaway pizzas. It occurred to Wallander that he ought to say something to cheer them up. But how did you lighten the mood after the killing of three innocent people on a summer picnic? Somewhere in the background was also the murder of one of their own.

Wallander said nothing, but he nodded to them and tried to show that he was there for them. Hansson looked at him with weary eyes.

"When are we meeting?" he asked.

Wallander glanced at his watch. "Now. Is Martinsson here?"

"He's on his way."

"Lisa?"

"In her office. I think things were hard for her in Lund. All the parents, couple after couple, stepped up to identify their child. Although I think Eva Hillström came by herself."

Wallander went straight to Lisa Holgersson's office. The door was slightly ajar, and he could see her behind the desk. Her eyes seemed wet. He knocked and looked in. She gestured for him to come in.

"Do you regret going to Lund?"

"There's nothing to regret. But it was as terrible as you said it would be. There are no words to offer someone at a time like this. Parents are called down on a summer's day to identify their dead child. The people who had fixed up the bodies had done a great job, but they couldn't completely hide the fact that they had been dead for a long time."

"Hansson said Eva Hillström came by herself."

"She was the most restrained, perhaps because she had feared the worst all along."

"She's going to accuse us of not moving fast enough on this. Perhaps with some justification."

"Is that really your opinion?"

"No, but I don't know how much my opinion matters. If we had had more personnel, if it hadn't been in the middle of everyone's holiday time . . . things might have been different. But there are always excuses. And now a mother is forced to confront her worst fear."

"I'd like to discuss the possibility of getting some reinforcements down here as soon as possible."

Wallander was too tired to argue, but he didn't agree with her. There was always the hope that greater numbers meant greater efficiency. But in his experience this was almost never the case. It was often a small, well-run investigative team that produced the best results.

"What do you think?"

Wallander shrugged. "I think you know my opinion on this. But I'm not going to object if you want reinforcements."

"I'd like to talk to the others about it tonight."

"They're exhausted," he said. "You won't get any rational answers. Why don't you wait until tomorrow?"

It was 10.45 p.m. Wallander got up and went to the conference room. Svedberg's chair was still empty. Nyberg came in straight from the crime scene and Wallander saw him shake his head. No new finds.

Wallander started by telling them about his visit to the hospital. He had brought the tape recorder and cassette with him. There was an eerie silence in the room when he played the recording of Svedberg's voice. After Wallander told them about his conclusions, he noticed that the exhaustion of the group seemed to lift a little. Svedberg had known something. Was that why he had been killed?

They slowly went over all the facts of the case again. The meeting stretched long into the night, and the team slowly overcame their tiredness and low spirits. They took a short break just after midnight. When they returned, Martinsson sat down in Svedberg's chair by mistake. He changed his seat when he realised what he had done. Wallander got up to go to the men's room and drink some water. His mouth was dry and his head ached, but he knew he had to push on. During the break he went to his office to call the hospital. After waiting for a long time he finally talked to the nurse who had checked his blood-sugar level.

"She's sleeping," she said. "She wanted a sleeping pill. Naturally we couldn't give her one, but she fell asleep anyway."

"Has anyone called her? Her mother?"

"Only a man who said he was her neighbour."

"Lundberg?"

"Yes, that was his name."

"The full impact of what has happened will probably only hit her tomorrow," Wallander said.

"What is it that's happened?"

Wallander couldn't think of any reason not to tell her. There was a stunned silence.

"I can't believe it," she said.

"I don't know," he said honestly. "I don't understand it any better than you."

He returned to the conference room. It was time for him to summarise the events as they knew them.

"I don't know why this happened," he started. "I see no possible motive and therefore no possible suspect. But I am aware of a chain of events, as you all are. This chain is not completely without gaps, but I'll tell you what I see. Correct me if I leave anything out."

He reached for some sparkling mineral water and filled

his glass. "Some time during the afternoon on 21 June, three young people drove out to Hagestad nature reserve. They probably arrived in two cars, both of which remain missing. According to Isa Edengren, who was supposed to have been with them but fell ill, they had chosen the place for their party in advance. They were going to make it a masquerade, which they had done before. We should try to understand this game as well as we can. I think there were very strong ties between these young people, something more than simple friendship.

"Their era this time was the 18th century, the age of Bellman. They wore costumes and wigs and played songs from *Fredman's Epistles*. We don't know if they were being observed at this point. The spot they had chosen was hidden from view. The killer appeared from somewhere and shot them. They were each shot in the forehead. We don't yet know what kind of weapon was used. Everything points to the killer carrying out the deed deliberately and without hesitation. We find them 51 days later. That's the most likely scenario, but until we know exactly how long they have been dead we cannot rule out that they may not have been killed at the Midsummer feast. It may have happened at a later date. We simply don't know. But we do know that the killer must have been privy to certain information. It's not really believable that this triple homicide was a chance occurrence. We can't rule out the possibility of a lunatic, since we can't rule anything out, but the signs point to a carefully planned and executed killing. The motive for this crime I cannot even begin to speculate about. Who would want to kill young people in the midst of the happiest time of their lives? I don't think I've ever been involved in a case like this before."

He looked around. He wasn't quite done with his

summary of the events, but he wanted to see if there were any questions. No one spoke.

"There is more to this story," he said. "We don't know if it is a beginning, an end, or a parallel event, but Svedberg was also murdered, and we found a photograph of these young people in his flat. We know that he was investigating their disappearance and that he started to do so as soon as he heard from Eva Hillström and the other parents. There is a connection here. We don't know what it is but we have to find it. That's where we have to begin."

He put his pencil down and leaned back in his chair. His back ached. He looked over at Nyberg.

"I should perhaps add that both Nyberg and I feel there is something artificial and arranged about the scene of the crime."

"I just can't understand how they could have lain there for 51 days without anyone finding them," Hansson said despondently. "A lot of people visit the reserve during the summer."

"I don't either," Wallander said. "There are three possibilities. We could be completely wrong about the time of death. Maybe it wasn't Midsummer's Eve; maybe it was later than that. Or else the scene of the crime and the place we found the bodies aren't the same. The third possibility is that these two places are one and the same, but someone moved the bodies and returned them at a later date."

"Who would do that?" Höglund asked. "And why?"

"That's what I think happened," Nyberg said.

Everyone looked at him. It was unusual for Nyberg to speak with such conviction so early on in an investigation.

"At first I just kept seeing the same thing Kurt did," he began. "That there was something fake about the whole scene, like a photographer had arranged it for the camera. Then I found some things that made me rethink."

Wallander waited with excitement, but it was as if Nyberg lost his train of thought.

"Go on," he said.

Nyberg shook his head. "It doesn't make any sense," he said. "Why would anyone move the bodies just to return them at a later date?"

"There might be a lot of reasons," Wallander said. "To delay a discovery or to give himself time to escape."

"Or to send a number of postcards," Martinsson said.

Wallander nodded. "We'll take this step by step. We don't know if our thinking is right or wrong."

"Well, it was the glasses that made me think again," Nyberg said slowly. "There was wine left in two of them. A little less in one, a little more in the other. It should have evaporated a long time ago, but what really surprised me was what wasn't there. There were no insects in the glasses, which there should have been. We know what happens if you let even an empty glass that has had wine in it sit out overnight. In the morning it's full of insects. But there was nothing in these glasses."

"What do you make of that?"

"That the glasses had been sitting out for only a couple of hours when Leman found the bodies."

"How many hours?"

"I can't tell you exactly."

"What about the remains of the food?" Martinsson objected. "The chicken was rotten, the salad mouldy, and the bread stale. Food doesn't go bad that quickly."

Nyberg looked at him. "But isn't that exactly what we're discussing now? That the scene that Mats and Rosmarie Leman discovered had been pre-arranged. Someone puts out a couple of glasses and splashes wine in the bottom.

The food has been decomposing elsewhere, and is distributed on the plates."

Nyberg sounded as certain as he had when he'd begun to speak. "We'll be able to prove it, if it is the case," he said. "We'll be able to determine exactly how long the wine we found in the glasses had been exposed to air. But I already know what I think. I think the Lemans would not have found anything at all if they had gone for their walk on Saturday morning."

The room was silent. Nyberg had followed his train of thought much further than Wallander had realised. It hadn't occurred to Wallander that the bodies might only have been lying out for about a day. The killer must have been close by. What Nyberg said also affected Svedberg's relationship to the crime. He could have killed them and hidden the bodies, but he could not have brought them out again.

"I can tell you feel sure of this," Wallander said. "What's the likelihood that you could be mistaken?"

"None. I may be wrong in the exact hours and times I've been suggesting. But it must have happened in the way I have described."

"Is the place we found them also the scene of the crime?"

"We're not finished yet," Nyberg said. "But it does seem as if blood has seeped through into the ground."

"So you think they were shot there and then moved?"

"Exactly."

"So where were they taken?"

They all sensed the importance of this question. They were charting the movements of the killer. Although they couldn't see him clearly, they were zeroing in on his actions. That was a crucial step.

"I think we should assume that this is the work of a man acting alone," Wallander said. "But there may have been more than one person involved. This seems more probable if it turns out that the bodies were moved and later replaced."

"Perhaps we're using the wrong words," Höglund said. "Perhaps instead of moved we should be saying concealed."

Wallander was thinking the same thing. "The spot is not deep inside the reserve," he said. "It's possible to drive a car up there, but it is not allowed and it would attract attention. The alternative is easy. The bodies could have been concealed somewhere in the area, perhaps quite close to the scene of the crime."

"The dogs didn't pick up any tracks," Hansson said. "Not that that means anything."

Wallander had made up his mind. "We can't wait for all the results to come in. I want to search the area again at dawn for somewhere the bodies may have been concealed. If we're right, it'll be nearby."

It was just after 1 a.m. Wallander knew everyone needed a few hours' sleep before the morning.

He was the last to leave the room. The night air was warm, with no hint of wind. He pulled the air deep into his lungs, walked behind the back of a police car, and relieved himself. He would miss his appointment with Dr Göransson in the morning. His blood-sugar level was way too high at 15.5, but how could he think about his health at a time like this?

He started to walk home through the deserted town. Something was bothering him, a fear he knew he shared with the others although no one had said so. They were close to tracking the killer's movements, but they had no idea what he was thinking or what motivated him. They had no idea if he was planning to strike again.

CHAPTER FIFTEEN

Wallander didn't make it into bed that night. As soon as he stopped outside his door on Mariagatan and fumbled for his keys, anxiety overtook him. He put the keys back in his pocket, walked over to his car and jumped in. Somewhere out there a killer was hiding in the shadows and he would remain there until they caught him. They had to find him. He simply couldn't be allowed to get away, to become one of the people who would haunt Wallander in his dreams.

As he drove through the calm night, he thought about a case in the early 1980s, shortly after he had moved to Ystad with Mona and Linda. Rydberg had called him late one night with the news that a young girl had been found dead in a field outside of Borrie. She had been bludgeoned to death. They drove out there together that November evening. Hard flecks of snow were drifting through the air.

The girl had taken the bus from Ystad after going to the cinema, got off at her normal stop, and followed her usual shortcut through the fields to the farm where she lived. When she hadn't arrived at the time she said she would be home, her father went down to the road to look for her, and found her.

The investigation went on for years and filled thousands of pages of reports, but they never found the killer, nor any possible motive. The only clue was a piece of a wooden clothes-peg found close to the dead girl's body which bore traces of blood. Apart from that there was nothing. Rydberg would often come to Wallander's office to talk about it. During his last days, when he was dying of cancer, he mentioned her again. Wallander understood that he didn't want him to forget about the dead girl in the field. Once he was gone, only Wallander would be left to solve the case. He seldom thought about her now, but occasionally she appeared in his dreams. The image was always the same. Wallander was leaning over her, with Rydberg somewhere in the background. She looked back at him but was unable to speak.

Wallander took the turn-off for the nature reserve. I don't want three young people haunting my dreams, he thought. Nor do I want Svedberg there. We have to find the one who did this.

He parked his car and saw to his surprise that the officer on duty was Edmundsson.

"Where's your dog?" Wallander asked.

"At home," Edmundsson said. "I don't see why he should have to sleep in the car."

Wallander nodded. "How is everything out here?"

"Only Nyberg is here, as well as those of us on duty."

"Nyberg?"

"He arrived a little while ago."

He's also haunted by anxiety, Wallander thought. It shouldn't surprise me.

"It's too hot to be August."

"Autumn will come, just you wait," Wallander said. "It'll come when you least expect it."

He turned on his torch and walked into the reserve.

The man had been hiding in the shadows for a long time. In order to enter the nature reserve without being seen, he had approached it from the sea. He followed the beach, climbed the dunes, and disappeared into the woods. To avoid running into the policemen or their dogs, he took a circuitous route towards the trail that led into the main hiking area. From there he could always make his way onto the road if the dogs picked up his scent. But he wasn't worried. They wouldn't expect him to be there.

Under the cover of darkness he saw police officers come and go along the path. Two of the officers were women. Shortly after 10 p.m. many of them left the reserve, and he sat down to drink the tea he had brought with him in a thermos. The order he sent to Shanghai had already been filled. He would pick it up early the next day. When he finished his tea, he packed the thermos away and made his way to the place where he had killed them. There were no more dogs in the area, so he felt safe. From a distance he could see big spotlights that were set up around the scene, casting an unearthly glow. It was like a theatre production, but one that was closed to the ordinary public. He was tempted to sneak close enough so he could hear what the policemen were saying and watch their faces. But he controlled himself, as he always did. Without self-control you couldn't be sure that you would get away and be safe.

The shadows danced in the spotlights. The police looked like giants, although he knew it was just an illusion. They fumbled around like blind animals in the world he had created. For a moment he allowed himself to enjoy a feeling of satisfaction. But only for a moment. He knew pride was dangerous and could make you vulnerable.

He returned to his lookout beside the main trail. He was thinking of leaving when someone walked by. The beam of a torch flickered over the ground. A face was visible for an instant and the man recognised him from the papers. His name was Nyberg and he was a forensic specialist. He smiled to himself. Nyberg might be able to identify the individual pieces, but he would never see the whole pattern.

He had finished putting his rucksack on and was about to cross the path when he heard another person approaching. Again a torch flickered between the trees and he jumped back into the shadows. The officer was large and moved heavily. The man felt a sudden impulse to make his presence known, to dash out like an animal of the night, before being swallowed up again by the darkness.

Suddenly the officer stopped. He let the torch shine on the bushes to the side of the trail. In a moment that lengthened into sheer terror the man thought that he had been caught. He was frozen and couldn't get away. Finally the light disappeared as the officer walked away. But then he stopped a second time, turned off the light, and waited in the dark. After a while he turned the torch back on and continued.

The man lay still for a long time, his heart pounding. What had caused the policeman to stop? He couldn't have heard anything, or seen him. For once his inner clock failed him. He had no idea how long he lay there before getting up, crossing the path, and making his way back down to the sea. It could have been an hour, maybe more. When he reached the beach it was starting to get light.

Wallander saw the lights from a distance. From time to time he heard Nyberg's tired and irritated voice. One officer was up on the path, smoking. He stopped again and listened. He didn't know where the feeling had come from, the sense that the killer was out there somewhere in the dark. Had he heard something? He stopped and felt a rush of fear. Then he realised that it must be his imagination. He stopped one more time, turned off the light, and listened. But there was only the sound of the sea.

He greeted the officer, who made an attempt to put out

his cigarette. Wallander stopped him. He was a young policeman by the name of Bernt Svensson.

"How's it going?" he asked.

"I think I saw a fox," Svensson said.

"A fox?"

"I thought I saw a shadow back there. It was bigger than a cat."

"There are no foxes in Skåne. They all died from the plague."

"I still think it was a fox."

Wallander nodded. "Then we'll say it was a fox. Just a fox."

He continued on down and into the ring of light. Nyberg was examining the place under the tree where the three bodies had lain. Even the blue cloth was gone now.

"What are you doing here?" he asked when he saw Wallander. "You should sleep. You have to have the energy to keep going."

"I know. But sometimes you can't sleep."

"Everyone should sleep," Nyberg said. His voice was cracking with fatigue. Wallander sensed how distraught he was.

"Everyone should sleep," he repeated. "And things like this shouldn't happen."

"I've been in the force for 40 years," Nyberg said. "I'm going to retire in another two."

"What will you do then?"

"Go crazy with boredom maybe," he said. "But you can bet I won't be standing around forests looking at the half-rotten corpses of some young people."

Wallander remembered what Sundelius had said. I used to go to work every day. Now I climb the walls.

"You'll find something," Wallander said encouragingly.

Nyberg muttered something unintelligible. Wallander tried to shake the tiredness out of his body.

"I came out to start planning the morning's activities," he said.

"You mean digging around for a possible hiding place?"

"If we're right about this, we should be able to deduce where he hid the bodies."

"He, or they. He may not have been alone," Nyberg answered.

"I think he was. It just doesn't make sense for two people to organise this kind of massacre. We're assuming the killer is a man, but I think that's a safe assumption. Women don't shoot people in the head. Especially young people."

"What about last year?"

Nyberg was referring to a case in which the killer of several people turned out to be a woman. But that did not change Wallander's mind.

"Not this time," he said. "So who are we looking for? An escaped lunatic?"

"Maybe. I'm not sure."

"But this gives us a starting point."

"Exactly. If he's alone, he has three bodies to hide. What does he do?"

"He won't move them very far, for practical reasons. He has to carry them, unless he brought a wheelbarrow, which would have drawn attention. I think he's a cautious person."

"So he buries them near here?"

"If he buried them at all," Wallander said. "Did you have the impression that the bodies had been exposed to animals or birds?"

"No. But I'm not a pathologist."

"Still, that confirms our idea that the bodies were in the ground. But animals can dig. That means the bodies have been protected somehow, by a box or plastic sheeting."

"I'm not an expert on these things," Nyberg said, "but

I do know that bodies in sealed containers decompose at a different rate to bodies exposed directly to the earth."

They were closing in on something that could be significant.

"Where does that lead us?" Wallander said.

Nyberg gestured with one arm.

"He wouldn't have gone uphill," he said and pointed back to the path. "Nor would he have crossed a path unless he had to."

They turned their backs to the hillside and looked past the lights, where insects danced in front of the hot lenses.

"To the left of us the ground slopes away steeply, then goes up again almost as sharply. I don't think he'd try there," Nyberg said.

"Straight ahead?"

"It's level, surrounded by thick brush."

"To the right?"

"Also brush, but not as thick. The ground is probably waterlogged from time to time."

"So probably somewhere straight ahead or to the right," Wallander said.

"To the right, I think," Nyberg said. "I forgot to mention something. If you go straight you hit another path."

"So we'll try to the right, once it gets light," Wallander said. "In a spot that looks like it might have been disturbed."

"I hope we're right," Nyberg said.

Wallander was so tired he could no longer speak. He decided to go back to his car and sleep for a few hours. Nyberg followed him up to the main path.

"I had a feeling there was someone sneaking around in the dark when I came up here," Wallander said. "And Svensson said he thought he saw a fox."

"Normal people have nightmares in their sleep," Nyberg

answered. "We have our nightmares when we're awake."

"I'm worried he's going to strike again," Wallander said. "Aren't you?"

Nyberg was silent for a moment before answering. "I'm always worried. But I also have the feeling that what happened here won't be repeated."

"I hope you're right," Wallander said. "I'll be back in a couple of hours."

He returned to the car park, without experiencing the feeling that someone was out there in the darkness. He curled up in the back seat of his car and fell asleep immediately.

It was broad daylight and someone was knocking on the window. He saw Höglund's face and hauled himself out of the car. His whole body ached.

"What time is it?"

"It's 7 a.m."

"Damn it, I've slept in. They have to start looking for a place to dig."

"They've already started," she said. "That's why I came to find you. Hansson's on his way."

They hurried up along the path. "I hate this," Wallander grumbled. "Sleeping in the back of a car, getting up unwashed and looking like hell. I'm too old for this. How am I supposed to think without even having a cup of coffee?"

"I think we can fix that," she said. "If the station hasn't supplied us with anything, you can have some of mine. I'll even give you a sandwich."

Wallander picked up his pace, but she still seemed to walk more quickly than he did. It annoyed him. They passed the place where he had felt as if someone was hiding in the bushes. He stopped and looked around, realising that it was the perfect lookout. Höglund looked at him expectantly, but Wallander didn't feel like explaining.

"Do me a favour," he said. "Get Edmundsson and his dog to search this place. Have them go 20 metres into the woods on either side."

"Why?"

"Because I want them to. That's all the explanation I can give right now."

"What do you want the dog to look for?"

"I don't know. Something that shouldn't be there."

She asked no further questions, and he already regretted not telling her more. It was too late now. They kept walking and she handed him a copy of the newspaper. It had a picture of "Louise" printed on the front page. He read the headline without stopping.

"Who's in charge of this?" he asked.

"Martinsson is organising and checking the leads as they come in."

"It's important that it's done right."

"Martinsson is very careful."

"Not always."

He heard how irritated and disapproving he sounded and knew there was no reason to take his tiredness out on her. But there was no one else around.

When all this is over I'll have to speak to her, he thought helplessly.

At that moment a jogger came towards them. Wallander reacted without a second thought by placing himself in the man's way.

"Haven't they sealed off the area? No one should be here except the police!"

The jogger was in his 30s and was wearing headphones. As he tried to run past, Wallander reached out to stop him. The jogger, thinking he was being attacked, hit back.

He caught Wallander on the side of his jaw. Wallander was taken by surprise and collapsed. When he got his bearings, Höglund had the man pinned to the ground with his arm twisted behind his back. The headphones had fallen onto the path, and Wallander heard to his surprise that the jogger had been listening to opera. Some officers came running down to help them and handcuffed the jogger. Wallander got up gingerly and felt his jaw. It hurt, and he had bitten the inside of his mouth, but his teeth were unharmed. He looked over at the jogger.

"The reserve has been sealed off," he said. "Did that fact escape you?"

"Sealed off?"

The man's surprise seemed genuine.

"Get his name," Wallander ordered. "Make sure the barriers are up. Then take him out and let him go."

"I'm going to report this," the jogger said angrily.

Wallander turned away and felt the inside of his mouth with a finger. Then he slowly turned back around to face him.

"What's your name?"

"Hagroth."

"What else?"

"Nils."

"And what is it you're going to report?"

"Excessive force. Here I am jogging peacefully and then I'm attacked without warning."

"You're wrong," Wallander said. "The person who was assaulted was me, not you. I'm a police officer and I was trying to stop you because you were inside a restricted area."

The jogger began to protest but Wallander lifted his hand. "You can get a year's jail time for assault of a police officer. It's a very serious offence. You're obliged to follow police orders and you were trespassing in a restricted area. You could get three years. Don't think you'll get away with a fine and a slap on the wrist. Do you have a previous criminal record?"

"Of course not."

"Then we'll say three years. But if you forget about this and stay away from here I'll think about letting it drop."

The jogger tried to protest again but once more Wallander's hand went up.

"You have ten seconds to make up your mind."

The jogger nodded.

"Take off the handcuffs," Wallander ordered. "See that you get him out of here and get his address."

Wallander continued walking up the path. His jaw hurt, but he was no longer tired.

"He wouldn't get three years," Höglund said.

"He doesn't know that," Wallander said. "And I don't think he's likely to go to any length to find out if it's true."

"I thought this was exactly the kind of thing the head of the national police wants us to avoid," she said. "Shaking the people's trust in the police."

"It'll be shaken more if we don't find whoever killed Boge, Norman and Hillström. Plus one of our colleagues."

When they finally arrived at the crime scene, Wallander poured coffee into a Styrofoam cup and went looking for Nyberg, who was supervising preparations for the dig. Nyberg's hair was standing on end, his eyes were bloodshot, and he was in a foul mood.

"I don't know why I'm the one who's suddenly in charge of this," he said. "Where the hell is everybody? Why is your face all bloody?"

Wallander felt his cheek with one hand. The corner of his mouth was bleeding.

"I got into a fight with a jogger," he said. "Hansson's on his way."

"A fight with a jogger?"

"It's a long story."

Wallander filled Höglund in on their conversation about where the bodies might be buried, and put her in charge of the search. He made some rapid calculations. With Höglund and Hansson at the crime scene, there was no reason for him to stay. If Martinsson was taking care of things back at the station, that meant Wallander could turn his attention to other tasks.

He dialled Martinsson's number. "I'm coming in," he told him. "Having Hansson and Ann-Britt here is enough."

"Any results?"

"It's too early for that. Have we heard anything from Lund?"

"I can try to call now."

"Good. Tell them it's urgent. What we really need is to establish a time of death. It would also be good to know who was killed first, if possible."

"Why is that important?"

"I don't know if it's important. But it's possible the killer was actually only after one of the three."

Martinsson promised to call Lund straight away.

Wallander put his phone back in his pocket. "I'm going back to Ystad," he told the others. "Let me know if you find anything."

He started walking back to the car and bumped into Edmundsson and his dog along the way. Höglund must already have made the call. Edmundsson had been equally swift.

"Did you fly him in?" Wallander asked, pointing at the dog.

"A colleague drove him in. What was it you wanted us to do?"

Wallander showed him the place and explained what he wanted. "If you find anything, you should let Nyberg know. When you're done, join the search up at the crime scene. They're looking for a place to start digging right now."

Edmundsson went pale. "Are there more bodies?" he asked.

His words jolted Wallander. He hadn't even considered this possibility, but he realised it was improbable.

"No," he said, "we don't expect to find more bodies, just a spot where they might have been buried for a while."

"Why would they have been buried?"

Wallander didn't answer. Edmundsson is right, he thought. Why would the killer hide the bodies? We've raised the question and tried to answer it, but it may turn out to be more important than we thought. He got into his car. His jaw still ached. He was about to start the engine when his phone rang. It was Martinsson.

He's got information from Lund, Wallander thought and felt a rising excitement.

"What did they say?"

"Who?"

"You haven't talked to Lund?"

"No, I haven't had time. I've just had a call."

Wallander could tell that Martinsson was worried, which was uncharacteristic.

Don't let it be someone else, he thought. Not more dead bodies. Not now.

"The hospital called," Martinsson said. "Isa Edengren has disappeared."

It was 8.03 a.m. on Monday, 12 August.

CHAPTER SIXTEEN

Wallander drove straight to the hospital, much too fast.
Martinsson was waiting for him when he arrived. He left
the car in a no-parking zone.

"What happened?"

Martinsson was carrying a notebook. "No one really
knows," he said. "She must have left around dawn, but no
one saw her leave."

"Did she call anyone? Did anyone come and pick her
up?"

"It's hard to get a straight answer. There are so many
patients in her ward, and almost no staff on night duty.
But she must have left before 6 a.m. Someone came in at
4 a.m. and saw her sleeping."

"Which of course she wasn't," Wallander said. "She was
waiting for the right moment to take off."

"Why?"

"I don't know."

"Do you think she'll try to kill herself again?"

"Possibly. But let's think this through. We tell her what
happened to her friends and the next day she makes her
escape. What does that mean?"

"That she's scared."

"Exactly. But what is she scared of?"

There was only one place Wallander could think of to
start looking for her, and that was the house outside Skårby.
He wanted Martinsson with him, if only so he wouldn't

have to be alone. When they arrived in Skårby, they stopped first at Lundberg's house. The man was out in the yard inspecting his tractor. He looked surprised when two cars pulled into his driveway. Wallander introduced Martinsson.

"You called the hospital last night and were told that Isa was OK, all things considered. Sometime early this morning, between 4 a.m. and 6 a.m., she disappeared. Escaped. What time do you get up?"

"Early. My wife and I are up by 4.30 a.m."

"And Isa hasn't turned up?"

"No."

"Did you hear any cars go by early this morning?"

The answer was very firm. "Åke Nilsson, who lives up the road, went by at about 5 a.m. He works at the slaughterhouse three days a week. But apart from him there was no one."

Lundberg's wife appeared at the door. She had heard the last part of the conversation.

"Isa hasn't been here," she said. "And there haven't been any cars, either."

"Is there anywhere else she might have gone?" Martinsson asked.

"Not that we know of."

"If she contacts you, you'll have to let us know," Wallander said. "It's very important for us to find out where she is. Is that clear?"

"She never calls," the woman said.

Wallander was already on his way back to his car. They drove to the Edengrens' house. He put his hand into the drainpipe and pulled out the spare keys. Then he showed Martinsson the gazebo in the back of the house. Everything seemed as it had when he was last there. They returned to the main house and unlocked the door. The house looked even bigger from the inside. No expense had been spared on the interior decorating but the impression was chilly, like a museum. There were few traces of the inhabitants. They walked through the rooms on the first floor, then went upstairs to the bedrooms. A large model aeroplane was suspended from the ceiling of one of the bedrooms. There was a computer on a desk, and someone had thrown a sweater over it. It was probably Jörgen's room, the brother who had committed suicide. Wallander went into the bathroom and saw a plug by the mirror. Reluctantly he pointed it out to Martinsson. It was probably here that Isa's brother had died.

"I bet that doesn't happen every day," Martinsson said. "Who kills himself with a toaster?"

Wallander was already on his way out of the bathroom. Next door was another bedroom. When he entered he knew it was Isa's.

"We have to search this room," he said.

"What are we looking for?"

"I don't know. But Isa was supposed to have been out there with them in the nature reserve. She tried to commit suicide, and now she's run away. We both think she's scared."

Wallander sat down at her desk while Martinsson started going through the dresser and the large cupboard that took up a whole side of the room. The drawers in the desk were unlocked, which surprised him. But after going through them he realised there was no need for privacy. The drawers were almost completely empty. He frowned. Had someone emptied them? He picked up a green writing pad. Underneath it was a poorly executed watercolour. "I.E. '95" was written in the corner. The watercolour depicted a coastal landscape of sea and cliffs. He put the pad back.

In a bookshelf next to the bed were several rows of books. He recognised some that Linda had read. He felt along the back of the shelves and found two that had fallen behind the others or were concealed. Both of them were in English. One had the title *Journey to the Unknown* by someone called Timothy Neil. The other was called *How to Cast Yourself in the Play of Life* by Rebecka Stanford. The book covers looked similar, with geometric signs, numbers, and letters that seemed to be suspended in a universe of some kind. Wallander took the books with him back to the desk. They were well-thumbed. He put on his glasses and read the blurb on the back cover of the first book. Timothy Neil discussed the importance of following the spiritual map as revealed by people's dreams. Wallander made a face and put the book down. Rebecka Stanford in turn discussed what she referred to as "chronological dissolution". Something caught his attention. There seemed to be a discussion of how groups of people could control time and move back and forth through the ages. She seemed to be arguing that this technique was useful for "self-actualisation in a time of increased meaninglessness and confusion".

"Have you ever heard of an author by the name of Rebecka Stanford?" Wallander asked Martinsson, who was standing on a chair looking through the contents of the highest shelf in the cupboard. He got down and came over to look at the book, then shook his head.

"It must be a young person's book. You'd better ask Linda," he said.

Wallander nodded. Martinsson was right; he should ask Linda, who read a lot. During their holiday on Gotland he had been surprised by all the books she had brought with her. He hadn't recognised the name of even a single author.

Martinsson returned to the cupboard, and Wallander turned to the shelf beside the bed. There were some photo albums there, which he brought back to the desk. Inside were pictures of Isa and her brother. The colours had started to fade. In one, the two of them were standing on either side of a snowman. They both held themselves stiffly, looking unhappy. After this photograph were several pages of Isa by herself. School photographs, images of Isa and her friends in Copenhagen. Then some more of her with Jörgen. Here he was older, perhaps 15, and sombre. Whether his attitude was affected or genuine, Wallander couldn't tell. The approaching suicide could be read in the pictures, Wallander thought, but did he know it himself? Isa was smiling in these pictures, while Jörgen looked miserable. Next were shots of a coastal landscape. Wallander was reminded of the watercolour painting. On one of the pictures he read "Bärnsö, 1989." Wallander kept leafing through the pages. There were no photographs of the parents, just Jörgen and Isa, her friends, and landscape shots of the same coastline and small islands.

"Where is Bärnsö?" Wallander asked.

"Isn't it one of the islands that gets mentioned in the marine weather report?"

Wallander wasn't sure. He looked for a long time at a picture of Isa standing on a rock just below the waves. It almost looked like she was walking on water. Who had taken it? Martinsson suddenly whistled with surprise.

"You'd better take a look at this," he said.

Wallander got up quickly. Martinsson held a wig in his hand that looked like the ones Boge, Norman and Hillström had been wearing. There was a slip of paper attached to a strand of hair. Wallander carefully removed it. *Holmsted's Costume Rental*, he read. *Copenhagen*. There was an address and phone number. He turned the slip over and saw that the wig had been rented on 19 June, to be returned on the 28th.

"Should we give them a call right now?" Martinsson asked.

"Or visit them in person," Wallander said, thinking. "No, let's start by calling."

"You'd better do it," Martinsson said. "Danes never understand my Swedish."

"You're the one who doesn't understand them," Wallander said gently. "Since you never listen properly."

"I'll find out where Bärnsö is. Why did you want to know that?"

"I'm trying to figure that out myself," Wallander answered and dialled the number. A woman answered. He introduced himself and explained what he wanted to know.

"The wig was rented by Isa Edengren, from Skårby, Sweden," he said.

"I'll check. Just a moment," she said.

Wallander waited. He could hear Martinsson asking someone for the number of the coast guard. The woman came back to the phone.

"There's no record of any rentals to Isa Edengren," she said. "Not on that day nor the days before."

"I'll give you another name to try," Wallander said.

"I'm the only person working here right now and I have some customers. Can it wait?"

"No. If you can't help me, I'll have to contact the Danish police."

She made no further protests and he gave her the other names – Martin Boge, Lena Norman and Astrid Hillström. Then he waited again. Martinsson sounded irritated. He didn't seem to be getting anywhere. The woman returned.

"Yes, that's right," she said. "Lena Norman came in and rented four wigs and some costumes on 19 June. It was all due back on 28 June but she hasn't shown up. We were just about to send off a reminder."

"Do you remember serving her? Was she alone?"

"My colleague was here that day. His name is Mr Sørensen."

"Can I talk to him?"

"He's on holiday until the end of August."

"Where is he?"

"He's on his way to the Antarctic."

"Where?"

"He's on his way to the South Pole. He's visiting some old Norwegian whale fishing stations along the way. Mr Sørensen's father was a whale fisherman. I think he was even the one who operated the harpoon."

"So there's no one at the shop who can identify Lena Norman, or tell me if she came in alone to rent the wigs?"

"No, I'm sorry. Of course, we would like to have them back. Otherwise we'll have to charge a replacement fee."

"It'll be a little while. They're involved in a case we're working on."

"Has anything happened?"

"You could say that, but I'll explain later. Please tell Mr Sørensen to contact the Ystad police as soon as he returns."

"I'll tell him. Wallander, was it?"

"Kurt Wallander."

Wallander hung up. So Lena Norman had been in Copenhagen. But had she gone there alone?

Martinsson came back into the room. "Bärnsö Island is off the coast of Östergötland," he said. "Or more precisely, it's part of the Gryt archipelago. There's also a Bärnsö way up north, but that's more of a reef."

Wallander told him about his conversation with the fancy dress shop in Copenhagen.

"We should talk to Lena Norman's parents," Martinsson said.

"I would have liked to wait a few days," Wallander said, "but I don't think that will be possible."

They both sat quietly for a moment, considering what lay ahead of them. At that moment they heard the front door open. They were both struck by the thought that it might be Isa Edengren. When they went to the top of the stairs, however, they saw Lundberg standing in the hall. When he caught sight of them he kicked off his boots and walked upstairs.

"Has Isa been in touch with you?" Wallander asked.

"No, it's something else. I don't mean to take up your time, but there was something you said when we were talking in the yard, about me calling the hospital to ask how Isa was."

"It was perfectly natural for you to want to know how she was doing."

Lundberg looked at Wallander with concern. "But that's just it. I didn't call, and neither did my wife. We didn't call to see how she was, although we should have."

Wallander and Martinsson exchanged glances.

"You didn't call?"

"No. Neither one of us."

"Is there another Lundberg who might have called?"

"Who would that be?"

Wallander looked thoughtfully at the man in front of him. There was no reason to doubt he was telling the truth. So someone else had called the hospital. Someone who knew that Isa was in close contact with the Lundbergs. Someone who also knew that she was there. But what had that person wanted to know? That Isa was getting better, or if she had died?

"I just don't understand. Who would pretend to be me?" Lundberg asked.

"You're the one who can best answer that question," Wallander said. "Who knew that Isa used to come to you when she had problems with her parents?"

"Everyone in the village knew," Lundberg said. "But I can't think of anyone who would have called and used my name."

"Someone could have seen the ambulance," Martinsson said. "Did no one call to ask what had happened?"

"Karin Persson called," Lundberg said. "She lives in the hollow down by the main road. She's very curious and keeps tabs on everyone. But I can't imagine she can make herself sound like a man on the phone."

"Was there no one else?"

"Åke Nilsson dropped by on his way back from work. He brought some pork chops. We told him what had happened, but he didn't even know Isa so he wouldn't have called."

"Anyone else?"

"The postman came by with some unexpected news. We won 300 kronor in the Lottery. He wanted to know if the Edengrens were home. We told him that Isa was in the hospital, but what reason would he have to call?"

"There was no one else?"

"No."

"You did the right thing in telling us about this," Wallander said firmly, ending the conversation. Lundberg went back down the stairs, pulled his boots back on and left.

"When I was out at the nature reserve last night,"

Wallander said, "I had the feeling that I was being watched by someone in the darkness. I thought I'd imagined it, but now I'm starting to wonder. This morning I even asked Edmundsson to examine the spot with his dog. Is someone keeping an eye on us?"

"I know what Svedberg would have said."

Wallander looked at Martinsson with surprise. "What would he have said?"

"It was something he said when we were working on the smuggling case, during the spring of 1988, if you remember. That we should stop from time to time and look back over our shoulders. Like the Indians."

"What would we see?"

"Someone who shouldn't be there."

"That would mean we should station men out here to keep watch over the house, in case someone decides to search Isa's room. Is that what you mean?"

"Something like that."

"There's no 'something' about it. You either think that's what we should do, or you don't."

"I'm just telling you what I think Svedberg would have said."

Wallander realised how tired he felt. His irritation lay just below the surface. He knew he should apologise to Martinsson, just as he should have explained himself to Höglund at the nature reserve. But he didn't.

They went back to Isa's room. The wig was lying on the desk next to Wallander's phone. He knelt down and looked under the bed, but found nothing. When he stood up he felt dizzy. He grabbed Martinsson's arm to steady himself.

"Don't you feel well?"

Wallander shook his head. "It's been years since I could

stay up this many nights in a row without really feeling it. It'll happen to you, too."

"We should ask Lisa for extra staff."

"She's already talked to me about it." Wallander said. "I told her we'd get back to her. Is there anything else we need to look at here?"

"I don't think so. There's nothing unusual in the cupboard."

"How about anything that seems to be missing? Anything that should be in a young woman's cupboard that isn't there?"

"Nothing that I can think of."

"Then let's get going."

It was close to 9.30 a.m. when they returned to their cars.

"I'll call Isa's parents myself," Wallander said. "The rest of you will have to take on Boge, Norman and Hillström's parents. I don't want to be responsible for what might happen if we don't get hold of Isa. They may know something, and so might the others in the photo that we found at Svedberg's flat."

"Do you think something's happened?"

"I don't know."

They drove away. Wallander thought back to the conversation with Lundberg. Who had made that call? He had a gnawing feeling that Lundberg had said something else that was important, but he couldn't think what it was. I'm tired, he thought. I don't listen to what people say and then I have the feeling that I missed something important.

When they arrived back at the station, they went off in separate directions. Ebba stopped him as he walked past the reception desk.

"Mona called you," she said.

Wallander came to a complete stop. "What did she want?"

"She didn't tell me."

Ebba gave him her phone number in Malmö. Wallander already knew it by heart, but Ebba was very thoughtful. She also handed him a number of other phone messages.

"Most of them are from reporters," she said consolingly. "You don't have to get back to them."

Wallander got some coffee and went into his office. He had just taken off his jacket and sat down when the phone rang. It was Hansson.

"There's nothing new to report," he said. "Just so you know."

"I want either you or Ann-Britt to come back to the station," Wallander said. "Martinsson and I can't quite keep up with everything that has to be done. For example, who's in charge of searching for the cars?"

"I am. I'm working on it. Has anything happened?"

"Isa Edengren escaped from the hospital this morning. It worries me."

"Which one of us would you rather have?"

Wallander would have preferred Höglund. She was a better police officer than Hansson. But he didn't say so.

"It doesn't matter. Just one of you."

He hung up and dialled Mona's number in Malmö. Every time she called, which wasn't often, he feared that something had happened to Linda. She answered on the second ring. Wallander always felt a twinge of sorrow when he heard her voice. Was it his imagination or was the feeling getting weaker? He wasn't sure.

"I hope I'm not bothering you," she said. "How are you?"

"I'm the one who called you," he said. "I'm fine."

"You sound tired."

"I am tired. You've probably seen in the papers that one of my colleagues is dead. Svedberg. Do you remember him?"

"Barely."

"What did you want?"

"I wanted to tell you that I'm going to get married again."

Wallander was quiet. For a moment he nearly hung up, but he stayed as he was, speechless.

"Are you there?"

"Yes," he said. "I'm still here."

"I'm telling you that I'm getting remarried."

"Who to?"

"Clas-Henrik. Who else would it be?"

"Should you really be marrying a golfer?"

"That's not a very nice thing to say."

"Then I should apologise. Does Linda know?"

"I wanted to tell you first."

"I don't know what to say. Perhaps I should congratulate you."

"That would be nice. We don't have to continue this conversation. I just wanted you to know."

"Why the hell would I want to know? What the hell do I care about you and your fucking golfer?"

Wallander was enraged. He didn't know exactly where it came from. Perhaps it was the tiredness, or the last remnant of pain at realising that now Mona was leaving him for good. The first time he had felt such pain was when she told him she wanted to leave him. And now, when she told him she was getting married again, he discovered that it was still there.

He slammed down the phone so hard that it broke. Martinsson was walking into his office as it happened, and he jumped when the receiver fell apart. Wallander pulled the phone out of the jack and threw the whole mess in the rubbish. Martinsson watched this, obviously afraid to incur Wallander's wrath. He raised his hands up in front of his chest and turned to leave.

"What did you want?"

"It can wait."

"My anger is a private matter," Wallander said. "Tell me what you want."

"I'm going to see Norman's family. I thought I'd start with them. Lillemor Norman may know where Isa has gone."

Wallander nodded. "Either Hansson or Ann-Britt will be in soon. Tell them to take care of the other families."

Martinsson nodded, then remained in the doorway. "You'll need a new phone," he said. "I'll see to it."

Wallander didn't answer. He waved for Martinsson to leave. He didn't know how long he sat there doing nothing. Once more he'd been forced to face the fact that Mona was still the woman he was closest to in his life. It was only when someone showed up at his door with a new phone that he got up and left. Without knowing why, he ended up wandering down the hall and coming to a halt outside Svedberg's office. The door was open slightly and he looked in. The sun coming in through the window revealed a thin layer of dust on the desk. Wallander closed the door and sat down in Svedberg's chair.

Höglund had already gone through all his papers. She was very thorough. It would be a waste of time to go over them again. Then he remembered that, like all of them, Svedberg had a locker in the basement. Höglund had probably checked it, but she had never mentioned having done so. Wallander went out to the reception area and asked Ebba for the keys.

"His spare keys are right here," she said with obvious distaste.

Wallander took them and was about to leave when she stopped him.

"When is the funeral going to be?"

"I don't know."

"It's not going to be easy."

"At least we don't have to face a widow and crying children," said Wallander. "But you're right. It's not going to be easy."

He went down the stairs and found Svedberg's locker. He didn't know what he was looking for; there was probably nothing to find. There were some towels, soap and a shampoo bottle, for Svedberg's Friday night saunas. There was also a pair of old trainers. Wallander felt with his hand along the top shelf. There was a thin plastic folder containing some papers. He took it out, put on his glasses, and looked through it. Inside was a reminder from Svedberg's mechanic to bring his car in for a tune. There were some handwritten notes that looked like shopping lists. But there were also some ticket stubs for the bus and the train. On 19 July Svedberg, or somebody, had taken the morning train to Norrköping. He had returned to Ystad on 22 July. He could tell from the way that the ticket was stamped that it had been used. The stubs from the bus were very blurry. He held them up to the light but couldn't read them. With the help of a magnifying glass he could just decipher the price and the words "Östgöta Public Transit". He called Ylva Brink, who was at home for once, but she had no idea what Svedberg would be doing in Östergötland. He had no family there as far as she knew.

"Maybe this Louise person lives there," she said. "Have you found out who she is yet?"

"Not yet, but you may be right."

Wallander got another cup of coffee. His mind kept returning to his conversation with Mona. He still couldn't comprehend how she could marry that skinny little golfer who supported himself by importing sardines. He returned to his office and kept staring at the ticket stubs. Suddenly he froze, the cup halfway to his mouth.

He should have thought of it at once. What was that island in Isa Edengren's photo album called? Bärnsö? Hadn't Martinsson said that Bärnsö was off the coast of Östergötland? He put the coffee cup down so roughly that some of the liquid spilled, and tried out his new phone by calling Martinsson.

"Where are you?"

"I'm having coffee with Lillemor Norman. Her husband will be home soon."

Wallander could hear from Martinsson's voice that the visit was difficult.

"I want you to ask her something," he said. "Now, while I'm still on the line. I want to know if she's heard of an island called Bärnsö, and if she knows of any connection between the island and Isa Edengren."

"Just that?"

"Just that. Do it now."

While Wallander was waiting, Höglund appeared in the doorway. Perhaps Hansson had sensed that Wallander would rather have her with him. She pointed to his coffee cup and disappeared. Martinsson came back on the phone.

"Well, that was unexpected," he said. "She says that the Edengrens not only have houses in Spain and France, but also one on Bärnsö Island."

"Good," Wallander said. "Finally things are starting to make some sense."

"Wait, there's more. Apparently the others have been there with her many times. Lena Norman, Boge and Hillström."

"I know someone else who's been out there," Wallander said.

"Who?"

"Svedberg. Between 19 and 22 July."

"What the hell? How do you know that?"

"I'll tell you when you get here. Now go back to what you were doing."

Wallander hung up, carefully this time. Höglund came in again. She sensed at once that something was up.

CHAPTER SEVENTEEN

Wallander was right. It had not occurred to Höglund to go down into the basement and look through Svedberg's things. He couldn't help feeling a sense of satisfaction that she had missed this. He thought of her as good at her job. But the fact that she had forgotten about the storage locker meant she wasn't infallible.

They quickly compared notes. Isa Edengren was gone. Wallander wanted the search for her to be their top priority. Höglund encouraged him to spell out what he thought might have happened to Isa. He couldn't get past the facts. Isa was supposed to have been at that party. She had tried to commit suicide. And now she had run away.

"There's a possibility we haven't considered," Höglund said. "Although it's unpleasant and rather improbable."

Wallander sensed what she was thinking. "You mean the possibility that Isa killed her friends? I've considered that, but she was genuinely ill on Midsummer's Eve."

"If that's when it really happened," Höglund said. "We still don't know that for sure."

Wallander knew she was right. "In that case we have even more reason to try to find her as soon as possible. We also shouldn't forget that someone called for her at the hospital posing as Lundberg."

She left his office to visit the Hillström and Boge families, as well as the young people from the photograph they'd found in Svedberg's flat. She promised that she'd ask about Bärnsö Island. Nyberg called just after she had gone. Wallander immediately thought they must have located the place where the bodies had been buried.

"Not yet," Nyberg said. "This process can take a long time. I'm calling because we've received some information on the gun that was found in Svedberg's flat."

Wallander reached for a notebook.

"The national register is a blessing," Nyberg continued. "The gun that was used to kill Svedberg was stolen two years ago in Ludvika."

"Ludvika?"

"The report was filed on the 19 February 1994 to the Ludvika police. It was handled by an officer called Wester. The man who reported the gun stolen was Hans-Åke Hammarlund. He was an avid hunter who kept all his weapons securely locked up in accordance with the law. On 18 February, he went into Falun on business. That night someone broke into his house. His wife, who was sleeping in an upstairs bedroom, didn't hear anything. When Hammarlund returned from Falun the next day, he discovered that a number of his guns were missing and filed the report the same day. The shotgun was a Lambert Baron, a Spanish make. The numbers match perfectly. None of the missing guns ever turned up, nor were they ever able to identify any suspects."

"So other weapons were stolen as well?"

"The intruder left behind a very valuable shotgun designed for shooting elk, but took two revolvers, or rather one pistol and one revolver. It's not clear from the report how the intruder entered the property, but I take it you understand what this may mean?"

"That one of the other weapons might have been the

one used in the nature reserve? Yes, we'll have to get that question answered as soon as possible."

"Ludvika is in the Dalarna region," Nyberg said. "That's quite far away from here, but weapons have a way of turning up where you least expect them."

"You don't think Svedberg stole the gun that was used to kill him?"

"When it comes to stolen weapons, the connections are rarely so straightforward," Nyberg replied. "Weapons are stolen, sold, used and resold. I think there may have been a very long chain of owners before this shotgun ended up in Svedberg's flat."

"It's still important," Wallander said. "I feel as though I'm trying to navigate through thick fog."

Nyberg promised to make the identification of the stolen guns a priority. Wallander was leaning over his notebook, trying to make an outline of recent events, when the phone rang again. This time it was Dr Göransson.

"You didn't come to your appointment this morning," he said sternly.

"I'm sorry," Wallander said. "I don't have much of an excuse."

"I know you're very busy. The papers are full of this terrible crime. I worked at a hospital in Dallas for a few years, and I think the headlines in the Ystad papers are getting frighteningly like those in Texas."

"We're working around the clock," Wallander said. "It's just the way it is."

"I still think you'll have to give your health a little of your time," Göransson said. "A mismanaged case of diabetes is no laughing matter."

Wallander told him about the blood test he had had in the hospital.

"That just emphasises what I'm saying. We have to do a complete check-up on you to see how well your liver, kidneys and pancreas are functioning. I really don't think it can wait any longer."

Wallander knew he'd have to go in. They decided that he would return the following morning at 8 a.m. He promised to come in on an empty stomach and to bring a urine sample.

Wallander hung up and pushed the notebook away. He saw clearly how badly he had been abusing his body these last few years. It had started when Mona told him she wanted a divorce, almost seven years ago. He was still tempted to blame her for it, but he knew deep down that it was his own doing.

He stared at the notebook for a moment longer, then started looking for the Edengrens. He checked the country codes in the phone book and saw that Isa Edengren's mother had been in Spain when he had talked to her last. He dialled the number again and waited. He was about to hang up when a man answered.

Wallander introduced himself. "I heard that you had called. I'm Isa's father."

He sounded as though he regretted this last fact, which enraged Wallander.

"I expect you're in the middle of making your arrangements to come home and take care of Isa," he said.

"Actually, no. It doesn't sound as if there's any immediate danger."

"How do you know that?"

"I spoke to the hospital."

"Did you say that your name was Lundberg when you made this call?"

"Why would I have done that?"

"It was just a question."

"Do you really have nothing better to do with your time than ask idiotic questions?"

"Oh, I do," Wallander said and stopped trying to conceal his anger. "For example, I may very well contact the Spanish police to enlist their aid in getting you on the next flight home."

It wasn't true, of course, but Wallander had had enough of the Edengrens' indifference towards their daughter in spite of their son's suicide. He wondered how people could have such a total absence of affection for their children.

"I find your tone insulting."

"Three of Isa's friends have been murdered," Wallander said. "Isa was supposed to have been with them when it happened. I'm talking about murder here, and you're going to cooperate with me or I'm going to go to the Spanish authorities. Am I making myself clear?"

The man seemed to hesitate. "What is it that's happened?"

"As far as I know, they sell Swedish papers in Spain. Can you read?"

"What the hell do you mean by that?"

"Exactly what I just said. You have a summer house on Bärnsö Island. Does Isa have the keys to it, or do you lock her out of that house, too?"

"She has the keys."

"Is there a phone on the island?"

"We use our mobile phones."

"Does Isa have one?"

"Doesn't everybody?"

"What's her number?"

"I don't know. I'm really not sure whether she has one."

"So which is it? Does she have a phone or not?"

"She has never asked me for money to buy one, and she couldn't afford one. She doesn't work, she doesn't do anything to try to get a grip on her life."

"Do you think it's possible that Isa has gone to Bärnsö? Does she often go there?"

"I thought she was still in the hospital."

"She's run away."

"Why?"

"We don't know. Is it possible that she would have gone to Bärnsö?"

"It's possible."

"How do you get there?"

"You take a boat from Fyrudden."

"Does she have access to a boat?"

"The one we have is currently being serviced in Stockholm."

"Are there any neighbours on the island I could get in touch with?"

"No, we're the only house on the island."

Wallander had been taking notes as they talked. For the moment he couldn't think of anything else to ask.

"You'll have to stay close to the phone so I can get hold of you," he said. "Is there any other place you can think of where Isa may have gone?"

"No."

"If you think of anything, you know where to reach me."

Wallander gave him the phone numbers to the station and his mobile phone, then hung up. His hands were damp with sweat. It was already past lunchtime, and Wallander ached from hunger and a headache. He ordered a pizza that arrived after 30 minutes, and ate it at his desk. Nyberg hadn't called back, and he wondered briefly if he should drive out to the nature reserve, but then decided against it. He wouldn't be able to speed anything up. Nyberg knew what he was doing. He wiped his mouth, threw out the pizza box, and went out to the men's room to wash his hands. Then he left the station, crossed the road, and started walking up towards the water tower. There he sat down in the shade and concentrated on a thought that kept returning to him.

His worst fear, that Svedberg was the one who killed the three young people, had started to fade. Svedberg was on the side of the pursuers in this case, still a little ahead of Wallander. It would be a while until they caught him up.

Svedberg could not be the murderer because he had been killed, too. Wallander's worst fear was starting to leave him, only to be replaced by another. Someone was observing their investigation, someone who kept himself very well informed. Wallander knew that he was right about this, even though he couldn't yet see how it all hung together.

The person who had killed Svedberg and killed the three young people had some means of access to the information he required. The Midsummer's Eve party was planned in complete secrecy and yet someone else knew about it, someone who realised that Svedberg was closing in on him.

Svedberg must simply have got too close, Wallander thought, without realising that he had wandered into forbidden territory. That was why he was murdered. There is no other reasonable explanation.

He could make sense of events up to this point, but beyond it the questions piled up one on top of the other. Why was the telescope at Björklund's house? Why had someone sent postcards from all over Europe?

I have to find Isa, he thought. I have to get her to tell

me what she doesn't even know she knows. And I have to follow in Svedberg's footsteps. What had he discovered that we still haven't seen? Or did he have access to some information from the very beginning that we don't have?

Wallander thought briefly about Louise, the woman in Svedberg's life, whom he had kept secret. There was still something about her picture that disturbed him, although he couldn't put his finger on it. The feeling was strong enough that he knew he mustn't give up on it, that he must bide his time. It occurred to him that there was a similarity between the young people in the reserve and Svedberg. They had all had secrets. Was this also significant?

Wallander got up and walked back to the police station. His body still ached from the hours he had spent sleeping curled up on the back seat of his car. His biggest anxiety still lay at the back of his mind – the fear that the killer would strike again.

When he got to the station he realised what he had to do. He had to drive up to Bärnsö and see if Isa Edengren was there. He had to choose between all the important tasks that lay before him. The most important was to find her.

Time was running out. He returned to his office and managed to get in touch with Martinsson, who had finally left the Norman family's home.

"Has anything happened?" Martinsson asked.

"Not nearly enough. Why haven't we heard anything from the pathologist? We're helpless until we have a time of death. Why aren't we getting any good leads? Where are the missing cars? We have to talk. Get here as soon as you can."

While they were waiting for Höglund, Wallander and

Martinsson called the young people in Svedberg's photograph. It turned out that they had all visited Isa on Bärnsö at one time or another. Martinsson spoke to the pathologist in Lund and was told that no results were available yet, either for the Svedberg case or the three young people. Wallander worked through a list of the leads that had come in from the general public. Nothing looked significant. The strangest thing was that no one had called to say they recognised the woman they were calling Louise. It was the first thing Wallander brought up with his colleagues in one of the smaller conference rooms. He put the photograph of her on the projector again.

"Someone must recognise her," he said. "Or at least think they do. But no one has called in."

"The picture has only been out there a few hours," Martinsson said.

Wallander dismissed this explanation. "It's one thing to ask people to recall an event," he said. "That can take time. But this is a face."

"Perhaps she's foreign?" Höglund suggested. "Even if she only lives in Denmark. Who bothers to read the Skåne papers over there? The photo won't be published in the national papers until tomorrow."

"You might be right," Wallander said, thinking of Sture Björklund, who commuted between Hedeskoga and Copenhagen. "We'll get in touch with the Danish police."

They looked at the picture of Louise for a long time.

"I can't escape the feeling that there's something unusual about her," Wallander said. "I just don't know what it is."

No one could say what it was. Wallander turned off the projector.

"I'm going up to Östergötland tomorrow," he said. "It's

possible that Isa might have gone there. We have to find her and we have to get her to talk."

"What exactly do you think she can tell us? She wasn't there when it happened."

Wallander knew that Martinsson's objection was reasonable. He wasn't sure that he could give him a good answer. There were so many gaps, so many thoughts that were closer to vague assumption than firm opinion.

"She is a witness, in a way," he said. "We're convinced that this is not a crime of opportunity. Svedberg's murder may still turn out to be just that, although I doubt it, but the deaths of these young people were well planned. The crucial thing here is that they made their own arrangements in secret, but someone else seems to have had access to that information – what they were thinking, where they were going to meet, perhaps even the exact time. Someone was spying on them. Someone managed to find out what they were up to. If it turns out that the bodies were buried fairly close to the place where they were killed, then we'll know this for sure. Holes don't dig themselves. Isa was part of these elaborate preparations. But she fell ill at the moment when everything was to begin. If she had been able to go, she would have. Her illness saved her life. And she is the one who can help us find out what happened that night. Somewhere along the way, without their realising it, she and the others crossed paths with the person who decided to take their lives."

"Is that what you think Svedberg believed?" Martinsson asked.

"Yes. But he knew something else as well. Or at least suspected it. We don't know how this suspicion arose in the first place, or why he conducted his whole investigation in secret. But it must have been important. He dedicated his entire holiday to it. He insisted on taking all of his holiday time. He had never done that before."

"Something's still missing," Höglund said. "And that's a motive. Revenge, hatred, jealousy. It doesn't add up. Who would've wanted to murder three young people? Or four, for that matter. Who could've hated them? Who had reason to be jealous? There's a brutality to this crime that goes beyond anything I've ever seen. It's worse than the case involving the poor boy who dressed up as an Indian."

"He may have chosen this party deliberately," Wallander said. "Although it's almost too terrible to imagine, he could have chosen his moment precisely because their joy was at its peak. Think how alone people can feel over Midsummer."

"In that case we're dealing with a madman," Martinsson said, visibly upset.

"A methodical and deliberate madman, yes," Wallander said. "But the important thing is to try to find the invisible common denominator in these crimes. The murderer got his information from some source. He must have had access to their lives. That's the key we're after. We have to look thoroughly into their lives. We'll find this point of intersection. We may already have come across it and not seen it."

"So you think Isa Edengren should be our focus," Höglund said. "In a way you think she's leading this investigation, and we're carefully following in her footsteps."

"Something like that. We can't overlook the fact that she tried to kill herself. We have to find out why. We also don't know how the killer feels about the fact that she survived."

"You're thinking about the person who called the hospital and pretended to be Lundberg," Martinsson said.

Wallander nodded. "I want one of you to talk to whoever took that call. Find out what the caller sounded like. Was he old or young? What dialect did he speak? Anything could turn out to be important."

Martinsson promised to take on this task. For the next hour they went over what else had to be covered. At one point Holgersson came in to talk about the arrangements for Svedberg's funeral.

"Does anyone know what kind of music he liked?" she asked.

"Strangely enough, Ylva Brink says she has no idea."

Wallander realised to his surprise that he had no idea either. Holgersson left again, after he had given her an update on the investigation.

"I wish we could know what exactly happened and why when we attend his funeral," Martinsson said.

"I doubt we will," Wallander said. "But that's what we'd all like."

It was 5 p.m. They were about to leave when the phone rang. It was Ebba.

"Please, no reporters," Wallander said.

"It's Nyberg. It sounds important."

Wallander felt a twinge of excitement. There was a hiss of static, then Nyberg's voice came on.

"I think we were right."

"Have you found the spot?"

"That's what we think. We're taking pictures now, and we're trying to see if we can get a footprint."

"Were we right about the location?"

"This is about 80 metres from where they were found. It's a very well selected spot. It's surrounded by thick shrubbery and no one would choose to walk through it."

"When are you going to start digging?"

"I was going to see if you wanted to come and take a look at it first."

"I'm on my way."

Wallander hung up. "They think they've found the place where the bodies were buried," he said.

They quickly decided that Wallander would go out there alone. The others had a number of tasks to take care of as soon as possible.

When he got to the nature reserve, he drove his car past the roadblocks all the way up to the crime scene. A forensic technician was waiting for him, and escorted him to a spot where Nyberg had cordoned off an area of about 30 square metres. Wallander saw at once that the spot was well chosen, just as he had said. He crouched down beside Nyberg, who started to point things out to him.

"The ground over here has been dug up," he said. "Clumps of grass have been taken out and replanted. If you look over there under the leaves you'll see dirt that's been swept aside. If you dig a hole and fill it with something else, there'll be earth left over."

Wallander brushed his hand along the ground. "It's been carefully done."

Nyberg nodded. "It's very precise," he said. "He didn't take any shortcuts. We would never have noticed this place without having set out to look for it."

Wallander got up. "Let's dig it up," he said. "We've got no time to lose."

The work went slowly. Nyberg directed the others. It was beginning to get dark by the time the first layer of earth had been removed. Spotlights were set up around the site. The earth underneath the sod was porous and came out easily. As they removed it, a rectangular hole became visible. By this time it was after 9 p.m. Holgersson had come out with Höglund and they watched in silence. By the time Nyberg was satisfied, Wallander knew what he was looking at. The rectangular hole in front of him was a grave.

They gathered in a semicircle around the edge.

"It's big enough," Nyberg said.

"Yes," Wallander said. "It's big enough. Even for four bodies."

He shivered. For the first time they were following closely in the killer's tracks. They had been right. Nyberg kneeled next to the hole.

"There's nothing here," he said. "It's possible that the bodies were sealed in airtight body bags. If there was also a tarpaulin tucked in around them under the sod, I doubt that even Edmundsson's dog would pick up anything. But of course we'll go over it, down to the last tiny speck of dirt."

Wallander walked back up to the main path with Holgersson and Höglund.

"What is this killer doing?" Holgersson asked, distaste and fear in her voice.

"I don't know," Wallander said. "But at least we have a survivor."

"Isa Edengren?"

Wallander didn't answer. He didn't need to. They all knew what he meant. The grave had been intended for her as well.

CHAPTER EIGHTEEN

At 5 a.m. on Tuesday, 13 August, Wallander left Ystad, deciding to drive along the coast, through Kalmar. He was already at Sölvesborg when he realised he had forgotten his promise to visit Dr Göransson at the clinic that morning. He pulled over by the side of the road and called Martinsson. It was just past 7 a.m. Wallander told him about the doctor's appointment and asked Martinsson to call and give an excuse.

"Tell him an urgent matter called me out of town," Wallander said.

"Are you sick?" Martinsson asked.

"It's a routine check-up," Wallander told him. "That's all."

Afterwards, when he had pulled back out onto the road, it occurred to him that Martinsson must have wondered why he didn't call Dr Göransson himself. Wallander asked himself the same question. Why couldn't he tell people that he had in all likelihood developed diabetes? He was having trouble making sense of his own actions.

He was thirsty, and his body ached. When he passed a roadside café he stopped and had breakfast. On the way out he bought two bottles of mineral water. He made it to Kalmar by 9 a.m. The phone rang. It was Höglund, who was going to help him with directions once he reached Östergötland.

"I talked to a colleague in Valdemarsvik," she said. "I

thought it would be best to make it sound like a personal favour."

"Good idea," Wallander said. "Police officers don't tend to like it when you trespass on their territory."

"Especially not you," she said with a laugh. She was right. He didn't like having police officers from other districts in Ystad.

"How do I get out to the island?" he asked.

"That depends on where you are right now. Are you far away?"

"I've just passed Kalmar. Västervik is 100 kilometres away, and then it's about another hundred after that."

"Then it'll be tight."

"What do you mean?"

"My contact in Valdemarsvik suggested that you take the post boat, but it leaves Fyrudden between 11 a.m. and 11.30."

"Is there no other way?"

"Oh, I'm sure there is. But you'll have to organise that once you get to the dock."

"I may be able to do that. Can't someone call the post office and tell them I'm on my way? Where does the post get sorted? In Norrköping?"

"I'm looking at a map right now," she said. "I think it would have to be in Gryt, if there's even a post office there."

"Where's that?"

"Between Valdemarsvik and Fyrudden harbour. Don't you even have a map with you?"

"Unfortunately I left it on my desk."

"Let me call you back," she said. "But I really think the best thing would be for you to go out with the post boat. If my colleague is right, it's the easiest way for people to get out to the islands. Those that don't have their own boats, of course, or anyone who's willing to come and get them."

Wallander understood what she meant.

"Good thinking," he said. "You mean that Isa Edengren may have taken the post boat herself?"

"It was just an idea."

Wallander thought for a moment. "But do you really think she made it up there by 11 a.m. if she left the hospital at 6 a.m.?"

"She may have," Höglund replied. "If she had a car, and Isa Edengren does have her licence. And we mustn't forget that she could have left the hospital as early as 4 a.m."

She promised to call him back. Wallander increased his speed. The traffic was getting heavier and there were a number of cars with trailers on the road. They reminded him that it was still summer, and holiday time. For a moment he considered turning on his police light, but decided against it. Instead he continued to increase his speed.

Höglund called him back after 20 minutes.

"I was right," she said. "The post gets sorted in Gryt. I even talked to the captain of the post boat. He sounded very nice."

"What was his name?"

"I didn't catch it. But he'll wait for you until midday. Otherwise he can come and get you later in the afternoon but I think that will cost you more."

"I was planning to write this trip off to expenses," Wallander said. "But I'll get there before midday."

"There's a car park next to the wharf," she said. "And the post boat is just across from it."

"Do you have his phone number?"

Wallander pulled over to the side of the road and wrote

down the number. As he sat there he was passed by a lorry he had finally managed to overtake a little earlier.

It was 11.40 a.m. when Wallander drove down the hill towards Fyrudden harbour. He found a car park and then walked out onto the pier. There was a soft wind. The harbour was full of boats. A man in his 50s was loading the last of his boxes into a large motorboat. Wallander hesitated, having imagined that the post boat would look different. He had even expected a flag bearing the post office logo. The man, who had just set down a crate of soda water, looked at Wallander.

"Are you the one going out to Bärnsö?"

"That's me."

The man stepped onto the dock and reached out his hand. "Lennart Westin."

"I'm sorry I'm a little late."

"Oh, there's no hurry."

"I don't know if the woman who called told you but I have to get back somehow, either later this afternoon or tonight."

"You aren't spending the night?"

The situation was starting to get confusing. Wallander didn't even know if Höglund had told him that he was a policeman.

"I should tell you I'm a detective with the Ystad homicide unit," Wallander said and got out his identification. "I'm working on a particularly difficult and unpleasant case at the moment."

This postman called Westin was a fast thinker.

"Is it that case involving the young people that I read about in the paper? Wasn't there a police officer killed, too?"

Wallander nodded.

"I thought I recognised them from the picture in the paper," Westin said. "At least one of them. I had the feeling I had given them a ride a year or so ago."

"With Isa?"

"Yes, that's right. They were with her. I think it was late autumn a couple of years ago. There was a storm coming in from the southwest. I wasn't sure we could pull up to the Bärnsö landing. It's a particularly exposed spot when the wind is blowing from that direction. But we made it. One of their bags fell in the water, and we managed to fish it out. That's why I remember. But you should never be too sure of your memory."

"I think you're probably right," Wallander said. "Have you seen Isa recently? Today or the day before?"

"No."

"Does she normally catch a ride out with you?"

"When her parents are out here, they collect her. Otherwise she gets a ride with me."

"So she's not here now?"

"If she is, she went out with someone else."

"Who would that have been?"

Westin shrugged. "There are always people around out here who would be willing to give her a ride. Isa knows whom to call. But I think she would have asked me first."

Westin glanced at his watch. Wallander hurried back to his car to get the little bag he had packed. Then he got on the boat. Westin pointed to the map beside the steering wheel.

"I could take you directly to Bärnsö but that would be out of my way," he said. "Are you in a hurry? If we go to Bärnsö on my regular route we'll be there in an hour. I have three other stops first."

"That's fine."

"When do you want me to pick you up?"

Wallander thought for a moment. Isa was most likely not on the island. He had drawn the wrong conclusion, which was a disappointment. But now that he was here he might as well search the house. He would probably need a couple of hours.

"You don't need to make up your mind right now," Westin said and gave him his card. "You can reach me over the phone. I can either come by this afternoon or this evening. I live on an island that's not too far away."

He pointed it out on the map.

"I'll call you," Wallander said and put the card away.

Westin started both the engines and set off.

"How long have you been delivering the post?" Wallander asked. He had to shout to make himself heard above the engine noise.

"Too long," Westin shouted back. "More than 25 years now."

"What do you do in the winter?"

"Hydrocopter."

Wallander felt his exhaustion lifting. The speed, the experience of being out on the water, gave him a surprising sense of well-being. When had he last felt like this? Perhaps during those days with Linda on Gotland. He knew it must be hard work delivering the post in the archipelago. But right now all suggestion of storms and autumn darkness seemed far away. Westin looked over at him, as if he knew what he was thinking.

"Maybe that would be something for me," he said. "Being a policeman."

Normally Wallander rushed to defend his profession. But here with Westin, as they sped across the smooth surface of the water, the familiar topic coaxed a different response from him.

"Sometimes I have my doubts," he shouted. "But when you reach 50 you're kind of on your own. Most doors are closed."

"I turned 50 this spring," Westin said. "Everyone I know out here threw a big party."

"How many people out here do you know?"

"Everyone. It was a big party."

Westin turned the wheel and slowed the boat down. Right next to a big cliff there was a red boathouse and a pier built out over a row of old stone structures.

"Båtmansö Island," Westin said. "When I was a child there were nine families living out here – more than 30 people. Now there are people out here over the summer, but come winter there's only one. His name is Zetterquist and he's 93 years old, but he still makes it through the winter. He's been widowed three times. He's the kind of old man you don't meet any more. I think the national board of health must have outlawed them."

His last remark took Wallander by surprise and made him laugh.

"Was he a fisherman?"

"He's been a jack-of-all-trades. He worked on a tugboat once upon a time."

"You know everybody. And they all know you?"

"That's the way it goes. If this old chap didn't show up to meet my boat, I'd go up and see if he was sick, or if he'd had a fall. If you're a country postman, either at sea or on land, you end up knowing everybody's business. What they're doing, where they're going, when they're due back. Whether or not you actually want to."

Westin had brought the boat softly alongside the

landing, and now he unloaded a couple of boxes. Quite a few people had gathered on the pier. Westin took the packet of post and walked up to a small red house.

Wallander stretched his legs on the pier, looking at a pile of old-fashioned stone sinkers. The air was cooler. Westin came back after a couple of minutes and they left. Their route took them through the varied landscape of the archipelago. After two more post stops, they approached Bärnsö. They came out on an open stretch of sea called Vikfjärden. Bärnsö lay strangely isolated, as if it had been thrown out of the community of islands.

"You must know the whole Edengren family," Wallander said, when Westin had pulled back the throttle and they were gliding towards the little dock.

"I suppose you could say that," Westin said. "Although I haven't had much contact with the parents. Honestly speaking, I think they're rather snobbish. But Isa and Jörgen have caught a ride with me many times."

"You know that Jörgen is dead," Wallander said carefully.

"I heard he was in a car accident," Westin said. "His father told me. I had to collect him once when there was something wrong with their boat."

"It's tragic when children die," Wallander said.

"I had always thought Isa was the one who would have an accident."

"Why is that?"

"She lives her life to the extreme. At least, if you believe what she says."

"She talks to you? Maybe as a postman you become something of a confidant."

"Hell, no," Westin said. "My son is Isa's age. They were together for a while a couple of summers ago. But it ended, like these things often do at that age."

The boat hit the edge of the pier. Wallander took his bag and got off.

"I'll give you a call this afternoon."

"I eat at 6 p.m.," Westin answered. "Before or after is fine."

Wallander watched the boat disappear around the point. He thought about how Westin had described Jörgen's death. His parents had changed the story. A toaster in the bath had become a car accident.

Wallander walked onto the green, lush island. Next to the dock was a boathouse and a small guest house. It reminded him of the gazebo in Skårby where he had found Isa. An old wooden rowing boat lay turned over on some trestles. Wallander caught a faint whiff of tar. Several large oak trees grew on the hillside leading up to the main house. It was a red two-storey house, old but in good condition. Wallander walked up to it, looking around and listening. There was a sailing boat in the distance, and the dying sound of an outboard motor. Wallander was sweating. He put the bag down, took his coat off and threw it over the railing of the front steps. The curtains were drawn in the windows. He went up the steps and knocked on the door. He waited. Then he banged on it with his fist. No one answered. He felt the handle. It was locked. For a moment he hesitated, then he walked around the back, feeling as though he was repeating his visit to Skårby. There was a garden with fruit trees behind the house – apples, plums and a lone cherry tree. Garden furniture was piled up under a plastic sheet.

A path led away from the house towards the thick woods. Wallander started walking down the path, and came to an old well and an earth cellar. The numbers 1897 were carved into the rock above the door, and the key was in the lock.

Wallander opened the door. It was dark and cool inside, and there was a smell of potatoes. When his eyes became accustomed to the dark he saw that it was empty. He closed the door and continued along the path, catching glimpses of the sea on his left. From the position of the sun he knew he was walking northwards. After about a kilometre he came to a junction where a smaller path led off to the left. He kept walking straight ahead, and after a couple of hundred metres came to the end. Ahead of him were smooth boulders and cliffs. Beyond them, just the open sea. It was the tip of the island. A seagull squawked above him, rising and falling on the wind. He climbed out onto the rocks, sat down, and wiped the sweat from his forehead, wishing that he'd brought some water with him. Gone were all thoughts of Svedberg and the dead young people.

He got up after a while and walked back. At the junction he took the smaller path, which led to a small, natural harbour. Some rusty iron rings were bolted into the rock face. The water was like a mirror, reflecting the tall trees. He turned and walked back to the main house. He checked his phone, went behind one of the oak trees, and took a piss. Then he got out a bottle of water and sat down on the main steps. His mouth was completely dry. As he put the bottle down something caught his attention. He stared at his bag that lay at the foot of the stairs. He was sure he had put it on the higher step. He got off the stairs and went over his actions in his mind.

First I put the bag down, then I removed my jacket and hung it on the railing, he thought. Then I moved the bag to the second step.

It had been moved. He looked around at everything with a new attentiveness. The trees, the bushes, the main house. The curtains were still drawn. He thought of the landing and the guest house, the guest house that reminded him of the gazebo in Skårby. He walked down the hill to the boathouse. The door was latched. He opened it and looked in. It was empty, but he could tell from the size of the berth and the ropes that it housed a big boat. Fishing nets were hanging on the walls. He went out again and locked the door. Part of the guest house was built out over the water with a ladder hanging over the end for swimming. He stood and stared at it for a moment. Then he walked up and felt the door. It was locked. He knocked lightly.

"Isa," he said. "I know you're in there."

He waited.

When she opened the door he didn't recognise her at first. She had tied her hair up in a knot. She was dressed in black, in some kind of overalls. Wallander thought her expression was full of animosity, but perhaps it was fear.

"How did you know I was here?" Her voice was hoarse.

"I didn't. Not until you told me."

"I haven't said anything. And I know you didn't see me."

"Policemen have the bad habit of noticing little things. Like someone lifting a bag, for instance. And not putting it back in the right place."

She stared back at him as if she couldn't understand what he had said. He saw that she was barefoot.

"I'm hungry," she said.

"So am I."

"There's food in the main house," she said and started walking. "Why did you come here?"

"We had to find you."

"Why?"

"Since you know what happened, I don't have to tell you."

She walked on in silence. Wallander looked at her. Her face was pale and drawn.

"How did you get out here?" he asked.

"I called Lage, who lives on Wettersö Island."

"Why didn't you get a ride with Westin?"

"I thought you might try to find out if I was here."

"And you didn't want to be found?"

She didn't answer this either. She unlocked the door and let them in, then walked around opening the curtains. She tugged at them in a careless way, as if she actually wanted to break everything around her. Wallander followed her into the kitchen. She opened the back door and connected a bottle of liquid gas to the stove. Wallander had already noticed that there was no electricity in the house. She turned around and looked at him.

"Cooking is one of the few things I can do."

She pointed out the refrigerator and a large freezer that were also hooked up to gas tanks. "They're full of food," she said disdainfully. "That's the way my parents want it. They pay someone to come out here and change the gas. They want food to be here in case they decide to come out for a couple of days. Which they never do."

She sounded like she was spitting. "My mother's an idiot," she said. "She's completely ignorant. She can't help it, I guess. My father, on the other hand, is not an idiot. But he's ruthless."

"I'd like to hear more."

"Not now. When we eat."

It was clear that she wanted him to leave the kitchen, so Wallander went out to the front of the house and called Ystad. He got hold of Höglund.

"I was right," he said. "She's here, just like we thought."

"Like you thought," she corrected him. "To tell the truth, I don't think any of us were so sure."

"Well, everyone's right some of the time. I think we'll be back in Ystad some time tonight."

"Have you talked to her?"

"Not yet."

She told him some calls had come in from people who thought they recognised the picture of Louise. They were still in the process of checking them. She promised to get back to him when they were finished.

Wallander went back into the house. He kept returning to the same thought. He had to get her to tell him what she didn't even know she knew.

She set the table in the large glassed-in veranda that had been added on to the side of the house. She asked him what he wanted to drink and he opted for water. She drank wine. He worried that she would get drunk and become impossible to talk to, but she had only one glass. They ate in silence. Afterwards, she put on some coffee. She shook her head when Wallander started clearing the table. A sofa and some chairs stood in a corner of the veranda. A lone sailing boat drifted by with limp sails.

"It's very beautiful here," he said. "This is a part of Sweden I haven't seen before."

"They bought the house 30 years ago," she replied. "They claim I was conceived out here, which may be true since I was born in February. They bought the house from an old couple who'd lived here their whole lives. I don't know how my father heard about it but one day he came to see them with a suitcase full of 100-kronor notes. It looks very impressive, but it doesn't necessarily mean it's a large sum of money. Neither of them had ever seen so much money in their lives. It took a couple of months to convince them, but they finally accepted the offer. I don't know what the exact amount was but I'm sure he paid nothing close to what it was worth."

"Do you mean that he swindled them?"

"I mean that my father has always been a scoundrel."

"If he simply made a good deal perhaps he should be called an ambitious businessman."

"My father has been involved in deals all over the world. He smuggled diamonds and ivory in Africa. No one really knows what he does now, but lately a lot of Russians have come out to visit him in Skårby. You can't tell me they're up to anything legal."

"As far as I know he's never been in trouble with us," Wallander said.

"Yes, he's good," she said. "And persistent. You can accuse him of a lot of things but he's not lazy. Ruthless people don't tend to rest on their laurels."

Wallander set his coffee cup down. "Let's talk about you instead," he said. "That's why I'm here, and it's been a long trip. We'll be heading back soon."

"What makes you think I'll be coming with you?"

Wallander looked at her for a long time before answering. "Three of your closest friends have been murdered," he said. "You were supposed to have been there when it happened. Both of us know what conclusion to draw from that."

She curled up in her chair and Wallander saw that she was frightened.

"Since we don't know why it happened, we have to take every precaution," he said.

The importance of what he was saying finally seemed to sink in. "Am I in danger?"

"We can't rule that out. We have no motive, therefore we have to consider all possibilities."

"But why would anyone want to kill me?"

"Why would anyone want to kill your friends? Martin, Lena, Astrid?"

She shook her head. "I don't understand it," she said.

Wallander moved his chair closer to hers. "Nonetheless you're the one who's going to help us," he said. "We're going to catch whoever did this. And to get him, we have to know why he did it. You got away. You're the one who's going to tell us."

"But when it's completely incomprehensible?"

"You have to think back," Wallander said. "Who could have targeted you as a group? What united you? Why? There is an answer. It has to be there."

He quickly changed tack, knowing that she was starting to listen to him. He didn't want to lose this opportunity.

"You have to answer my questions," he said. "And you have to tell the truth. I'll know if you're lying. And I don't want that."

"Why would I lie?"

"When I found you, you had just tried to commit suicide," he said. "Why? Did you already know what had happened to your friends?"

She looked at him with surprise. "How could I have known that? I had the same questions as everybody else."

Wallander knew she was telling the truth. "Why did you want to kill yourself?"

"I didn't want to live any more. Is there ever any other reason? My parents have ruined my life, just like they ruined Jörgen's. I just didn't want to live any more."

Wallander waited. Maybe she would keep talking. But she didn't say anything else.

For the next three hours he led her step by step through the events of the summer. He didn't leave anything untouched, however minor. He went through everything, sometimes more than once. There were no limits to how far back he could go. When had she first met Lena Norman? Which year, which month, what day? How had they meet, how did they become friends? When she said she couldn't remember, or if she became unsure of herself, he slowed down and started again. An unclear memory could be overcome with patience. The whole time he was trying to get her to think about whether there had been anyone else there.

"A shadow in the corner," he said. "Was there a shadow in the corner? Anything you're forgetting?"

He asked about everything that might have seemed unexpected. As time went on she started to understand his methods, and then it was easier. Shortly after 5 p.m. they decided to stay the night and leave Bärnsö the following day. Wallander called Westin, who promised to come and get them when Wallander called. He didn't ask about Isa, but Wallander was sure he had known she was out there all along. They took a walk on the island, talking the whole time. Now and again Isa interrupted herself to point out places where she had played as a child. They walked out to the northernmost point. To his surprise she pointed to a shelf in the rock where she claimed to have lost her virginity one summer, but she didn't say with whom.

When they returned to the house it was starting to get dark. She walked around turning on the kerosene lamps, while Wallander called Ystad and talked to Martinsson. Nothing much had happened. No one had identified Louise. Wallander told him he was staying the night, and that he would return with the girl the next day.

Isa and Wallander continued their conversation all evening, pausing only to have tea and sandwiches.

Wallander walked out in the dark and relieved himself against a tree. The wind moaned in the treetops. Everything was quiet. He was beginning to understand their games – the way they dressed up, had parties, and travelled to different ages. When the conversation approached the party that had turned out to be their last, Wallander proceeded with painstaking care. Who could possibly have known about their plans? No one? He simply couldn't accept her answer. Someone must have known.

It was 1.30 a.m. when they stopped for the night. Wallander was so tired that he felt nauseated. She still hadn't come up with anything, but they were going to keep going in the long car trip to Ystad. He wasn't going to give up.

She showed him to a bedroom on the second floor. She was sleeping downstairs. She said good night and gave him a kerosene lamp. He made his bed and opened the window. It was very dark outside. He lay down in the bed and blew out the lamp. He heard her cleaning up in the kitchen, then the sound of the front door being locked. Then nothing.

Wallander fell asleep immediately.

No one noticed the boat that crossed Vikfjärden late that evening with its lights turned off. And no one heard it as it glided into the natural harbour on the west side of Bärnsö Island.

CHAPTER NINETEEN

Linda screamed.

She was somewhere close by. Her scream forced its way into his dreams. When he opened his eyes he had no idea where he was, but the faint scent from the kerosene lamp made him realise that it couldn't have been Linda who had screamed. His heart was pounding. It was quiet outside, just the whisper of the wind in the trees. He listened. Had it been a dream? He sat up and fumbled for the matches that he had placed beside the lamp on the table, lit it, and got dressed. He was putting his shoes on when he heard the sound. Something banging against the side of the house. Maybe the sound of a washing line hitting a drainpipe. But it was coming from downstairs. He got up, still with one shoe in his hand, and went over to the door. He opened it carefully and the sound came more clearly. The kitchen. The kitchen door must be open and banging in the wind. His fear came back with a vengeance. He hadn't been dreaming. The scream had been real.

Instead of putting his shoe on, he kicked off the other one, and walked downstairs with the lamp in his hand. He stopped halfway down and listened. The lamplight flickered over the walls. His hands were shaking. He realised that he had nothing to defend himself with. He tried to gather his thoughts. Nothing could happen out here. They were alone on the island. Maybe a bird had cried outside his window. And there was another possibility – that he wasn't the only one who had nightmares.

He went all the way downstairs and stopped outside her door, listened, then knocked. No answer. It's too quiet, he thought. He felt the handle. It was locked. Now he didn't hesitate. He banged the door and rattled the handle. Nothing. He went out to the kitchen. The back door was open and he closed it. He looked in the kitchen drawers and found a screwdriver, and used it to open her door. The bed was empty, the window open without being fastened. He tried to think what might have happened. He remembered seeing a big torch in the kitchen. He got it, and took a hammer as well. He opened the back door, and shone the light out into the darkness.

Once he was outside he realised that he was barefoot. A bird flew away from somewhere nearby. The sound of the wind was stronger. He called Isa's name, but there was no answer. He shone the light below her window. There were footprints on the ground, but they were so faint that he couldn't see where they led. He shone the light out into the darkness and called out again. Still no answer. His heart was pounding. He went back to the kitchen door and examined the lock. It had been forced, just as he'd thought. His fear grew stronger. He turned around and lifted his hammer, but there was no one there. He returned to the house. His phone was on the table next to his bed. He tried to imagine what had happened.

Someone breaks in through the kitchen door. Isa wakes because someone is trying to get into her room. Then she jumps out the window.

He couldn't think of any other explanation. He looked at his watch. It was 2.45 a.m. He dialled Martinsson's home number. He answered on the second ring. Wallander knew he had a phone by his bed.

"It's Kurt. I'm sorry to wake you."

"What's wrong?" Martinsson was still half-asleep.

"Get up," Wallander said. "Splash some cold water on your face. I'll call back in three minutes."

Martinsson started to protest, but Wallander hung up and looked at his watch. In exactly three minutes he called back, worrying about the battery to his phone running out.

"Listen carefully," he said. "I can't talk for long, my battery is going to run out. Do you have a pen and paper?"

Martinsson was wide awake now.

"I'm writing this down as we speak."

"Something's happened out here. I don't know what. Isa Edengren screamed, and I woke up. Now she's gone. The back door to the house has been forced. There's someone else on the island besides us. Whoever it is, he's come for her. I'm afraid she's in danger."

"What do you want me to do?"

"For now, just get the phone number of the coast guard in Fyrudden. Be prepared for my next call."

"What are you going to do?"

"Find her."

"If the killer's out there it'll be dangerous. You need help."

"And where would that come from? Norköpping? How long would that take?"

"You can't search an entire island by yourself."

"It's not that big. I'm going to hang up now, I want to conserve the battery."

Wallander put his shoes on and slipped the phone into his pocket, tucked the hammer into his belt, and left the house. He walked down to the landing and shone the torch. No boat. The boathouse and guest house were empty. He was calling her name. He ran back up to the main house, and started down the path. The bushes and trees looked white in the strong light. There was no one in the earth cellar.

He continued, calling her constantly. When he came to the junction in the path, he hesitated. Which way should he go? He looked at the ground, but couldn't see any prints. He headed for the northern tip of the island. He was out of breath when he reached the end. The wind coming in off the open sea was icy. He let the beam from the torch play over the rocks. Two eyes gleamed in the light. It was a little animal, a mink perhaps, that scuttled away between the rocks. He walked to the very end of the rocks, shining his light in the crevices. Nothing. He turned around to start back.

Something made him stop. He listened. The waves hit the shore in a rhythmic motion, but there was another sound. At first he didn't know what it was. Then he realised that it was an engine. The sound came from the west.

The harbour, he thought, and started running. I should have taken the other path.

He stopped only when he was about to reach the shore. He stepped out and flashed his light over the water. There was nothing there, and the sound had disappeared. A boat has just left, he thought. His fear increased. What had happened to her? He walked back along the path, trying to decide how to continue his search. Did the coast guard have dogs? Even though the island was small, he wouldn't be finished until morning. He tried to think out how she would have reacted. She had fled her bedroom in panic. The person trying to break in had blocked her way up to his room. She jumped out the window and took off into the darkness. He doubted that she'd had a torch.

Wallander reached the junction again. Suddenly he knew. As they were walking around the island, she had mentioned a favourite hiding place she and Jörgen had when they were little. He thought back to where they had been standing when she had pointed to the rock face that was the highest point on the island. It had been closer to the house, and he remembered two juniper trees. He left the path. Fallen trees and thick shrubbery slowed his progress. There were large boulders strewn about, and he shone his light on them as he walked by. As he was nearing the beginning of the rock face, he caught sight of a deep crevice behind some ferns. He walked up to the rock wall, parted the ferns, and shone his torch inside.

She was there, curled up against the side of the rock, wearing only a nightgown. Her arms were wrapped around her legs and her head was leaning against one shoulder. It looked like she was sleeping, but he knew at once that she was dead. She had been shot in the head.

Wallander sank down on the ground. The blood rushed to his head. He felt like he was dying, and he didn't really mind. He had failed. He hadn't managed to keep her safe. Even the hiding place where she had played as a child hadn't protected her. He hadn't heard a shot. The gun must have had a silencer.

He got up and leaned against a tree. The phone slid out of his grasp. He leaned down, picked it up, and started staggering back towards the house as he called Martinsson.

"I'm too late," he said.

"Too late for what?"

"She's dead. Shot, just like the others."

Martinsson didn't seem to understand. Wallander had to repeat himself.

"My God," Martinsson said. "Who killed her?"

"A man in a boat," Wallander said. "Call the police in Norrköping. They'll have to do this. And talk to the coast guard."

Martinsson promised to do what he said.

"You might as well wake up the others," he said. "Lisa Holgersson, everyone. Once I get some help out here I'll call you again."

The conversation was over. Wallander sat on a chair in the kitchen, with the beam resting on a tapestry with the words "home sweet home". After a while he forced himself to get up, go into her room, and pull the blanket from her bed. Then he went out into the dark. Once he got back to the crevice he wrapped the blanket around her.

He sat down by the ferns that covered the opening. It was 3.20 a.m.

The wind picked up in the early, pale dawn. Wallander heard the coast guard arriving and went to the landing. The policemen approached him with suspicion. Wallander could understand their reaction. What was a police officer from Skåne doing out here on one of their islands? If he had been on holiday, it would have been different. He led them to the crevice, and turned away as they lifted the blanket. One of the officers demanded to see Wallander's police ID. Wallander lost his temper. He tore his wallet from his pocket and threw his ID card on the ground. Then he walked away. His fury left him almost immediately, replaced by a paralysing fatigue. He sat down on the front steps to the house with a bottle of water.

Harry Lundström came and found him. He'd seen

Wallander lose his temper and had thought how tactless it had been to ask him for his police badge at that moment. It was clear, after all, that he was a fellow police officer. The call had come from the Ystad police, with very specific information. A detective by the name of Kurt Wallander was on Bärnsö Island. He had found a dead girl, and he needed assistance.

Harry Lundström was 57 years old. He had been born in Norrköping and was considered the best detective in the city by everyone but himself. When Wallander flew into a rage, Lundström had understood his reaction. He didn't know what events lay behind the murder, but he knew that it had to do with the dead police officer and the three young people. Beyond that it was very unclear. But Harry Lundström had a huge capacity for empathy. He could imagine what it might have felt like to find a girl dressed only in her nightgown, curled in a crevice, with a bullet hole in her head.

Lundström sat down next to Wallander on the steps.

"That was a thoughtless thing of them to do," he said. "Asking for your ID like that."

He stretched out his hand and introduced himself. Wallander immediately felt that he could trust him.

"Should I speak to you?"

Lundström nodded.

"Then let's go inside," Wallander said.

They sat in the living room. After he'd called Martinsson on Lundström's phone, and arranged for Isa's parents to be notified of her death, he took more than an hour to explain who the dead girl was, and the circumstances surrounding her murder. Lundström listened without taking notes. Now and again they were interrupted by officers with questions. Lundström provided simple and clear instructions. When Wallander had finished talking, Lundström asked about a few details. Wallander thought that they were exactly the questions he would have asked himself.

It was already 7 a.m. and through the windows they could see the coast guard's boat scraping against the dock.

"I'd better get back up there," Lundström said. "You can stay here, of course. You've seen more than enough."

The wind was very strong now, and Wallander shivered.

"It's an autumn wind," Lundström said. "The weather has started to turn."

"I've never been in this archipelago before," Wallander said. "It's very beautiful."

"I played handball when I was young," Lundström said. "I had a picture of the Ystad team on my bedroom wall, but I've almost never been to your parts."

As they walked along the path, they could hear dogs barking in the distance.

"I thought it would be best to comb the island," Lundström said, "in case the killer is still here somewhere."

"He arrived by boat," Wallander said. "He anchored on the west side."

"If we had more time, we'd arrange to put some of the nearby harbours under surveillance," Lundström said. "But it's too late now."

"Maybe someone saw something," Wallander said.

"We're on to it," Lundström said. "I've considered the possibility. Someone may have seen a boat anchoring here late last night."

Wallander remained at a distance while Lundström walked up to the crevice and had a brief discussion with his colleagues. He felt sick to his stomach. What he wanted most of all was to get off the island as soon as possible.

His feeling of being somehow responsible for the crime was very strong. They should have left the island last night. He should have realised the danger of staying. The murderer seemed always to be in a position of knowing what they were doing. It had also been a mistake to let her sleep downstairs. He was aware that blaming himself was unreasonable, but he couldn't help it.

Lundström reappeared, and at the same time an officer with a dog came from the opposite direction. Lundström stopped him.

"Find anything?"

"There's no one on the island," the officer said. "She traced him to a bay on the west side, but the scent ended there."

Lundström looked at Wallander. "You were right," he said. "He came and left by boat."

They walked down to the main house again. Wallander thought about what Lundström had just said.

"The boat is important," he said. "Where did he get hold of it?"

"I was just thinking the same thing," Lundström said. "If we assume that the killer is not from around here, which I think we have to, then we have to find out where he got the boat from."

"He stole it," Wallander said.

Lundström stopped. "But how did he find his way here in the middle of the night?"

"He may have been out here before, and there are maps."

"Do you really think he's been out here before?"

"We can't rule that out."

Lundström started walking again.

"A stolen or borrowed boat," he said. "It must have happened near here. Either in Fyrudden, Snäckvarp or

Gryt. If he didn't steal it from a private dock, that is."

"He can't have had a lot of time," Wallander said. "Isa ran away from the hospital yesterday morning."

"Criminals in a hurry are always the easiest to trace," Lundström said.

They reached the landing and Lundström talked to a police officer who was adjusting one of the ropes. They took shelter from the wind by the boathouse.

"There's no reason to keep you here," Lundström said. "I assume that you want to go home."

Wallander felt a need to describe his feelings. "It shouldn't have happened," he said "I feel responsible. We should have left here yesterday. And now she's dead."

"I would have done the same thing that you did," Lundström said. "This was where she ran to. This was where you could start to get her talking. You couldn't have known what was going to happen."

Wallander shook his head. "I should have realised how much danger she was in."

They walked up to the house, and Lundström said he would do his best to ensure cooperation between the Norrköping and Ystad police.

"I'm sure there'll be the odd complaint about our not being informed that you were up here, but I'll see that they keep quiet."

Wallander got his bag and they returned to the landing. The coast guard would drop him back on the mainland. Lundström remained on the landing and saw them off. Wallander lifted his hand in a gesture of gratitude.

He threw his bag in the car and went to pay his parking ticket. As he was walking back he saw Westin on his way into the harbour. Wallander walked out to meet him, noting Westin's sombre expression as he stepped ashore.

"I take it you've heard the news," Wallander said.

"Isa is dead."

"It happened last night. I woke up when she screamed, but I was too late."

Westin looked at him grimly. "So it wouldn't have happened if you hadn't come out here last night?"

There it is, Wallander thought. The accusation. The one I can't defend myself against.

He took out his wallet. "How much do I owe you for yesterday's trip?"

"Nothing," Westin said.

Westin began to walk away. Wallander remembered that he had one more question to ask him.

"There's one more thing," he said.

Westin turned.

"Sometime between 19 and 22 July, you took someone to Bärnsö."

"In July I had a lot of passengers every day."

"This was another detective," Wallander said. "His name was Karl Evert Svedberg. He spoke with an even stronger Skåne accent than I do. Do you remember him?"

"Was he wearing his uniform?"

"I doubt it."

"Can you describe him?"

"He was almost completely bald, about as tall as me, solid but not overweight."

Westin thought it over.

"Between 19 and 22 July?"

"He would probably have crossed in the afternoon or early evening on the 19th. I don't know when he came back, but it would have been the 22nd at the latest."

"I'll check my records," Westin said. "But I don't remember off hand."

Wallander followed him out to the boat. Westin got out a notebook that lay under his chart, and came out of the wheelhouse.

"There's nothing here," he said. "But I do have a vague recollection of him. There were a lot of people on board, though. I might be confusing him with someone else."

"Do you have access to a fax machine?" Wallander asked. "We can send you a picture of him."

"I can get faxes at the post office."

Another possibility occurred to Wallander.

"You might already have seen a picture of him," he said. "Maybe on TV. He's the police officer who was murdered in Ystad a couple of days ago."

Westin frowned. "I heard about that," he said. "But I can't remember seeing a picture."

"You'll get one over the fax," Wallander said. "Give me the number."

Westin wrote it down for him in his notebook and tore out the page.

"Do you know if Isa was out here between 19 and 22 July?"

"No, but she was here a lot this summer."

"So it's a possibility?"

"Yes."

Wallander left Fyrudden. He stopped at a petrol station in Valdermarsvik, then took the coast road. There wasn't a cloud in the sky. He rolled down the window. When he reached Västervik he realised that he didn't have the energy to continue. He had to eat something, and sleep. He found a roadside café and ordered an omelette, some mineral water and a cup of coffee. The woman who took his order smiled at him.

"At your age you shouldn't stay up all night," she said.

Wallander looked at her with surprise. "Is it so obvious?"

She bent down and got her bag from behind the counter, then fished out a make-up mirror and handed it over to him. She was right. He was pale and had dark circles under his eyes. His hair was a mess.

"You're right," he said. "I'll have my omelette, then I'll catch up on a bit of sleep in my car."

He went outside and sat down in the shade. She brought the food out on a tray.

"There's a small room off the kitchen with a bed in it," she said. "You could use it for a while if you'd like."

She walked away without waiting for an answer. Wallander watched her departing figure with surprise. After he'd finished eating he walked over to the door of the kitchen. It was open.

"Is the offer still open?" he asked.

"I don't go back on my word."

She showed him the room and the bed, which was a simple folding cot with a blanket.

"It's better than the back seat of your car," she said. "Of course, policemen are used to sleeping anywhere."

"How do you know I'm a policeman?"

"I saw your police ID in your wallet when you paid. I was married to a policeman, so I recognised it."

"My name is Kurt. Kurt Wallander."

"I'm Erika. Sleep well."

Wallander lay down on the bed. His whole body ached and his head felt completely empty. He knew he should call the station and let them know that he was on his way, but he couldn't be bothered. He closed his eyes and fell asleep.

When he woke he had no idea where he was. He looked down at his watch. It was 7 p.m. He sat up with a jerk. He had slept for more than five hours. Cursing, he got the phone and called the station. Martinsson didn't answer, and so he tried Hansson.

"Where the hell have you been? We've been trying to reach you all day. Why wasn't your phone on?"

"There must have been something wrong with it. Has anything happened?"

"Nothing more than us wondering where you were."

"I'll be there as soon as I can. By 11 p.m. at the latest."

Wallander hung up. Erika appeared in the doorway.

"I think you needed that," she said.

"An hour would have been plenty. I should have asked you to wake me."

"There's coffee, but no hot food. I've closed for the day."

"You've been waiting for me?"

"There are always things that need doing around here."

They went out into the empty restaurant, and she brought him a cup of coffee and some sandwiches, and sat down across from him.

"I just heard on the radio about the girl who was killed in the archipelago, and the police officer who found her," she said. "I take it that was you."

"Yes, but I'd rather not talk about it. So, you were married to a policeman once?"

"When I lived in Kalmar. I moved here after the divorce, when I had the money to buy this place."

She told him about the first few years, when the restaurant didn't make enough money. But it was doing better now. Wallander listened, but all the while he was looking at her. He wanted to reach out and touch her, to hold on to something normal and real. He sat with her for half an hour, then paid and walked to his car. She followed him out.

"I don't really know how to thank you," he said.

"Why do people always need to thank each other?" she said. "Drive carefully."

Wallander reached the station at 11 p.m. and met with everyone in the large conference room. Nyberg and Holgersson were there. During the drive back, he had thought through everything that had happened, beginning on the night that he had woken thinking that something was wrong with Svedberg. He still felt guilty about Isa, but now he also felt anger at her death. His rage caused him to speed up without noticing it, and at one point he found himself doing more than 150 kilometres per hour.

His rage stemmed not only from her senseless murder, but also from his feeling of failure at their inability to see which way to turn. And now Isa Edengren had been shot out on Bärnsö Island, practically before his eyes.

Wallander told everyone about the events on the island. After answering their questions and listening to a report on developments in Ystad, he summed up the situation in a few sentences. It was well past midnight.

"Tomorrow we have to start from the beginning," he said. "We have to start from the beginning and work from there. We'll find the killer sooner or later. We have to. But I think that the best thing to do now is to go home and get some sleep. It's been hard up till now, and I think that it's just going to get harder."

Wallander finished. Martinsson looked as though he was about to speak, but then changed his mind. Wallander was the first to leave. He closed his office door, making it clear that he didn't want to be disturbed. He sat down and thought about what he hadn't brought up at the meeting, what they would have to discuss the following day.

Isa Edengren was dead. Did that mean that the killer had completed his task, or was he now preparing for something else?

No one knew the answer.

Part Two

CHAPTER TWENTY

On the morning of Thursday, 15 August, Wallander finally went back to Dr Göransson's office. He didn't have an appointment but was seen immediately. He hadn't slept well and was extremely tired, but he left the car at home. He knew that each new day would carry with it fresh excuses for not exercising. This day was just as inconvenient as any other, so he might as well start getting used to it.

The weather was still beautiful and calm. As he walked through the town he tried to recall when they had last had an August this warm. But his mind kept turning back to the investigation, and not just during his waking hours. It haunted him in his sleep as well.

Last night he had dreamed of Bärnsö. He kept hearing her scream. When he woke up he was halfway out of bed, drenched in sweat, his heart pounding. It had taken him a long time to fall back to sleep.

He sat at the kitchen table for a while after he woke. It was still dark outside. He couldn't think of a time when he'd felt as helpless as he did at that moment. It wasn't just the fatigue caused by the little icebergs of sugar floating around in his blood. It also came from a feeling of having been overtaken by age. Was he really too old? He wasn't even 50.

He wondered if he was simply starting to crumble under the weight of all the responsibility and was now on a downward trajectory to a point where only fear remained.

He was very close to making a new decision: to give up. To ask Holgersson to put someone else in charge.

The question was who to appoint in his place. Martinsson and Hansson both came to mind, but Wallander knew neither one of them was up to it. They would have to bring someone in from outside, which was not ideal. That would be like labelling themselves inadequate.

He didn't come to any conclusion. When he decided to go to the doctor it was in the hope that he'd hear the words that would free him, give him the chance to be forced to take leave on medical grounds.

But it turned out that Dr Göransson had no such plans for him. After telling Wallander that his blood sugar was still too high, that he was leaking sugar into his urine and had worryingly high blood pressure, he simply gave him a prescription for some medication and ordered him to make a radical change in his diet.

"We have to attack your symptoms from all sides," he said. "They're connected and have to be treated as such. But it's not going to be possible unless you take charge of your health."

He gave him the phone number of a dietician. Wallander left the office with the prescription in hand. It was a little after 8 a.m. and he knew he should go directly to the station, but he didn't feel ready. He went up to the café by the main square and had a cup of coffee, but this time he passed on the pastry.

What do I do now, he thought. I'm in charge of solving one of the most brutal serial killings in Sweden in years. Every police officer's eye is on me, since one of the victims was in the force. The press are hounding me. I'll probably be criticised by the victims' parents. Everyone expects me to find the killer in a few days and to have collected the kind of evidence against him that would make even the most hardened prosecutor weep. The only problem is that in reality I have nothing. Soon I'll gather my colleagues together and we'll start again. We aren't even close to anything like a breakthrough. What we're in is a vacuum.

He finished his coffee. A man was reading the paper at the next table. Wallander saw the big black headlines, and left the café in a hurry. Since he had time to spare, he decided to squeeze in an errand before returning to the station. He went to Vädergränd and rang the doorbell at Bror Sundelius's house. There was a chance that Sundelius didn't welcome surprise visits, but Wallander knew it would not be because he wasn't up yet.

The door opened. Even though it was only 8.30 a.m., Sundelius was dressed in a suit. The knot of his tie was an exercise in perfection. He opened the door wide without hesitation, invited Wallander in, and disappeared into the kitchen for coffee.

"I always keep the water hot," he said, "in case I have unexpected visitors. The last time that happened was about a year ago, of course, but you never know."

Wallander sat down on the sofa and pulled the cup towards him. Sundelius sat down across from him.

"Last time we spoke we were interrupted," Wallander said.

"The reason for that has become exceedingly clear," Sundelius replied dryly. "What kind of people do we let into this country anyway?"

His comment puzzled Wallander.

"There's no evidence that this was the work of an immigrant," he said. "Why would you think that?"

"It seems obvious to me," Sundelius said. "No Swede could have done anything like this."

He knew the best thing to do was to steer the conversation to safer ground. Sundelius did not seem like the kind of man who was easily swayed in his convictions. But Wallander couldn't keep himself from articulating his objections.

"Nothing points to a killer of foreign extraction. That much we know. Let's talk about Karl Evert instead. You knew him quite well?"

"He was always 'Kalle' to me."

"How long had you known each other?"

"Which day did he die?"

Wallander was puzzled again. "We haven't established that yet. Why?"

"If you had, I would have been able to give you an exact answer. Let me provisionally say that we knew each other 19 years, seven months, and around 15 days when he passed away so tragically. I have kept careful records my whole life. The only data I won't be able to record is the exact time of my own death, unless I commit suicide, which I have no plans to do. But my lawyer has instructions to burn all my notebooks when I die. They are of value only to me, not anyone else."

Wallander was starting to sense that Sundelius was one of these old people who did not get enough chances to talk to others. Wallander thought briefly of his father – one of the few people he had known who had been an exception to this rule.

"You were both interested in astronomy, is that correct?"

"That is correct."

"You don't have a Scanian accent. You moved here at some point?"

"I moved here from Vadstena on 12 May 1959. My furniture arrived on the 14th. I thought I would stay a few years, but it has been much longer than that."

Wallander cast his gaze hastily around the room. He didn't see any pictures of family. Sundelius wasn't wearing a ring.

"Are you married?"

"No."

"Divorced?"

"I'm a bachelor."

"Like Svedberg."

"Yes."

He might as well come right to the point. He still had a copy of the picture of Louise in his breast pocket. He took it out and laid it on the table.

"Have you ever seen this woman before?"

Sundelius put on some glasses after polishing the lenses with his handkerchief, and studied it carefully.

"Isn't that the same picture that was published in the paper the other day?"

"That's right."

"Members of the public were asked to call the police if they had any information regarding who she was."

Wallander nodded. Sundelius laid the photograph back on the table.

"So I should already have contacted you if I had known anything about her."

"Do you?"

"No. And I have a gift for faces. It's a necessity for a banker."

Wallander couldn't help himself. Why would bank directors need to have a gift for faces? He asked the question and got another long answer.

"There was a time when I was young when it was the only kind of credit information there was," Sundelius said. "That was before our society started recording its citizens' every move. We speak of before and after the birth of Christ, but it would be more accurate to speak of before and after the invention of personal identification numbers. When I was young, you had to make your decision on the spot. Was the person standing before you honest? Did he mean what he said? Did he have integrity, or was he a liar? I remember an old clerk in Vadstena who never gathered any credit reports on his clients, and this even after the regulations were tightened and it was easier to collect such information. However large the loan in question, he would simply study the person's face. And he was never wrong, not once over the course of his whole career. He rejected the scoundrels, and helped the honest and hardworking. Of course, he could never foresee a person's luck."

Wallander nodded and continued. "This woman has been connected with Kalle," he said. "According to reliable information, they saw each other for about ten years. Or, to be more precise, they had a relationship for ten years. Kalle remained a bachelor, but he was apparently involved with this woman for a very long time."

Sundelius froze with the coffee cup halfway to his mouth. When Wallander finished speaking, he slowly lowered it onto the saucer.

"That was not very reliable information," he said. "You're wrong."

"In what way?"

"In all ways. Kalle didn't have a girlfriend."

"We know these meetings took place in secret."

"They didn't take place at all."

Sundelius was sure of himself. But Wallander also

sensed something else in the tone of his voice. At first he couldn't tell what it was. Then he realised that Sundelius was upset. He maintained his self-control, but an edge had crept into his voice.

"Let me make it clear that none of his colleagues nor anyone else knew about this woman," Wallander said. "Only one person knew about her. So we're all very surprised."

"Who knew about her?"

"I'd rather not tell you for now."

Sundelius looked at Wallander. There was something resolute and yet vacant in his gaze. But Wallander was sure: the indignation and irritation were there. It was not his imagination.

"Let us leave this unknown woman for a while," Wallander said. "How did you meet?"

Sundelius's manner was altered. Now his answers came reluctantly and without his previous fluency. He had been led into an area where he hadn't been expecting to go.

"We met in the home of mutual friends in Malmö."

"Is that what it says in your notebook?"

"I really don't know why the police would be interested in what my calendar does or does not say."

Now he's completely dismissive, Wallander thought. A photograph of an unknown woman changes everything. He continued carefully.

"But it was at that time that you started maintaining a friendship?"

Sundelius seemed to have realised that his new attitude was noticeable. He resumed his calm and friendly manner, but Wallander still felt his attention was elsewhere.

"We would study the night sky together. That was all."

"Where did you go?"

"Out into the countryside, where it's dark. Especially in

the autumn. We would go to Fyledalen, among other places."

Wallander thought for a moment. "You were surprised when I first contacted you," he said. "You said you were surprised that I hadn't been in touch earlier, since Kalle didn't have many close friends. Did you count yourself among them?"

"I remember what I said."

"But now you describe a relationship based on a mutual interest in the night sky. Was that all it was?"

"Neither he nor I was the intrusive type."

"But it hardly qualifies you as a close friend, does it? Nor as the kind of friend we as his colleagues would have heard about."

"It was what it was."

No, Wallander thought. It wasn't. But I still don't know what it was.

"When was the last time you saw each other?"

"In the middle of July. The 16th, to be precise."

"You went to look at the stars?"

"We went out to Österlen. It was a very clear night, although summer is not the best time."

"How was he?"

Sundelius looked at him blankly. "I don't understand the question."

"Was he his normal self? Did he say anything unexpected?"

"He was exactly as he always was. You don't talk much when you look at stars. At least we never did."

"And after that?"

"We didn't see each other again."

"Had you decided when you would see each other again?"

"He said he was going away for a few days and that he had a lot to do. We said we would be in touch in August, when he was due to take his holidays."

Wallander held his breath. Three days later Svedberg had gone to Bärnsö. What Sundelius had just said seemed to indicate that Svedberg had already decided to go. He'd said he had a lot to do, and that he was due to take his holiday in August, although he was actually in the middle of his holiday already.

Svedberg was lying, Wallander thought. Even to Sundelius, who was his friend, he had lied about the way he was spending his holiday. He didn't tell people at work either. For the first time Wallander felt that he was very close to a revelation. But he still didn't see what it could be.

Wallander thanked him for the coffee. Sundelius followed him to the door.

"I'm sure we'll be seeing each other again," Wallander said as he took his leave. Sundelius had completely regained his composure.

"I'd be grateful if you would let me know when the funeral is going to be."

Wallander promised him he would be notified. He walked along Vädergränd and sat down on a bench outside Café Bäckahästen. As he watched the ducks swimming in the pond, he went over his conversation with Sundelius. There were two moments of particular significance: one when Wallander had showed him the photograph, the other when he had realised that Svedberg was lying. He stayed with the photograph for a moment. It wasn't just the picture that had upset him; it was also the fact that Wallander had spoken of a ten-year love affair.

Perhaps it's that easy, he thought. Maybe there wasn't

one love affair but two. Could Sundelius and Svedberg have had a relationship? Was there something to the rumour that Svedberg was gay? Wallander grabbed a handful of gravel and let it fall through his fingers. He still had doubts. The photograph was of a woman, and Sture Björklund was very sure of the fact that a woman called Louise had long been a part of Svedberg's life. That raised another important question. Why did Sture Björklund know about this woman when no one else did?

Wallander wiped off his hands and got up. He remembered the prescription, and stopped at a pharmacy to have it filled. When he took out the prescription slip, he noticed that his phone was turned off. He continued on to the station at a more rapid clip. His conversation with Sundelius had propelled him deeper into the investigation.

When Wallander walked through the station doors, Ebba told him that everyone was looking for him. He told her to tell people that they were meeting in half an hour. On his way to his office he bumped into Hansson.

"I was just coming to find you. Some results have come in from Lund."

"Can the pathologist give us a time of death?"

"It seems like it."

"Then let's have a look."

Wallander followed Hansson to his office. When they walked past Svedberg's office, he noticed to his surprise that the nameplate was already gone. His surprise turned into dismay, then anger.

"Who removed Svedberg's nameplate?"

"I don't know."

"Couldn't the bastards at least have waited until after the funeral?"

"The funeral is on Tuesday," Hansson said. "Lisa said that the minister of justice will be attending."

Wallander knew her from her TV appearances to be a very determined and self-confident woman. Right now her name escaped him. Hansson hastily brushed some racing forms off his desk and got out the pathologist's report. Wallander leaned against the wall while Hansson was rifling through the report.

"Here we are," he said finally.

"Let's start with Svedberg."

"He was hit with two shots from the front. Death was instantaneous."

"But when?" Wallander said impatiently. "Skip the rest unless it's important. I want a time."

"When you and Martinsson found him he couldn't have been dead more than 24 hours, and not less than ten."

"Are they sure? Or will they change their minds?"

"They seem sure. And just as sure that Svedberg was sober when he died."

"Were there speculations to the contrary?"

"I'm just stating what the report says. His last meal, taken a couple of hours before he died, was of yogurt."

"That suggests he died in the morning."

Hansson nodded. Everyone knew that Svedberg ate yogurt for breakfast. When he was forced to work a night shift he always put a container of yogurt in the fridge in the canteen.

"There it is," Wallander said.

"There's a lot more," Hansson continued. "Do you want the details?"

"I'll go over those myself later," Wallander said. "What does it say about the three young people?"

"That it's difficult to ascertain their time of death."

"We knew that already. But what's their conclusion?"

"Their tentative conclusion is that there needs to be further research done, but they don't rule out the possibility that the victims could have been killed as early as 21 June, Midsummer's Eve, with one stipulation."

"That the bodies weren't left out in the open air."

"Exactly. Of course, they're not sure."

"But I am. Now we can finally draw up a time frame. We'll start with that at the meeting."

"I haven't located the cars yet," Hansson said. "The killer must have disposed of them too somehow."

"Maybe he buried them as well," Wallander said. "Whatever he did with them, they have to be found as soon as possible."

He walked back to his office, got out his medication, and read the label. It was called Amaryl, and the instructions said to take it with food. Wallander wondered when he would have a chance to eat next. He got up with a heavy sigh and walked to the canteen, where he found some old biscuits on a plate. He managed to get them down and took his pills when he was finished.

He returned to his office, gathered up his papers, and went to the conference room. Just as Martinsson was about to close the door, Lisa Holgersson turned up with Thurnberg, the chief prosecutor, in tow. Wallander realised when he saw him that he hadn't really kept him informed of the investigation's progress. As might be expected, Thurnberg had a disapproving look on his face. He sat as far from Wallander as he could get.

Holgersson told them that Svedberg's funeral was to be held on Tuesday, 20 August, at 2 p.m.

She looked at Wallander. "I'll give a speech," she said. "So will the minister of justice and the national chief of police. But I wonder if one of you shouldn't also say a few words. I'm thinking especially of you, Kurt, since you've been here the longest."

Wallander held up his hands. "I can't give a speech," he said. "Standing in church next to Svedberg's coffin, I won't be able to get a single word out."

"You made a great speech when Björk retired," Martinsson said. "One of us should say something, and it ought to be you."

Wallander knew he couldn't do it. Funerals terrified him.

"It's not that I don't want to do it," he said pleadingly. "I'll even write the speech. I'm just not going to be able to deliver it."

"I'll do it if you write it." Höglund said. "I don't think anyone should be forced to speak at a funeral unless they want to. It can be so overwhelming. I can give the speech, unless anyone objects."

Wallander was sure that neither Hansson nor Martinsson actually thought this was the best solution. But neither one of them said so, and it was agreed that Höglund would speak.

Wallander quickly turned the discussion to the case. Thurnberg sat motionless at his end of the table, an inscrutable expression on his face. His presence made Wallander nervous. There was something disdainful, even hostile, in his manner.

They went through the latest developments. Wallander gave them an abbreviated version of his conversation with Sundelius, completely leaving out Sundelius's reaction to hearing of Svedberg's ten-year relationship with an unknown woman.

Leads kept being phoned in to the station, but there were no credible reports about the woman's identity yet. Everyone agreed that this was unusual. They decided to send the picture to the Danish papers, as well as to Interpol.

After a couple of hours, they reached the matter of the pathologist's report and Wallander suggested they take a short break. Thurnberg got up immediately and left the room. He hadn't said a single word. Lisa Holgersson lingered after the others had left.

"He doesn't seem very happy," Wallander said, referring to Thurnberg.

"No, I don't think he is," she answered. "I think you should talk to him. He thinks this is taking too long."

"We're working as hard as we can."

"But do we need reinforcements?"

"We'll discuss this issue, of course, but I can tell you right now that I for one am not going to oppose it."

His answer seemed to relieve her. He went out and got a cup of coffee. Then they all filed back into the room. Thurnberg returned to the same seat, his face as blank as before. They began to go through the autopsy report. Wallander sketched the possible time frame on the board.

"Svedberg was killed not more than 24 hours before we found him. Everything indicates that he was killed in the morning. As far as the young people go, it turns out that our hypothesis works better than we had imagined. It doesn't supply us with a motive or a killer, but it does tell us something significant."

He sat down before he continued. "These young people made the arrangement for their celebration in secret. They chose a place where they were sure they would be left alone. But someone knew about their plans. Someone kept himself incredibly well informed, and had the time to make meticulous preparations. We still have no motive for what happened in the nature reserve, but we have a killer who didn't give up until he had traced the only remaining survivor of this night and killed her too. Isa Edengren.

He knew she fled to Bärnsö, and he found her out there among all those islands. This gives us a place to start. We're looking for a person who knew about the plans for the Midsummer celebration. Someone close to the source."

No one spoke for a long time.

"Where do we find this person who had access to so much information?" Wallander said. "That's where we have to start. If we do, then sooner or later we'll find out where Svedberg fits into the picture."

"We already have," Hansson said. "We know he started his investigation only a few days after Midsummer."

"I think we can say more than that," Wallander said. "I think Svedberg had a definite suspicion who killed, or was about to kill, the young people in the reserve."

"Why did the killer wait so long to kill Isa Edengren?" Martinsson asked. "He took more than a month to do it."

"We don't know why," Wallander agreed. "She wasn't particularly hard to find."

"And one more thing," Martinsson added. "Why did he dig up the bodies? Did he want them to be discovered?"

"There's no other explanation," Wallander said. "But it raises another set of questions about what motivates this killer. And in what way he and Svedberg had anything to do with each other."

Wallander sat back and looked at everyone gathered around the table.

Svedberg knew what had happened to the young people when they didn't return after Midsummer, he thought. Svedberg knew who the killer was, or at least had a very strong suspicion. That's why he was killed. There just isn't any other explanation. Which brings us to the most important question of all. Why didn't he want to tell us who the killer was?

CHAPTER TWENTY-ONE

Shortly after 2 p.m., Wallander asked Martinsson a question regarding a call that had come in from a man who had a news-stand in Sölvesborg. This man had stopped at Hagestad's nature reserve on the afternoon of Midsummer's Eve on his way to a party in Falsterbo. He had realised he was going to be too early, and had stopped to take a break. He thought he remembered two cars parked at the entrance. But Wallander never heard what additional details the man remembered. When he finished asking Martinsson his question, he fainted.

One moment he was waving his pencil in Martinsson's direction. The next he fell back in his chair, his chin to his chest. For a split second no one knew what had happened. Then Holgersson and Höglund reacted almost simultaneously, before the others. Hansson later confessed that he had thought Wallander had had a stroke and died. What the rest of them thought, or feared, he never heard. They dragged him out of the chair and laid him out on the floor, loosened his collar, and took his pulse. Someone grabbed a phone and called an ambulance. But Wallander came to before it arrived. As they helped him to his feet, he was already thinking that his blood-sugar level must have dropped. He drank some water and took some lumps of sugar from a tray on the table. He was starting to feel his normal self again.

Everyone around him looked worried. They thought he

should go down to the hospital for an examination or at the very least go home and rest. But Wallander didn't want to do either. He excused the episode as due to lack of sleep and then returned to the matter at hand with such determined energy the others had to back down.

The only one who didn't show signs of either worry or fear was Thurnberg. He hardly had any reaction at all. He stood up when Wallander was laid on the ground, but he didn't leave his place. No one really noticed a significant shift in expression either.

When they took a break Wallander went to his office and called Dr Göransson, and told him about the fainting episode. Dr Göransson did not seem surprised.

"Your blood-sugar level will continue to fluctuate," he said. "It'll take us a while to get it stabilised. We may have to reduce your medication if it keeps happening, but until then keep an apple handy in case you get dizzy."

After that day Wallander walked around with lumps of sugar in his pocket, as if he were expecting to see a horse. He didn't tell anyone about his diabetes. It was still his secret.

The meeting dragged on until 5 p.m., but by then they had managed to go through every aspect of the investigation thoroughly. There was a new infusion of energy in the room. They decided to call for reinforcements from Malmö, although Wallander knew that it was the people gathered around the table who would remain the core members of the investigative team.

Thurnberg remained behind after everyone had filed out of the room, and Wallander realised he must want to have a word with him. As he made his way to the other side of the table, he thought regretfully of Per Åkeson, who was somewhere under an African sun.

"I've been expecting a debriefing for quite a while," Thurnberg said. His voice was high-pitched and always sounded on the verge of cracking.

"We should have done this earlier, of course," Wallander said in a friendly tone. "But the direction of the investigation has shifted dramatically over the last couple of days."

Thurnberg ignored Wallander's last comment. "In the future I expect to be continuously apprised of the situation without having to ask. The justice department is naturally very interested when a police officer is killed."

Wallander felt no need to answer. He waited for him to continue.

"The investigation up to this point can hardly be called successful or even as thorough as one would hope," Thurnberg said, gesturing to a long list of points he had written on a pad of paper in front of him. Wallander felt as if he was back at school being told he had failed a test.

"If the criticisms are warranted we'll take the steps necessary to remedy the situation," he said.

He tried hard to sound calm and friendly, but he knew he would be unable to conceal his anger much longer. Who did this visiting prosecutor from Örebro think he was? How old was he? He couldn't be more than 33.

"I'll see to it that you have my list of complaints about the handling of the case on your desk tomorrow morning," Thurnberg said. "I'll be expecting a written response from you."

Wallander stared back at him quizzically. "Do you really mean you want us to waste time writing letters to each other while a killer who's committed five brutal murders is still running around out there?"

"What I mean is that the investigation so far has not been satisfactory."

Wallander hit the table with his fist and got up so violently that the chair fell to the ground. "There are no perfect investigations!" he roared. "But no one is going to accuse me or my colleagues of not having done everything that we can."

Thurnberg's expression finally changed. His face drained of all colour.

"Go ahead and send me your little note," Wallander said. "If you are right, we'll do as you say. But don't expect me to write you any letters in reply."

Wallander left the room and slammed the door shut behind him.

Höglund was on her way into her office and turned around when she heard the noise.

"What was that all about?" she asked.

"It's Thurnberg," Wallander said. "The bastard's whining about the investigation."

"Why?"

"He doesn't think we're thorough enough. How could we possibly have done more?"

"He probably just wants to show you who's boss."

"In that case he's picked the wrong man."

Wallander went into her office and sat down heavily in her visitor's chair.

"What happened in there?" she asked. "When you fainted."

"I haven't been sleeping well," he said, dodging her question. "But I feel fine now."

He got the same feeling he had when he was in Gotland with Linda. She didn't believe him either. Martinsson poked his head round the door.

"Am I interrupting anything?"

"No, it's good that you're here," Wallander said. "We should talk. Where's Hansson?"

"He's working on the cars."

"He should be here too," Wallander said. "But you'll have to fill him in later."

He gestured to Martinsson to close the door, then told them about his conversation with Sundelius, and his feeling that Svedberg might have been gay after all.

"Not that it matters one way or the other," he added. "Police officers are allowed to have whatever sexual orientation they like. The reason I'm not going public with this is that I don't want to start unnecessary rumours. Since Svedberg didn't talk about his sexuality while he was alive, I don't see the need for public speculation now that he's dead."

"It complicates this matter with Louise," Martinsson said.

"He may have been a man of many interests. But what is it that Sundelius knows? I had a strong feeling that he wasn't telling me everything. That means we have to dig deeper into both their lives. Are there other secrets? We have to do the same thing with these young people. Somewhere there's a point of intersection. A person who is a shadow to us right now, but who is there just the same."

"I have a vague recollection that someone lodged a complaint against Svedberg with the justice department's ombudsman a number of years ago," Martinsson said. "I forget what it was about."

"We should look into it, like everything else," Wallander said. "I thought we could divide these things up. I'll take Svedberg and Sundelius. I also have to talk to Björklund again, since he's the only one who knows anything about Louise."

"It's incomprehensible that no one's seen her," said Höglund.

"It's not just incomprehensible," Wallander said. "It's an impossibility. We just have to find out why."

"Haven't we gone a little easy on Björklund?" Martinsson asked. "After all, we found Svedberg's telescope at his house."

"He's innocent until proven guilty," Wallander said. "It's a hackneyed phrase, but there's some truth to it."

He got up. "Remember to tell Hansson about this," he said and left the room.

It was 5.30 p.m. and he hadn't eaten anything all day except the dry old biscuits in the canteen. The thought of going home and cooking a meal was too overwhelming. Instead he went down to the Chinese restaurant on the main square. He drank a beer while he was waiting. Then another. When the food came he ate too fast, as usual. He was about to order dessert when he stopped himself, and headed home. It was another warm evening and he opened the door to the balcony. He tried to call Linda three times, then gave up. Her phone was constantly busy. He was too tired to think. The TV was on, with the sound down. He lay down on the sofa and stared up at the ceiling. Shortly before 9 p.m. the phone rang. It was Lisa Holgersson.

"I think we have a problem," she said. "Thurnberg spoke to me after your argument."

Wallander grimaced, sensing what she was about to say. "Thurnberg was probably upset because I shouted at him. I made a lot of noise, thumped my fist on the table, that sort of thing."

"It's worse than that," she said. "He says you're not fit to be in charge of the investigation."

That came as a surprise. Wallander hadn't thought Thurnberg would go so far. He should have felt angry, but instead he was frightened. It was one thing to question your own abilities, but had it never occurred to him that someone else might do so.

"What were his reasons?"

"Mostly things to do with the running of the investigation. He's particularly concerned about the fact that he's been kept so poorly informed."

Wallander protested. What more could they have done?

"I'm just telling you what he said. He also thinks it was a serious lapse of judgment not to contact the police in Norrköping before you went up to Östergötland. He questions the validity of the trip itself, in fact."

"But what about the fact that I found Isa?"

"He thinks the police in Norrköping could have done that, while you were down here leading the team, and he seems to imply that she might have lived if this had been the case."

"That's absurd," Wallander said flatly. "I hope that's what you told him."

"There's one last thing," she said. "Your health."

"I'm not sick."

"Look, you fainted right in front of everyone. In the middle of a meeting."

"That could happen to anyone who is overworked."

"I'm telling you what he said."

"But what did you say to him?"

"That I would speak to you. And consider it."

Suddenly Wallander felt unsure of her opinion. Could he still assume she was on his side? His suspicion flared up in an instant, and it was strong.

"So now you've talked to me," he said. "What do you think?"

"What do you think?"

"That Thurnberg is an annoying little man who doesn't

like me or any of the others. Which is mutual, by the way. I think he looks on his time here simply as a springboard to greater things."

"That's hardly an objective statement."

"But true. I believe I did the right thing in going up to Bärnsö Island. The investigation here continued just the same. There was no reason to notify the police in Norrköping because no crime had been committed, nor was there any reason to assume one would occur. On the contrary, there was every reason in the world to keep things quiet. Isa Edengren could easily have become even more frightened."

"Thurnberg understands all that," she said. "And I agree with you that he can seem very arrogant. What seems to worry him most is your health."

"I don't think he's worried about anyone but himself. The day I'm no longer up to leading the investigation I promise you'll be the first to know."

"I suppose Thurnberg will have to accept that as his answer for now. But it might be best if you kept him better informed from now on."

"It's going to be hard for me to trust him in the future," Wallander said. "I can stand a lot of things, but I hate it when people go behind my back."

"He hasn't gone behind your back. Telling me about his concerns was the right thing to do."

"No one can force me to like him."

"That's not what this is about. But I think he's going to react to any signs of weakness from now on."

"What the hell do you mean by that?"

The sudden flare of anger came from nowhere, and Wallander didn't manage to control it.

"You don't have to get upset. I'm just telling you what's happened."

"We have five murders to solve," Wallander said. "And a killer who's cold-blooded and well-organised. There are no apparent motives and we don't know if he's going to strike again. One of the victims was a close colleague. You have to assume people are going to get a little upset. This investigation isn't exactly a tea party."

She laughed. "I haven't heard that expression used before in this context."

"Just so you understand where I'm coming from," Wallander said. "That's all."

"I wanted to let you know about this as soon as possible."

"I know, I'm grateful that you did."

When the conversation was over, Wallander went back to the sofa. His suspicions still hadn't left him, and he was already plotting how he would get even with Thurnberg. Perhaps it was out of self-defence, perhaps self-pity. The thought of being relieved of his responsibilities frightened him. Being in charge of an investigation like this meant being under an almost unbearable strain, but the thought of humiliation was worse.

Wallander felt a great desire to talk to someone, anyone who could give him the kind of moral support he needed. It was 9.15 p.m. Who could he call? Martinsson or Höglund? Most of all he wanted to talk to Rydberg, but he lay in his grave and couldn't speak. He thought of Nyberg. They never really talked about private matters, but Wallander knew Nyberg would understand. His irascible and outspoken nature was an advantage in this situation. Above all, Wallander knew Nyberg respected his abilities. He doubted that Nyberg would be able to stand working under anyone else.

Wallander dialled Nyberg's home number. As usual he

answered the phone in an irritable voice. Wallander often said to Martinsson that he'd never heard Nyberg sound friendly on the phone.

"We need to talk," Wallander said.

"What's happened?"

"Nothing to do with the case. But I need to see you."

"Can't it wait?"

"No."

"I can be at the station in 15 minutes."

"Let's meet somewhere else. I thought we could go out and have a beer."

"We're going to a bar? What's this all about?"

"Do you have any suggestions where we could go?"

"I never go out," Nyberg said dismissively. "At least not in Ystad."

"There's a new restaurant and bar by the main square," Wallander said. "By the antiques shop. I'll see you there."

"Do I have to wear a suit and tie?"

"I can't imagine you would," Wallander answered.

Nyberg promised to be there in half an hour. Wallander changed his shirt, then left the flat on foot. There weren't many people in the restaurant. When he asked, they told him it closed at 11 p.m. He realised he was quite hungry, flipped through the menu, and was shocked by the prices. Who could afford to eat out any more? But he wanted to treat Nyberg to something to eat.

Nyberg arrived in exactly half an hour. He was dressed in a suit and tie, and had even slicked his normally wayward hair down with water. The suit was a little old and looked too big. Nyberg sat down across from Wallander.

"I had no idea there was a restaurant here," he said.

"It opened fairly recently," Wallander answered. "Five or so years ago. Let me treat you to something."

"I'm not hungry," Nyberg said.

"Then have a starter," Wallander said

"I'll leave it up to you," Nyberg said and pushed his menu away.

They had a couple of beers while they waited for the food to arrive. Wallander told him about his conversation with Holgersson. He recounted it in detail, but he also added the things he had thought and not said.

"It doesn't sound like the kind of thing you should pay much attention to," Nyberg said when Wallander had finished. "But I understand why it upset you. Internal disputes are the last thing we need right now."

Wallander pretended to take Thurnberg's side for a moment. "Do you think maybe he's right? Should someone else take charge?"

"Who would that be?"

"Martinsson?"

Nyberg stared back at him in disbelief. "You're joking."

"What about Hansson?"

"Maybe in ten years. But this is the worst case we've ever had. That's not a good time to suddenly weaken the leadership of the investigation."

The food appeared on the table and Wallander kept talking about Thurnberg. But Nyberg gave only one-word answers and offered no further comments. At last Wallander realised he was going too far. Nyberg was right. There was nothing more to say. If necessary, Nyberg would back him up. A couple of years earlier Wallander had taken up the matter of his unreasonable workload with Holgersson, soon after she had replaced Björk as chief of police. Nyberg's situation improved after that. They had never talked about it, but Wallander was sure Nyberg knew the part he had played in the matter.

Nyberg was right. They shouldn't waste any more of their energy on Thurnberg, but save it for more pressing matters. They ordered more beers and were told it was the last round. Wallander asked Nyberg if he wanted coffee, but he declined.

"I have more than 20 cups a day," he said. "To keep my energy up. Actually, maybe just to keep going."

"Police work wouldn't be possible without coffee," Wallander said.

"No work would be possible without coffee."

They pondered the importance of coffee in silence. Some people at a nearby table got up and left.

"I don't think I've ever been involved in anything quite as strange as these murders," Nyberg said suddenly.

"Neither have I. It's senseless brutality. I can't imagine a motive."

"It could simply be for the love of killing," Nyberg said. "A killer with a lust for blood who carefully plans and arranges his crimes."

"You may be right," Wallander said. "But how did Svedberg get onto him so fast? That's what I can't understand."

"There's only one rational explanation, which is that Svedberg knew whoever it was. Or had a definite suspicion. Then the question of why he didn't want to tell anyone about this becomes crucial, perhaps the most important question of all."

"Could it be that it was someone we know?"

"Not necessarily. There's another possibility. Not that Svedberg knew who it was, or that he had definite suspicions, but that he feared it was someone he knew."

Wallander saw the logic of Nyberg's statement. To suspect someone and to fear something were not necessarily the same thing.

"That would explain the need for secrecy," Nyberg continued. "He's afraid the killer is someone he knows, but he's not sure. He wants to be convinced before he tells us about it, and he wants to be able to bury the whole thing in silence if his fears turn out to be mistaken."

Wallander watched Nyberg attentively. He was seeing a connection that had not been apparent to him earlier.

"Let's assume that Svedberg hears about the disappearance of the young people," he said. "Let's assume that he is driven by fear that is grounded in a reasonable suspicion. Let's even assume that he knows he's right and that he knows who is responsible for their disappearance. He doesn't even have to know they're dead."

"It isn't very likely that he knew," Nyberg said. "Since he would then have felt compelled to come clean. I can't imagine that Svedberg would have been able to carry a burden like that."

Wallander nodded. Nyberg was right.

"So he doesn't know they're dead," he said. "But he has strong fears and enough conviction to confront this particular person. Then what?"

"He's killed."

"The scene of the crime is hastily rearranged, so that our first thought was that there had been a burglary. And something's missing: the telescope. Which is then hidden in Sture Björklund's shed."

"The door," Nyberg said. "I'm convinced that the killer was let into Svedberg's flat. Or maybe even had his own set of keys."

"It must be someone he knows, someone who's been there before."

"Someone who knows he has a cousin. The killer tries

to push the blame onto him, by planting the telescope at Björklund's place."

The waitress came over with the bill, but Wallander was reluctant to end their conversation.

"What's the common denominator? We really have only two people in the picture: Bror Sundelius and an unknown woman by the name of Louise."

Nyberg shook his head. "A woman didn't commit these murders," he said. "Although we said the same thing a couple of years ago and were proved wrong."

"It can hardly have been Bror Sundelius either," Wallander said. "His legs are bad. There's nothing wrong with his mind, but his health isn't the best."

"Then it's someone we still don't know about," Nyberg said. "Svedberg must have had other people he was close to."

"I'm going to go back a little," Wallander said. "Tomorrow I'm going to start searching Svedberg's life."

"That's probably the right way to do it," Nyberg agreed. "I'll check on the results of our forensic tests, especially the fingerprinting. Hopefully that'll tell us more."

"The weapons," Wallander said. "They're important."

"Wester in Ludvika is very pleasant," Nyberg said. "I'm getting full cooperation."

Wallander pulled the bill towards him. Nyberg wanted to split it with him.

"We could try to put it on the expense account," Wallander said.

"You'll never get this through," Nyberg said.

Wallander felt around for his wallet. It wasn't there. Suddenly he saw it in his mind's eye, lying on the kitchen table.

"I still want to treat you, but it seems I've left my wallet at home."

Nyberg took out his wallet and counted out 200 kronor. But the bill was almost twice that.

"There's a cashpoint around the corner," Wallander said.

"I don't use cards like that," Nyberg said firmly.

The waitress, who had turned the lights on and off several times, approached them. They were the only people left. Nyberg showed her his ID, which she regarded sceptically.

"We don't let guests have tabs here," she said.

"We're police officers," Wallander said angrily. "I just happen to have left my wallet at home."

"We don't give credit," she said. "If you can't pay I'll have to report you."

"Report us to who?"

"The police."

Wallander almost lost his temper, but Nyberg restrained him. "This could get interesting."

"Are you paying or not?" the waitress asked.

"I think you should call the police," Wallander said pleasantly.

The waitress walked off and made the call, making sure to lock the front door first.

"They're on their way," she said. "You'll have to stay until then."

They waited five minutes, then a police car pulled up outside and two officers got out. One of them was Edmundsson. He stared at Wallander and Nyberg.

"We seem to have a little problem," Wallander said. "I've left my wallet at home and Nyberg doesn't have enough cash to cover the bill. This lady doesn't give credit, nor was she impressed by Nyberg's ID."

Edmundsson took this in, then burst into laughter. "What's the bill?" he asked.

"It's 400 kronor."

He took out his wallet and paid.

"It's not my fault," the waitress said. "My boss says we should never give credit."

"Who owns this place?" Nyberg asked.

"His name's Fredriksson. Alf Fredriksson."

"Is he a big man?" Nyberg asked. "Does he live in Svarte?"

The waitress nodded.

"Then I know him," Nyberg said. "Nice man. Say hello to him from Nyberg and Wallander."

The squad car was already gone when they walked out onto the street.

"This is the strangest August I've ever known," Nyberg said. "It's already the 15th and it's still warm."

They parted ways when they got to Hamngatan.

"We just don't know if he's going to strike again," Wallander said. "That's the worst thing."

"That's why we have to get him," Nyberg said. "As fast as we can."

Wallander walked home slowly. He was inspired by his talk with Nyberg but felt no real peace of mind. He didn't want to admit it, but Thurnberg's reaction and his conversation with Holgersson had depressed him. Was he being unfair to Thurnberg? Was he right? Should someone else be in charge of this investigation?

When Wallander got home he put on a pot of coffee and sat down at the kitchen table. The thermometer outside the window read 19°C. Wallander got out a pad of paper and a pencil, then looked for his glasses, and found a pair under the sofa.

Coffee cup in hand, he found himself walking around the kitchen table a couple of times as if to coax himself into the right frame of mind for the task ahead. He had never written a speech in memory of a murdered colleague before. Now he regretted having agreed to do it. How did you describe the feeling of finding your colleague with his face blown off in his flat only one week earlier?

Finally he sat down and got started. He could still remember when he first met Svedberg, 20 years earlier, when Svedberg had already begun to bald. He was halfway through when he tore everything up and started again. It was after 1 a.m. when he'd finished. This time it was good enough.

He walked out onto the balcony. The town was quiet, and it was still quite warm. He recalled his conversation with Nyberg and let his mind wander. Suddenly the image of Isa Edengren was there, curled up in the cave that had protected her as a child but no longer could. Wallander went back in, leaving the door to the balcony open. There was a thought that wouldn't go away. That the man out there in the darkness was preparing to strike again.

CHAPTER TWENTY-TWO

It had been a long day. There were many packages, certified letters, and international money orders. He wasn't done with the bookkeeping until it was almost 2 p.m.

His old self would have been irritated by the fact that the work took longer than expected. Now it didn't affect him any more. The enormous change he'd undergone had made him impervious to time. He realised there was no such thing as past or future. There was no time that could be lost or won. The only thing that counted was action.

He put away his postbag and cashbox, then showered and changed his clothes. He hadn't eaten since early that morning, before he'd driven to the depot to start sorting his post. But he wasn't hungry. This was a feeling that he remembered from his childhood. When something exciting lay in store for him, he lost his appetite. He went into the soundproofed room and turned on all the lights. He'd made the bed before leaving that morning, and now he spread the letters out over the dark-blue bedspread. He sat cross-legged in the middle of the bed. He had read these letters before. That was the first step, to pick out letters that caught his eye. He opened them carefully, without doing any damage to the envelope. He copied them and then he read them. He didn't know exactly how many letters he had opened, copied and read this past year. It must have been close to 200. Most of them were nothing special. They were vacuous, boring. It wasn't until he had opened the letter from Lena Norman to Martin Boge . . .

He interrupted the thought. That was over and done with. He didn't need to think about them any more. The last phase had been so difficult and tiring. First there was the trip to Östergötland, then he had hunted around for a suitable boat in the darkness, one that was big enough to take him to the little island at the far edge of the archipelago.

It had been a bothersome undertaking, and he hadn't liked having to put in the extra effort. It meant overcoming his own resistance, something he tried to avoid. He looked at the letters spread around him on the bed. Choosing a couple that were planning to get married had not occurred to him until sometime in May. The idea came to him by chance, like so much else in life. During his years as an engineer, chance had not been allowed in his orderly existence. Now everything had changed. The interplay of luck and coincidence meant a person's life was a steady stream of unexpected opportunities. He could pick and choose what he wanted.

The little raised flag on the letter box told him nothing. But when he knocked on the door and entered the kitchen, he found more than a hundred invitations lying on the table. The bride-to-be let him in. He could no longer remember her name, but he remembered her joy, and it enraged him. He took her letters and posted them, and if he hadn't been so embroiled in complicated plans for participating in the upcoming Midsummer celebration he would perhaps have become involved in her wedding.

New opportunities kept presenting themselves. All six envelopes in front of him were wedding invitations. He had read their letters, got to know each couple. He knew where they lived, what they looked like, and where they were to be married. The invitations in front of him were merely printed cards, there to remind him of the different couples.

Now he faced his most important task, deciding which of the couples was the happiest. He went through the envelopes one by one, reminding himself of other letters that they had written, to each other or their friends. He savoured the moment, suffused with contentment. He was in charge. In this soundproofed room he could not be touched by the things that had made him suffer in his earlier life – the feeling of being an outsider and being misunderstood. In here he could bear to think about the great catastrophe, when he was shut out and declared superfluous.

Nothing was hard any more. Or almost nothing. He still couldn't bear to think about how he had subjected himself to humiliation for more than two years. He had answered ads in the paper, sent in his CV, gone to countless interviews.

That was before he cut himself off from his former existence and left everything behind. Becoming another.

He knew he was one of the lucky ones. Today he would never have got a job as a substitute postman. There were blocks to most professions. People were laid off. He noticed this as he went along his post route. People sat in their houses waiting for letters. More and more of them ended up on the outside and had not yet learned how to break free.

He finally picked the couple getting married on Saturday, 17 August, at their home just outside Köpingebro. They had invited a lot of people. He couldn't even remember how many invitations they had given him. But both of

335

them had been standing there when he came in through the door, and their happiness seemed limitless. He could have killed them on the spot. But as usual he controlled himself. He congratulated them, and no one could have guessed what he was really thinking.

It was the most important art a person could learn: self-control.

On Friday morning, Wallander began the task of mapping out Svedberg's life in earnest. He arrived at the station shortly after 7 a.m. and went about his task with some reluctance. He didn't know exactly what he was looking for, but somewhere in Svedberg's life there had to be a point leading to the reason for his murder. It was like trying to find a trace of life in a person who had already died.

What interested him most this morning was a man called Jan Söderblom, who Ylva Brink said knew Svedberg when he was young, during his days of compulsory military service and police training. The connection was severed when Söderblom married and moved away, she thought to Malmö or Landskrona. What interested Wallander was that Söderblom had become a police officer just like Svedberg. He was about to call the station in Malmö when Nyberg appeared at the door. Wallander could tell from his expression that something was up.

"Things are happening," Nyberg said and waved some faxes at him. "We can start with the murder weapons, if you like. Turns out the revolver stolen in Ludvika along with the shotgun could have been the same as the one in the nature reserve."

"Could have been?"

"In my language that means it's the one."

"Good," Wallander said. "We needed that."

"Then there are the fingerprints," Nyberg continued. "We found a good right thumbprint on the shotgun. We found another good thumbprint on a wineglass out in the reserve."

"Same thumb?"

"Yes."

"Previous record?"

"Not in our files. But we're going to send that thumbprint all around the world if we have to."

"So it is the same man," Wallander said slowly. "At least we know that much."

"There were no fingerprints on the telescope, however, other than Svedberg's own."

"Does that mean he hid it at Björklund's place himself?"

"Not necessarily. The person could have been wearing gloves."

"We have this thumbprint on the shotgun," Wallander said. "But what about in Svedberg's flat in general? We have to know who created that chaos, if it was Svedberg or someone else. Or both."

"We'll have to wait on that, but they're working on it."

Wallander got up and leaned against the wall. He felt that there was more to this.

"We found none of Svedberg's prints on the shotgun," Nyberg said. "That may or may not mean anything."

"We've come a long way," Wallander said. "We have a single killer."

"Maybe we should notify the chief prosecutor," Nyberg said, smiling. "That might cheer him up."

"Or not. We're not living up to our bad reputation. But we'll make sure he gets his report."

Nyberg left the room and Wallander grabbed the phone,

called Malmö and asked to speak to Officer Jan Söderblom. Sure enough there was a detective by that name who worked mainly on theft cases, but he was on holiday on a Greek island until the following Wednesday. Wallander left a message that he wanted to speak to him as soon as possible. He also made a note of Söderblom's home phone number. He had just hung up when Höglund knocked on the half-open door. She held his speech about Svedberg in her hands.

"I've read it," she said. "And I think it's honest and moving. I suppose those two things always go together. No one's touched simply by empty talk of eternity and light conquering the darkness."

"It's not too long?" Wallander asked anxiously.

"I read it aloud to myself and it took less than five minutes. I don't usually speak at funerals, but I think it's just the right length."

She was about to slip out again when Wallander told her Nyberg's news.

"That's a huge step forward," she said when he had finished. "If we could only find the person or people who stole the guns."

"It'll be hard, but of course we'll try. I was wondering if it wouldn't be worth it to put pictures of the guns in the papers. Both the revolver and the shotgun."

"There's a press conference at 11 a.m.," she said. "Lisa has been overrun by the press lately. Maybe we should tell them about the weapons. What do we really have to lose by telling them there's a connection between the two cases? It'll be murder on a scale this country hasn't seen for a long time."

"You're right," Wallander said. "I'll be there."

She lingered in the doorway. "Then there's the elusive

Louise," she said. "Whom no one seems to have seen. There have been a lot of calls but nothing reliable."

"That's strange," Wallander said. "But someone somewhere knows her. We talked about trying Denmark."

"Why not all of Europe?"

"Yes," he agreed. "Why not? But let's start with Denmark and let's do it now, as soon as possible."

"I'm on my way to Lund to go through Lena Norman's flat," she said. "But I'll ask Hansson to do it."

"Not Hansson," Wallander said. "He's still working on finding the cars. There has to be someone else who can do it."

"We're going to need those reinforcements," Höglund said. "Lisa says some people are arriving from Malmö this afternoon."

"We need Svedberg," Wallander said. "That's what it is. We just aren't used to not having him around."

They were silent for a while after this; then she left. Wallander opened the window. It was still warm, and there was only a gentle breeze. The phone rang. It was Ebba. She sounded tired, and Wallander thought how much she had seemed to age during the last few years. Before, she had always helped them keep their spirits up. Now she was often down herself, and sometimes she forgot to pass along their messages. She was due to retire next summer, but no one could bring themselves to think about it.

"There's a call here from an officer called Larsson. He says he's from the police in Valdemarsvik," she told him. "Can you take it? Everyone else is busy."

Larsson spoke with an Östgöta dialect.

"Harry Lundström from Norrköping told us to inform you about anything stolen around Gryt on the day that girl was shot out on Bärnsö Island."

"That's right."

"We may have something that will interest you, stolen from Snäckvarp. The owner can't say exactly when, because he wasn't there when it happened. But it was found in an inlet just south of Snäckvarp. It's a six-metre fibreglass boat with a raised steering platform."

Wallander felt his usual insecurity in discussing boats.

"Is it big enough to take out to Bärnsö?"

"If the wind wasn't too strong it could take you all the way out to Gotland."

Wallander thought for a moment. "Any fingerprints?" he asked.

"We've checked," Larsson said. "There was oil on the steering wheel so we found a couple of good prints there. They're already on their way over to you, via Norrköping. Harry is the one in charge of the whole thing."

"Was there a road near where the boat was found?" Wallander asked.

"The boat was hidden in a mass of reeds. But you can walk to Snäckvarp in about ten minutes and there's a dirt road from there."

"This is important," Wallander said.

"How are things going? Are you closing in on the killer?"

"Yes, but these things take time."

"I never met the girl, but I had a run-in with Edengren a couple of years ago."

"Oh, what happened?"

"Illegal fishing. He was putting nets and eel traps in other people's water."

"Isn't it free fishing out there?"

"It varies. Not that he bothered to find out. If I may speak plainly, I thought he was a royal pain in the arse. But of course I feel sorry for him now, with the girl and all."

"Was that it? Illegal fishing?"

"As far as I know."

Wallander thanked him for the call. Then he tried to reach Harry Lundström in Norrköping, and was directed to his mobile phone. Lundström was in a car somewhere out in Vikboland. Wallander told him they had a positive ID on the murder weapon from the reserve, and that they would soon know about the gun used on Bärnsö Island. Lundström in turn told him they weren't sure of any prints found on the island, but he assumed the stolen boat in Snäckvarp was the one the killer had used.

"People out here on the islands are getting worried," he said. "You have to get this man."

"Yes," Wallander said. "Yes, we do. And we will."

He went and got a cup of coffee when he was done with the conversation. It was already 9.30 a.m. Something occurred to him, and he went back to his office and looked up the number for the Lundberg family in Skårby. The wife answered. Wallander realised he hadn't spoken to them since Isa was murdered, and so he began by offering her his condolences.

"Erik is still in bed," she said. "He doesn't have the energy to get up. He says we should sell the house and move away. Who could do something like this to a child?"

Isa was like a daughter to her, Wallander thought. I should have thought of it earlier.

He couldn't really answer her question, but he sensed that she held him responsible for Isa's death.

"I called to see if her parents have come home," he said.

"They came back last night."

"That was all I wanted to know," he said. He expressed his regrets once again and then hung up.

He planned to drive out to Skårby immediately after the

press conference. He wanted to go right away, but there wasn't time. He picked up the phone and called Thurnberg. Without mentioning what he had heard the previous night, he gave him a short update on the latest findings from the forensic investigation. Wallander concluded by stressing that the findings meant they could now concentrate on searching for a single killer. Thurnberg said he looked forward to seeing the written report, and Wallander promised to send him a copy.

"There will be a press conference at 11 a.m.," Wallander said. "I think we should reveal these latest findings to the press and have pictures of the guns published."

"Do we have any pictures of them available now?"

"We'll get them tomorrow at the latest."

Thurnberg made no objections, and said he would participate in the press conference. They kept the conversation brief, but Wallander noticed by the end that he had broken into a sweat.

They held the press conference in the largest room available. Wallander couldn't remember another case ever getting so much attention. As usual he got terribly nervous when he walked up to the podium. To his surprise, Thurnberg began. That had never happened in all the years he had worked there. Per Åkeson always let Wallander or the chief of police take on that task. Thurnberg spoke as if he was accustomed to speaking to the press. It's a new era, Wallander thought. He wasn't sure that he didn't feel a tiny bit envious. He listened carefully to what Thurnberg said, and couldn't deny that he expressed himself well.

Next it was his turn to speak. He had made some notes on a piece of paper to remind himself of what to say, but now, naturally, couldn't find it. He told them they had traced the murder weapons to Ludvika, with a possible link to a robbery in Orsa. He also told them that they were still waiting for a positive ID on the weapon used on Bärnsö Island in the Östergötland archipelago. As he spoke he thought of Westin, the postman who had taken him out to the island. Why he thought of him at that moment he couldn't say. He also talked about the findings regarding the stolen boat. When he finished, there were many questions. Thurnberg handled most of them, with Wallander jumping in from time to time. Martinsson was listening to the proceedings from the very back of the room.

Finally a woman from one of the evening papers indicated that she wanted to ask a question. Wallander had never seen her before.

"Would it be accurate to say that the police have no leads at this time?" she said, turning directly to Wallander.

"We have many leads," Wallander said. "We're just not close to making an arrest."

"It seems to me that the police investigation hasn't yielded any results. It seems more than likely that this killer will strike again. After all, I think it's clear to all of us that we're dealing with a madman."

"We don't know that," Wallander answered. "That's why we're keeping our approach as comprehensive as we can."

"That sounds like a strategy," the reporter said. "But it could also give the impression that you don't know where to turn, that you're helpless."

Wallander glanced at Thurnberg, who encouraged him to continue with an almost invisible nod of his head.

"The police are never helpless," Wallander said. "If we were, we wouldn't be police officers."

"Don't you agree that you're looking for a madman?"

"No."

"What else could this person be?"

"We don't know yet."

"Do you think you'll catch whoever did this?"

"Yes, without a doubt."

"Will he strike again?"

"We don't know."

There was a brief pause. Wallander got up, which the others took as a signal that the conference was over. Wallander thought Thurnberg had probably intended to end it in a more formal manner, but Wallander left the room before Thurnberg had a chance to talk to him. TV news teams were waiting to interview him in the reception area. Wallander told them to speak with Thurnberg. Later Ebba told him that Thurnberg was more than happy to oblige.

Wallander went into his office to get his coat. He tried to think what it was that made him think of Westin during the press conference. He knew it was significant. He sat down at his desk and tried to coax the thought to the surface, but it wouldn't come. He gave up. As he was putting his coat on, Hansson called.

"I found the cars," he said. "Norman's and Boge's: a 1991 Toyota and a Volvo that's one year older. They were in a car park down by Sandhammaren. I've already called Nyberg. He's on his way there."

"So am I."

At the edge of town, Wallander pulled over at a take-away bar and ate a hotdog. It had become habit now to buy one-litre bottles of mineral water. He had forgotten to take the medication that Dr Göransson had prescribed for him, and he didn't have it with him.

He drove back to Mariagatan in a bad temper. There was a heap of post on the floor in the hall, and he noticed a post-card from Linda, who was visiting friends in Hudiksvall, and a letter from his sister Kristina. Wallander took the post with him into the kitchen. His sister had put the name and address of a hotel on the back of the envelope. It was in Kemi, which Wallander knew was in northern Finland. He wondered what she was doing there, but he let the post wait, and took his medicine instead. Before he left the kitchen, he glanced at the post lying on the table and again his thoughts returned to Westin. Now he was able to catch hold of the thought.

There was something Westin had said during their trip out to Bärnsö Island, something that Wallander's subconscious had been turning over and was trying to send to the surface. He tried to reconstruct their conversation in the noisy wheelhouse without success. But Westin had said something important. He decided to call him after he had looked at the two cars.

Nyberg was already there when Wallander got out of his car. The Toyota and Volvo were parked next to each other. Police tape was plastered all around the area and the cars were being photographed. The doors and boots were wide open. Wallander walked up to Nyberg, who was getting a bag out of his car.

"Thanks again for meeting me last night," he said.

"An old friend came down to see me from Stockholm in 1973," Nyberg replied. "We went out to a bar one evening. I don't think I've been out since then."

Wallander remembered that he hadn't paid Edmundsson back.

"Well, anyway, I had a nice time," he said.

"There's already a rumour going around that we were caught trying to get out of paying the bill," Nyberg said.

"Just as long as Thurnberg doesn't get wind of it. He might take it the wrong way."

Wallander walked over to Hansson, who was making some notes.

"Any doubt they're the right ones?"

"The Toyota is Lena Norman's, the Volvo belongs to Martin Boge."

"How long have they been here?"

"We don't know. In July the car park is full of cars coming and going. It's only in August that it starts to slow down and that people start noticing which cars haven't been moved."

"Is there any other way to find out if they've been here since Midsummer?"

"You'll have to talk to Nyberg about that."

Wallander went back to Nyberg, who was staring at the Toyota.

"Fingerprints are the most important," Wallander said. "The cars must have been driven here from the reserve."

"Someone who leaves his prints on a boat might well leave us a greeting on a steering wheel."

"That's what I'm hoping."

"That probably also means our killer is fairly sure his prints don't appear in any records, either here or abroad."

"I was thinking the same thing," Wallander said. "We'll just have to hope you're wrong."

Wallander didn't need to stay any longer. As he passed the turn-off to his father's house, he couldn't resist having a look. There was a For Sale sign by the driveway. He didn't stop. Seeing the sign gave him a funny feeling. He had just made it back to Ystad when the mobile phone rang. It was Höglund.

"I'm in Lund," she said. "In Lena Norman's flat. I think you should come here."

"What is it?"

"You'll see when you get here. I think it's important."

Wallander wrote down the address and was on his way.

CHAPTER TWENTY-THREE

The block of flats was on the outskirts of Lund. It was four storeys high, one of five buildings comprising a large housing estate. Once, many years ago when Wallander had come down to Lund with Linda, she had pointed them out to him and told him they were student flats. If she had chosen to study in Lund, she would have lived in a place like this. Wallander shivered, imagining Linda out in the reserve.

He didn't have to guess which building it was, as a police car was parked outside one of them. Wallander put his phone in his pocket and got out. A woman was stretched out in the sun on one of the lawns. Wallander wished he could lie down beside her and sleep for a while. His tiredness came and went in heavy waves. An officer stood inside the doorway, yawning. Wallander waved his identification in front of him and the officer pointed up the stairs absentmindedly.

"All the way up. No elevator."

Then he yawned again and Wallander felt a sudden urge to whip him into shape. Wallander was the superior officer, and one from another district at that. They were trying to catch a man who had killed five people so far. He didn't need to be greeted by an officer who yawned and could hardly bring himself to speak.

But he said nothing. He walked up the stairs. Apart from the loud, raucous music coming from one flat, the building seemed abandoned. It was still August and the autumn term had not yet begun. The door to Lena Norman's flat was slightly ajar but Wallander rang the bell anyway.

Höglund came to the door herself. He tried to read her expression without success.

"I didn't mean to sound so dramatic over the phone," she said quickly. "But I think you'll understand why I wanted you to see this."

He followed her into the flat, which hadn't been aired out for a while. The air had that characteristic but indescribable dry quality he had so often encountered in concrete buildings. He had read somewhere that the FBI had developed a method for determining how long a house had been locked up. He didn't know whether Nyberg had the technique at his disposal.

At the thought of Nyberg he made another mental note to repay Edmundsson. The flat had two rooms and a kitchen. They reached the combined living room and study. The sun was shining in through the window and dust drifted slowly in the still air. There were a number of photographs tacked up on one wall. Wallander put on his glasses and peered at them. He recognised her at once. Lena Norman was dressed up in a scene that looked like it was supposed to be from the 17th century. Martin Boge was also in the picture, which was taken with what appeared to be a castle in the background. The next picture was also of a party. Lena Norman was in that one too, and now Astrid Hillström was there. They were indoors somewhere, half-naked. Wallander guessed they were staging a bordello scene. Neither Norman nor Hillström was particularly convincing. Wallander straightened up and cast a glance over the entire wall.

"They play different roles at their parties," he said.

"It goes further than that," she said and went over to a desk that stood at right angles to one of the windows. It was covered with binders and plastic folders.

"I've gone through this material," she said. "Not completely, of course, but what I've seen so far worries me." Wallander lifted his hand to interrupt her.

"Wait a second. I need to drink a glass of water, and use the bathroom."

"My father has diabetes," she said.

Wallander froze on his way to the door. "What do you mean by that?"

"If I didn't know any better I'd think you had it too, the way you drink water these days. And need to go to the loo constantly."

For a moment Wallander thought he was going to break his silence and tell her the truth: that she was right. But instead he just muttered something inaudible and left the room. When he came out of the kitchen, the toilet was still flushing.

"The flushing mechanism is broken," he said. "I guess that's not our problem."

She was looking at him as if she was expecting him to talk.

"Why are you worried?" he asked.

"I'll tell you what I've found so far," she said. "But I'm convinced there's more, and that it'll become apparent when we've gone through everything."

Wallander sat down on a chair by the desk. She remained standing.

"They dress up," she started. "They have parties, and move between our own time and that of past ages. From time to time they even go into the future, but not very often. Probably because it's harder – no one knows how people will dress in a thousand years, or even 50. We know all this, of course. We've talked to the friends who weren't with them at Midsummer. You even had a chance to talk to Isa Edengren. We know they rented their costumes in Copenhagen. But there's a deeper level to this."

She picked up a folder covered in geometric figures. "They appear to have belonged to a sect," she said. "It has its roots in the United States, in Minneapolis. It strikes me as an updated version of the Jim Jones cult or the Branch Davidians. Their rules are horrifying, something akin to the threatening letters people who have broken chain mail or pyramid schemes hand over to us. Anyone who divulges their secrets will suffer violent retribution – always death, of course. They pay dues to the head office that in turn sends out lists of suggestions for their parties and explains how to maintain their secrecy. But there is also a spiritual dimension to their activities. They think that people who practise moving through time like this will be able to choose the age of their rebirth at the moment of their death. It was highly unpleasant reading. I think Lena Norman was the head of the Swedish chapter."

Wallander was listening with rapt attention. Höglund had called him down here with good reason.

"Does the organisation have a name?"

"I don't know what it would be in Swedish. In English they call themselves the Divine Movers."

Wallander flipped through the folder she had given him. There were geometric figures everywhere, but also pictures of old gods and the mutilated bodies of tortured people. He put the material down with disgust.

"Do you think what happened in the nature reserve was

a result of vengeance? That they had divulged the secret and had to be killed?"

"In this day and age I hardly think that can be ruled out."

Wallander knew she was right. Only a short time ago a number of members of a sect in Switzerland and France had committed mass suicide. In May, Martinsson had taken part in a conference in Stockholm devoted to the role of the police in stemming this increased activity. It was getting harder, since modern sects no longer circled around a single crazed individual. Now they were well-organised corporations that had their own lawyers and accountants. Members took out loans to pay fees they couldn't really afford. It wasn't even clear these days if the emotional blackmail that took place could be classified as criminal activity. Martinsson had told Wallander after he returned from the conference that new laws would have to be enacted if they were to have any hope in prosecuting these soul-sucking vampires who were profiting from the increased sense of helplessness in society.

"This is an important discovery," he said to Höglund. "We're going to need help with this. The national police have a special division devoted to working on new sects. We'll also need help from the United States on the Divine Movers. Above all, we have to get the other young people involved in this to talk, get them to divulge their carefully guarded secrets."

"They take their vows and then eat horse liver. Raw," she said, leafing through the folder.

"Who officiates at these ceremonies?"

"It must be Lena Norman."

Wallander shook his head, baffled. "And she's dead now. Do you think she would have broken her vows? Was there someone waiting to replace her?"

"I don't know. Maybe we'll find a name among these papers when we've had a chance to go through them properly."

Wallander stood up and looked out the window. The woman was still down on the lawn. He thought of the woman he had met at the roadside restaurant outside Västervik. He searched for her name for a while before it came to him: Erika. He had a sudden longing to see her again.

"We probably shouldn't get too distracted by all this," he said in an absentminded way. "We shouldn't rule out our other theories."

"Which are?"

He didn't need to spell it out for her. The only possible theory was a deranged killer acting alone. The theory you always worked with when you had no leads.

"I have difficulty seeing Svedberg getting tangled up in all this," he said. "Even though he's surprised us."

"Maybe he wasn't directly involved," Höglund said. "He may simply have known someone who was."

He thought again of Westin, the seafaring postman. Wallander was still desperately trying to catch hold of something he had said during that boat trip. But it remained out of reach.

"There's really only one thing we need to know," Wallander said, "as in all complicated cases. One thing, that would set everything else in motion."

"The identity of Svedberg's killer?"

He nodded. "Exactly. Then we would have an answer to everything, except perhaps the question of the motive. But we could piece that together as well."

Wallander returned to the chair and sat down. "Did you have time to talk to the Danes about Louise?"

"The photograph will be published tomorrow."

Wallander got up again. "We have to go through this flat thoroughly," he said. "From top to bottom. But I think I'll be of more use in Ystad. If we have time, we'll contact Interpol today and get the Americans involved. Martinsson will love taking charge of that."

"I think he dreams about being a federal agent in the United States," Höglund agreed. "Not just a policeman in Ystad."

"We all have our dreams," Wallander said, in an awkward and completely unnecessary attempt to come to Martinsson's defence. He gathered the papers from the desk while Höglund looked around the kitchen for some plastic bags to put them in. They talked for a while in the small hall before he left.

"I keep having this feeling that I'm overlooking something," Wallander said. "I think it has something to do with Westin."

"Westin?"

"He was the one who took me out to Bärnsö Island. He's the postman in the archipelago. He said something when we were standing in the wheelhouse. I just can't remember what it was."

"Why don't you call him? The two of you might be able to reconstruct the conversation. Maybe simply hearing his voice will bring whatever it was back to you."

"You may be right," Wallander said doubtfully. "I'll call."

Then he remembered another voice. "What happened with Lundberg? I mean the person who wasn't him, but who pretended to be. The one who called the hospital and asked about Isa."

"I passed that on to Martinsson. We exchanged a couple of tasks; I can't remember now what they were. I took on

353

something he hadn't had time to do. He promised to talk to the nurse."

Wallander sensed a note of criticism in her voice. They all had so much to do. The tasks were piling up.

Wallander drove back to Ystad, thinking over the latest events. How did the revelations in Lena Norman's flat alter the picture? Were these parties much more sinister than he had thought? He recalled the time a few years earlier, when Linda had undergone what might be described as a religious crisis. It was right after the divorce. Linda was as lost as he was, and one night he had heard a soft mumbling from inside her bedroom that he thought must be prayer. When he found books in her room about Scientology, he'd become seriously concerned. He tried to reason with her without much success. Finally Mona sorted things out. He didn't know exactly what happened, but one day the soft mumbles behind her door stopped and she went back to her old interests.

He shivered at the thought of sects. Were the answers to this case lying somewhere in these plastic bags? He accelerated. He was in a hurry.

The first thing he did back at the station was to find Edmundsson and pay him the money he owed. Then he went to the conference room where Martinsson was briefing the three police officers from Malmö who were joining the investigation. Wallander had met one of them before, a detective in his 60s by the name of Rytter. He didn't recognise either of the other two, who were younger. Wallander said hello, but didn't stay. He asked Martinsson to try to catch him sometime later that evening. Then he went to his office and started going through the papers from Lena Norman's flat. He was about half finished when Martinsson appeared. It was a little after 11 p.m. Martinsson was pale and bleary-eyed. Wallander wondered how he looked himself.

"How's it going?" he asked.

"They're good," Martinsson said. "Especially the old guy, Rytter."

"They're going to make a real difference," Wallander said enthusiastically. "It will give us the break we need."

Martinsson pulled off his tie and unbuttoned his collar.

"I have a project for you," Wallander said. He told him in some detail about the materials that had turned up in Lena Norman's flat. Martinsson became more and more interested. The thought that he would be contacting colleagues in the U.S. was clearly invigorating.

"The most important thing is to get a clear picture of these people," Wallander said.

Martinsson looked at his watch. "I guess this isn't the best time of day to get in touch with the U.S., but I'll give it a shot."

Wallander got up and gathered the papers together, and they went to copy the material that Wallander hadn't had time to look through.

"Apart from drugs, sects are the thing I'm most afraid of for my children," Martinsson said. "I'm afraid of them getting pulled into some religious nightmare they won't be able to get out of, where I won't be able to reach them."

"There was a time when I had those exact worries about Linda," Wallander said. He didn't say anything more, and Martinsson didn't ask any questions.

The copier suddenly stopped working. Martinsson reloaded it with a new sheaf of blank paper. Wallander left Martinsson and returned to his office. A report on the charges once filed against Svedberg was lying on his desk. He read through it quickly to get a sense of what had happened. It was dated 19 September 1985. A man named Stig Stridh, the complainant, was assaulted by his brother, an alcoholic, who had come to ask him for money. He knocked out two of Stridh's teeth, stole a camera, and demolished a large part of his living room. Two police officers, one by the name of Andersson, showed up at the flat and took down details of the incident. Stridh was called down to the police station on 26 August for a meeting with Inspector Karl Evert Svedberg. Svedberg explained to him that there would not be an investigation into the case since there was no evidence. Stridh argued vehemently that a camera was missing and a large part of his living room was damaged, and that the two officers had seen his cuts and bruises. According to Stridh, at this point Svedberg's manner became threatening and he ordered him to drop the charges. Stridh left and later wrote a letter to Björk, in which he complained about the treatment he had received.

Two days later Svedberg showed up at Stridh's door and repeated his threats. After some deliberation with friends, Stridh had decided to file charges against Svedberg with the department of justice. Wallander read the report with a growing sense of disbelief. Svedberg's response to the report was brief and denied all charges. Svedberg's behaviour in the case simply couldn't be explained. But this was exactly the kind of thing they had to get to the bottom of.

It was past midnight when Wallander had finished reading the report. He hadn't managed to fit in the visit to Isa Edengren's parents. He couldn't find a Stig Stridh in the phone book. Both matters would have to wait until the morning. Now he had to get some sleep. He took his coat and left the station. There was a faint breeze outside, but it was still warm. He found his car keys and unlocked the door.

Suddenly he jerked around. He couldn't say what had frightened him. He listened hard and stared into the shadows at the edge of the car park. There was no one there, he told himself. He got into his car. I'm always afraid that he's out there, close by, he thought. Whoever he is, he keeps himself well informed, and I'm afraid he will kill again.

CHAPTER TWENTY-FOUR

On Saturday, 17 August, Wallander woke to the sound of rain drumming against the bedroom window. The alarm clock read 6.30 a.m. Wallander listened to the sound of the rain. Soft morning light was streaming in through a gap in the curtains. He tried to recall when it had last rained. It had to have been before the night when he and Martinsson found Svedberg's body, and that was eight days ago. It's an unfathomable length of time, he thought. Neither long, nor short. He went out to the bathroom and had a pee, then drank some water at the kitchen counter and returned to bed. The fear from the night before was still with him, just as mysterious, just as strong.

He was showered and dressed by 7.15 a.m. For breakfast he had a cup of coffee and a tomato. The rain had stopped and the thermometer read 15°C. The clouds were already starting to clear. He decided to make his calls from the flat rather than the station. First he would call Westin, then the operator to try and get Stig Stridh's phone number. He had already found the piece of paper with Westin's numbers on it. He was counting on Westin having Saturdays off, but he probably wasn't the type to stay in bed, either. Wallander took his coffee with him into the living room and dialled the first of the three numbers on the scrap of paper. A woman answered after the third ring. Wallander introduced himself and apologised for calling so early.

"I'll get him," she said. "He's chopping wood."

Wallander thought he could hear the sound of wood splitting in the background. Then the sound stopped and he heard children's voices. Westin finally came to the phone, and they exchanged greetings.

"You're chopping wood," Wallander said.

"The cold weather always comes sooner than you think," Westin said. "How are things going? I've been trying to follow the case in the papers and on the news. Have you caught him yet?"

"Not yet. It takes time. But we'll get him."

Westin was silent on the other end. He probably saw right through Wallander's optimism, which was as hollow as it was necessary. Pessimistic policemen rarely solved complicated crimes.

"Do you remember any of our conversation when we were heading out to Bärnsö?" Wallander asked.

"Which part?" Westin answered. "We talked all the way there, if I recall. Between stops."

"One of our conversations was a little longer – I think it was the very first part of the trip."

Suddenly Wallander remembered. Westin had slowed the boat down and they were coasting in towards the first or perhaps the second island. It had a name that reminded him of Bärnsö.

"It was one of the first stops," Wallander said. "What were the names of those islands?"

"You must be thinking of Harö or Båtmansö Island."

"Båtmansö. That was it. An old man lived there."

"Zetterquist."

It was starting to come back to him now. "We were on our way in towards the dock," he said. "You were telling me about Zetterquist, who spends the winters out there all alone. Do you remember what you said?"

359

Westin laughed, but in a jovial way. "I'm sure I could have said any number of things."

"I know this seems strange, but it's actually quite important," Wallander said.

Westin seemed to sense that Wallander was serious. "I think you asked me what it was like to deliver the post," he said.

"Then I'll ask you that same question. What's it like being a postman in the islands?"

"It gives you a sense of freedom, but it's also hard work. And no one knows how long I'll keep my job. I wouldn't put it past them to cut my route entirely and stop servicing the archipelago. Zetterquist once told me he might even have to put in an advance order to have his body collected, just to make sure he wasn't left lying out there indefinitely when his time came."

"You didn't say that. I would have remembered it. I'll ask you again. What's it like to be a postman in the islands?"

Westin hesitated this time. "I don't recall saying much else."

But Wallander knew there had been something else. Something mundane, about what delivering post to people who lived out there was like.

"We were on our way in towards the landing," Wallander said. "That much I remember. The boat had slowed down a lot and you were telling me about Zetterquist."

"Maybe I said something about how you end up looking out for people. If they don't come down to meet you, you go up and make sure they're all right."

Almost, Wallander thought. We're almost there now. But you said something more, Lennart Westin. I know you did.

"I can't think of anything else. I really can't," Westin said.

"We're not giving up just yet. Try again."

But Westin couldn't come up with anything else and Wallander wasn't able to coax it out of him.

"Keep at it," Wallander said. "Call me if it comes back to you."

"I'm not normally the curious type, but why is this so important?"

"I don't know," Wallander said simply. "But when I do, I'll tell you, I promise."

Wallander felt despondent after the call. Not only had he been unable to get Westin to remember what he'd said, it was probably irrelevant anyway. His thoughts of giving up, and letting Holgersson put someone else in charge returned more strongly. But then he thought of Thurnberg and felt an even stronger urge to prove him wrong. He called the operator and asked for a number for Stig Stridh. It was unlisted but not private. He dialled the number and counted nine rings before someone answered. The voice was old and drawling.

"Stridh."

"This is Inspector Kurt Wallander from the Ystad police."

Stridh sounded like he was spitting when he replied. "It wasn't me who shot Svedberg, but maybe I should have."

His attitude angered Wallander. Stridh should show more respect, even if Svedberg had acted inappropriately towards him in the past. He had trouble holding back his irritation.

"You filed charges against Svedberg ten years ago. They were dismissed."

"I still can't understand how they could do that," Stridh said. "Svedberg should have lost his job."

"I'm not calling to discuss the decision," Wallander said curtly. "I want to talk to you about what happened."

"What's there to talk about? My brother was drunk."

"What's his name?"

"Nisse."

"Does he live in Ystad?"

"He died in 1991. Cirrhosis of the liver, what a surprise."

Wallander was momentarily at a loss. He had assumed the call to Stig Stridh was the first step towards eventually meeting the brother who played the leading role in the whole strange episode.

"You have my condolences," Wallander said.

"The hell I do. But whatever. I'm not particularly sorry. I get left in peace now and I have the place to myself. At least more often."

"What do you mean by that?"

"Nisse has a widow, or whatever one should call her."

"Is she his widow?"

"That's what she says, but he never married her."

"Do they have children?"

"She did, but not with him. That was just as well. One of hers is doing time."

"What for?"

"Robbed a bank."

"What's his name?"

"It's a she. Stella."

"Your brother's stepdaughter robbed a bank?"

"Is that so strange?"

"It's unusual for a woman to commit that kind of crime. Where did it take place?"

"In Sundsvall. She fired a number of shots at the ceiling."

A vague recollection of this event was coming back to Wallander. He looked for something to write with. Wallander turned back to the matter at hand. Stridh's answers came slowly and with great unwillingness. It took what seemed like an eternity, but Wallander finally had a clearer picture of the events. Stig Stridh had been married, had two grown sons who now lived in Malmö and Laholm. His brother, Nils, called Nisse, who was three years younger, became an alcoholic early on. He began a career in the military but was discharged on account of his heavy drinking. At first Stig tried to be patient with his brother, but the relationship deteriorated, not least because he always came asking for money. Tensions had reached breaking point eleven years earlier. This was the point Wallander wanted to reach.

"We don't have to go through the events in detail," he said. "I just want to know one thing: why do you think Svedberg acted the way he did?"

"He said we had no evidence, but that was bullshit."

"We know that. We don't have to go into it. What I want to know is why you think he acted like this."

"Because he was an idiot."

Wallander was prepared for the answers to anger him, and he knew that Stig had good reasons for his hostility. Svedberg's behaviour had been incomprehensible.

"Svedberg was no idiot," Wallander said. "There must be another explanation. Had you ever met him before?"

"When would that have been?"

"Just answer my questions," Wallander said shortly.

"I'd never met him before."

"Have you had any run-ins with the law yourself?"

"No."

That answer came a little too fast, Wallander thought. It isn't true.

"Stick to the truth, Stridh. If you tell me lies I'll have you hauled straight down to the station in the blink of an eye."

It worked. "Well, I did a little car-dealing in the 1960s,"

he said. "There was some trouble once about a car that was supposed to be stolen, but that's all."

Wallander decided to take him at his word.

"How about your brother?"

"He probably did all kinds of things, but he never did any time for anything except his drinking."

Again, Wallander felt that Stridh was telling the truth. The man didn't know of a connection between his brother and Svedberg. It's hopeless, he thought. I'm banging my head against the wall. Wallander ended the conversation, having decided to talk to Rut Lundin, the "widow".

He left the flat and walked to the station.

Shortly after 11 a.m., as he went to get another cup of coffee, he realised that most of his colleagues were around, including the officers from Malmö, and took the opportunity to call a meeting in the conference room. He started by going through his own attempts to shed light on the events surrounding the complaint filed against Svedberg eleven years ago. Martinsson told him that Hugo Andersson, the policeman who'd answered Stridh's call that night, now worked as a janitor at a school in Värnamo. The officer who'd been his partner was a policeman by the name of Holmström, who now worked in Malmö.

Martinsson promised to check up on both of them. Wallander told them he was driving out to meet Isa Edengren's parents. After the meeting, Wallander shared a pizza with Hansson. All day he had been trying to keep track of how much water he had drunk and how many times he'd relieved himself, but he had already lost track. He called Rut Lundin. Once she understood why he was calling, she answered most of his questions – but she had nothing useful to add. He asked her specifically about Nisse's drinking buddies, and she said she remembered a few. When he pressed her for names, she said she needed time to think. He told her he would drop by later that afternoon.

At 4 p.m. he called Björk, their former chief of police, who now lived in Malmö. They started by catching up on the latest gossip, and Björk expressed deep sympathy at their having to deal with the case at hand. They talked at length about Svedberg. Björk said he was planning to attend the funeral, which surprised Wallander, although he didn't know why. Björk had nothing to say about the complaint filed against Svedberg. He couldn't remember any more why Svedberg had dismissed the investigation, but since the department of justice hadn't intervened, he was sure the whole thing was above board.

Wallander left the station at 4.30 p.m., on his way to Skårby. First he stopped by Rut Lundin's flat to pick up the list of names she had promised him. When he rang her doorbell she opened the door at once, as if she had been waiting for him in the hall. He could see that she was drunk. She thrust a piece of paper in his hand and said it was all she could remember. Wallander saw she didn't want him to come in, so he thanked her and left.

Back out on the footpath, he stopped under the shade of a tree and read through what she had written. He immediately saw a name he recognised about halfway down the list. Bror Sundelius. Wallander caught his breath. A pattern was finally starting to emerge. Svedberg, Bror Sundelius, Nisse Stridh. He didn't get any further. The phone in his pocket rang.

It was Martinsson, and his voice was shaking.

"He's done it again," he said. "He's done it again."

It was 4.55 p.m. on Saturday, 17 August 1996.

CHAPTER TWENTY-FIVE

He knew he was taking a risk. He hadn't done that before, since taking risks was beneath him and he had devoted his whole life to learning how to escape. But he was attracted by the challenge, and the situation was much too tempting.

He had almost lost control when he came by to pick up their invitations. Their joy was so great that it felt like a physical blow, an act specifically aimed at humiliating him, which of course it was.

Then, when he read the letter, he made up his mind. Between the ceremony at the church and the reception, they were going to stop off at a nearby beach to have their wedding portraits taken. The photographer was very clear in his directions and had even drawn a little map for them. The couple agreed. They would meet him there at 4 p.m., weather permitting.

He went there to scout it out. The photographer's directions were so clear that he had no problem in locating the exact spot. The beach was big, with a camping ground at one end. At first, he wasn't sure that he'd be able to carry out his plans, but then he saw that they would be quite sheltered in their spot among the sand dunes. There would be others on the beach, but they would keep their distance while the photographs were being taken. The challenge was figuring out which direction to approach them from. Disappearing afterwards would be relatively easy, since it was only about 200 metres to the car. If anything went wrong and he was chased, he had his gun. Someone might notice what kind of car he was driving, but he would have three different cars standing by so he could switch them.

He didn't solve the question of his approach on the first visit. But on the second visit, he saw what he had overlooked on the first. He saw the dramatic solution that would enable him to transform the comedy into tragedy.

Suddenly everything was planned and he was running out of time. Cars had to be stolen and parked in their various locations. A small revolver wrapped in plastic had to be buried in the sand. He also put a towel in with it.

The only thing he couldn't count on was the weather, but August had been beautiful this year.

They were married in the church where she had been confirmed nine years earlier. The minister who had officiated then had died, but she had a relative who was a minister and he agreed to step in. Everything went according to plan. The church was bursting with family and friends, and once the photo session was over they would have a big reception. The photographer was at the church with them taking pictures. He had already planned out the pictures he wanted to take at the beach. He had used the spot before and it worked well. He had never been as lucky with the weather as today.

They arrived at the beach just before 4 p.m. The camping ground was full of people, and a number of children were playing on the beach. A lone swimmer was out in the water. It took the photographer only a few minutes to set up his gear, which included the tripod and the light reflectors. They were completely undisturbed.

Everything was ready. The photographer paused behind

the camera while the bridegroom helped his bride check her make-up in a small mirror. The swimmer was on his way up out of the water. His towel lay on the beach. He sat down on it, with his back to them. The bride thought it looked like he was digging a hole in the sand. They were ready. The photographer told them what he had planned for the first photo. They debated whether they should be serious or smiling, and the photographer suggested trying it both ways. It was 4.09 p.m. They had plenty of time.

They had just taken the first picture when the man on the beach below them got up and started walking. The photographer was getting ready to take the next picture but at that moment the bride saw that the man had changed his course and was heading towards them. She held up her hand to stop the photographer from taking the picture, thinking it best to wait until he had passed. He was almost upon them now, carrying his towel like a shield in front of his body. The photographer smiled at him and turned back to the couple. The man smiled in return, unwrapped the towel from his gun, and shot the photographer in the neck. He quickly advanced a couple of steps and shot the bride and groom in turn. All that was heard were some dry crackles. He looked all around. No one had noticed anything.

He continued on over the sand dunes and waited until he was out of sight of the camping ground. Then he started running. He reached the car safely, unlocked it, and jumped in. The whole thing had taken less than two minutes.

He realised that he was cold. It was another risk he had taken, as he could have caught cold. But the temptation had simply been too great. It was wonderful to emerge from the water like that, like the invincible person he really was.

At the edge of Ystad he stopped the car and pulled on the tracksuit he had laid out on the back seat. Then he settled in to wait.

It took a little longer than he expected. Was it one of the children playing on the beach, or someone at the camping ground taking a walk? He would read about it in the papers soon enough.

Finally he heard the noise of the sirens. It was just before 5 p.m. The vehicles drove past him at high speed, among them an ambulance. He felt like waving at them, but controlled himself. He drove home. He had again achieved what he had set out to do. And escaped again, with dignity.

Wallander was picked up outside Rut Lundin's building. The officers assigned to get him didn't know anything other than that they were to take him to Nybrostrand. From the information on the police radio, he gathered that several people were dead. He hadn't managed to get anything more out of Martinsson. Wallander leaned back in his seat. Martinsson's words still echoed in his head. "He's done it again."

He opened the door before the car had even come to a halt. A woman stood there crying, her hands in front of her face. She was wearing shorts and a T-shirt with a slogan supporting Sweden joining NATO.

"What happened?" Wallander asked.

People from the camping ground were rushing around, waving and gesturing. They were running all over the sand dunes. Wallander made it out there before the rest. He stopped dead. The nightmare was repeating itself. At first he couldn't take in what he was seeing, and then he understood that three bodies lay before him. There was a camera on a tripod.

"They had just been married," he heard Höglund say, somewhere nearby. Wallander walked closer and crouched down. All three of them had been shot. The shots had struck the bride and groom in the forehead. The bride's white veil was stained with blood. He touched her arm very carefully. It was still warm. He stood up again and hoped he wouldn't get dizzy. Hansson arrived, as well as Nyberg. He walked over to them.

"It's him again. This happened minutes ago. Are there any tracks? Has anyone seen anything? Who found them?"

Everyone around him seemed dumbstruck, as if they had been looking to him to supply them with the answers.

"Don't just stand there – move!" he shouted. "It just happened! This time we've got to get him!"

Their paralysis lifted, and after a couple of minutes Wallander was able to get a clearer idea of what had happened. The couple had come here to have their wedding pictures taken. They had gone into the sand dunes. A child playing on the beach had left his friends because he needed to pee. He had discovered the dead bodies and run screaming to the camping ground. No one had heard shots, and no one had noticed anything unusual. Several witnesses confirmed that the photographer and the couple had arrived alone.

"Some of the children saw a man swimming in the water," Hansson said. "According to their accounts, he came up out of the sea, sat down in the sand, and then disappeared."

"What do you mean, 'disappeared'?" Wallander was having trouble concealing his impatience.

"A woman who was hanging up her laundry when the couple arrived said the same thing," Höglund said. "She thought she saw a swimmer, but when she looked again he was gone."

Wallander shook his head. "What does that mean? That he drowned? Buried himself in the sand?"

Hansson pointed to the stretch of beach that lay directly below the crime scene.

"The place he sat down was right there," he said. "At least according to one child who seems believable. He had his eyes open."

They walked down on the beach. Hansson ran over to a dark-haired boy and his father. Wallander made them all walk in a wide circle to avoid ruining the tracks in the sand and making it harder for the dog to pick up a scent. They could see the marks of someone sitting in the sand, the remains of a little hole and a piece of plastic sheeting.

Wallander shouted for Edmundsson and Nyberg to join him.

"This plastic reminds me of something," he said, and Nyberg nodded. "Maybe it matches the plastic sheeting we found in the nature reserve."

Wallander turned to Edmundsson. "Let her smell this and see what she finds."

They walked off to the side and watched the dog, who immediately took off into the sand dunes. Then she veered to the left. Wallander and Martinsson followed at a distance. The dog was still excited. They arrived at a small road, and there the scent ended. Edmundsson shook his head.

"A car," Martinsson said.

"Someone may have seen it," Wallander said. "Get every police officer out here to work on this: we're looking for a man in a bathing suit. He left about an hour ago in a car that was parked here."

Wallander ran back to the crime scene. One of the forensic technicians was making a mould of a footprint in the sand. Edmundsson's dog was searching the area.

Hansson was just ending a conversation with a woman from the camping ground. Wallander waved him over.

"More people saw him," Hansson said.

"The swimmer?"

"He was down in the water when the couple arrived. Then he walked up onto the beach. Someone said it looked as though he started to build a sand castle, then got up and disappeared."

"No one's seen anyone else in the area?"

"One man, who is clearly under the influence, claimed two masked men were riding down the beach on bicycles, but I think we can safely disregard this."

"Then we'll stick with the swimmer for now," Wallander said. "Do we know who the victims are?"

"The photographer had this invitation in his pocket," Höglund said and handed it over to Wallander. He was overcome by such a wave of despair that he wanted to scream.

"Malin Skander and Torbjörn Werner," he read out loud. "They were married at 2 p.m. this afternoon."

Hansson had tears in his eyes. Höglund was staring at the ground.

"They were man and wife for two whole hours," he said. "They came down here to have their pictures taken. Who was the photographer?"

"We found his name on the inside of the camera bag," Hansson said. "His name was Rolf Haag and he had a studio in Malmö."

"We have to notify the next of kin," Wallander said. "The press will be all over this place before we know it."

"Shouldn't we put up roadblocks?" Martinsson asked. He had just joined them.

"Why? We have no idea what the car looked like. Even though we know when this happened, it's already too late."

"I just want to nail the bastard," Martinsson said.

"We all do," Wallander said. "So let's go through everything we know at this point. The one lead we have is a lone swimmer. We have to assume he's our man. We know two things about him: he's well informed and plans his crimes meticulously."

"You think he was out there swimming in the ocean while he waited for them?" Hansson asked hesitantly.

Wallander tried to imagine the chain of events. "He knew the newly-weds were having their wedding pictures taken here," he said. "On the invitation it said the reception was starting at 5 p.m. He knew the photo session would be around 4 p.m. He waited out in the water, having parked his car nearby in a spot where he could get down to the beach without walking through the camping ground."

"He had his gun with him the whole time he was out in the water?" Hansson was clearly sceptical, but Wallander was starting to see how it hung together.

"Remember that this is a well-informed and meticulous killer," he said. "He's waiting for his victims out in the water. That means he's only wearing a bathing suit, and with his hair wet his whole appearance is altered. No one pays any attention to a swimmer. Everyone saw him and knew he was there, but no one could describe him."

He looked around and they nodded in agreement. None of the witnesses had managed to describe him yet.

"The newly-weds arrive with their photographer," Wallander said. "That's his cue to come up out of the water and sit down on the beach."

"He has a towel," Höglund added. "A striped one. Several people recalled that detail."

"That's good," Wallander said. "The more detail the

better. He sits down on his striped towel, and what does he do?"

"He starts to dig in the sand," Hansson said.

The pieces were starting to fit together. The killer followed his own rules, and often varied them, but Wallander was starting to see a pattern.

"He's not building a sand castle," he said. "He's uncovering a gun that he's buried in the sand under a piece of plastic sheeting."

Now they followed his train of thought. Wallander continued slowly. "He planted the gun there at some earlier point," he said. "He just has to wait for the right moment, when no one happens to be walking by. He gets up, probably shielding the gun from view with his towel. He fires the gun three times. The victims die immediately. He must have had a silencer on the gun. He continues past the sand dunes, gets to the road where his car is parked, and escapes. The whole thing doesn't take longer than a minute. But we don't know where he went."

Nyberg walked over and joined them.

"We don't know anything about this killer, other than what he's done," Wallander said. "But we're going to find similarities between these crimes, and new details will emerge."

"I know something about him," Nyberg interjected. "He uses snuff. There's some down there in the hole in the sand. He must have tried to kick some sand over it, but the dog found it. We're sending it to the laboratory. You can find out quite a lot about a person from his saliva."

Wallander saw Holgersson approaching from a distance, with Thurnberg a couple of steps behind. The sense of failure washed over him again. Even though he had acted in good faith, he had failed. They hadn't found the man who had killed their colleague, three young people in a nature reserve, a girl curled up in a cave on an island in the Östergötland archipelago, and now some newly-weds and their photographer. There was only one thing he could do, and that was ask Holgersson to put someone else in charge. Maybe Thurnberg had already asked the national police to step in.

Wallander didn't have the energy to go over the events with them. Instead, he walked to Nyberg, who was turning his attention to the tripod.

"He was able to take one picture before it happened," Nyberg said. "We'll get it developed as soon as possible."

"They were married for two hours," Wallander said.

"It seems like this madman hates happy people, sees it as his life's calling to turn joy into misery."

Wallander listened absently to Nyberg's last comment, but he didn't reply. He still didn't have the energy to comprehend the enormity of what had happened. He had been convinced that the killer would strike again, but he was hoping he would be proved wrong.

A good policeman always hopes for the best outcome, Rydberg had often said. And what else? That fighting crime is simply a question of endurance; about which side can outlast the other.

Holgersson and Thurnberg appeared at his side. Wallander had been so lost in thought that he jumped.

"The road should have been blocked off," Thurnberg said, by way of greeting.

Wallander looked back at him stonily. At that moment he decided two things. He wasn't going to relinquish leadership in this case willingly, and he was going to start speaking his mind, the latter effective immediately.

"Wrong," he answered. "The roads shouldn't have been

blocked off at all. You can of course order us to do so, but it won't receive my endorsement."

This wasn't the answer Thurnberg was expecting, and he looked taken aback.

He was too puffed up, Wallander thought with satisfaction. He was so puffed up by his own sense of importance that he burst. Wallander turned his back on Thurnberg. Holgersson looked paler than he'd ever seen her before. He could see his own fear in her eyes.

"It's the same man?"

"I'm sure of it."

"But a couple of newly-weds?"

It was the first thought that had come to him as well.

"You could say that wedding clothes are a kind of costume."

"Is that what he's after?"

"I don't know."

"What else could it be?"

Wallander didn't answer. The only possibility he could see was a madman. A madman who wasn't a madman, but who had killed eight people, including a police officer.

"I've never been involved in anything so horrible in my whole life," she said. After a moment she added, "I heard they were married nearby."

"In Köpingebro," Wallander told her. "The reception is about to begin."

She looked at him and he knew what she was thinking.

"I'm going to ask Martinsson to contact the photographer's family," he said. "He can contact the Malmö police for help. You and I will drive out to Köpingebro."

Thurnberg stood a short distance away, talking to someone on his mobile phone. Wallander wondered who it was.

He gathered everyone around him and asked Hansson to take charge until he returned.

"Answer all of Thurnberg's questions," Wallander said. "But if he tries to tell you what to do, let me know."

"Why on earth would a chief prosecutor try to tell the police how to do their work?"

Now there's a good question, Wallander thought. But he left without answering and joined Holgersson, who was waiting silently in her car.

At 10 p.m. on Saturday, 17 August, it began to rain. Wallander was already back at the crime scene. Notifying the next of kin, entering that room of joy with his brutal news, was even worse than he had imagined. Holgersson was strangely passive during the visit, perhaps because her encounters with the parents of the young people in the reserve the week before had drained her of any remaining energy. Maybe we have a set quota for these kinds of experiences, Wallander thought. I must have met mine by now.

It was a relief to get back to Nybrostrand. Holgersson had already returned to Ystad by then. Wallander had been in touch with Hansson by phone several times, but there was nothing new to report. Hansson told him that Rolf Haag was unmarried and childless. Martinsson had delivered the news to his aged father, who was in a nursing home. A nurse assured Martinsson that the old man had long since forgotten he even had a son.

Nyberg had just been given a freshly developed copy of the one photograph Rolf Haag had taken. The bride and groom smiled into the camera. Wallander looked at it intently for a moment. He suddenly remembered something Nyberg had said to him earlier.

"What was it you said?" he asked. "When we were standing here before. You had just discovered that he had managed to take a picture."

"I said something?"

"It was some kind of comment."

Nyberg thought hard. "I think I said that the killer didn't like happy people."

"What did you mean by that?"

"Svedberg is the exception, of course. But with the young people in the nature reserve, I think their celebration could be characterised as joyous."

Wallander sensed he was on to something. He looked at the wedding picture again, then gave it back to Nyberg and was about to say a few words to Höglund when Martinsson pulled him aside.

"I thought you should know that someone has filed charges against you."

Wallander stared back at him.

"Against me? Why?"

"For assault."

Martinsson scratched his head apologetically. "Do you remember that jogger in the nature reserve? Nils Hagroth?"

"He was trespassing."

"Well, he filed the charges anyway. Thurnberg's got wind of it and seems to take it seriously."

Wallander was speechless.

"I just wanted to tell you," Martinsson said. "That's all."

It was raining harder now. Martinsson left.

A police spotlight illuminated the place where, a few hours earlier, a couple of newly-weds had been murdered. It was 10.30 p.m.

CHAPTER TWENTY-SIX

It stopped raining shortly after midnight. Wallander walked down to the sea to think. It was what he most needed to do at this point. A fresh smell was rising up from the ground after the rain. There were no more wafts of rotting seaweed. The hot weather had lasted for two weeks. Now that the rain had passed, it was warming up again and there was still no wind. The waves against the shore were almost imperceptible.

Wallander pissed into the water. In his mind's eye he could see the little white grains of sugar congealing in his veins. He was constantly dry-mouthed, had trouble keeping his eyes focused on an object, and feared that his blood-sugar levels were increasing.

As he walked along the dark beach, his thoughts returned to the latest events. He was convinced that the lone swimmer, the man with the striped towel, was the one they were looking for. There was no other plausible suspect. He was the one who had been in the nature reserve, probably hidden behind the tree that Wallander had pinpointed. Later he had been in Svedberg's flat. And now he had emerged from the ocean. His weapon was concealed in the sand, his car parked on a nearby road.

The swimmer had been to this place more than once. He must have gone to the same spot and dug a hole in the sand. It could even have been in the middle of the night. Wallander felt he was getting closer to unlocking the secret now, but he wasn't quite there yet. The answer is quite simple, he thought. It's like looking for the pair of glasses on your nose.

He began walking slowly back. The spotlights shone in the distance. Now he tried following in Svedberg's footsteps. Who was the person he had let into his flat? Who was Louise? Who had sent those postcards from all over Europe? What was it you knew, Svedberg? Why didn't you want to tell me, even though Ylva Brink says I was your closest friend?

He stopped. The question he'd posed suddenly seemed more important than before. If Svedberg hadn't wanted to tell anyone what he was up to, it could only have been because he was hoping he was wrong. There was simply no other reason for it. But Svedberg had been right, and that was why he was killed.

Wallander had almost reached the police barricades. There was still a little group of people gathered around the perimeter, trying to see something of the sombre tragedy that had taken place. When Wallander came over the sand dunes, Nyberg had just finished making some notes.

"We have some footprints," Nyberg said. "I mean that quite literally, since the killer was barefoot."

"Have you pieced together what happened?"

Nyberg put the notebook away. "The photographer was hit first," he said. "There's no doubt about that. The bullet entered his neck at an angle, so he may have had his back partially turned. If the first shot had been aimed at the couple, he would have turned around and been shot from the front."

"And next?"

"It's hard to say. I think the groom was probably the

next to go. A man is more of a threat, physically. Then the girl last."

"Anything else?"

"Nothing you don't already know. This killer is in total control of his weapon."

"His hand doesn't shake?"

"Hardly."

"You see a calm and determined killer?"

Nyberg looked grimly at Wallander. "I see a cold-blooded and heartless madman."

When Wallander returned to the police station, the phones were going mad. One of the officers on duty gestured for him to come over. Wallander waited while he finished a phone call about a drunk driver sighted in Svarte. The officer promised to send out a squad car as soon as possible, but Wallander knew no squad car would be making it to Svarte for another 24 hours.

"A police officer from Copenhagen called you. The name was something like Kjær or Kræmp."

"What was it about?"

"The photograph of that woman."

Wallander took the piece of paper with the name and number on it and sat down at his desk to make the call without even removing his coat. The call had come in just before midnight. Kjær or Kræmp might still be there. The call was answered and Wallander said who he was looking for.

"Kjær."

Wallander was expecting a man's voice, but Kjær was a woman.

"This is Kurt Wallander from Ystad. I'm returning your call."

"We have some information for you about the picture

of that woman. We've had two calls from people who claim to have seen her."

Wallander banged the table with his fist.

"At last."

"I've spoken with one of the callers myself. He seemed very reliable. His name is Anton Bakke. He's a manager at a company that makes office furniture."

"Does he know her personally?"

"No, but he was absolutely convinced he had seen her here in Copenhagen at a bar, close to the Central Station. He's seen her there several times."

"It's extremely important that we speak to this woman."

"Has she committed a crime?"

"We don't know that yet, but she is wanted in connection with a growing murder investigation. That's why we sent you her photograph."

"I heard about what happened over there. Those young people in the park. And the police officer."

Wallander told her about the latest events.

"And you think this woman had something to do with it?"

"Not necessarily, but I would like to ask her some questions."

"Bakke says there have been periods when he went to this bar as often as several times a week. He saw her there about half the time."

"Was she usually alone?"

"He wasn't sure, but he thought she sometimes came with someone else."

"Did you ask him when he saw her last?"

"When he was there last, sometime in the middle of June."

"What about the other caller?"

"It was a taxi driver who claimed he gave her a ride in Copenhagen a couple of weeks ago."

"A taxi driver sees a lot of people. How can he be sure?"

"He remembered her because she spoke Swedish."

"Where did he pick her up?"

"She waved him down on the street one night, or rather, early one morning. It was around 4.30 a.m., and she said she was catching the first ferry back to Malmö."

Wallander knew he had to make a decision. "We can't ask you to arrest her," he said. "But we do need you to bring her in. We must talk to her."

"We should be able to do that. We can invent a reason."

"Just tell me when she next shows up at that bar. What was its name?"

"The Amigo."

"What kind of a place is it?"

"It's pretty nice, actually, even though it's down on Istedgade."

Wallander knew that the street was in downtown Copenhagen.

"I appreciate your help on this."

"We'll let you know when she turns up."

Wallander wrote down Kjær's full name and her phone numbers. Her first name was Lone. Then he hung up.

It was 1.30 a.m. He rose slowly to his feet and went to the men's room, then drank some water in the canteen. Some dried-up sandwiches lay on a plate, and he picked one of them up. He heard Martinsson's voice out in the hall, speaking to one of the Malmö officers. They came into the canteen a few minutes later.

"How's it going?" he asked, between bites of the sandwich.

"No one's seen anyone other than that one swimmer."

"Do we have a description of him yet?"

"We're trying to piece together everything we've received so far."

"The Danish police called. They may have found Louise."

"Really?"

"Seems like it."

Wallander poured himself a cup of coffee. Martinsson was waiting for him to continue.

"Have they arrested her?"

"They have no grounds to do so. But reports have come in from both a taxi driver and a man who saw her in a bar. They recognised her from the photograph in the paper."

"So her name really is Louise?"

"We don't know that yet."

Wallander yawned. Martinsson did the same. One of the Malmö officers tried to rub the tiredness from his eyes.

"I'd like to see everyone in the conference room," Wallander said.

"Give us 15 minutes," Martinsson said. "I think Hansson's on his way over now, and I'll call Ann-Britt at home."

Wallander took his coffee with him to his office. He looked up and studied the map of Skåne hanging on his wall. First he located Hagestad, then Nybrostrand. Ystad lay nestled in between. The area was small, but this fact didn't lead anywhere in itself. Wallander finally picked up his notebook and walked over to the conference room. He was met by tired, despondent faces. Their clothes were wrinkled, their bodies heavy.

Our killer's probably sleeping peacefully as we speak, Wallander thought, while we're fumbling around in his footsteps.

They went through the various points that were currently

under investigation and reported the latest findings. The biggest breakthrough was the fact that no one had seen anyone other than the lone swimmer. That strengthened the case against him.

Wallander looked through his notes. "Unfortunately our description of him is strange and rather contradictory," he said gloomily. "The witnesses can't seem to agree whether he has very short hair or is bald. Those who think he has hair can't agree on the colour. Everyone, however, seems to concur that he doesn't have a round face. It seems to be long, or 'horsey', as two independent witnesses have said. Furthermore, everyone seems to agree that he wasn't very tanned. He was of average height – though in reality that could mean anything between a dwarf and a giant. He was of average build and there was nothing remarkable about the way he moved. No one has been able to say what colour his eyes were. The area of greatest confusion is in regard to his age. We have reports that range from 20 to 60. More people have his age between 35 and 45, but no one seems to have any grounds for these statements."

Wallander pushed the notebook away. "In other words, we really have no description at all," he said.

The silence lay heavy in the room. Wallander realised he had to try to lighten the mood.

"We have to remember that it's impressive how much information we've been able to gather in such a short time," he said. "We'll be able to do even more tomorrow. And it's an enormous step to be able to focus on one suspect. I wouldn't hesitate for a moment to call this a breakthrough."

At 2.40 a.m. he called the meeting to an end. Martinsson was the only one who stayed on. He wanted to fill Wallander in on the information he had received regarding the Divine

Movers. He started going through the reports that had come in from the United States and Interpol, but Wallander interrupted him impatiently.

"Has there ever been an incidence of violent crime?" he said. "Have members of this sect ever been the targets of attack?"

"Not from what I can see so far. But I've been told that more files are on their way, both from Washington and Brussels. I'll read through them tonight."

"You should go home and sleep," Wallander said sternly.

"I thought this was important."

"It is, but we can't do everything at once. We have to concentrate on Nybrostrand right now. That's where we got the closest to this madman."

"So, you've changed your mind?"

"What do you mean?"

"Well, now you're talking about a 'madman.'"

"A murderer is always crazy. But he can also be cunning and cowardly. He can be like you and me."

Martinsson nodded tiredly and didn't manage to stifle his yawn.

"I'm going home," he said. "Remind me why I ever became a policeman."

Wallander didn't answer. He went into his office to get his coat and remained standing in the middle of the room. What should he do now? He was too tired to think, but he was also too tired to sleep. He sat down in his chair and looked at the picture of Louise that was lying on his desk. He was struck again by the feeling that there was something strange about her face, but he still couldn't put his finger on it. In an absentminded way he picked up the photo and slipped it into his coat pocket. He closed his eyes to let them rest from the light, and fell asleep almost immediately.

He woke with a start without knowing where he was. It was just before 4 a.m. He had slept for almost an hour. His body ached, and he sat for a long time without a single thought in his head. Then he went to the men's room and splashed cold water on his face. Although he was still plagued by indecision, he knew he needed to sleep, if only for a few hours. He needed to bathe and change his clothes. Without having made a firm decision, he left the station and headed home.

But once he was in his car, he turned in the direction of Nybrostrand. There would be nobody there at 4 a.m., only the officers assigned to guard the area. Being alone at the crime scene could make it easier to see new details. It didn't take him long to get there. As he expected, there were no longer any onlookers crowded around the police barricades. One squad car, with someone sleeping behind the wheel, was parked down on the beach. Another officer was outside it, smoking a cigarette. Wallander walked over and said hello. He saw that it was the same man who had been assigned to the nature reserve that night.

"Everything looks pretty quiet," he said.

"Actually the last of the gawkers didn't leave until just a little while ago. I always wonder what they expect to see."

"They probably get a thrill from being in the presence of the unthinkable," Wallander said. "Knowing that they themselves are safe."

He crossed the police line to the crime scene. A lone spotlight was illuminating the well-trodden grass. Wallander walked over to where the photographer had stood, then slowly turned around and walked down the dune to where the hole was.

The guy with the striped towel knew everything, Wallander thought. He wasn't just well informed, he knew everything down to the last detail. It was as if he had been there when they made their plans.

Was that a possibility? If the killer was Rolf Haag's assistant, that would explain his knowledge of this photo session. But how would such an assistant know about the party in the nature reserve? And Bärnsö Island? And what about Svedberg?

Wallander dropped the thought for now, although he meant to take it up again. He walked back up the side of the dune, thinking about the motive for killing young people dressed up in costume. Svedberg was the exception, but this was easy enough to interpret. Svedberg had never been a target; he had simply come too close to the truth.

It occurred to him that Rolf Haag could be dismissed: he had simply been in the way. That left six victims. Six young people in different kinds of costume, six very happy people. He thought about Nyberg's words: seems like this madman hates happy people. So far it made some sort of sense, but it wasn't enough.

He walked up to the road where the getaway car must had been parked. Again, the killer had planned things down to the last detail. There were no houses nearby, no potential witnesses. He returned to the crime scene, where the officer on duty was still smoking.

"I'm still thinking about the gawkers," he said, throwing the butt on the ground and grinding it into the sand, where many others were already strewn about. "I guess we would be there too if we hadn't joined the force."

"Probably," Wallander said.

"You see so many strange people. Some of them pretend not to be interested, but they hang around for hours. One of the last people to leave this evening was a woman. She was already here when I arrived."

Wallander was only half-listening, but decided he may as well stay and chat while he was waiting for dawn.

"At first I thought it was someone I knew," the policeman said. "But it wasn't. I just thought I had seen her somewhere before."

It took a while for his words to sink in. Finally Wallander looked over at the policeman.

"What was that last thing you said?"

"I thought the woman hanging around here was someone I had seen before. But it wasn't."

"You thought you had seen her somewhere before?"

"I thought maybe she was someone I was related to."

"Well, which was it? Someone you thought you knew, or someone you thought you had seen before?"

"I don't know. There was something familiar about her, that's all."

It was a long shot, perhaps just grasping at straws, but Wallander hauled out the photograph of Louise that he had tucked into his coat pocket. It was still dark, but the policeman took out his torch.

"Yeah, that's her. How did you know?"

Wallander held his breath. "Are you sure?"

"Absolutely. I knew I had seen her somewhere before."

Wallander swore under his breath. A more attentive officer might have identified her on the spot and alerted the others. But he knew that was unfair. There were so many people coming and going. At least this policeman had noticed her.

"Show me where she was standing."

The policeman shone a torch over to a spot close to the beach.

"How long was she here?"

"Several hours."

"Was she alone?"

The policeman thought for a moment. "Yes." His tone was definite.

"And she was one of the last to leave?"

"Yes."

"Which direction did she go?"

"Towards the camping ground."

"Do you think she was staying there?"

"I didn't see exactly where she was headed, but she didn't look like a camper."

"Well, what do campers look like, in your opinion? And how was she dressed?"

"She was dressed in a blue suit of some kind, and in my experience campers tend to wear casual clothing."

"If she turns up again, let me know immediately," Wallander said. "Tell the others. Do you have this picture in the car?"

"I'll wake up my partner. He'll know."

"Don't bother."

Wallander gave him the photograph he had been holding. Then he left. It was almost 5 a.m., and he was already feeling less tired. His sense of excitement was mounting. The woman called Louise was not their lone swimmer. But she might just know who he was.

CHAPTER TWENTY-SEVEN

He woke up when the phone rang, sat up in bed with a jerk, then staggered out into the kitchen. It was Lennart Westin.

"Were you sleeping?" Westin asked apologetically.

"Not at all," Wallander answered. "But I was in the shower. Can I call you back in a couple of minutes?"

"No problem. I'm at home."

There was a pen on the table, but no piece of paper in sight, not even the newspaper. Wallander wrote the number down on the table. Then he hung up and put his head in his hands. He had a pounding headache and he was more tired now than before he had gone to bed. He rinsed his face with cold water, looked around for some aspirin, and put water on for coffee. But there was no more coffee. That was the last straw. Almost 15 minutes went by before he called Lennart Westin back. The kitchen clock read 8.09 a.m. Westin answered.

"I think you must have been asleep after all," he said. "But you did say to call if I thought of anything that might be important."

"We work around the clock," Wallander said. "It's hard to get enough sleep. But I'm glad you called."

"It's two things, really. One is about that policeman who came by earlier, the one who was shot. When I woke up this morning, I remembered something he had said as we were going out to the islands."

Wallander stopped him and went to the living room to get a notebook.

"He asked me if I had ferried any women to Bärnsö Island recently."

"And had you?"

"Yes, as a matter of fact."

"Who?"

"A woman called Linnea Vederfeldt, who lives in Gusum."

"Why was she going out to Bärnsö?"

"Isa's mother had ordered new curtains for the house. She and Vederfeldt knew each other from childhood. She was going out there to measure everything."

"Did you tell Svedberg this?"

"I didn't think it was any of his business, so I avoided going into details."

"How did he react?"

"Well, that's just it. He insisted that I tell him more about her. Finally I told him she was a childhood friend of Isa's mother and then he completely lost interest."

"Did he ask anything else?"

"Not that I can think of. But he became agitated when he realised that I had taken a woman out to Bärnsö. I remember it so clearly now that I don't know how I ever forgot it."

"What do you mean by agitated?"

"I'm not so good at describing these things, I guess. But I would say 'afraid' even."

Wallander nodded. Svedberg had been afraid it was Louise.

"What about the other thing? You said there were two."

"I must have slept really well. This morning I also thought of what it was I said to you as we were approaching that first landing. I said that you end up knowing everything about people, whether or not you want to. Do you remember that?"

"Yes."

"That's all. I hope it helps."

"Yes, it does. I'm glad you called."

"You should come out here sometime in the autumn," Westin added. "When it's quiet."

"Do I take that to mean you're inviting me?" Wallander asked.

"Take it any way you like," Westin laughed. "But you can normally take me at my word."

After they had finished the conversation, Wallander walked slowly into the living room. He remembered the conversation now, about delivering post in the islands. Suddenly he caught hold of the thought he had been trying to grasp for so long. They were looking for a killer who planned everything about his terrible crimes down to the last detail. This approach depended on his being able to get access to very specific information about his victims' lives without their knowing. Like being able to read other people's post. Wallander stood frozen in the middle of the living room. Who would have unlimited access to other people's letters? Lennart Westin had suggested a possibility: a postman. Someone who opened letters on the way, read them, sealed them again, and made sure they got to the intended address. No one would ever know they had been opened.

Something told Wallander it couldn't be this simple. This wasn't the way things worked. It was too far-fetched. Nonetheless, it answered one of the most difficult questions in the investigation: how the killer managed to gather all his information.

All trace of sleepiness was gone now. He realised he had

hit on a possible explanation. There were weaknesses, of course, not least the consideration that the victims did not live along a single postal route. But perhaps it wasn't actually a postman. Could it be someone who sorted the post before it was carried out?

He quickly showered, put his clothes on, and left. It was 9.15 a.m. when he walked through the main doors of the police station. He felt the need to discuss his latest ideas with someone, and he knew exactly who that person was. He found her in her office.

"I hope I don't look like you do," said Höglund as he walked through her door, "if you'll excuse me for being so blunt. Did you sleep at all last night?"

"A couple of hours."

"My husband's leaving for Dubai in four days. Do you think we'll have closed the door on this hell by then?"

"No."

"Then I don't know what I'm going to do," she said and let her arms fall by her sides.

"You'll just work when you can, it's as simple as that."

"It's not simple at all," she replied. "But men rarely understand that."

Wallander didn't want to be pulled into a conversation about the problems of finding childcare, so he quickly changed the topic to the latest events. He told her about the policeman who had seen Louise out at Nybrostrand. He also told her about his conversation with Lone Kjær.

"So Louise exists. I was beginning to think she was a ghost."

"We still don't know if that really is her name, but she exists. I'm sure of it. And she's very interested in our investigation."

"Is she our killer?"

"I suppose we can't rule her out completely, but she could also be someone who has found herself in Svedberg's situation."

"Following in someone else's tracks?"

"Yes, something like that. I want everyone alerted to the fact that she may return to the crime scene."

Wallander now turned the conversation to Westin's phone call. Höglund listened attentively, but he could tell that she was sceptical.

"It's worth looking into," she said when he finished. "But I see a number of potential problems with your idea. For one, do people even write letters any more?"

"It's not perfect, but I see it more as an answer to part of the problem. An idea that may complete the picture, rather than give us the entire solution."

"We've come across a couple of postmen in the course of this investigation already, haven't we?"

"There have been two," Wallander said. "Westin, and the postman that Isa's neighbour, Erik Lundberg, mentioned had come by the day that Isa was taken to the hospital."

"Maybe we should find out if his voice matches the one that made the phone call to the hospital."

It took a moment for Wallander to follow her. "You mean the person who said he was Lundberg?"

"Yes. The postman knew she was in the hospital since Lundberg told him. He also knew that Lundberg knew."

Wallander's head was starting to spin. Was there something to all this? His fatigue was returning and he wasn't sure he could trust his own ability to reason any more.

"Then there's this matter with Svedberg," he said. He told her about the charges that had been filed. "I don't understand why he wouldn't investigate the alleged attack by Nils Stridh on his brother. He even resorted to threatening Stig Stridh, to protect Nils Stridh at all costs. Why? He was lucky the whole thing was dropped by the authorities. He could have been severely reprimanded."

"It doesn't sound like Svedberg at all."

"That's what makes me suspicious. He must have felt pressured to act in that way."

"By Nils Stridh?"

"Who else could it have been?"

They thought for a moment. "It sounds like blackmail to me," she said finally. "But what could Stridh have known about Svedberg?"

"That remains to be seen. But I think Bror Sundelius knows more than he's telling."

"We should put a little pressure on him."

"We will," Wallander answered. "As soon as we have some time to spare."

They had a meeting at 10 a.m. Martinsson, Hansson and the three officers from Malmö were there. Nyberg was still at the crime scene and Holgersson had barricaded herself in her office. She was dealing with the press. Thurnberg was keeping his distance, although Wallander caught sight of him in the hall. The meeting took a light-hearted turn when someone started passing around the complaint that had been filed by the jogger, Nils Hagroth, about Wallander's assault on him at the nature reserve. Wallander was the only one who failed to find it funny, not because he was bothered by the report itself, but because he didn't want his team to become distracted.

They had a lot to do. Wallander and Höglund would drive out to Köpingebro to talk with Malin Skander's parents, while Martinsson and Hansson would handle

Torbjörn Werner's relatives. Wallander nodded off the moment he got into Höglund's car, and she let him sleep.

He woke up when she stopped the car, at a farm just outside Köpingebro. Although it was a beautiful day, an unnatural quiet reigned in the house and garden. All the doors and windows were shut. As they walked up to the main house, a man wearing a dark suit came walking towards them. He was well into middle age, tall and strongly built. His eyes were red. He introduced himself as Lars Skander, father of the bride.

"You'll have to talk to me," he said. "My wife isn't up to it."

"We offer you our condolences," Wallander said. "We're also sorry we couldn't leave you in peace, but it's imperative that we get answers to a few questions."

"Of course, if it can't wait." Lars Skander didn't try to hide either his bitterness or his sorrow. "You have to get this maniac."

The look he gave them was pleading. "How can someone do this? How can someone murder two people about to have their wedding pictures taken?"

Wallander was afraid that the man was going to break down, but Höglund took charge of the situation.

"We're only going to ask you a few essential questions," she said. "Only as much as we need in order to catch whoever did it."

"Can we sit outside?" Lars Skander asked. "It's so oppressive inside."

They walked in silence to the garden at the back of the house. A table and four chairs stood under an old cherry tree.

"Can you think who might have done this?" Wallander asked after they had gone through the most straightforward details about the murdered couple. "Did they have any enemies?"

Lars Skander stared back at him, uncomprehending. "Why would Malin and Torbjörn have had enemies? They were friends with everyone. You couldn't find more peace-loving people."

"It's an important question. I need you to think very carefully before answering."

"I have thought about it. I can't think of a single person."

Wallander moved on. Information, he thought. What we need to know is how the killer got the information he needed.

"When did they choose the day for their wedding?"

"I can't recall exactly. Sometime in May, I think. First week of June at the latest."

"When did they decide upon Nybrostrand as the place where their wedding pictures would be taken?"

"That I don't know. Torbjörn and Malin planned everything carefully in advance, and Torbjörn and Rolf Haag went way back, so I'm sure the plans for the photography were made early."

"Two months ago, then?"

"Something like that."

"Who knew that the wedding pictures were going to be taken on the beach?"

The answer came as a surprise. "Almost no one."

"Why not?"

"They wanted to be left alone during that time, between the church and the reception. Only they and Rolf knew where they were going. They said it would be like a secret honeymoon for a couple of hours."

Wallander and Höglund exchanged glances.

"This is extremely important," Wallander said. "I have to make sure I've understood you correctly. Apart from

Malin and Torbjörn, only the photographer knew where the pictures were going to be taken?"

"That's right."

"And the location was chosen sometime at the end of May or beginning of June."

"Originally, they were going to have the pictures taken up by the Ale stones," Lars Skander said. "But then they changed their minds. It's become commonplace for couples to have their pictures taken up there, apparently."

Wallander frowned. "So you did know where they were going to have the pictures taken."

"I knew about the Ale stones plan. But then they changed their minds, like I said."

Wallander drew his breath in sharply. "When was it that they changed their minds?"

"Just a couple of weeks ago."

"And the new location was kept a secret?"

"Yes."

Wallander studied Lars Skander without speaking. Then he turned to Höglund. He knew they were thinking the same thing. The location had been changed only a few weeks ago, and the couple had been sure it was their secret. But someone had still managed to trespass into their private plans.

"Call Martinsson," Wallander said to Höglund. "Get him to confirm this with the Werner family."

She got up and walked away to make the call.

We haven't been this close before, Wallander thought. He tried to go through all the possibilities in his head. He still didn't know for sure if Rolf Haag had an assistant or not, and it was still possible that a close friend had known about the plans, despite what Lars Skander had told them.

At that moment, a window on the top floor of the house was flung open. A woman leaned out, screaming.

CHAPTER TWENTY-EIGHT

Wallander would retain the image of the screaming woman in his head for a long time. It had been one of the most beautiful days of an unusually warm summer, the garden was green and lush, and Höglund was leaning against the pear tree talking on her mobile phone while he sat across from Lars Skander in a white wooden chair. Both he and Höglund immediately thought it was too late, that the woman who had flung open the window was about to hurl herself down onto the flagstones. They would never get to her in time.

There was a moment of complete calm, as if everything was frozen. Then Höglund dropped her phone and ran towards the window, while Wallander yelled something – he hardly knew what. Lars Skander got to his feet very slowly. The woman in the window continued to scream. She was the mother of the dead bride, and her pain cut that warm August day like a diamond cuts glass. They agreed afterwards that it was her scream that shook them the most.

Höglund disappeared into the house, while Wallander remained under the window with outstretched arms. Lars Skander stood at his side like a ghost, staring up at the distraught woman in the window. Then Höglund appeared out of nowhere behind her and pulled her into the room. Everything went quiet.

When Wallander and Lars Skander entered the bedroom, Höglund was sitting on the floor with her arms around the woman. Wallander went back downstairs and called an ambulance. They returned to the garden at the back of the house once the ambulance had come and gone. Höglund picked up the phone that lay in the grass.

"Martinsson had just answered when it happened. He must have wondered what was going on," she said.

He sat back down in one of the chairs. "Call him," he said.

She sat down across from him. A bee buzzed back and forth between them. Svedberg had a phobia of bees. Now he was dead. That's why they were there, in the Skanders' garden. Many others were also dead. Too many.

"I'm afraid he's going to strike again," Wallander said. "Every second I think I'll get a call telling me he's done it again. I'm going crazy looking for signs that the nightmare will soon be over, that we won't have to kneel over any more bodies of people who have been shot, but I can't find them."

"All of us have that fear," she replied.

That was all that needed to be said. Höglund called Martinsson who, as expected, demanded to know what had happened. Wallander moved his chair over into the shade and took hold of his thoughts.

If the decision to move the photo session to Nybrostrand was made only a couple of weeks ago, who would have had access to that information? Why hadn't anyone confirmed whether or not Rolf Haag had an assistant?

Höglund finished her conversation and also moved her chair into the shade.

"He'll call me back," she said. "Apparently the Werners are both very old. Martinsson can't tell whether they're in shock or just senile."

"What about the question of Rolf Haag's assistant?"

Wallander asked brusquely. "The Malmö police were going to take care of that for us. Do you remember Birch? We worked with him on a case last year."

"How could I forget?"

Birch was a police officer of the old school. It had been a pleasure to meet him.

"He moved to Malmö," she said. "I think he was put in charge of this."

"Then he's already done the work," Wallander said firmly.

He took up his phone and dialled the Malmö police station. He was in luck: Birch was in his office. After exchanging greetings, Birch got straight to the point.

"I called Ystad with my report," he said. "It hasn't reached you?"

"Not yet."

"Then I'll tell you the main points of interest. Rolf Haag's studio is located close to the Nobel plaza, and his main occupation was studio photography, though he also published some travel books."

"I'm going to interrupt you here," Wallander said. "What I really need to know is whether or not he had an assistant."

"Yes, he did."

"What's his name?" Wallander gestured for Höglund to give him a pen.

"Her name is Maria Hjortberg."

"Have you talked to her?"

"I couldn't. She's at her parents' house outside Hudiksvall for the weekend. It's a small place in the woods and they have no phone. She's coming back to Malmö this evening and I'm planning to meet her at the airport. But I very much doubt she's the person who shot her boss and this young couple."

This wasn't the answer that Wallander was looking for, and it irritated him, which he thought was probably a sign that he was a bad policeman.

"What I need to know is whether someone else knew where the wedding pictures were going to be taken."

"I searched the studio last night," Birch said. "It took half the night. I found a letter from Torbjörn Werner to Haag dated 28 July. In it he confirmed the time and place for the photo session."

"Where was it posted?"

"Ystad appears at the top of the page."

"There's no envelope? No postmark?"

"There's a big bag of paper in Haag's office, so it could be in there. Otherwise, I'm afraid it might already have been thrown away. It was written several weeks ago, after all."

"I need that envelope."

"Why is it so important? Can't we assume it was posted in Ystad, since that's where it was written?"

"I need to know if the envelope was opened by someone before it reached Haag. I want our forensics team to have a look at it, if only to rule out this possibility."

Birch didn't need further explanation. He promised to go down to the studio at once.

"That's some theory you've got," he said.

"It's all I have right now," Wallander answered.

Birch promised to call if he found anything.

It was already midday. Wallander went home, fried some eggs for lunch, then lay down to rest for half an hour. At 1.10 p.m. he was back at the police station.

Going through the notes in his office, he decided that the theory about someone having opened the letters needed to be explored before they dismissed it. He went out to the front desk and talked to the girl who filled in for Ebba on the weekends. He asked her if she knew where the post in Ystad was sorted. She didn't.

"Maybe you could find that out for me," Wallander said.

"But it's Sunday," she said.

"A regular working day, as far as I'm concerned."

"But surely not for the post office."

Wallander was starting to get angry, but he controlled himself.

"Post is collected even on Sundays," he said. "At least once. That means that someone is working down at the post office today."

She promised to try to find the answer to his question. Wallander hurried back to his office, feeling that he had disturbed her. Just as he closed his door, it struck him that he was wrong about one thing. He had told Höglund that two postmen already figured in this investigation. But there were actually three. What was it Sture Björklund had said that day? He had the feeling that someone had been at his house when he wasn't there. His neighbours knew how much he valued his privacy. The only person who came by regularly was the postman.

Could it have been the postman who put Svedberg's telescope in Björklund's shed? It wasn't just a wholly unreasonable idea, it was crazy. He was grasping at straws. He growled angrily to himself and started leafing through the various reports that lay on his desk. Before he'd got very far, Martinsson appeared in the doorway.

"How did it go?" Wallander asked.

"Ann-Britt told me about the woman who tried to jump out the window. We didn't have quite as bad a time of it, but it's so tragic. Torbjörn had just taken over the farm. The old couple were getting ready to hand over all the responsibility to the next generation. One son died in a car crash a few years ago. And now they have no one."

"The killer doesn't consider things like that," Wallander said.

Martinsson walked over and stood by the window. Wallander could see how shaken he was. Once upon a time, he had been an eager young recruit with all the best intentions – and at a time when becoming a police officer was no longer seen as something noble. Young people seemed to despise the profession, in fact. But Martinsson held fast to his ideals and genuinely wanted to be a good policeman. It was only during the last few years that Wallander had noticed his faith starting to slip. Now Wallander doubted that Martinsson would make it to retirement.

"He's going to do it again," Martinsson said.

"We don't know that for sure."

"Why wouldn't he? He kills for the sake of killing – there's no other motive."

"We don't know that. We just haven't found his motive yet."

"You're wrong."

Martinsson's last words were delivered with such force that Wallander took them as an accusation.

"In what way am I wrong?"

"Until a few years ago, I would have agreed with you: there's an explanation for all violence. But that just isn't the case any more. Sweden's undergone a fundamental change. A whole generation of young people is losing its way. They don't know what's right or wrong. And I don't know what is the point of being a policeman any more."

"That's a question only you can answer."

"I'm trying."

Martinsson sat down. "You know what Sweden has

become?" he asked. "A lawless nation. Who would have thought that could ever happen?"

"We're not quite there yet," Wallander said. "Even though I agree with you that it's where things seem to be heading. This is why it's so important for us not to give up."

"That's what I used to say to myself. But I'm not sure I think it's possible for us to make a difference any more."

"There isn't one police officer in this country who hasn't asked himself these same questions," Wallander said. "But that doesn't change the fact that we have to keep working, we have to resist the direction our society has taken. We have to stop this madman, and we're very close to him right now. We're going to get him."

"My son is convinced that he wants to be a policeman too," Martinsson said after a while. "He asks me what it's like. I never know what to say."

"Send him to me," Wallander said. "I'll have a talk with him."

"He's eleven."

"That's a good age."

"All right, I'll send him."

Wallander took advantage of the shift in their conversation to return to the matter at hand.

"How much did the Werners know about the photo session?"

"Nothing more than the time."

Wallander let his hands fall onto the table.

"Then we have a breakthrough. Tell everyone I want a meeting at 3 p.m. this afternoon."

Martinsson nodded and got ready to leave. He turned when he reached the door.

"Do you mean what you said about talking to my son?"

"I'll do it the moment all this is over," Wallander said.

"I'll answer all his questions and even let him try on my policeman's cap."

"You have one of those?" Martinsson asked with surprise.

"Somewhere. I just have to find it."

Wallander went to the meeting that afternoon with the feeling that he was going to end up having another confrontation with Thurnberg. Apart from the unfortunate incident in Nybrostrand, there had been no further contact. Wallander was still unsure what would come of the charges the jogger had filed against him. Although Thurnberg hadn't said anything about it, Wallander felt that there was an ongoing war between them.

After the meeting, he realised he was wrong. Thurnberg surprised him by offering support when the others faltered or started to disagree. Whenever he made a comment, it was short and to the point. Perhaps Wallander had been too quick to judge him. Was Thurnberg's arrogance just a bluff, perhaps a sign of insecurity?

Wallander paused for a moment as they were getting ready to leave, wondering if he should say something to Thurnberg. But he couldn't think of anything.

It was now 4.30 p.m. In two hours, Haag's assistant would be arriving at the airport. Wallander tried to call Birch, but there was no answer. He decided to do something he had never done before. He had an old alarm clock in his desk drawer, and he got it out and set it. He locked the door of his office, stretched out on the floor, and pushed an old briefcase under his head for a pillow. Someone knocked on the door right before he fell asleep, but he didn't answer. If he was going to have the energy to keep working, he would need an hour of sleep.

* * *

A rapid succession of disjointed images passed before him. A glimpse of his father, the smell of turpentine, the holiday in Rome. Suddenly Martinsson was there, standing at the foot of the Spanish Steps. He looked like a small child. Wallander called out to him, but Martinsson couldn't hear him. Then the dream was gone.

It took some effort to get to his feet. His joints cracked as he walked to the men's room. He hated this crippling fatigue. It was getting harder and harder to bear as he got older. He splashed cold water on his face and took a long leak. He avoided looking at his face in the mirror. He reached Sturup Airport at 6.45 p.m. When he entered the arrivals area, he spotted Birch's imposing figure almost immediately. He was leaning against the wall, his arms crossed. When he saw Wallander, his sombre face broke into a wide smile.

"You're here as well?"

"I thought you wouldn't mind the company."

"Let's go and grab a cup of coffee. Her plane's not due in for a while."

As they stood in line at the cafeteria, Birch told him he hadn't found the envelope Wallander was hoping for. "But I did talk to one of our forensic technicians," Birch said, as he helped himself to a piece of cake and a Danish pastry, "and he told me I'd never be able to tell if a letter had been opened and resealed. There have been new advances in this area, it seems. No more steam, like in the old days."

"I need that envelope," Wallander said. He forced himself not to follow Birch's example and kept to a cup of coffee. They walked over to the gate. Birch wiped crumbs from his mouth.

"I'm not sure I understand the relevance of the envelope. Of course, I'm also wondering why you decided to come out here. Maria Hjortberg must be important."

Wallander began to tell him about the latest developments as passengers started to stream in from the plane. Birch surprised Wallander by pulling a piece of paper from his coat pocket with Maria Hjortberg's name on it. He walked out into the middle of the gate area and held it up, while Wallander watched from the side.

Maria Hjortberg was a very beautiful woman, with intense dark eyes and long dark hair. She had a rucksack slung over one shoulder. She probably still didn't know that Rolf Haag was dead, but Birch was already telling her. She shook her head in disbelief. Birch took her rucksack, then led her over to Wallander and introduced him.

"Is anyone coming to pick you up?" Birch asked.

"I was going to take the bus."

"Then we'll give you a ride. Unfortunately we have some questions to ask you and they can't wait. But we can do this either at the police station or the studio."

"Is it really true?" she asked in a dazed voice. "Is Rolf really dead?"

"Yes. I'm sorry," Birch said. He asked her if she had more luggage, but she didn't. "How long have you worked as his assistant?"

"Not very long. Since April."

Her answer came as a relief to Wallander. Her grief wouldn't be too intense – unless, of course, she had been in a relationship with him. She told Birch that she preferred to speak to them at the studio.

"You take her in your car," Wallander said to Birch. "I have some phone calls to make."

* * *

Two hours later it became clear that Maria Hjortberg didn't have any crucial information to give them. She hadn't even known about Rolf Haag's photo session at Nybrostrand. He had told her that he would be attending a wedding on Saturday, but she had thought it was a personal invitation, not a job. She had never heard of Malin Skander or Torbjörn Werner. They had a calendar in the office where they noted their appointments, but there was nothing down for Saturday, August 17. When Birch showed her the letter he had found, she merely shook her head.

"He opened all the post," she said. "I helped him with the photo sessions, that was all."

"Who else could have seen this letter?" Wallander asked. "Who else has access to this studio? A cleaner?"

"We do our own cleaning. And clients didn't go into the office."

"So it was just you and Rolf?"

"Yes, although I was hardly ever here."

"Have there been any burglaries?"

"No."

"I looked for the envelope that this letter came in," Birch said. "I couldn't find it anywhere."

"It must have been thrown away," she said. "Rolf likes to keep things tidy. The rubbish is collected every Monday."

Wallander looked at Birch. There was no reason for her to lie. He didn't think they could get any further.

"How close was your relationship?" he asked.

She understood what he was getting at, but didn't seem to mind. "It was nothing personal," she said. "We worked well together and I learned a lot from him. I'm hoping to set up my own studio one day."

It was over. Birch said he would drive her home while

Wallander drove back to Ystad. They parted outside on the street.

"I still don't understand it," she said. "I spent the last two days in an isolated house in an equally isolated forest, and I come back to this."

She began to cry and Birch put an arm around her protectively.

"I'll take her home now," he said. "Will you give me a call later?"

"I'll call you from Ystad," Wallander said. "Where are you going to be?"

"I'm going to search his flat later tonight."

Wallander made sure that he had Birch's mobile number, then crossed the street to his car. It was 10.30 p.m.

Before he had a chance to start the car, the phone buzzed in his pocket and he answered.

"Is this Kurt Wallander?"

"Yes."

"Lone Kjær here. I just wanted to tell you that the woman we're calling Louise is at the Amigo right now. What do you want us to do?"

Wallander made a quick decision. "I'm already in Malmö. I'll be right over. If she leaves, have someone follow her."

"There's a boat leaving at 11 p.m., I think. That brings you to Copenhagen at around 11.45 p.m. I'll meet you on this side."

"Just don't lose her," Wallander said. "I need this one."

"We'll watch over her well, I promise."

Wallander hung up and stared unseeing into the darkness, his excitement growing.

CHAPTER TWENTY-NINE

Wallander picked her out as soon as he got off the boat. She was wearing a leather coat, she had short blond hair, and she was younger than he imagined, and smaller. But there was no doubt that she was in the force. Why, he couldn't have said, but he could always pick out the police officer in a group of strangers.

He stopped in front of her and they exchanged greetings.

"Louise is still at the bar," she said.

"If that really is her name," Wallander said.

"Why is she so important to your investigation?"

Wallander had been thinking about this on the way over. He couldn't connect her to the crimes in any way. All he wanted to do was talk to her. He had so many questions.

"I think she may have interesting information for us. Of course, a bar is hardly the best place for this kind of a conversation."

"You can always use my office."

A police car was waiting for them, and they drove away in silence. Wallander thought about the last time he had been in Copenhagen. It was when he'd attended a performance of *Tosca* at Det Kongelige theatre. He'd gone to a bar after the performance and was dead drunk by the time he caught the last boat for Malmö.

Lone Kjær was speaking to someone on the car radio.

"She's still there," she said, pointing out the window. "It's across the street. Do you want me to wait for you?"

"Why don't you come in?"

The broken neon sign simply read "igo". Wallander was about to meet the woman he'd been wondering about since he'd found her photograph in Svedberg's secret compartment under the floorboards.

They opened the door, pushed aside the heavy red curtain, and entered the bar. It was warm and smoky inside, the lighting was tinged red, and it was full of people. A man walked towards them on his way out.

"All the way at the end of the bar," he said to Lone Kjær.

Wallander nodded to him, then left Kjær by the door and started making his way through the crowd.

He caught sight of her. She was sitting at the far end of the bar. Her hair looked just as it had in the photograph. Wallander stood frozen, watching her. She looked like she was alone, although there were people on either side of her. She was drinking a glass of wine. When she turned her head in his direction, he slipped behind a tall man who was drinking a beer. When Wallander looked again she was staring down at her glass of wine. Wallander turned, nodded to Kjær, and made his way over to Louise.

He was in luck. Just as he reached her, the man on her left stood up and left. Wallander sank down on the bar stool, and she glanced at him quickly.

"I think your name is Louise," Wallander said. "My name is Kurt Wallander, and I'm a police officer from Ystad. I need to speak to you."

She tensed up for a moment, then relaxed and smiled.

"All right, but I'd like to visit the ladies' room first, if you don't mind. I was just about to get up when you sat down."

She got up and walked towards the back of the room, where there were signs to the men's and women's lavatories.

The bartender caught Wallander's eye, but he shook his head to indicate he wouldn't be ordering anything. She doesn't speak with a Scanian dialect, he thought. But she is Swedish.

Kjær came closer. Wallander gave her a sign that everything was proceeding smoothly. The clock hanging on the wall advertised a brand of whisky that Wallander had never heard of. Four minutes went by. Wallander looked over at the area leading to the lavatories. A man walked by, then another. He tried to concentrate on his questions, wondering which he should ask first.

Seven minutes had gone by now, and he realised something was wrong. He got up and walked towards the lavatories. Kjær appeared at his side.

"Go into the ladies' room and look around."

"Why? She hasn't come out again. I would have seen her if she had tried to leave."

"Something's wrong," Wallander said. "I want you to check for me."

Kjær went into the women's lavatory and Wallander waited. She was back again almost immediately.

"She's not in there."

"Damn it," Wallander said. "Is there a window in there?"

Without waiting for an answer he jerked the door open and went in. Two women were adjusting their make-up in front of the mirror. Wallander hardly noticed them. Louise was gone. He ran out again.

"She must still be here somewhere," Kjær said in disbelief. "I would have seen her."

"But she isn't," Wallander said.

He made his way to the front door through a throng of people that seemed to be getting thicker all the time. The bouncer looked like a wrestler.

"Ask him," Wallander said. "We're looking for a woman with medium-length dark hair. Did anyone like that leave recently? It would have been ten minutes ago at the most."

Kjær asked the bouncer but he shook his head, and said something that Wallander didn't catch.

"He's sure," she yelled over the noise in the room.

Wallander turned and started pushing his way through the crowd again. He was looking for her, but part of him knew she was already gone.

Finally he gave up, and made his way over to the bartender. He couldn't see the glass of wine Louise had been drinking.

"Where's the glass that was here?" he asked.

"I've already washed it."

Wallander waved to Kjær and she came over. He pointed to the top of the bar.

"I don't know how likely we are to get anything, but let's try for some fingerprints."

"It'll be a first for me," she said. "I've never had to cordon off a section of a bar before. But I'll make sure it's done."

Wallander left and walked out into the street. He was drenched with sweat and shaking with anger. How could he have been so stupid? That smile, her willingness to speak with him, just a trip to the ladies' room first. Why hadn't he seen through it?

Kjær came out after ten minutes. "I really don't know how she did it," she said. "I know I would have seen her if she had tried to leave."

But the pieces were starting to fit together. Slowly Wallander understood what must have happened. There was only one answer. It was so unexpected that he needed time to grasp its full implication.

"Can we go to your office?" he asked. "I need time to think."

When they got there, Kjær brought him a cup of coffee and repeated her question.

"I just don't understand how she got away without being seen."

"That's because she never left," Wallander said. "Louise is still in there somewhere."

She looked at him with surprise. "Still there? Then why did we come here?"

Wallander shook his head dully. He was frustrated at his lack of awareness. He had sensed that there was something strange about her hair the first time he'd seen her picture in Svedberg's flat.

I should have seen it back then, he thought. That it was a wig.

She repeated her last question.

"In a way, Louise is still in the bar," he answered, "because Louise is just an act, put on by someone else. A man. That wrestler who was guarding the door said three men left the bar during the last ten minutes. One of them was Louise, with her wig in her pocket and all her make-up wiped off."

She didn't believe him, and he was too tired to go into more detail. The important thing was that he knew it. Still, he owed her an explanation. She had helped him. Although it was past midnight, he continued to explain.

"When she went into the lavatory, she took off her make-up and the wig, and then she walked out again," Wallander said. "She probably altered something about the way her clothing looked as well. Neither of us noticed anything, because we were waiting for a woman to come out. Who would have noticed a man?"

"The Amigo doesn't have a reputation as a transvestite bar."

"He may simply have gone there to play the role of a woman," Wallander said thoughtfully. "Not to be among his own kind."

"What does this mean for your investigation?"

"I don't know. It probably means a great deal, but I haven't thought it through yet."

She looked down at her watch.

"The last boat to Malmö has already left. The earliest leaves at 4.45 a.m. in the morning."

"I'll stay in a hotel," Wallander said.

She shook her head. "You can sleep on the sofa at my place," she said. "My husband comes home around this time. He's a waiter. We have sandwiches and a beer together before we go to bed."

They left the police station.

Wallander slept uneasily. At one point he got up and walked over to the window. He stared down at the empty street and wondered why all city streets resembled each other at night. He kept waiting for someone to appear, but all was quiet. He felt his anxiety grow stronger. The victims so far had been dressed up in costume. Just like Louise. When Wallander had told her who he was, she left.

It was him, he thought. There's no other explanation. I had the killer by my side without knowing it. But I didn't manage to see through his disguise, and he disappeared. Now he knows we're closing in, but he also knows we haven't guessed his real identity.

Wallander went back to the sofa and dozed until it was time to take the ferry back to Malmö.

He called Birch when he got to the other side, hoping he was an early riser. Birch answered and said he was just drinking his morning coffee.

"What happened to you last night? I thought we were going to be in touch."

Wallander explained what had happened.

"Were you really that close?"

"I let myself be fooled. I should have stood guard by the lavatories."

"It's easy to say so in hindsight," Birch said. "You're back in Malmö now, aren't you? You must be tired."

"The worst thing is that I can't get the car started. I left my lights on."

"I'll come over. I have jump leads," Birch said. "Where are you?"

Wallander gave him directions.

It took Birch less than 20 minutes to get there, during which time Wallander napped in his car.

Birch looked closely at Wallander. "You should really try to sleep for a few hours," he said. "It won't help matters if you collapse."

While they put the jump leads on, Birch told him he had searched Haag's flat but hadn't found anything significant.

"We'll do another search of the studio and his flat," Birch said. "And we'll stay in touch."

"I'll tell you how things go at our end," Wallander said.

He left Malmö. It was 6.25 a.m. At the turn-off for Jägersro, he pulled over to the side of the road and called Martinsson.

"I've been trying to reach you," Martinsson said. "We were supposed to have a meeting last night, but no one could contact you."

"I was in Denmark," Wallander said. "Tell everyone I want a meeting at 8 a.m."

"Has anything happened?"

"Yes, but I'll tell you about it later."

Wallander continued on towards Ystad. The weather was still beautiful. There were no clouds in the sky and no wind. He was feeling less tired, and his mind was starting to work again. He went through the meeting with Louise over and over, trying to home in on the face behind the wig and make-up. Sometimes he almost had it.

He reached Ystad at 7.40 a.m. Ebba was at the front desk. She sneezed.

"Caught a cold?" he asked. "In the middle of summer?"

"Even an old bag like me can have allergies," she replied good-naturedly. Then she looked sternly at him.

"You haven't had a wink of sleep, have you?"

"I was in Copenhagen. That's not conducive to a good night's sleep."

She didn't seem to see the humour in this. "If you don't start taking your health seriously, you'll pay for it," she said. "Mark my words."

He didn't answer. He was sometimes annoyed by her ability to see right through him. She was right, of course. He thought about the clumps of sugar in his bloodstream.

He got himself a cup of coffee and went into his office. Soon his colleagues would be waiting for him in the conference room. He would have to tell them what had happened the night before, how the killer had been there, gone to the lavatory, and disappeared.

A woman went up in smoke by taking on the form of a man. There was no Louise any more. All they had was an unknown man who simply removed his wig and disappeared without a trace. A man who had already killed eight people, and who might be preparing to strike again.

He thought about Isa Edengren, curled up in the cave behind the ferns, and shivered.

What do I tell them, Wallander thought. How do I find the right path through this unknown territory? We're pressed for time and can't afford to think through every possibility, every possible lead. How can I know which is the right way?

Wallander left his own questions unanswered and went to the men's room. He stared at his image in the mirror. He was swollen and pale, with watery bags under his eyes. For the first time in his life, the sight of his face made him nauseated.

I have to catch this killer, he thought. If only so I can go on medical leave and start taking control of my health.

It was now just after 8 a.m. Wallander left the men's room.

Everyone was already in the conference room when he entered. He felt like the tardy schoolboy, or perhaps the flustered teacher. There was Thurnberg, fingering his perfectly knotted tie. Holgersson smiled her quick, nervous smile. The others greeted him to the best of their exhausted capability: simply by being there.

Wallander sat down and told them exactly where things stood. How he had been inches away from the killer, and how he had let him slip away under his very nose. He told the story calmly, starting with Maria Hjortberg and ending with Louise's smile and her apparent willingness to talk to him, saying she just had to visit the lavatory first.

"He must have removed the wig while he was in there," he said. "It was the same one as in the picture, by the way. He must have wiped off his make-up as well. He's careful by nature, and he must have foreseen the risk of being recognised. He probably had some make-up remover with him. I didn't notice him slip out because I was waiting for a woman."

"What about his clothes?" Höglund said.

"Some kind of trouser suit," Wallander said. "And low-heeled shoes. I suppose it might have been obvious that he was a man if one knew to look carefully. But you couldn't see while he sat at the bar."

Höglund's was the only question.

"I have no doubts that he's the one," Wallander said after a pause. "Why else would he leave like that?"

"Did you consider the fact that he might have been on your boat this morning?" Hansson asked.

"I did think of it," Wallander said. "But by then it was too late."

They should blame me for this, he thought. For this and for many other aspects of the investigation. I should have known it was a wig from the moment I first saw the photograph. If we had known we were looking for a man from the beginning it would all have been different. The search for him would have taken precedence over everything else. But I didn't see it. I didn't understand what I was looking at.

Wallander poured himself a glass of mineral water. "We have to assume he could strike again at any moment, so we have no time to lose. We have to re-examine the facts of this investigation to see if we can find any trace of this man."

"The photograph," Martinsson said. "We can manipulate it on the computer and make it look more like a man."

"That's at the top of our list right now," Wallander said. "We'll have that done as soon as we leave this meeting. A face can be significantly altered with make-up and a wig, but it can't be completely changed."

There was a new surge of energy in the room. Wallander didn't want to keep them any longer, but Holgersson sensed he was about to bring the meeting to a close, and raised her hand.

"I want to remind you that Svedberg's funeral is tomorrow at 2 p.m. With the best interests of this investigation in mind, I'm cancelling the reception afterwards."

No one had any comments. Everyone seemed eager to leave.

Wallander went to his office to get his coat. There was something he wanted to follow up on even though it would most likely lead nowhere. He was just about to leave when Thurnberg appeared.

"Do we really have the resources to manipulate that photograph here?" he asked.

"Martinsson knows the most about that sort of thing," Wallander said. "If he has any doubts about his ability to do the job properly, he'll turn it over to the technicians, don't worry."

Thurnberg nodded. "I just wanted to make sure." But he clearly had something else to say. "I don't think you should blame yourself for letting him slip away in the bar. You couldn't have been expected to see through his disguise."

It seemed as if he really meant it. Was this his way of making amends? Wallander decided to accept him at face value.

"I appreciate your opinion," he said. "This investigation has been far from clear-cut."

"I'll get in touch if I think of anything that might be helpful," Thurnberg said.

Wallander left the station. He hesitated for a moment in the car park before deciding to walk. All he had to do was walk downtown, and he had to keep moving or else sleep would overtake him.

It took him ten minutes to reach the red building that was the central postal depot. Post was being unloaded from yellow postal vans. Wallander had never been down here before. He looked around for an entrance and found one. It was locked. He pressed a small buzzer and was let in.

The man who greeted him was the manager, a young man hardly more than 30 years old. His name was Kjell Albinsson, and he made a good impression. Albinsson escorted him to his office, where a fan placed on top of a filing cabinet was going at high speed. Wallander got out a pen and paper, wondering how he should go about phrasing his questions, such as "Do your postal workers ever open other people's post?" It was an impossible question to ask, an insult to the profession. Wallander thought of Westin, who would no doubt have been deeply offended. He decided instead to start from the beginning.

It was 10.43 a.m. on Monday, 19 August.

CHAPTER THIRTY

A map hung on the wall in Albinsson's room. Wallander started there, asking him about the rural postal routes. Albinsson wanted to know why the police were so interested in this information, and Wallander came close to telling him. Then he realised how preposterous it would sound if he said that the police suspected one of his staff of being a mass murderer, so he kept his explanations as vague as possible, making sure that Albinsson knew not to expect further clarification.

Albinsson described the various routes to him with great enthusiasm. Wallander took occasional notes.

"How many postmen work here?" Wallander asked after Albinsson had finished with the map and sat down at his desk.

"Eight."

"Do you have their names written down anywhere? Photographs would be helpful too."

"The Post Office is a proactive business these days," Albinsson said. "We have an information brochure that I think is just what you're looking for."

As Albinsson left the room, Wallander thought to himself that he had just had a stroke of luck. From the photographs of the postal workers he would immediately be able to determine if the man in Copenhagen worked here or not. Then he would have identified the killer in a single stroke.

Albinsson came back with the brochure, and Wallander looked around for his glasses, to no avail.

"Maybe mine will work," Albinsson suggested. "What's your prescription?"

"I don't know, around ten-point-five, I think."

Albinsson looked at him curiously. "That would mean you were blind," he said. "I take it you mean one-point-five. I'm a two, so go ahead and try them."

Wallander put on the glasses and found that they helped. He unfolded the brochure and looked closely at the pictures of the eight postal workers. There were four men and four women. Wallander studied the men's faces, but none of them bore any likeness to Louise. He hesitated for a moment at the face of a man called Lars-Göran Berg, but quickly realised that it couldn't be him. He looked briefly at the women, and recognised one who regularly delivered post to his father's house in Löderup.

"Can I keep this?" he asked.

"You can have more copies if you like."

"Just one will do."

"Have I answered all your questions?"

"Not quite. There's one more point I need to cover. All of the post is sorted here in this building, right? Do the postmen sort their own post?"

"Yes."

He gave the glasses back to Albinsson. "That's all. I won't keep you from your work any longer."

He stood up. "What is it you're trying to find out?" Albinsson asked.

"Just what I said. This is a routine check."

Albinsson shook his head. "I don't believe that. Why would the chief inspector on a pressing murder case drop by as a matter of routine? You're trying to solve the murder of one of your colleagues, as well as that of those young-sters in the Hagestad nature reserve, and the newly-weds. Your visit here has something to do with all that, doesn't it?"

"That wouldn't change the fact that this is still a routine check," Wallander said.

"I think you're looking for something in particular," Albinsson said.

"I've told you as much as I can."

Albinsson didn't ask any more questions. They parted at the front door, and Wallander walked out into the sunny yard. What a strange August this is, he thought. The heat just won't let up, and there's never even a hint of a breeze.

He walked back to the station, wondering whether to wear his uniform at Svedberg's funeral. He also wondered whether Höglund was regretting having promised to give a speech, let alone one she hadn't written herself.

When he walked into reception, Ebba said that Holgersson wanted to speak to him. Ebba seemed depressed.

"How are things with you these days?" he asked. "We never have time to talk any more."

"Things are as they are," she said.

It was the kind of thing his father used to say when he spoke of getting old.

"As soon as all this is over, we'll talk," he said.

She nodded. Wallander sensed that something was differ-ent about her, but he had no time to ask more. He went to Holgersson's office. Her door was wide open as usual.

"This is a significant breakthrough," she said as soon as he had sat down in the comfortable armchair across from her. "Thurnberg is impressed."

"Impressed by what?"

"You'll have to ask him that. But you're living up to your reputation."

Wallander was surprised. "Are things really so bad?"

"I'd say just the opposite."

Wallander made an impatient gesture with his hand. He didn't want to talk about his own performance, especially since he knew it was seriously flawed.

"The national chief of police will officiate at the funeral tomorrow," she said, "together with the minister of justice. They're landing at Sturup tomorrow morning at 11 a.m. I'll be there to greet them and escort them back here. They have both requested a briefing on the state of our investigation, so I've scheduled that for 11.30 a.m., in the large conference room. It'll be you, me, and Thurnberg."

"Could you handle it on your own, or with Martinsson? He can speak more eloquently than I can."

"You're the one in charge of the investigation," she said. "It'll only take half an hour, then we'll break for lunch. They fly back to Stockholm straight after the funeral."

"I'm dreading this funeral," Wallander said. "It's different when the dead person has been brutally murdered."

"You're thinking about your old friend Rydberg?"

"Yes."

The phone rang and she picked it up, listened for a moment, and then asked the caller to get back to her later.

"Have you chosen the music?" Wallander asked.

"We let the cantor choose it for us. I'm sure it'll be appropriate. What is it usually? Bach and Buxtehude? And then the old standard hymns, of course."

Wallander got up to leave. "I hope you'll make the most of this opportunity," he said. "What with the national chief of police and the minister of justice here."

"What opportunity?"

"To tell them they can't let things go on like this. The cuts in staff and funding are starting to look like a conspiracy to make us unable to do our jobs, not like a matter of fiscal responsibility. The criminal element is taking over. Tell them it will be the end of all of us if they don't do something to stop it. We're not quite there yet, but we will be soon."

Holgersson shook her head in amazement. "I don't think we see eye to eye on this."

"I know you've noticed it too."

"Why don't you tell them yourself?"

"I probably will. But I have a killer to track down in the meantime."

"Not you," she corrected him. "We."

Wallander went to Martinsson's office. Höglund was with him and they were studying a picture on the computer screen: Louise's face. Martinsson had erased her hair.

"I'm using a programme developed by the FBI," Martinsson told him. "We can add details such as hairstyles, beards and moustaches. You can even add pimples."

"I don't think he had any of those," Wallander said. "The only thing I'm interested in is what was under his wig."

"I called a wigmaker in Stockholm about that," Höglund said. "I asked him how much hair you could hide under a wig, but it was hard to get a clear answer from him."

"So he could have bushy hair for all we know," Wallander said.

"The programme can do other things, too," Martinsson said "We can fold out the ears and flatten the nose."

"We don't have to fold out or flatten anything," Wallander said. "The photograph is already so similar to his face."

"What about the eye colour?" Martinsson asked.

428

Wallander thought for a moment. "Blue," he answered.

"Did you see her teeth?"

"Not her teeth. His teeth."

"Did you see them?"

"Not very closely. But I think they were white and well kept."

"Psychopaths are often fanatics about oral hygiene," Martinsson said.

"We don't know if he's a psychopath," Wallander said.

Martinsson entered the information about eyes and teeth into the computer.

"How old was she?" Höglund asked.

"You mean he," Wallander said.

"But the person you saw was a woman. You only realised later that she had to be a man."

She was right. He had seen a woman, not a man, and that was the image he had to return to in order to judge the person's age.

"It's always hard to tell with women who wear a lot of make-up," he said. "But the photograph we have must be fairly recent. I would say around 40 years old."

"How tall was she?" Martinsson asked.

Wallander tried hard to remember. "I'm not sure," he answered. "But I think she was quite tall, between 170 and 175 centimetres."

Martinsson entered in the numbers. "What about her body?" he said. "Was she wearing falsies?"

Wallander realised he hadn't noticed very much about her at all.

"I don't know," he said.

Höglund looked at him with a hint of a smile. "The latest studies indicate that the first thing a man notices about a woman is her breasts," she said. "He registers whether they are small or large, then usually proceeds to her legs, and finally her behind."

Martinsson chuckled from his place at the computer. Wallander saw the absurdity of the situation. He was supposed to describe a woman who was actually a man, but who should still be regarded as a woman, at least until Martinsson had finished entering the data into the computer.

"She was wearing a jacket," he said. "Maybe I'm an unusual male, but I really didn't notice her breasts. And the bar hid most of her body. I didn't see much of her when she stood up and went to the ladies' room, because she was swallowed up by the crowd. It was a full house."

"We have quite a lot already," Martinsson said reassuringly. "We just have to work out what kind of hairstyle he had under the wig."

"There must be a hundred different styles," Wallander said. "Let's try circulating the face without any hair. Someone may recognise his features."

"According to the FBI, that's almost impossible."

"Let's do it anyway."

Something else occurred to Wallander. "Who questioned the nurse who received the call from the man pretending to be Erik Lundberg?"

"I did," Höglund said.

"What did she remember about his voice?"

"Not very much. He had a Scanian accent."

"Did it sound real?"

She looked at him with surprise. "Actually, no. She said there was something funny about his dialect, although she couldn't put her finger on it."

"So it could have been fake?"

"Yes."

"Was it a low or high voice?"

"Low."

Wallander thought back to his time in the Amigo. Louise had smiled at him, then excused herself, and her voice had been deep, although she had tried to make it sound feminine.

"I think we can assume it was him," Wallander said. "Even though we have no proof."

He told them about his visit to the postal depot. "I've only been able to find one common denominator so far," he said. "Isa Edengren and Sture Björklund had the same postman. The other people in this investigation bring the number of postmen involved to three, in addition to someone who works outside of Ystad altogether. It therefore seems reasonable to ditch this theory, since it's absurd to think there's a conspiracy between postal workers."

He sat back in his chair and looked at the other two. "I see no pattern yet," he said. "We have costumes and secrets, but nothing more."

"What happens if we ignore the costumes?" Höglund said. "What do we have then?"

"Young people," Wallander said. "Happy people, having a party or getting married."

"You don't think Haag is a target?"

"No. He falls outside the parameters."

"What about Isa Edengren?"

"She was supposed to have been there."

"That changes our picture," Höglund said. "A new motive emerges. She's not allowed to escape, but escape what? Is it revenge, or hatred? There also doesn't seem to be any point of connection between the young people and the wedding couple. And then there's Svedberg. What lead was he following?"

"I think I can answer the last question," Wallander said. "At least for now. Svedberg knew this man who dresses as a woman. Something made him suspicious. Over the course of the summer, his investigation confirmed his suspicion. That's why he was killed – he knew too much. But he didn't have time to tell us what he knew."

"But what does it all add up to?" Martinsson said. "Svedberg told his cousin he was involved with a woman called Louise. Now it turns out she's a man. Svedberg must have known that after all these years, so where does that lead us? Was Svedberg a transvestite? Was he homosexual after all?"

"A number of explanations are possible," Wallander said. "I doubt that Svedberg had a passion for dressing up in women's clothing, but he may very well have been homosexual without any of us knowing about it."

"One person in our investigation seems to be growing in importance," Höglund said.

Wallander knew to whom she was referring: Bror Sundelius.

"I agree," he said. "We need to maintain that end of the investigation, not as an alternative but as part of our search for the killer. We need to know more about the people involved in charges filed against Svedberg. He may very well have been the victim of blackmail or had some other reason to keep Stridh quiet."

"If Bror Sundelius has deviant tendencies then it all starts to make sense," Martinsson said.

Wallander bristled at Martinsson's words. "In this day and age, homosexuality can hardly be regarded as 'deviant'," he said. "Maybe in the 1950s, but not now. That people might still want to conceal their sexual preferences is another matter entirely."

Martinsson registered Wallander's disapproval, but said nothing.

"The question is what connected these three men, Sundelius, Stridh, and Svedberg," Wallander said. "A bank director, a petty criminal and a policeman, whose surnames all start with the letter 'S'."

"I wonder if Louise was in the picture at that point," Höglund said.

Wallander made a face. "We have to call him something else," he said. "Louise disappeared in the lavatory of that bar back in Copenhagen. We'll confuse ourselves if we don't use another name."

"What about Louis?" Martinsson said. "That would make it easy."

They all agreed, and Louise was renamed. Now they were looking for a man called Louis. They decided that Martinsson should spend part of his time keeping an eye on Sundelius. Wallander left the room and went back to his office. He bumped into Edmundsson on his way.

"We didn't find anything in that area of the nature reserve you wanted us to search," he said. It took Wallander a moment to remember what this had been about.

"Nothing?"

"We found a wad of chewing tobacco by a tree," Edmundsson said. "That was it."

Wallander looked closely at him. "I hope you collected that wad of chewing tobacco, or at least alerted Nyberg."

Edmundsson surprised him with his answer. "Actually, I did."

"This could be more important than you realise," he said.

He kept walking towards his office. He was right. The killer had been there that night, hiding where he had the best view of their comings and goings. He had spat out a wad of chewing tobacco, just like on the beach. And later he had turned up outside the police barricades at Nybrostrand, although this time he was disguised as a woman.

He's following us, Wallander thought. He's somewhere close by, both a step ahead and a step behind. Is he trying to find out what we know? Or is he trying to prove to himself that we can't find him?

Something occurred to him and he called Martinsson. "Is there anyone who has shown an unexpected interest in our investigation?"

"You mean like a journalist?"

"Let people know to be on the lookout for someone who takes an interest in the case, something out of the ordinary. I don't think I can give you a more precise description – just someone who seems odd."

Martinsson promised to pass it on. Wallander hung up.

It was midday and he felt nauseated with hunger. He left the station and walked to a restaurant in the middle of town. He got back at 1.30 p.m., took off his coat, and looked through the brochure that he had picked up at the post office.

The first postman was called Olov Andersson. Wallander picked up the receiver and dialled his number, wondering how long he could keep going.

He returned to Ystad shortly after 11 a.m. Since he didn't want to risk running into the policeman who had found him in Copenhagen, he took the ferry from Helsingør. When he arrived at Helsingborg, he took a taxi to Malmö where his car was parked. The unexpected inheritance he'd received from a relative meant he no longer had to worry about money. He watched the car park from a distance before approaching his car. There had never been a moment when he doubted that he would get away with it, just as he hadn't doubted the fact that he would get away the night before at the Amigo. That had been a major triumph. He hadn't expected a policeman to stroll in and sit down beside him, but he hadn't panicked or lost control of himself, only done what he had long ago planned to do in such a situation.

He walked calmly into the women's lavatory, took off his wig and tucked it inside his shirt above his belt, removed his make-up with the cream he always carried with him, and then left, timing his departure so it coincided with a man leaving the men's room. He still had the ability to escape. It had not failed him.

When he was certain that the car park wasn't under surveillance, he got into the car and drove to Ystad. Once he was back at home he'd taken a long shower and crawled into bed in the soundproofed room. There was so much he had to think through. He didn't know how that policeman Wallander had found him. He must inadvertently have left a trace of himself behind. That upset him more than it worried him. The only thing he could think of was that Svedberg had kept a photo of him in his flat after all. A photograph of Louise. He hadn't found it during his search. Nonetheless, this thought calmed him. The policeman was expecting to talk to a woman. Nothing suggested that he had seen through the disguise, although by now he might have put two and two together.

The thought of his narrow escape excited him. It spurred him on, although he now encountered a problem. He hadn't selected any more people to kill. According to his original plans, he was going to wait for a whole year before acting again. He needed to plan his next move carefully so he could outdo himself. He would wait just long enough for people to start to forget about him, and then he would show himself again.

But his recent encounter with the policeman changed everything. Now he couldn't stand the idea of waiting a whole year before striking again. He stayed in bed all afternoon, analysing his situation methodically. There were a number of courses of action to be evaluated. A few times he almost gave up.

At last he thought he had hit upon a solution. It went against the original plan, which was its biggest flaw, but he felt he had no alternative. It was also a great temptation. The more he thought about it, the more it struck him as ingenious. He would create something completely unexpected, a riddle no one would see through.

It would have to be Wallander, the policeman, and soon. Svedberg's funeral was tomorrow. He would need that day for his preparations. He smiled at the thought that Svedberg would actually come to his aid. During the funeral, the policeman's flat would be empty. Svedberg had told him on several occasions that Wallander was divorced and lived alone. He would wait no longer than Wednesday. The idea filled him with exhilaration. He would shoot him first, and then give him a disguise. A very particular disguise.

CHAPTER THIRTY-ONE

Monday had been a wasted day. That was the first thought that went through Wallander's mind when he woke up Tuesday morning. For the first time in a long while he felt fully rested, as he'd left the station at 9 p.m. the night before.

It was 6 a.m. and he lay motionless in his bed. Through the gap in the curtains he saw blue sky. Monday had been a wasted day because it hadn't brought them closer to their goal. He'd spoken to two of the postal workers assigned to rural routes, but neither one had been able to tell him anything of significance. Around 6 p.m., Wallander had conferred with the other members of the investigative team. By then they had covered all six postal workers. But what were they supposed to have asked, and what answers had they been expecting?

Wallander was forced to admit that his hunch had been wrong. And it wasn't just the postmen who had proved a dead end; Lone Kjær had called from Copenhagen to say that they hadn't been able to recover any prints from the bar top at the Amigo. They had even worked on the bar stool. Wallander knew it had been unlikely that they'd get anything, but he'd still been hoping that they would. A print would have identified the killer beyond doubt. Now they had to carry around that vague and disconcerting anxiety that this lead would also turn out to be false; that the man in the dark wig was only a step along the path, not the answer itself.

They'd spent a long time wondering whether or not to publish the digitally enhanced picture of Louis – too long for Wallander's liking. He'd sent for Thurnberg. The members of his team had wildly differing opinions, but Wallander had insisted that it should be published. Someone might recognise the face now that the wig was gone. All they needed was one person. Thurnberg had joined the discussion for the first time, supporting Wallander. In his opinion, the picture should be released to the press as soon as possible.

They decided to wait until Wednesday, the day after the funeral.

"People love these composite sketches," Wallander had said. "It doesn't matter if it really looks like him or not. There's something extraordinary, almost magical about this act of throwing out a half-finished face in the hope that someone will bite."

They had worked non-stop all Monday afternoon. Hansson had searched the various databases of the Swedish Police for information on Bror Sundelius. As expected, there was nothing. In terms of digital records at least, he was clean. They'd decided that Wallander would go back and talk to him on Wednesday, pressing him harder this time. Wallander knew that Sundelius was coming to the funeral, and he'd reminded the others of this fact.

Other things had come up on that Monday afternoon, even though Wallander now saw the day as a waste. Shortly after 4 p.m., a journalist from one of the national papers had called him to say that Eva Hillström had been in contact with them. The parents of the young murder victims were planning to criticise the police investigation. They didn't think the police had done enough, and they felt they had been denied information that they'd had a right to. The reporter had told him that their criticism was strong. In addition, Eva Hillström seemed to regard Wallander as the person responsible, or rather, the one who was not responsible enough. It would be a big article, and it would come out the day after next. The reporter had called to give Wallander a chance to respond to the allegations. Somewhat to his own surprise, Wallander had sharply declined to comment. He'd said he would be in touch when he had read the article and seen for himself what the parents had to say. If he had any reason to disagree with their claims, he would send a rebuttal. End of story.

After speaking to the journalist he'd felt a new knot in his already overtaxed stomach. This one took up residence right next to the fear that the killer was going to strike again. He'd gone over it all again in his mind, asking himself if they could have done more, if they had really done everything in their power up to this point. The reason that they hadn't caught the killer yet was because the investigation was so complicated, not because of laziness, lack of focus, or poor police work. They had so little to go on. The internal blunders made along the way were another matter. The perfect investigation didn't exist; not even Eva Hillström could claim otherwise.

After the 6 p.m. meeting, when they had ruled out the postal workers and studied different images of Louis with exhausted eyes, Wallander told them about his conversation with the newspaper reporter. Thurnberg, immediately concerned, had questioned Wallander's decision not to respond to the allegations.

"There just isn't time to do everything at once," Wallander had said. "We're so overworked right now that even these allegations will have to wait."

"The national chief of police is going to be here tomorrow," Thurnberg had replied, "and the minister of justice. It's particularly unfortunate that this article is going to coincide with their visit."

Wallander had suddenly understood Thurnberg's real concern. "Not even a shadow of these allegations falls on you," he'd said. "It seems that Eva Hillström and the other parents are critical of the work of the police, not the chief prosecutor's office."

Thurnberg had had nothing else to say. Shortly afterwards they'd called it a day. Höglund had followed Wallander out into the hall and told him that Thurnberg had been asking questions about events in the nature reserve on the day the jogger, Nils Hagroth, claimed to have been assaulted by Wallander. On hearing this, Wallander had been hit by another a wave of exhaustion. Didn't they have enough on their plates without Nils Hagroth's absurd charges? That had been the moment when, despite the consistently high level of activity, the entire day had begun to seem like a waste.

Wallander reluctantly got out of bed at 7.30 a.m. He was already dreading this day. His uniform hung on the cupboard door. He had to put it on now, because there wouldn't be enough time between his meeting with the national chief of police and the minister of justice and the funeral itself. He looked at himself in the mirror after he put it on. The trousers strained alarmingly across his belly. He would have to leave the top button undone. He couldn't remember when he had last worn his uniform but it must have been a long time ago.

On the way to the station he stopped at a news-stand and bought a paper. The reporter had not been exaggerating.

It was a big article, with pictures. The parents' allegations were threefold. First, the police had waited too long before acting on the disappearance of their children. Second, they felt the investigation had not been as organised as it could have been. Third, they felt they had been poorly informed of the developments in the case.

The national chief isn't going to be very happy, Wallander thought. It's not going to matter if we tell him that these allegations are unjust. The fact that they've been made will hurt the police.

Wallander approached the station feeling shaken and angry. It was just before 8 a.m. It was going to be a long and depressing day, although the weather was still warm and beautiful.

Holgersson called him from her car at 11.30 a.m. They were on their way from Sturup and would arrive at the station in five minutes. Wallander walked out to reception to greet them. Thurnberg was already there. They exchanged pleasantries, neither of them mentioning the article. The car pulled up outside and everyone got out. The national chief of police and the minister of justice were appropriately dressed for a funeral. Everyone was introduced, and they all proceeded to Holgersson's office for coffee. Before they entered the room, Holgersson pulled Wallander aside.

"They read the article on the plane," she said, "and the national chief is not pleased."

"What about the minister?"

"She seemed more eager to hear your side of the story before giving an opinion."

"Should I say something?"

"No. Only if they bring it up."

They sat down with their coffee and Wallander received

their condolences for Svedberg's death. After that, it was his turn to say something. As usual he had forgotten to bring the piece of paper he'd scribbled some notes on. But it didn't really matter. He knew what he wanted to tell them: that they had a lead. They had identified the killer. Things were picking up, there were new developments.

"This whole matter is very unfortunate," the national chief said when Wallander finished. "A policeman and some innocent youngsters murdered. I hope we can count on you to wrap this up shortly. I'm pleased to hear you have a breakthrough."

It was clear that he was extremely anxious.

"No society will ever be free of lunatics," the minister said. "Mass murders happen in democracies and dictatorships the world over."

"And lunatics don't act according to a predictable pattern," Wallander added. "They can't be easily categorised. They plan their deeds carefully, often appearing from nowhere, with no previous criminal record."

"Community policing," the national chief said. "That's where it has to start."

Wallander didn't quite understand the link between lunatics and community policing but he said nothing. The minister asked Thurnberg some questions, then it was over. As they were about to leave for lunch, the national chief noticed that some papers were missing from his briefcase.

"I have a temporary secretary right now," he said glumly. "I never know where anything is. I hardly have time to learn their names before they leave again."

As they toured the station, the minister of justice fell in beside Wallander.

"I heard someone's filed charges against you. Is there anything to it?"

"I'm not concerned about it," Wallander said. "The man was trespassing at the scene of a murder investigation. There was no assault involved."

"I didn't think so," she said encouragingly.

Once they had returned to the reception area, the national chief asked Wallander the same question.

"The timing is very unfortunate," he said.

"It's always unfortunate," Wallander said. "But I have to give you the same answer that I gave the minister. The allegations of an assault are unfounded."

"Then what was it?"

"A man who was trespassing on the scene of a police investigation."

"It's important for the police to maintain a good relationship with the public and the media."

"Once this case is completed, I'll issue a statement to the papers," Wallander said.

"I'd like to see that before it goes to press," the national chief said.

Wallander promised to oblige. He declined to accompany them to lunch, and stopped by Höglund's office instead. It was empty. He returned to his own office and sat down at his desk. The germ of an idea was dancing somewhere deep in his mind, but he couldn't quite catch it. Was it something the minister had said? The national chief? It was gone.

At 2 p.m., Saint Mary's Cathedral by the main square was full of people. Wallander was one of the pallbearers. The coffin was white and simply adorned with roses. They carried it into the church.

Wallander searched the crowd for a man's face, although he wasn't expecting Louis to be there. He didn't see him.

But Bror Sundelius was there. Wallander greeted him. Sundelius asked him how the investigation was proceeding.

"We've had a breakthrough," Wallander replied. "That's all I can tell you."

"Just be sure you get him," Sundelius said.

Svedberg's murder had obviously shaken him. Wallander wondered if Sundelius knew what Svedberg had known. Did he feel the same fear? He must talk to him again as soon as possible.

Wallander sat in the front row of the cathedral with a sense of dread in his stomach. Dread at the idea of his own annihilation. He wondered if funerals really had to be such an ordeal. The minister of justice spoke about democracy and the right to a secure life, the national chief of police about the tragic nature of this death. Wallander wondered if he was going to weave in a piece about community policing, then decided he was being unfair. There was no reason for him to question the man's sincerity. When the national chief was finished, it was Ann-Britt Höglund's turn. Wallander had never seen her in her uniform before. She read Wallander's words in a loud, clear voice, and to his surprise he didn't cringe when he heard them.

It was towards the end of the service, right before the processional, when Wallander finally seized the thought that had been skirting the edges of his consciousness. The national chief had said something while rifling through his papers, something about temporary employees who came and went and whose names one never learned before they were gone. At first he didn't know why this comment had stayed with him, but then he suddenly saw the connection. Postal workers must have substitutes who filled in for them when they were away.

It was past 5 p.m. when Wallander was able to return home and take off his tight uniform. He called the postal depot, but no one answered. Before trying to reach Albinsson, he showered and changed, found a pair of glasses and looked in the phone book. Kjell Albinsson lived in Rydsgård. He dialled the number and Albinsson's wife answered. Her husband was playing football for the post office team. She didn't know where the game was being played, but she promised she would have him return Wallander's call.

Wallander heated up tomato soup and ate some slices of crisp bread, then lay on his bed, exhausted despite his good night's sleep. The funeral had tired him out. He was woken by the phone at 7.30 p.m. It was Kjell Albinsson.

"How was the game?" Wallander asked.

"Not so good. We were playing a slaughterhouse team. They have some good players. But it was only a pre-season game. The regular season doesn't start for a while."

"It's a great way to stay in shape."

"Or get your bones broken."

Wallander decided to launch straight into his question. "There was one thing I forgot to ask you the other day. I take it you sometimes employ substitute postal workers."

"That's right. Both short-term and long-term."

"Who do you normally use?"

"We prefer to use people with experience, and we've been pretty lucky. With today's unemployment, we have many to choose from. There are two people who do most of our substituting. One is a woman called Lena Stivell. She had a permanent position, but chose to go to part-time and then to occasional work."

"Is the other one also a woman?"

"No, he's a man called Åke Larstam. He used to be an engineer, but he retrained."

"To become a postal worker?"

"It's not as strange as it sounds. The hours are good and you meet a lot of people."

"Is he working at the moment?"

"He subbed for someone about a week ago. I'm not sure what he's up right now."

"Is there anything else you can tell me about him?"

"He's a very private person, but conscientious. I think he's about 44 years old, and he lives here in Ystad – at number 18, Harmonigatan, if I'm not mistaken."

Wallander thought for a moment. "And these substitutes might be placed on any of your routes?"

"It's supposed to work that way. You never know when someone's going to come down with a cold."

"Which route was Larstam working on last time?"

"The district to the west of Ystad."

Wrong again, Wallander thought. Neither the nature reserve nor Nybrostrand lay to the west.

"Thanks, that's all I wanted to know," he said. "I appreciate you taking the time to call me back."

Wallander hung up and decided to return to the station. The investigative team had no plans to meet that evening, but he would use the time to re-examine material in the case files. The phone rang. It was Albinsson again.

"I made a mistake," he said. "I mixed up Lena's and Åke's assignments. Lena took the route to the west of Ystad."

"And was Åke Larstam also working?"

"That's where I was wrong. He last subbed on a route in Nybrostrand."

"When was that?"

"In July. The assignment was only for a couple of weeks."

"Do you remember the route he had before that?"

"He had a long-term assignment out towards Rögla. That must have been from March to June."

"Thanks for telling me," Wallander said.

He replaced the receiver. Åke Larstam had recently been delivering post in the area where Torbjörn Werner and Malin Skander lived. Before then, he had been delivering post in an area that included Skårby, where Isa Edengren lived. It was probably mere coincidence, but he couldn't help taking out the phone book and looking for Larstam's entry. There was no one by that name in the book. He called information and was told that Larstam had an unlisted number.

Wallander dressed and went down to the station. To his surprise, Höglund was also there. She was in her office, looking through a thick pile of papers.

"I didn't think anyone else would be here," he said.

She was still dressed in her uniform. Wallander had already complimented her on her speech earlier in the day.

"My babysitter is there tonight," she said. "I have to make the most of it. There's so much paperwork to do."

"Same here. That's why I came down too."

He sat down in her visitor's chair. She saw he wanted to discuss something with her, and she pushed her pile of paper to the side. Wallander told her about the idea he'd had after hearing the national chief mention his temporary secretary. Then he described his conversation with Albinsson.

"From his description, he hardly sounds like a mass murderer," she said.

"Who does? My point is that we finally have someone whose activities we can trace to three of the victims' homes."

"So what are you suggesting we do?"

"I just came here to talk to you about it, nothing more."

"We've talked to the regular postal workers, so we should talk to these substitutes too. Is that what you want?"

"I don't think we need to bother with Lena Stivell."

Höglund looked down at her watch. "We could take a short walk," she said. "Get some fresh air. We could walk by Harmonigatan and ring Larstam's bell. It's not that late."

"Even I hadn't thought that far," he said. "But I like your idea."

It took them ten minutes to walk to Harmonigatan, which lay in the western part of the city. Number 18 was an older, three-storey block of flats. Larstam lived on the top floor. Wallander rang the bell and they waited. He rang it again.

"I suppose he isn't home," she said. Wallander crossed the street and looked up at the flat. Two of the windows were lit. He went back and tried the front door. It was open, so they walked in. There was no elevator. They walked up the wide stairs. Wallander rang the doorbell, and they heard it ring inside. Nothing happened. He rang it three times. Höglund bent down and looked through the post slot.

"There's no sound," she said. "But the light's on."

Wallander rang the bell one last time, then Höglund banged on the door.

"We'll have to try again tomorrow," she said.

Wallander was struck by the feeling that something wasn't quite right. She noticed it immediately.

"What are you thinking?"

"I don't know. That something doesn't add up."

"He's probably not home. The manager at the post office

said that he's not working at the moment. He might have gone somewhere for a few days. That's a logical explanation."

"You're probably right," Wallander said doubtfully.

She started down the stairs. "Let's try again tomorrow," she said.

"That is if we don't try to go in tonight anyway."

She looked up at him with genuine surprise. "Are you suggesting that we break in? Is he even a suspect?"

"It's just that we happen to be here now."

She shook her head vigorously. "I can't let you do it. It goes against all the rules."

Wallander shrugged. "You're right. We'll try again tomorrow."

They returned to the station. During the walk they discussed how the workload should be distributed over the next couple of days. They parted in reception, and Wallander returned to his office to deal with some pressing paperwork.

Shortly before 11 p.m. he dialled the number of the Stockholm restaurant where Linda worked. For once he succeeded in getting through, but Linda was very busy. They agreed that she would call him in the morning.

"How is everything?" he asked. "Have you decided where you're going to go?"

"Not yet. I will."

The conversation gave him a burst of energy. He returned to his paperwork. At 11.30 p.m., Höglund came to say she was leaving.

"I'll try to be here before 8 a.m.," she said. "We can start by visiting Larstam again."

"We'll fit it in when we have the time," Wallander said.

Wallander waited for five minutes, then took a set of

skeleton keys out of his desk drawer and left the office. He had already made up his mind while they were deliberating outside Larstam's door. If she didn't want to be party to breaking in, he would do it alone. There was something about Åke Larstam that bothered him.

He walked back to Harmonigatan. It was just before midnight and there was a soft, easterly breeze. Wallander thought he could feel a touch of autumn chill in the air. Maybe the heat wave was nearing its end. He rang the bell from downstairs and noted that the same lights were on. When there was no answer, he pushed open the front door and walked up the stairs.

He had a feeling of being back where it all began; of reliving the night when he and Martinsson had gone up to Svedberg's flat. He shuddered, then listened intently outside the door of the flat. Not a sound. He carefully opened the post slot. No sound, just a soft beam of light. He rang the doorbell and waited, then rang it again. After waiting for five minutes, he got out the skeleton keys, and looked closely at the door. It was fitted with the most elaborate set of locks he had ever seen in his life. Åke Larstam was clearly a person who valued his privacy. There was no way he would be able to open these locks with his skeleton keys. At the same time, the need to get inside seemed more pressing than ever. He hesitated for only a moment before getting out his phone and calling Nyberg.

Nyberg answered in his usual irritated tone. Wallander didn't need to ask if he had been asleep.

"I need your help," he said.

"Don't tell me it's happened again," Nyberg groaned.

"No one's dead," Wallander said. "But I need your help opening a door."

"You don't need a technician for that."

"In this case I do."

Nyberg growled on the other end, but he was fully awake now. Wallander described the locks to him and gave him the address. Nyberg promised to come. Wallander walked quietly down the stairs and waited for him out on the street. He would need to explain to him what was going on, and Nyberg was probably going to protest loudly. With good reason.

Wallander knew he was doing something he shouldn't.

Nyberg arrived within ten minutes. Wallander guessed he was wearing pyjamas under his coat. As he had expected, Nyberg immediately issued a furious protest.

"You can't just break into the homes of innocent people."

"I need you to open the door," Wallander said. "Then you're free to go. I take full responsibility, and I won't tell a soul you've been here."

Nyberg still expressed his reluctance, but when Wallander insisted he walked up the stairs and studied the locks carefully.

"No one will believe you," he said. "There's no way you'd get past this on your own."

Then he got to work. At just before 1 a.m., the door finally opened.

CHAPTER THIRTY-TWO

The first thing he noticed was the smell. After he stepped into the hall, he stood absolutely still to and listened for sounds within the flat. That's when it hit him. Nyberg stayed where he was on the other side of the door. The smell was overpowering.

He realised that it was merely the smell of a place that was never aired. The air had actually gone bad. Wallander gestured for Nyberg to follow him in, which he did unwillingly. Wallander told him to wait there and walked into the rest of the flat on his own. There were three rooms and a little kitchen, all clean and orderly. The neatness contrasted strongly with the bad air.

The door to one of the rooms differed from the others. It looked as if it had been specially made. When Wallander pushed it open he saw that it was extremely thick. It reminded him of a door to a recording studio, like the ones he had seen on the few occasions he'd done radio interviews. Wallander stepped inside. There was something strange about the room. There were no windows and the walls were reinforced. There was a bed and a lamp in the room, nothing else. The bed was made, but there was a faint imprint of a body on the bedspread. It took him a while to put it together: the room looked as it did because it had been soundproofed. His curiosity piqued, Wallander walked through the rest of the flat again, hoping to find a picture of the man who lived there. There were shelves full of porcelain figures, but not a single photograph. Wallander came to a halt in the living room, suddenly overtaken by the sense that he was violating someone's privacy.

He had no business being here. He should leave at once. But something held him back. He returned to the hall where Nyberg was waiting.

"Five more minutes," he said. "That's all."

Nyberg didn't reply. Wallander returned to the flat, conducting a methodical search now. He knew what he was looking for. He went through the three cupboards one by one. In the first two he found only men's clothing. He was about to close the door of the third when he caught sight of something. He reached into one end of the cupboard, where some clothes had been hung behind the others, and pulled out a hanger. It held a red dress. He started going through the drawers with equal concentration, feeling underneath the neatly folded piles of men's clothing. The sense that time was running out, that he had to hurry, spurred him on. Again, he came up lucky. Various articles of women's underclothing were hidden away. He returned to the third cupboard, crept around on hands and knees, and found some women's shoes. He was careful to return things as they had been. Nyberg came out into the living room as he worked.

Wallander could see that he was furious. Or possibly afraid.

"It's been almost 15 minutes," he hissed. "What the hell are we doing here?"

Wallander didn't answer. Now he was looking around for a desk. There was an old secretary's desk in the corner. It was locked. He motioned for Nyberg to work on it, but Nyberg objected.

Wallander interrupted his protests, giving him the shortest possible answer he could think of.

"Louise lives here," he said. "You know, the woman in the picture we found in Svedberg's flat. The woman in Copenhagen. The one who doesn't really exist. She lives here."

"You could have said that a little earlier," Nyberg said.

"I didn't know for sure," Wallander said. "Not until this moment. Could you open that desk for me, without leaving any marks?"

Nyberg unlocked it quickly with his tools. The lid folded down into a writing surface.

It had often seemed to Wallander that police work was characterised by a series of expectations that were inevitably disappointed. What he had been expecting at this particular moment, he was later unable to determine, but it could not have been what actually awaited his gaze.

There was a plastic folder full of newspaper clippings, all related to the murder investigation. There was a copy of Svedberg's obituary, which Wallander hadn't seen until then.

Nyberg was waiting behind him. "You should take a look at this," Wallander said slowly. "It'll explain what we're doing in this flat."

Nyberg took a few steps forward, flinched, then looked at Wallander.

"We could leave," Wallander said, "and put the house under surveillance. Or we could call for reinforcements and start going through the flat right away."

"He's killed eight people," Nyberg said. "That means he's armed and dangerous."

It hadn't occurred to Wallander that they might be in danger. That made up his mind for him: they'd get reinforcements. Nyberg closed the desk. Wallander went into the kitchen, where he had seen some glasses on the counter. He wrapped one of them in paper and put it in his pocket. He was about to leave the kitchen when he noticed that the back door was slightly ajar. He felt a wave of fear so powerful it almost knocked him over. He thought someone was about to push the door open and shoot. But nothing happened. Gingerly he approached the back door and nudged it gently. The back stairs were empty. Nyberg was already on his way out of the flat by the front door. Wallander joined him.

They listened carefully. Nothing. Nyberg softly closed the front door. He examined the threshold with a torch.

"There are a few scratches," he said. "But they're not noticeable unless you're really looking for them."

Wallander thought about the back door that had been slightly ajar. He decided to keep it to himself for now. When they got to the station, Wallander literally ran down the corridor to his office. The first person he called was Martinsson, since he wanted him there as soon as possible.

During the next ten minutes he talked to a number of sleepy people who became surprisingly alert when he told them about his find. Martinsson was the first to arrive, then Höglund and the others in rapid succession.

"I'm lucky," she said. "My mother's visiting."

"I went back to Harmonigatan," Wallander said. "I had the feeling it couldn't wait."

By 2 a.m., everyone was assembled. Wallander looked around the table. He wondered briefly how Thurnberg had found the time to get such a perfect knot in his tie. Then he told them about his discovery.

"What made you go over there in the middle of the night?" Hansson asked.

"I'm usually sceptical of my intuition," Wallander said. "But this time I was right."

He shook off his tiredness. Now he had to shape his investigative team into hunters, stalking their prey in ever-narrowing circles until he was caught.

"We don't know where he is right now," he said. "But the back door was open. Given the nature of the locks on his front door, I think we can assume he heard us working on them and fled. In other words, he knows we're closing in on him."

"That means he's not likely to return," Martinsson said.

"We don't know that for sure. I'd like to put the place under surveillance. One car is fine, as long as there are several others close by."

Wallander brought his palms down heavily on the table.

"This man is extremely dangerous," he said. "I want everyone to be fully armed."

Hansson and one of the reinforcements from Malmö volunteered to take the first watch. Nyberg said he would take them to the flat and see if there had been any change in the lights in the window.

"I want to talk to Kjell Albinsson in Rydsgård," Wallander continued. "A car should be sent out to bring him in."

No one remembered Albinsson. Wallander explained that he was the manager at the postal depot and moved on.

"We need to check if Åke Larstam turns up in any police records," he said. "That's your responsibility, Martinsson. It may be the middle of the night to everyone else, but to us it's a normal working day. Feel free to call anyone you can think of who may have important information. Albinsson will give us some details about Larstam, but it may not be enough. This man dresses up as a woman and takes on other personas. His name may not even be Larstam. We have to look everywhere we can think of for clues. Everywhere."

Wallander now took out the glass he had taken from the flat and placed it on the table.

"If we're lucky, there are prints on this glass," he said. "And if I'm right, they're going to match the ones we found in Svedberg's flat, as well as the ones in the nature reserve."

"What about Sundelius?" Höglund asked. "Shouldn't we wake him up as well? He may know something about Larstam."

Wallander nodded and glanced briefly at Thurnberg, who seemed to have no objections.

"Why don't you do the honours, Ann-Britt? Don't let him off easily this time. He's been hiding something from us, I'm sure of it. Now we have no more time for secrets."

Thurnberg nodded. "That sounds reasonable enough," he said. "But let me just ask this: is there any possibility that we're mistaken?"

"No," Wallander said. "We're not mistaken."

"I just want to make sure, since the only thing we really have on this man is a file of newspaper clippings."

Wallander felt perfectly calm as he answered. "It's him. There's not a single doubt in my mind."

They made the conference room their provisional head-quarters. Wallander was still in his chair at the end of the table when they brought in Kjell Albinsson. He was very pale and seemed bewildered at having been woken up in the middle of the night and brought to the police station. Wallander asked someone to bring him a cup of coffee. In the background he saw Höglund go by with an indignant Sundelius.

"I want to explain the whole situation to you," he began.

457

"We think Åke Larstam is the person who killed a police officer by the name of Svedberg a few weeks ago, the same man who was buried yesterday."

Albinsson went whiter still. "That's just not possible."

"There's more," Wallander said. "We're also convinced he killed three young people in Hagestad's nature reserve, as well as a young woman on an island in the Östergötland archipelago, and finally a couple of newly-weds out in Nybrostrand. What I'm telling you is that this person has killed eight people in a relatively short space of time, making him one of the worst mass murderers that Sweden has ever had."

Albinsson simply shook his head. "There has to be some mistake. It can't be Åke."

"I wouldn't be talking with you now if I wasn't utterly certain. You must take my word for it, and make sure you answer my questions as thoroughly as you can. Do you understand?"

"Yes."

Thurnberg walked in and sat across the table from Albinsson without a word.

"This is chief prosecutor Thurnberg," Wallander said. "The fact that he's here means you're not being charged with anything."

Albinsson didn't seem to understand. "I'm not charged with anything?"

"That's what I said. Now try to concentrate on my questions."

Albinsson nodded. The realisation of where he was and why seemed slowly to be sinking in.

"Åke Larstam lives at number 18, Harmonigatan," Wallander said. "We know he isn't there now, and we suspect he's fled. Do you have any idea where he might have gone?"

"I don't really know him outside work."

"Does he have a summer house? Any close friends?"

"Not that I know of."

"You must know something."

"There's some information about him in the employee records. But all that's kept at the depot."

Wallander swore under his breath. He should have thought of that himself. "Then we'll get it," he said. "Now."

He called in some patrol officers and sent them off with Albinsson. When he returned to his seat, Thurnberg was making notes on a pad.

"How did you enter the flat in the first place?" he said.

"I broke in," Wallander said. "Nyberg was present but the responsibility was wholly mine."

"I hope you're right about Larstam. Otherwise this is going to look very bad."

"I envy you that you should have time to think about such things right now."

"You have to understand my position," Thurnberg said. "Sometimes people make mistakes."

Wallander controlled his temper with some difficulty.

"I don't want another murder on my hands," he said. "That's the bottom line. And Åke Larstam is the man we've been looking for."

"No one wants any more murders," Thurnberg said. "But we also don't want any more police errors."

Wallander was about to ask Thurnberg what he meant by this when Martinsson came in.

"Nyberg called," he said. "The lights in the window haven't changed."

"What about the neighbours?" Wallander asked.

"Where do you want me to start?" Martinsson asked. "With Larstam and the police records? Or with the neighbours?"

"You should do both at the same time. But if we can find anything on Larstam in our files, it would be useful."

Martinsson left and silence filled the room. Somewhere a dog barked and Wallander wondered absently if it was Kall. It was just before 3 a.m. Wallander left to get some coffee. The door to Höglund's office was closed. She was in there with Sundelius. For a moment he wondered if he should go in, but he decided against it.

Wallander returned to the conference room and saw that Thurnberg had left. He glanced at his pad to see what Thurnberg had written. *Dashes, ashes, lashes.* A random series of rhyming words. Wallander shook his head.

Five minutes went by, then Albinsson came in. He was less pale now. He held a yellow folder in his hands.

"These are confidential records," he said. "I should really consult the postmaster before handing them over."

"If you do that I'll get the chief prosecutor back in here," Wallander said, "and have you arrested for obstruction of justice and aiding a criminal."

Albinsson seemed to take this seriously. Wallander stretched out his hand and took the file. The records confirmed what Albinsson had already told him. From the beginning of March to the middle of June Larstam had worked on the Skårby route. In July he had delivered post in Nybrostrand.

There was little personal information. Åke Larstam had been born on 10 November 1952, in Eskilstuna. His full name was Åke Leonard Larstam. He had graduated from high school in 1970, had done his compulsory military training in Skövde the following year, then had enrolled at the prestigious Chalmers School of Engineering in Gothenburg in 1972. He had graduated from Chalmers in 1979 and taken a job in Stockholm with Strand Consulting. He'd worked there until 1985, when he'd given notice and started to retrain for the postal service. That year he had moved first to Höör and then to Ystad. He was unmarried and had no children. The space allotted to "emergency contact" was blank.

"Doesn't this man even have any relatives?"

"Apparently not," Albinsson said.

"But he must have socialised with someone."

"He was very private, as I said."

Wallander put down the file. All of the facts would be verified, but for now Wallander had to concentrate on finding where Larstam was.

"No one is completely without personal relationships," Wallander said. "Who did he talk to? Who did he have coffee with? Did he have any strong opinions? There has to be something more you can say about him."

"We talked about him sometimes," Albinsson said. "He was so hard to get to know. But since he was always so friendly and helpful, everyone left him alone. You can grow fond of people you know nothing about."

Wallander thought about what Albinsson had just said. Then he chose a different tack.

"Some of these jobs were long-term, some just a matter of days. Did you ever know him to turn down an assignment?"

"No."

"So he didn't seem to have another job?"

"Not that we knew about. He could get ready at a few hours' notice."

"That means you always managed to get hold of him."

"Yes."

"He was always at home waiting for the phone to ring?"

Albinsson was very serious when he answered. "It seemed like that."

"You've described him as conscientious, helpful, careful and responsible. And introverted. Did he ever do anything that surprised you?"

Albinsson thought for a while. "He sang to himself."

"Sang?"

"Yes. He hummed melodies under his breath."

"What kinds of things?"

"Mainly hymns, I think. He would do it as he was sorting the post, or as he was walking out to his car. I don't know how to describe it. He sang in a very low voice, probably because he didn't want it to bother anyone."

"He sang hymns?"

"Or religious songs."

"Was he religious?"

"How would I know that?"

"Just answer the question."

"There's a thing called freedom of religion in this country. Åke Larstam could be a Buddhist for all I know."

"Buddhists don't go around shooting people," Wallander said sharply. "Did he have any other peculiar characteristics?"

"He washed his hands a lot."

"Anything else?"

"The only time I saw him in a bad mood was when people around him were laughing. But that seemed to pass quickly enough."

Wallander stared at Albinsson. "Can you elaborate on what you just said?"

"Not really. It's just what I told you."

"He didn't like people being happy?"

"I wouldn't say that, but he seemed to withdraw more when other people were laughing. I suppose you could call that being happy. It seemed to irritate him."

Wallander had a flashback to the crime scene at Nybrostrand. Nyberg had turned to him and said that the killer didn't seem to like happy people.

"Did he ever show any violent tendencies?"

"Never."

"Any other tendencies?"

"He had no tendencies. You hardly noticed him."

Wallander sensed there was something else that Albinsson was trying to get at. He waited.

"Maybe you could say that his strongest characteristic was the fact that he didn't seem to want to be noticed. He was the kind of person who never turns his back to a door."

"What do you mean by that?"

"That he always wanted to know who was coming and going."

Wallander thought he knew what Albinsson was saying. He looked at his watch. It was 3.41 a.m. He called Höglund.

"Are you still with Sundelius?"

"Yes."

"I'd like to see you out in the hall for a moment."

Wallander got up. "Can I go home now?" Albinsson asked. "I know my wife must be worried."

"Please feel free to call her. But you can't go home just yet."

Wallander went out into the hall and closed the door. Höglund was already waiting for him.

"What did Sundelius say?"

"He claims he doesn't know who Åke Larstam is. He keeps repeating that he and Svedberg never did anything but look at stars, and that once they went to a natural healer together. He's very upset. I don't think he's comfortable talking to a female police officer."

Wallander nodded thoughtfully. "I think we can send

him home for now," he said. "He probably didn't know Larstam. I think what we have is two separate nests of secrets. We have Larstam, who eavesdropped on his victims' most intimate affairs. And we have Svedberg, who kept a part of his life secret from Sundelius."

"And what would that have been?"

"Just think about it."

"You mean there's a love triangle of sorts behind all this?"

"Not behind. In the middle of."

She nodded. "I'll send him home. When are Hansson and the others supposed to be relieved?"

Wallander realised he had already made up his mind.

"They can stay. We're going in. Åke Larstam isn't coming back tonight. He's holed up somewhere – the question is where. If we're going to find the answer, our best place to start is in his flat."

Wallander returned to the conference room while Albinsson was talking on the phone to his wife. Wallander signalled for him to finish his call.

"Have you been able to think of anything else?" he asked. "Where could Åke Larstam have gone?"

"I don't know. But that makes me think of another way to describe him."

"How?"

"That he was always trying to hide."

Wallander nodded. "I'll have someone take you home now," he said. "But give me a call if you think of anything else."

They went back into Åke Larstam's flat at 4.15 a.m. Wallander gathered everyone outside the door to the soundproofed bedroom.

"We're looking for two things," he said. "The first is where he could be hiding. Does he have a secret hiding place? How do we force him to show himself? The second is whether he is planning to kill again. That's the most important point. It would also be useful if anyone found a picture of him."

He took Nyberg aside when he finished. "We need fingerprints," he said. "Thurnberg is nervous. We have to have something that places Larstam at the scene of the crime. This has to take precedence over anything else."

"I'll see what I can do," Nyberg said.

"Don't see what you can do, just do it," Wallander said.

Wallander went into the soundproofed room and sat down on the bed. Hansson appeared in the doorway, but Wallander waved him away.

Why build a soundproofed room? To keep sounds out, or to keep them in? Why, in a town like Ystad? Traffic is never that bad. His thoughts wandered. The bed was uncomfortable to sit on. He got up and looked under the sheets. There was no mattress, just the hard platform of the bedframe. He's a masochist, Wallander thought. Why? He stooped to peer under the bed. There was nothing there, not even a speck of dust. Wallander tried to summon forth the spirit of the man who lived here. Åke Larstam, 44 years of age. Born in Eskilstuna, a graduate of Chalmers. An engineer turned postal worker. You suddenly go out and kill eight people. Apart from Svedberg and the photographer, your victims were all dressed up. The photographer just happened to be in the way, and you killed Svedberg because he was on to you. His worst fears were confirmed. But the others were dressed up, and they were happy. Why did you kill them? Was it in here, in your soundproofed chamber, that you planned everything?

Wallander didn't feel any closer to the killer's thoughts. He walked out into the living room, and looked around at all the porcelain figures. Dogs, roosters, dolls in 19th-century dress, gnomes and trolls. It's like a doll's house, Wallander thought. A doll's house inhabited by a lunatic with bad taste. He wondered why Larstam kept all these kitsch souvenirs.

Höglund came in from the kitchen and interrupted his train of thought. Wallander knew immediately that she had found something.

"I think you'd better take a look at this," she said. Wallander followed her into the kitchen. One of the drawers had been pulled out and placed on the table. At the top of a pile of papers in the drawer was a piece of mathematical paper. Something was written on it in pencil. If that was Larstam's handwriting, he wrote in an unusually spiky style. Wallander put on his glasses and read what it said.

There were only ten words, forming a macabre poem of sorts. *Number 9. Wednesday 21. He giveth and He taketh away.* The meaning was immediately clear to Wallander, as it must have been to Höglund.

"He's already killed eight people," Wallander said. "This is about victim number nine."

"It's the 21st today," she said. "And it's Wednesday."

"We have to find him," Wallander said, "before he gets a chance to do this."

"What about the last part? What does he mean by 'He giveth and He taketh away'?"

"It means Larstam hates happy people. He wants what they have to be taken from them."

Wallander told her what Albinsson had said.

"How do you go about locating happy people?" she asked.

"You go out and look for them."

He felt the knot in his stomach return.

"One thing is strange," she said. "This number nine sounds like a single person. But if you disregard Svedberg, he's always gone for a group of some sort in the past."

"You're right to disregard Svedberg. He's not part of the pattern. It's a good point."

It was 4.20 a.m. Wallander walked over to the window and looked out into the night. It was still dark. Åke Larstam was out there in that darkness. Wallander felt a sudden twinge of panic. We're not going to get him in time, he thought. We're going to be too late. He's already chosen his victim and we have no idea who it is. We're scurrying around like blind mice, not knowing where to turn. We know nothing.

Wallander put on a pair of rubber gloves and starting going through the rest of the papers in the drawer.

CHAPTER THIRTY-THREE

The sea. That would be his place of last resort, if it ever came to that. He imagined himself walking straight out, slowly sinking down to the place where eternal darkness and silence reigned. A place where no one would ever find a single trace of him.

He took one of his cars and drove down to the sea, just west of Ystad. Mossbystrand was deserted this August evening. Few cars went by on the road to Trelleborg. He parked so that none of the lights from oncoming traffic would hit him, and so that he could make a quick getaway if he was being followed.

There was one detail about the latest events that disturbed him. He had been lucky. If his bedroom door had been completely closed, as it usually was, he would never have heard them breaking into the flat that evening. He had woken up with a start, realised what was happening, and slipped out the back door. He had no idea if he had remembered to close it behind him. The only thing that he had grabbed, apart from some clothes, was his gun.

Although he had been shaken, he'd forced himself to drive calmly. He didn't want to risk having an accident.

Now it was 4 a.m. and it would be a while before the sun came up. He thought about everything that had happened and wondered if he had made a mistake. But he couldn't find anything. He was not going to alter his plans.

Everything had gone well. During Svedberg's funeral he

had gone to the policeman's flat on Mariagatan. It was easy enough to pick the lock. He'd looked through the flat and quickly established that the man lived alone. Then he'd made his plans. It was easier than he expected; he found a set of spare keys to the flat in a kitchen drawer. He wouldn't have to pick the lock next time. For fun he lay down on the policeman's bed, but it was much too soft. He felt as though he was drowning.

Afterwards he had gone home, showered, eaten and rested in the soundproofed room. Later he'd done something that he had been planning to do for a long time. He polished all his porcelain figurines. That had taken quite a while. When he was done, he'd eaten his supper and gone to bed. He had been sleeping for several hours when he'd heard the policemen at the door.

He thought about the fact that the police were in his flat right now, pulling out drawers, dirtying the floor, moving his porcelain figurines around. It enraged him, and he could hardly control his desire to rush back and shoot them all. But self-preservation was more important than revenge, and he knew they would find nothing in the flat to help them in their search. He kept no photographs there, no private documents, nothing. They didn't know about the safe-deposit box he kept at the bank under an assumed name. That's where all the important documents were, such as his car registration and his financial information.

They would probably be in his flat for many hours but sooner or later the policeman would return home, exhausted after his sleepless night. And he would be there waiting for him.

He returned to the car. The most important thing was for him to catch up on the sleep he had missed. He could of course sleep in one of his cars, but there was a slight chance that he could be discovered. He also disliked the idea of curling up in the back seat. It was undignified. He wanted to stretch out in a real bed, one where he could remove the mattress to give him the firm support he liked.

He considered checking into a hotel under a false name, but dismissed the possibility when he had a sudden flash of inspiration. There was one place he could go where no one would disturb him. And there was always the back door if someone turned up unexpectedly. He started the engine and turned on the headlights. It was almost time for the sun to rise. He needed to sleep, to rest in preparation for the coming day.

He turned on to the main road and drove back to Ystad.

It was close to 5 a.m. when Wallander started to realise how best to describe the kind of person Åke Larstam was. He was someone who left no trace of himself. They had nearly finished their search of the flat and hadn't managed to find even one object that revealed anything about the person who lived there. There was no post, not even a piece of paper with Åke Larstam's name on it.

"I've never seen anything like it," Wallander said. "Åke Larstam doesn't seem to exist. We can't find a single document that verifies his existence, even though we know he's real."

"Maybe he keeps another flat somewhere," Martinsson said.

"Maybe he has ten other flats," Wallander answered. "He might have all kinds of villas and summer houses, but if so we have nothing here that will lead us to them."

"Perhaps he took everything with him when he fled,"

Hansson said. "He may have known we were closing in on him."

"The state of this flat doesn't suggest that," Wallander said. "I think he lived like this. The man has a professionally soundproofed room. But you may be right. I hope you are; then perhaps we'll find something after all."

The piece of paper lay on the table in front of them.

"Are we misinterpreting it?" Höglund asked.

"It says what it says. Nyberg claims it was written recently. He can tell that from the consistency of the graphite, or something like that."

"Why do you think he wrote it?"

Martinsson was the one who asked the last question, and Wallander knew it was an important one.

"You're right," he said. "It stands out as the only personal item we've found. What does it mean? I'm assuming that he was here when Nyberg and I were at the door. The unlocked back door seems to imply a hasty departure."

"Then this was something he left behind inadvertently?" Martinsson asked.

"That's the most plausible explanation. Or rather the most obvious. But is it the right one?"

"What would the alternative be?"

"That he wanted us to find it."

No one seemed to grasp what Wallander was getting at. He knew it was a flimsy theory.

"What do we know about Åke Larstam? We know he's good at getting the information he needs. He ferrets out other people's secrets. I'm not saying he has access to our investigation, but I think the information he does have is aided by a fair amount of foresight. He must have considered the possibility that we would find him. The fact that I turned up at that bar in Copenhagen, if nothing else, would have forced him to think about this. What does he do? He prepares to flee, but first he prepares a greeting for us. He knows we'll find it, since there's nothing much else here to find."

"But that still doesn't tell us why," Martinsson said.

"He's teasing us. That's not so unusual. Lunatics like this often enjoy taunting the police. He must have exulted over his triumph in Copenhagen. There he was, parading around as Louise just after the Danish papers had run her picture, and he still managed to get away."

"It still strikes me as strange that we would find this piece of paper on the very day he's planning to kill again."

"He couldn't have known when we would get here."

But the words sounded unconvincing even to his ears. Wallander let it drop.

"We have to take his threats seriously," he said. "We have to assume he intends to strike again."

"Do we have any leads whatsoever?" The question came from Thurnberg, who had appeared in the doorway.

"No," Wallander said. "We have nothing. We might as well be honest about that."

No one said anything. Wallander knew he had to counteract the sense of hopelessness that was spreading through the team. It was 5.20 a.m. Wallander suggested that they report back at 8 a.m. That would give everyone an opportunity to rest for an hour or so. They would station a couple of officers outside the block of flats, and they would also start questioning the neighbours about Larstam.

Nyberg waited until everyone except Wallander had left the room.

"He keeps a clean house," he said. "But we have finger-prints."

"Anything else?"

"Not really."

"Any weapons?"

"No, I would have already told you about something like that."

Wallander nodded. Nyberg's face was ashen with exhaustion.

"I think you were right about the killer and happy people."

"Will we find him?"

"Sooner or later. But I dread what may happen today."

"Couldn't we make some kind of announcement?"

"Saying what exactly? That people should avoid laughing today? He's already chosen his victim. It's probably someone who isn't giving a thought to the idea of being followed."

"I guess we might have a better chance of locating his hideout if we keep quiet."

"That's my thought, too. I just don't know how much time we have."

"Shouldn't we also consider the possibility that he may not have an extra flat or summer house to run to? What then? Where would he go?"

Nyberg was right. Wallander hadn't considered this possibility. The fatigue had wrung his brain dry. "What do you think?" he asked.

Nyberg shrugged. "We know he has a car. Maybe he's curled up in the back seat. It's still warm enough to sleep outside. That's another possibility. Or he may have a boat. There are a number of options."

"Too many," Wallander said. "We have no time to look for him."

"I understand the hell you're in right now," Nyberg said. "Don't think I don't."

It was rare for Nyberg to express anything remotely close to emotion. Wallander sensed his support, and for once felt somewhat less alone.

Once Wallander was out on the street, he was no longer sure what to do. He knew he needed to go home, shower, and sleep for at least half an hour. But anxiety drove him to keep going. A squad car took him back to the station. He felt queasy and thought about trying to eat something, but instead he drank some more coffee and took his medication. He sat down at his desk and started working through the file again. He saw himself back at Svedberg's flat, with Martinsson close behind. Åke Larstam was the one who had been there and killed Svedberg. Wallander still couldn't see their relationship clearly, but the photo Svedberg had was of Larstam dressed as a woman. Now he knew why the flat had looked the way it did. Larstam's greatest fear was leaving traces of himself. After shooting Svedberg, he had turned the flat upside down looking for that photograph. But Svedberg had had a secret of his own.

The team met promptly at 8 a.m. When Wallander saw the fatigue and anxiety on the faces around him, he worried that he had failed them. Not that he had led them down the wrong path, but that he hadn't led them down the right one. They were still fumbling around in a no-man's-land, not knowing which way to turn. He had one clear thought in his head.

"From now on we work together," he said. "This room will be our headquarters and our meeting place."

The others went to their offices to get the materials they needed. Only Martinsson lingered in the doorway.

"Have you slept at all?" he asked.

Wallander shook his head. "You have to," Martinsson said firmly. "We can't do this if you collapse."

"I can keep going a while longer."

"You've already crossed the line. I slept for an hour. It helped."

"I'll take a walk soon," Wallander said. "I'll go home and change my shirt."

Martinsson looked as if he was going to add something, but Wallander held his hand up to stop him. He didn't have the energy to listen. He didn't know if he was ever going to have the energy to get up from his chair again. They all filed back into the room and closed the door. Thurnberg loosened his tie and actually looked tired. Holgersson sent a message saying that she was in her office dealing with the press.

Everyone looked at Wallander.

"We have to try to understand the way he thinks," he said. "And we have to figure out where can we look for answers. We're not only going to look back through our files on this investigation; some of us will have to examine this man's past. We need to know if he has any living relatives at all, if anyone remembers him from his time at Chalmers, or his old workplace. Where did he retrain to become a postal worker? Our biggest problem is time. We have to assume that the note we found was a message to us about his intentions. Somehow we have to decide what information to look for first."

"We should find out about his parents," Höglund said. "We can only hope his mother is still alive. A mother knows her children; we've learned that lesson."

"Why don't you look into that?" Wallander said.

"One more thing," she said. "I think there's something

strange about his career switch from engineer to postal worker. That needs to be explored."

"I recently heard about a bishop who started driving a taxi," Hansson said.

"This is different," she said. "I heard about that bishop, too. He was already 55 – maybe he wanted to try something completely different before he got too old. But Åke Larstam made his switch before he turned 40."

Wallander sensed that this was important. "You mean that something happened?"

"Yes, something significant had to have happened to make him change his life so completely."

"He moved, too," Thurnberg said. "That suggests that Ann-Britt is right."

"I'll look into this myself," Wallander said. "I'll call that engineering firm – what was it called?"

Martinsson flipped through his papers. "Strand Consulting. He left in 1985, which means he was then 33 years old."

"We'll start there," Wallander said. "The rest of you will keep looking through the material we already have. You're trying to find out where he might be, and who his next victim is."

"What about bringing in Kjell Albinsson again?" Thurnberg asked. "He might think of something else, particularly if he participates in our discussion."

"You're right," Wallander said. "We'll bring him back. Someone also has to run Larstam's name through the database."

"His name isn't there," Martinsson said. "I've already checked."

Wallander was surprised that he had found the time to do it, but then he realised that Martinsson must have lied when he said he had slept for an hour. He had been working as hard as Wallander, but had lied out of consideration. He didn't know if he should be touched or angry. He decided against both, and pushed on.

"Get me the number of that firm."

He dialled the number that was read out to him and reached a recording stating that the number had been changed. He dialled the new number, which was in Vaxholm, an island very close to Stockholm. This time someone answered.

"Strand Consulting," a female voice said.

"My name is Kurt Wallander. I'm a detective with the criminal division in Ystad. I need some information about a former employee at your company."

"And who might that be?"

"An engineer by the name of Åke Larstam."

"There's no one here by that name."

"I know. That's what I just said. He's a former employee. Please listen."

"There's no need to take that tone with me. How do I know you're really from the police, anyway?"

Wallander was about to pull the phone out of the wall but managed to calm himself.

"Of course you have no way of knowing who I am," he said. "But all the same, I need information on Åke Larstam. He left the firm in 1985."

"That was before my time. You'd better speak with Persson."

"Why don't I give you my number? That way he can double-check that I'm calling from the Ystad police station."

She wrote down the number.

"This is an urgent matter. Is Persson available?"

"He's meeting with a client right now, but I'll have him call you when he's done."

"That's not soon enough," Wallander said. "He'll have to interrupt his meeting and call me back immediately."

"I'll tell him it's important, but that's all I can do."

"Then tell him this: if he doesn't return my call in three minutes, a police helicopter will be dispatched from Stockholm to bring him in for questioning."

Wallander hung up, aware that everyone was staring at him. He looked over at Thurnberg, who burst out laughing.

"I'm sorry about that," Wallander said. "I had to say something."

Thurnberg nodded. "I didn't hear you say anything."

The phone rang in less than two minutes. The man on the other end said he was Hans Persson. Wallander told him what he needed to know, without saying that Åke Larstam was wanted for murder.

"According to our information, he stopped working for you in 1985," Wallander said.

"That's right. It was in November, if I recall."

"You remember?"

"Vividly."

Wallander pushed the receiver closer to his ear.

"Why was it so memorable? What happened?"

"He was fired. He's the only engineer I've ever let go. I should explain at this point that I founded this company. There's never been a 'Strand' here, I just thought Strand sounded better than Persson."

"So you fired Åke Larstam. Why?"

"It's hard to explain, but he just didn't fit in here."

"Why not?"

"It will sound strange when I explain it."

"I'm a policeman, I'm used to strange things."

"He wasn't independent enough. He always agreed with

everything, even when we knew he had a different opinion. It isn't possible to have constructive discussions with people who are only out to please others. You can't get anywhere with them."

"That's how he was?"

"Yes. It just wasn't working out. He never came up with any ideas of his own."

"How were his technical abilities?"

"Excellent. That was never the issue."

"How did he react to his termination?"

"He didn't show any emotion at all, as far as I could tell. I was expecting to keep him on for another half a year at least, but he left immediately. He walked out of my office, got his coat, and just left. He didn't even pick up the severance pay due to him. It was as if he vanished into thin air."

"Did you have any contact with him after that?"

"I tried to, but I never managed to speak with him in person."

"Did you know he went to work for the post office?"

"I heard about it. There was some paperwork that came through from the employment office."

"Did he have any close friends that you were aware of?"

"I knew nothing about his personal life. He wasn't particularly close to anyone at this office. Sometimes he looked after other people's flats when they were gone, but otherwise I think he simply kept to himself."

"Do you know if his parents were still alive, or if he had any siblings?"

"I have no idea. His life outside this office was a complete blank. That's a real problem at a small firm."

"I understand. Thanks for your help."

"You'll understand if my curiosity has been piqued," Persson said. "Can you tell me what this is about?"

"You'll hear about it soon enough," Wallander said. "I can't tell you more than that right now."

Wallander hung up abruptly. He was struck by something Persson had said, something about how Larstam looked after other people's flats when they were away on holiday. He hesitated, but decided it should be looked into.

"Has anything been done with Svedberg's flat?" he asked.

"Ylva Brink said at the funeral that she was going to empty it soon, but she hasn't started yet."

Wallander thought about the keys that were still in his desk drawer.

"Hansson," he said. "You and someone else should go down to his flat and look around. See if you can tell if anyone's been there recently. The keys are in my top drawer."

Hansson left with one of the officers from Malmö. It was just before 9 a.m. Höglund was trying to find Larstam's parents. Martinsson went back to double-check the database. Wallander went to the men's room, refusing to look at himself in the mirror. When he returned to the conference room, someone was passing around a plate of sandwiches, but he shook his head. Höglund appeared in the doorway.

"Both of his parents are dead," she said.

"Any siblings?"

"Two older sisters."

"Find them."

She left, and Wallander thought about his own sister, Kristina. How would she describe him if the police came around asking questions?

He heard someone shouting in the corridor. Wallander got up quickly as a policeman appeared in the door.

"Gunfire," he shouted. "Down at the main square."

Wallander knew what it meant. "It must be Svedberg's flat," he shouted back. "Anyone injured?"

"I don't know. But the gunfire has been confirmed."

Four cars with blaring sirens were on their way in less than a minute. Wallander sat in the back seat with his gun held tightly in his hand. Larstam was there, he thought. What had happened to Hansson and the colleague from Malmö? He feared the worst, but pushed the thought away. It was too unbearable.

Wallander was out of the car before it came to a halt. A crowd had gathered at the door to the block of flats on Lilla Norregatan. Wallander dived through the crowd at full speed, bellowing, he was later told, like a charging bull. Then he saw both Hansson and the officer from Malmö. They were unhurt.

"What happened?" Wallander yelled.

Hansson was pale and shaking. The Malmö officer was sitting on the kerb.

"He was there," Hansson said. "I had just unlocked the door and stepped inside. He appeared out of nowhere and fired his gun. Then he was gone. It was pure luck we weren't hit. We turned and ran. It was sheer luck."

Wallander didn't say anything, but he knew luck had nothing to do with it. Larstam was an excellent marksman. He could have taken out both of them if he had wanted to. But he hadn't. Someone else was marked as his victim.

The flat was now empty. The back door was ajar. A greeting, Wallander thought when he saw it. A second door left open. He's showing us how good he is at getting away.

Martinsson emerged from Svedberg's bedroom.

"He's been sleeping in there," he said. "Now at least we know how he thinks. He takes shelter in empty nests."

"We know how he thought," Wallander corrected. "He won't do the same thing twice."

"Are you sure?" Martinsson said. "He's probably trying to figure out how we think. Maybe it makes sense to leave some men here. We don't expect him to return here, so that may be exactly what he does."

"He can't read our thoughts."

"It seems to me," Martinsson said, "that he gets pretty damn close to that. He always manages to stay one step ahead of us and one step behind at the same time."

Wallander didn't reply. He was thinking the same thing.

It was 10.30 a.m. There was only one thing Wallander was sure of and that was that Larstam had not yet killed victim number nine. If he had, Hansson would have been number ten, and their colleague from Malmö number eleven.

Why is he waiting, Wallander thought. Because he has to? Is his victim out of reach, or is there another explanation? Wallander left Svedberg's flat with nothing but more questions. I might as well face it, he thought. I'm back to square one.

CHAPTER THIRTY-FOUR

He felt a sense of regret when it was over. Should he have aimed at their heads after all? He knew that it had to be the police. Who else would have reason to visit Karl Evert's flat, now that he was dead and buried? He also knew that they were trying to track him down. There was no other reasonable explanation.

Once again he had managed to escape, something that was both reassuring and satisfying. Although he hadn't expected them to come looking for him there, he had taken the necessary precautions by unlocking the back door and propping a chair against the front door. It would fall to the ground if someone tried to enter. The gun lay loaded on the bedside table. He slept with his shoes on.

The noise from the street disturbed him. It wasn't like sleeping in his soundproofed room. How many times had he tried to convince Karl Evert to renovate his bedroom? But nothing had come of it, and now it was too late.

The images had been blurry and indistinct, but he'd known he was dreaming of his own childhood. He was standing behind the sofa. He was very young. Two people were fighting, probably his parents. There was the harsh, domineering voice of a man. It swooped over his head like a bird of prey. Then there was a woman's voice, weak and afraid. When he heard it, he thought he was hearing his own voice, though he was still safely hidden behind the sofa.

That was when he was woken by the sounds from the hall. They entered his dreams by force. By the time the chair fell over, he was on his feet, the gun cocked in his hand. It would have meant changing his plans, but he should have shot them. He had left the building, his gun tucked into his coat pocket. The car was parked down at the railway station. He'd heard sirens in the distance. He'd driven out past Sandskogen, towards Österlen. He stopped in Kåseberga and took a walk down to the harbour. He thought about what he should do next. He needed more sleep, but it was getting late and he had no idea when Wallander would return home. He had to be there when he did. He had already decided that it should happen today, and he couldn't risk changing his plans.

When he arrived at the far end of the pier, he made up his mind. He drove back to Ystad and parked at the back of the block of flats on Mariagatan. No one saw him slip in through the front door of the building. He rang the doorbell and listened carefully. No one was home. He unlocked the door, walked in, and sat down on the sofa in the living room. He put his gun down on the coffee table. It was a few minutes after 11 a.m.

Hansson and the Malmö officer were still so shaken that they had to be sent home. This meant that the team shrank by two people, and Wallander detected a new level of tension among members of the group when they gathered after the chaotic events at Lilla Norregatan.

Holgersson took him aside to ask if it was time to send for more reinforcements. Wallander wavered, exhausted and starting to doubt his judgment, but then answered with an emphatic no. They didn't need reinforcements, they just needed to focus.

"Do you really think we can find him?" she asked. "Or are you just hoping there will be another breakthrough?"

"I don't know," he admitted.

They sat back down at the conference table. Martinsson had still not been able to find anything on Larstam in the police registers, so he turned the matter over to a subordinate who would search the files in the basement. Höglund hadn't yet managed to find anything on the two sisters. Now that Hansson was out of the game, Wallander asked her to hold off on that. He needed to have her close by; the sisters would have to wait. They had to concentrate on finding Larstam before he turned to victim number nine.

"We have to ask ourselves what we know," Wallander said, for the umpteenth time.

"He's still in town," Martinsson said. "That must mean he's preparing to strike somewhere close by."

"He's not unaffected by us," Thurnberg said, who rarely commented on the action. "He knows we're on his heels."

"It's also possible he likes it this way," Wallander said.

Kjell Albinsson, who was sitting silently in a corner of the room, now indicated that he wanted to speak. Wallander nodded to him and he got up and approached the table.

"I don't know if this is anything," he said. "But I just remembered that last summer someone at work claimed to have seen Larstam down at the marina. That might mean he owns a boat."

Wallander hit the table with the flat of his hand. "How seriously can we take this?"

"It was one of the other postmen who saw him. He was sure it was him."

"Did he ever actually see Larstam climb onto one of the boats?"

"No, but he said he was carrying a container of petrol."

"Then it can't be a sailing boat," said one of the Malmö officers. But this comment met with a storm of protests.

"Sailing boats often have engines as well," Martinsson said. "We can't rule anything out, even a little sea plane."

Martinsson's last suggestion met with even more protests. Wallander silenced them.

"A boat is a good hiding place," he said. "The question is how much stock we put in this."

He turned to Albinsson again. "Are you sure you're right?"

"Yes."

Wallander looked over at Thurnberg, who nodded.

"Get some plainclothes officers to look around the marina," Wallander said. "Make the whole thing as discreet as possible. If there's even a hint of a suspicion that Larstam is there, they should turn back. We'll have to decide how to proceed at that point."

"There are probably a lot of people down there," Höglund said, "with this weather we've been having."

Martinsson and one of the Malmö officers headed down to the marina. Wallander asked Albinsson to sit at the table.

"If you have any more of these boat stories up your sleeve, I'd love to hear them."

"I've been trying to think of everything I can, but it's just making me realise how little I knew about him," Albinsson said.

Wallander checked his watch. It was 11.30 a.m. We're not going to get him in time, he thought. At any moment the phone will ring with the news of another murder.

Höglund started talking about Larstam's motive.

"It must be some kind of revenge," Wallander said.

"For what?" she asked. "Because he was fired from his job? What would the newly-weds have to do with that?"

Wallander got up to get some coffee and Höglund came along.

"You're right. There's another motive here," Wallander said, as they were nursing their mugs of coffee in the canteen. "There may be an element of revenge at the bottom of it, but Larstam kills people who are happy. Nyberg was struck by this thought in Nybrostrand. Albinsson confirmed it. Åke Larstam doesn't like it when people laugh."

"Then he's more disturbed than we realised. You don't kill people just because they're happy. What kind of world is this?"

"Good question," Wallander said. "We ask ourselves what kind of world we live in, but it's too painful to face the truth. Maybe our worst fears have already been realised – maybe the justice system has collapsed. More and more people are feeling overlooked and superfluous, and that feeds the escalation of senseless violence we're seeing. Violence has become part of our daily reality. We complain about the way things are, but sometimes I think things are even worse than we're admitting."

Wallander was about to continue with this line of thought when he was told that Martinsson was on the phone. He spilled coffee on his shirt as he ran back to the conference room.

"We haven't found anything," Martinsson said. "There isn't a boat registered under Larstam's name."

Wallander thought for a moment. "He may have registered his boat under someone else's name," he said.

"These marinas are so small that people generally know each other," Martinsson said. "I doubt he would have felt safe using an assumed name."

But Wallander wasn't prepared to let go of the idea just yet. "Did you check under Svedberg's name?"

"I did, actually. But there wasn't anything."

"I want you to check the register one more time. Try anyone's name who's been associated with this investigation, either centrally or otherwise."

"You're thinking of names like Hillström and Skander?"

"Exactly."

"I see what you're saying, but do you really think it's a reasonable assumption?"

"Nothing is reasonable. Just do it. Call me if you find anything."

Wallander hung up, and looked down at the large coffee stain on his shirt. He was fairly sure he had at least one clean shirt in his cupboard, and it would take him only 20 minutes to go home and change. But he decided to wait until he heard from Martinsson again.

Thurnberg came over. "I'd like to send Albinsson home," he said. "I don't think he has anything to add at this point."

Wallander got up, walked over to Albinsson, and shook his hand. "You've been a great help to us."

"I still don't understand any of this."

"None of us do."

"Nothing should go further than this room," Thurnberg said.

Albinsson promised to keep quiet.

"Does anyone know where Nyberg is?" Wallander asked.

"He's using the phone in Hansson's office."

"That's where I'll be if Martinsson calls."

Wallander went to Hansson's office, where Nyberg sat

488

with the telephone receiver pressed to his ear. He was writing something on a pad. He looked up when Wallander came in.

"We'll know whether or not it's Larstam's thumb before the end of the day," Nyberg said when he'd hung up.

"It is his thumb," Wallander said. "We just need confirmation."

"What will you do if it isn't his thumb?"

"Resign from this investigation."

Nyberg pondered these words. Wallander sat down in Hansson's chair.

"Do you remember the telescope?" Wallander asked. "Why was it over at Björklund's house? Who put it there?"

"You don't think it was someone other than Larstam, do you?"

"Why did he put it there?"

"Maybe to cause confusion. Perhaps a half-hearted attempt to pin the blame on Svedberg's cousin."

"He must have thought of everything."

"If he hasn't, we'll get him."

"His prints should be on the telescope."

"If he didn't think to wipe it off first."

The phone rang and Wallander grabbed it. It was Martinsson.

"You're right," he said.

Wallander jumped to his feet so fast the chair was knocked over.

"What do you have?"

"A berth registered in Isa Edengren's name. I even saw the contract and it looks like he imitated her signature. I recall what her handwriting looked like. Someone in the office remembers the person who signed it. He says it was a dark-haired woman."

"Louise."

"Exactly. She even told them her brother would often be using the boat."

"He's good," Wallander said.

"It's a small wooden boat," Martinsson said. "Big enough for a couple of sleeping berths below deck. There's another boat on one side but nothing on the other."

"I'm coming down," Wallander said. "Keep your distance, and above all stay vigilant. We have to assume he's being very careful now and he won't approach the marina unless he's sure the coast is clear."

"I guess we haven't kept as low a profile as we should have."

Wallander hung up and told Nyberg what had happened. He returned to the conference room and placed Höglund and Thurnberg in charge of coordinating assistance in the event that he needed it.

"What will you do if you find him?" she asked.

Wallander shook his head. "I'll think about that when I get there."

It was almost 1 p.m. when Wallander arrived at the docks. It was warm, and there was an occasional breeze from the southwest. He took out the binoculars he had remembered to bring and took his first look at the boat.

"It looks empty," Martinsson said.

"Is there anyone on the boat to the left?" Wallander asked. "No."

Wallander let the binoculars glide over the rest of the boats. There were people on many of them.

"We can't risk any shots being fired," Martinsson said. "But I also don't see how we can evacuate the entire marina."

"We can't wait," Wallander said. "We have to know if he's there or not, and if he is, we have to bring him in."

"Should we start cordoning off the area around the boat?"

"No," Wallander said. "I'm climbing aboard."

Martinsson jumped. "Are you insane?"

"It would take us at least an hour to secure the area. We don't have the luxury of time in this case. I'm going in, and you'll have to back me up from the pier. I'll be as quick as I can. I doubt he's keeping a lookout. If he's there, he's probably sleeping."

"I can't let you do this," Martinsson said. "It's suicide."

"Keep in mind that Larstam didn't kill Hansson or the Malmö officer, and not because he missed. Neither was his ninth victim. This man is very particular about who he kills, and when."

"So he won't shoot you?"

"I think I have a good chance, that's all."

But Martinsson wasn't about to give in. "He has no escape route this time. What's he going to do? Jump into the water?"

"We have to take that chance," Wallander said. "I know that his not having an escape route could change everything."

"It's irresponsible."

Wallander's mind was made up. "All right then, we'll proceed with the necessary caution. Return to the station and see to it that we get the proper reinforcements. I'll stay here and keep an eye on the boat."

Martinsson left. Wallander instructed the Malmö officer to guard the car park. He walked out onto the pier, thinking that he was about to violate the most fundamental rule of police work. He was about to confront a ruthless killer, alone, without a single person to back him up, in an area that wasn't properly secured. Some children were playing on the pier. Wallander made himself sound as stern as possible and ordered them to move their games. His hand squeezed the gun in his pocket. He had already disengaged the safety catch. He studied the boat carefully and realised there was no way to approach it from the pier. If Larstam was on board he would see him. The only chance he had was to approach the boat from behind, but for that he needed a dinghy. He looked around. There was a party going on in the boat next to him, and a little red dinghy lay tied to its side. Wallander didn't hesitate. He climbed aboard and showed the surprised revellers his police identification.

"I need to borrow your dinghy," he said.

A bald man with a glass of wine in his hand stood up.

"Has there been an accident?"

"No," Wallander said. "But I have no time to explain it to you. Everyone stays put, no one climbs out onto the dock. Understood?"

No one argued with him. Wallander stepped clumsily into the dinghy and fumbled with the oars, dropping one. As he reached for it, the gun almost slid out of his pocket. He swore and broke out into a sweat. Eventually he got the oars under control and made his way into the harbour. He wondered if the dinghy was going to sink under his weight, but managed to approach the back of Larstam's boat without a mishap. He grabbed it with one hand and felt his heart pounding. He secured his dinghy, careful to avoid setting the other boat in motion. Then he stopped and listened. The only sound he heard was his own heart. Gun in hand, he slowly undid the fastenings of the covering on the back of the boat. Still no sound. Once he had undone a big enough portion of the covering he faced the hardest part. Now he had to flip the covering off and then throw himself to one side to avoid the person who might be waiting inside with a gun aimed at his head. His mind was blank, and the hand holding his gun was trembling and sweaty.

All at once he performed the manoeuvre. The dinghy rolled so hard he thought he was going to end up in the water. But he grasped a railing on the side of the boat and kept his balance. Nothing happened. He peeked inside and saw that the boat was empty. The small doors to the lower cabin were open, and he could see all the way in. No one was there. He climbed aboard, still holding his gun in front of him. It was two steps down to the bunk area. He saw that the bunks were not made up. The mattresses were covered with plastic.

The man with the bald head grabbed the mooring line when Wallander returned the dinghy. "Now maybe you'll tell us what that was all about," he said.

"No," Wallander replied.

He was in a hurry now. The others might already be on their way and he had to stop them. Larstam wasn't in the boat. That could mean they were one step ahead of him for the first time. Wallander paused on the pier and called Martinsson.

"We're on our way," Martinsson said.

"Abort!" yelled Wallander. "I don't want to see a single car! Come down here alone."

"Has anything happened?"

"He's not here."

"How do you know for sure?"

"I just know."

Martinsson was silent. "You went aboard," he said finally.

"We're under pressure," Wallander said. "We'll discuss this some other time."

Martinsson arrived in five minutes and Wallander told him about his hunch that they were one step ahead of Larstam at last. When Martinsson caught sight of the flapping covering at the back of the boat, he shook his head in disapproval.

"We'll have to fix that," Wallander said quickly. "You stand guard in case he's on his way."

Martinsson stayed on the pier while Wallander climbed aboard and into the cabin. He looked around but saw nothing. When he had fastened the covering, he returned to the pier.

"How did you manage it?" Martinsson asked.

"I borrowed a dinghy."

"You're crazy."

"Maybe. But I don't think so."

Wallander walked up to the Malmö officer guarding the car park and told him to keep an eye on the harbour and the marina. He also called the station and posted more officers on the job.

"You should go home and change your shirt," Martinsson said, staring at Wallander.

"I will," he said. "I just want to talk this through with the others."

No one at the station asked him how he had got onto the boat. No one seemed to think to ask him if he had done it alone. Martinsson sat through the meeting as if he had been struck dumb. Wallander realised how upset he was, but he would have to deal with that later.

"We have to keep looking for him," Wallander said. "He used Isa Edengren's name to rent his berth. He doesn't seem to be following a pattern, but somewhere we're going to run across a clue that will blow this whole case wide open. I'm sure of it."

Wallander felt for a moment as if he were preaching to the converted, but he didn't know what else to do.

"Why did Larstam choose Isa Edengren's name?" he said. "Is it a coincidence, or is there something more here?"

"Isa's funeral is the day after tomorrow," Martinsson said.

"Call her parents. Tell them I want them to come down so someone can ask them about the boat."

Wallander got to his feet. "Right now I'm going to excuse myself for 20 minutes so I can run home and change my shirt."

Ebba came into the room with a plate full of sandwiches. "If you give me your keys, I'll go and get it for you," she said. "It's no bother."

Wallander thanked her but declined her offer. He needed to get away, if only for a short while. He was about to leave the room when the phone rang. Höglund answered and immediately gestured for him to stay in the room.

"It's the Ludvika police," she says. "That's where one of Åke Larstam's sisters lives."

Wallander decided to stay. He looked around for Ebba, but she had left. Martinsson took over the call from Ludvika, while Höglund called Isa Edengren's parents. Wallander stared down at his coffee stain. Martinsson hung up.

"Berit Larstam," he said. "She's 47, an unemployed social worker. She lives in Fredriksberg, wherever that is."

"That's where the weapons were stolen," Wallander said. "Maybe Larstam was visiting his sister at the time."

Martinsson waved a small piece of paper at him, then dialled the number.

Wallander felt he was no longer needed for the moment. He looked for Ebba in reception, but couldn't see her, so he returned to the conference room.

"Axel Edengren, the father, has promised to come in," Höglund said. "I think we can expect a pompous arse who doesn't think much of the police."

"What makes you say that?"

"He lectured me at length about how incompetent we were. I almost lost my temper."

"That's what you should have done."

Martinsson ended his conversation. "Åke Larstam visited her about once every three years. They weren't particularly close."

Wallander stared at him with surprise. "Is that all?"

"What do you mean?"

"Didn't you ask her anything else?"

"Of course I did, but she asked if she could return my call later. She was in the middle of something."

Wallander was starting to get irritable, and Martinsson was on the defensive. Tension filled the air. Wallander left and went to reception. Ebba was there.

"I think I will ask you to get it for me after all," he said, handing her the keys. "There should be a clean shirt in the cupboard. If not, you'll have to take the cleanest one you find from the hamper."

"I'll take care of it."

"Can anyone give you a ride?"

"I have my trusty old Volvo," she said. "You haven't forgotten about it, have you?"

Wallander smiled. He watched her as she walked out the front doors. He thought again about how hard these last few years had been on her. He returned to the conference room and apologised to Martinsson for his bad temper. They continued their work.

CHAPTER THIRTY-FIVE

Ebba still wasn't back with his shirt by the time Axel Edengren arrived at the station. Wallander started wondering what was taking so long. Was she having trouble finding a clean shirt? Wallander felt somewhat ill at ease as he walked out to reception to greet Axel Edengren. Not so much because of the large coffee stain on his chest as because of his recollection of the strange way in which the Edengrens had treated their daughter. Wallander wondered what kind of man he was about to meet, and for once the reality matched his expectations. Axel Edengren was a big, powerfully built man, with a spiky crew-cut and intense blue eyes. He was one of the largest men Wallander had ever seen, and there was something unappealing about his bulk. His handshake was dismissive. As Wallander showed him to his office, he felt as though he was being followed by a bull about to skewer him with his horns. Axel Edengren started speaking before they sat down.

"You were the one who found my daughter," he said. "What brought you to Bärnsö in the first place?" He used the polite form of the Swedish "you" in addressing Wallander.

"Please feel free to use the informal 'you' with me," Wallander said.

Edengren's reply was swift and unexpected. "I prefer to use the polite form of address with people I don't know, and whom I plan to meet only once. What were you doing in Bärnsö, Inspector?"

Wallander felt a spark of anger, but he didn't think he had the energy to wield his usual authority.

"I had reason to believe Isa had gone there. And it turned out I was right."

"I've heard about the sequence of events. I can't believe you allowed it to happen."

"I didn't let anything happen. If I had had even the slightest inkling of what was about to happen, I would have done everything in my power to prevent it. I assume that goes for you too, not only in the case of Isa, but with Jörgen."

Edengren flinched at the sound of his son's name. It was as if he had been knocked to his knees while running at top speed. Wallander took the opportunity to turn the conversation around.

"We're pressed for time, so let me simply express my condolences for what happened. I met Isa several times and thought she was a nice young woman."

Edengren was about to say something, but Wallander pressed on. "There's a berth at the marina here in Ystad that has been rented in Isa's name."

Edengren regarded Wallander with suspicion. "That's a lie."

"No, it's quite true."

"Isa doesn't have a boat."

"That's what I thought. Do you have a berth here?"

"No, my boats are in a marina in Östergötland."

Wallander had no reason to doubt him. "We think someone else rented the berth in your daughter's name."

"Who would that be?"

"The person we believe killed your daughter."

Edengren stared at him. "Who is that?"

"His name is Åke Larstam."

There was no reaction. Edengren didn't recognise the name.

"Have you arrested him?"

"Not yet."

"Why not? You believe he killed my daughter, don't you?"

"We haven't managed to locate him. That's why we asked you to come down. We're hoping you can make our task easier."

"Who is he?"

"For security reasons I can't give you all the information right now. Let's just say he's been working as a postman for the past couple of years."

Edengren shook his head. "Is this some kind of joke? The postman killed my daughter?"

"Unfortunately it's no joke."

Edengren was about to ask him something else, but Wallander stopped him. The moment of low energy had passed.

"Did Isa have any contact with the sailing club that you know of? Did any of her friends have boats?"

Edengren's answer came as a surprise. "Not Isa, but Jörgen did. He had a sailing boat. In the summer he kept it in Gryt. He sailed all around Bärnsö. The rest of the year it was kept down here."

"But Isa never used the boat?"

"Only with her brother. They got along well together, at least most of the time."

For the first time Wallander sensed something like sorrow in his voice. There was nothing to read on the surface, but Wallander thought there was probably a volcano of feelings locked up inside his enormous body.

"How long did Jörgen sail for?"

"He started in 1992. He had a little informal sailing club with regular meetings. They had parties and sent letters back and forth in bottles. Jörgen was often the secretary. I had to show him how to write up the minutes."

"Do you still have those records?"

"I remember putting all the minutes in a box after he died. They must still be there."

I need names, Wallander thought.

"Can you think of the names of any of his friends?"

"Some, but not all."

"But the names are probably recorded in the minutes."

"Probably."

"Then I'd like you to go and get them," Wallander said. "It could be important."

Wallander offered to send a police car to Skårby, but Edengren wanted to get them himself. He turned around in the doorway.

"I don't know how I'm going to stand it," he said. "I've lost both my children. What else is there?"

He didn't wait for an answer, and Wallander would not have been able to give him one. He got up and walked to the conference room. Ebba wasn't there, and no one had seen her. Wallander called his home number. The phone rang eight times but no one answered. Ebba must be on her way back.

Edengren returned after 40 minutes, and handed Wallander a big brown envelope.

"That's all I have. I think there are eleven sets of minutes in there. They seem not to have taken it so seriously."

Wallander leafed through the papers. They were type-written and contained a number of mistakes. He found seven names altogether, but recognised none of them. Another dead end, he thought. I'm still looking for a pattern, but Åke Larstam doesn't follow one. He went to the conference room, showed the material to Martinsson and asked him to look over the names. Wallander was about to walk out the door when Martinsson gave a yell. Wallander turned and walked back. Martinsson pointed to the name "Stefan Berg".

"Wasn't one of the postmen called Berg?"

It had slipped Wallander's mind, but he now realised that Martinsson was right.

"I'll call him," Martinsson said.

Wallander returned to Edengren. He paused before walking into the room. Was there anything else he needed to ask? He didn't think so. He pushed open the door. Edengren was standing at the window and turned when he heard Wallander come in. To his surprise, Wallander saw that his eyes were red.

"You're free to go home now," he said. "We have no reason to keep you."

Edengren looked searchingly at him. "Will you get him? The bastard who killed Isa?"

"Yes, we'll get him."

"Why did he do it?"

"We don't know."

Edengren shook his hand and Wallander followed him out to reception. Still no sign of Ebba.

"We'll stay in Sweden until after the funeral," Edengren said. "Then I don't know. Maybe we'll leave Sweden, sell the house in Skårby and in Bärnsö too. The thought of going back there is too unbearable."

Edengren left without waiting for a response. Wallander stood for a long time after he had gone. When he returned to the conference room, Martinsson was getting off the phone.

"We were right," he said. "Stefan Berg is the postman's son. He's enrolled in a college in Kentucky right now."

"Where does that lead us?"

"Nowhere, really. Berg told me everything he could, I think. He said he often talked about himself and his family when he was at work. That means Åke Larstam would have had many opportunities to hear about Stefan and the sailing club."

Wallander sat down. "But where does it really lead us? Is there anything here that can point us in the right direction?"

"It doesn't seem like it."

Wallander suddenly erupted and swept the pile of papers in front of him onto the floor.

"We're not going to find him!" he yelled. "Where the hell is he? Who the hell is the ninth victim!"

The others in the room looked at him to see if he was done. Wallander threw his arms out in apology and left the room. He started walking up and down the hall. He checked to see if Ebba had come back, but she was still gone. She probably had trouble finding a clean shirt and went to buy me a new one, he thought.

It was 3.27 p.m., and there were only eight and a half hours left for Åke Larstam to do what he had promised to do.

Wallander went back to the conference room and waited until he caught Höglund's eye. When she came over to talk to him, he told her to get Martinsson and join him in his office.

"Let's think this through together," Wallander said when they were assembled. "We still have two questions. We need to know where he is, and who he's planning to kill. Even if he's planning his deed for the stroke of midnight, we have less than nine hours to go."

He knew that Martinsson and Höglund must have thought of this as well, but it seemed as if the full implications were only hitting them now.

"Where is he?" Wallander repeated. "What is he thinking? We found him in Svedberg's flat, which suggests he didn't think we would look for him there. But we did. Then there's his boat. But he may already assume it's too dangerous to use it. Then what will he do?"

"If his earlier crimes are anything to judge by," Martinsson said, "he'll choose a victim and a situation that poses little threat to himself. The way in which he's toying with us is different. He knows we're after him. He knows we've seen through his disguise."

"He's asking himself how we think," Höglund said.

Wallander felt that they were all thinking along the same track now. "You're Larstam," he said. "What are you thinking?"

"He's intending to go through with number nine. He's fairly sure we don't know who that is."

"How can he be so sure of that?"

"Because if we knew, we would have surrounded that person with police protection. He's made sure of the fact that this hasn't been done."

"We could also come to a different conclusion," Martinsson said. "He could be concentrating on finding a secure hiding place. He may not be overly concerned about getting to number nine yet."

"That may be what he wants us to think," Höglund said.

"So we have to think differently," Wallander said. "We have to take yet another step into the unknown."

"He must have chosen the most unlikely place for us to look for him."

"In that case he should be here, in the basement of the station," Martinsson said.

Wallander nodded. "Or some symbolic equivalent to the station. What could that be?"

None of them had a suggestion.

"Does he assume we know what he looks like as a man by now?"

"He can't take any chances."

Wallander suddenly thought of something. He turned to Martinsson. "Did you ask his sister for a photograph?"

"I did, but she said the only one she had was of Larstam as a 14-year-old, and that it wasn't a very good one."

"No help there then."

"Where is Åke Larstam at this exact moment?"

No one had an answer, because there was nothing to go on. Just this strenuous speculation. Wallander felt a hint of panic. Time was ticking inexorably by.

"What about the person he's after?" Wallander said. "He's killed six young people so far, as well as an older photographer and a middle-aged policeman. I think we should discount the last two. That leaves us with six young people, killed on two separate occasions in two groups."

"Three," Höglund objected. "He killed Isa Edengren on a separate occasion, alone on an island in the middle of nowhere."

"That tells us that he finishes what he starts," Wallander said. "He follows through, whatever it takes. Is there anything unfinished in his present situation? Or is he embarking on a new project?"

Before anyone could answer this last question, there was

a knock on the door. It was Ebba. She held a shirt on a hanger in her hand.

"I'm sorry it took so long," she said. "I took the opportunity to run some other errands, and then I had a lot of trouble with the lock on your front door."

Wallander frowned. There was nothing wrong with his lock as far as he knew. Ebba must have tried the wrong key. He took the shirt and thanked her for her efforts. Then he excused himself to go and change.

"Even when you're on your way to your own execution, it feels good to be wearing a clean shirt," he said when he came back. He stuffed the stained shirt in his desk drawer. "Where were we?"

"There's no unfinished business that we can think of," Martinsson said. "No one except for Isa was also due to attend the Midsummer celebration. And only two people get married at a time."

"We have to start again," Wallander said. "The worst possible case. We have nothing to go on."

The room became silent. There seemed to be nothing else to say. Of two impossible alternatives, we have to choose the one that seems less impossible, he thought.

"We're never going to figure out where he's hiding," he said finally. "Our only choice is to focus on his potential victim. This is what we have to concentrate on from now on, before he has a chance to do his deed. Are you with me?"

Wallander knew this was still an impossible task.

"Do you think it will do any good?" Höglund asked.

"We can't give up," Wallander replied.

They started again. It was past 4 p.m. Wallander's stomach ached from hunger and anxiety. He was so tired it was starting to feel like his natural state. He sensed the same desperate fatigue in the other two.

"In broad strokes," Wallander prompted, "what do we have? Happy people. Joyful people. What else?"

"Young people," Martinsson said.

"People in costume," Höglund added.

"I don't think he repeats himself," Wallander said. "But we can't be sure of that. The question then is where we can find out about happy, young people in costume who are gathering for some reason today, other than for a wedding or a midnight picnic in a nature reserve."

"Perhaps someone's having a masquerade?" Martinsson suggested.

"The newspaper," Wallander said suddenly. "What's going on in Ystad tonight?"

He had hardly finished the sentence before Martinsson had rushed out of the room.

"Should we return to the conference room?" Höglund asked.

"Not just yet. We'll go back soon enough. But I'd like to have something to bring to the table, even if it's just a red herring."

Martinsson stormed back into the office with the *Ystad Allehanda* in his hand. They laid it on the table and leaned over it. There was a fashion show in Skurup that immediately drew Wallander's attention.

"Models are dressed up," he said. "And we can assume they're generally feeling good about themselves."

"That's not until next Wednesday," Höglund said. "You misread it."

They kept flipping the pages, then all three of them saw it at the same time. That evening there was going to be an event at the Continental Hotel for the "Friends of Ystad" Society. Members were asked to attend in 17th-century dress. Wallander was doubtful from the start. Something told him it wasn't right, but Martinsson and Höglund didn't share his doubts.

"This must have been planned in advance," Martinsson said. "He's had a long time to make his preparations."

"The members of this type of society are rarely very young," Wallander said.

"The ages are often quite mixed," Höglund said. "That's my impression, anyway."

Wallander couldn't shake off his doubts, but they didn't have anything to lose. The dinner was scheduled for 7.30 p.m. They had a couple of hours to go. Just in case, they finished looking through the paper to see if there were any other events to consider, but found nothing.

"It's up to you," Martinsson said. "Do we focus on this or not?"

"It's not my decision," Wallander said. "It's ours. And I agree with you: what do we have to lose?"

They returned to the conference room. Wallander wanted both Thurnberg and Holgersson to be present, so someone was sent to get them. While they were waiting, Martinsson was trying to find out who was responsible for arranging the party that evening.

"Call the hotel," Wallander said. "They'll know who made the reservation."

Although Martinsson was standing right next to him, Wallander heard himself raise his voice. The fatigue and tension were taking their toll.

When Thurnberg and Holgersson entered the room, Wallander made a point of closing the door, underscoring the seriousness of the moment. He described the reasoning that had led them to the conclusion that Åke Larstam was planning to strike at a party at the Continental Hotel later that evening. They could be wrong in their assumptions; it might turn out to be another dead end. But it was all they had. The alternative was simply to wait. He thought Thurnberg would have strong objections and might dismiss the plan out of hand, but to his great surprise Thurnberg approved. He used the same argument they had: what else was there to do?

At these words they were under way. It was 5.15 p.m. and they had two hours to make their preparations. Wallander took Martinsson and went down to the Continental, while Höglund remained in the conference room. They called in reinforcments for the evening and Wallander insisted everyone be equipped with the highest level of protection. Åke Larstam was a dangerous man.

"I don't think I've ever worn a bulletproof vest," Wallander said. "Except during training exercises."

"It'll help, if he's still using his gun," Martinsson said. "The only problem is that he shoots people in the head."

Martinsson was right. Wallander made a call from the car and ordered helmets to go with the vests. They parked outside the main entrance to the hotel.

"The manager of the restaurant is called Orlovsky," Martinsson said.

"I've met him before," Wallander said.

Orlovsky had been notified of their visit and was waiting for them in the lobby. He was a tall, trim man in his 50s. Wallander decided to tell him exactly what was going on. Together they walked into the room where preparations for the evening's festivities were under way.

"We need to be as efficient as possible," Wallander said. "Could someone show Martinsson around while you and I talk?"

Orlovsky beckoned to a waiter who was setting the table. "He's been here for 20 years."

The waiter's name was Emilsson. He looked surprised at the request but obediently accompanied Martinsson out of the room. Wallander told Orlovsky enough to let him know what was going on.

"Wouldn't it be best to cancel the event altogether?" Orlovsky asked when Wallander had finished.

"Perhaps. But we won't do that unless we decide that the security of the guests will be compromised, and we're not quite there yet."

Wallander wanted to know how the guests would be seated and asked to see the seating arrangement. They were expecting 34 people. Wallander paced around the room and tried to imagine Larstam's preparations. He doesn't want to be caught, Wallander thought. He'll have his avenue of escape well prepared. I doubt he's planning to kill all 34 people, but he'll need to get close to the tables.

A thought struck him. "How many waiters will be working tonight?" he asked.

"Six altogether."

"Do you know them all personally?"

"All except one who's been hired for this evening."

"What's his name?"

Orlovsky pointed to a small, pudgy man of around 65 who was setting out the glasses.

"His name is Leijde and he's often called in to help with larger dinners. Would you like to talk to him?"

Wallander shook his head. "What about the kitchen staff? The bartender? Who's working the coat check?"

"They're all permanent employees."

"Do you have any guests staying at the hotel?"

"A couple of German families."

"Will anyone else be here tonight?"

"No, the whole dining area has been reserved for the

509

party, although we have room for more. That leaves only the receptionist."

"Is it still Hallgren?" Wallander said. "I've met him before."

Orlovsky confirmed that Hallgren still worked there. Martinsson and the waiter Emilsson returned from the kitchen. Emilsson went back to setting the table, while Martinsson sat down to sketch an approximation of the dining area, lavatories, and kitchen with Orlovsky's help. Wallander wondered briefly if the staff should be given protective gear as well, but decided against it. It would tip Larstam off. All of a sudden Wallander had the distinct impression that he was somewhere close by, that he was surveying the comings and goings at the hotel.

Time was running out. Wallander and Martinsson returned to the station, where they were told that reinforcements were on their way. Höglund and Holgersson had moved quickly.

Martinsson's sketch was put onto a transparency. "Here's what we're going to do," Wallander said. "At some point Larstam will try to enter the hotel. Meanwhile we have to surround the entire building, although I want our men to be invisible, hard as I know that is. Otherwise we'll scare him off."

He looked around, but no one had any comments. He continued. "If he somehow manages to break through our outer ring of officers, we'll have a team placed inside the dining room. I suggest Martinsson and Höglund dress up as members of the waiting staff."

"With a bulletproof vest and helmet?" Martinsson said.

"No. If he enters the dining room, we have to get him at once. All exits from the dining room have to be blocked. I'm going to be circulating the entire area, since

I'm the only person who can actually identify him."

Wallander paused. Before the meeting broke up he had one more thing to add.

"We can't overlook the fact that he may be dressed up as a woman. Not Louise, but someone else. We can't even know he's going to turn up for sure."

"What if he doesn't?"

"Then we go home and get a good night's sleep. That's what we need most, after all."

They took up their positions at the hotel a little after 7 p.m. Martinsson and Höglund put on waiters' uniforms, and Wallander positioned himself behind the reception desk. He was in radio contact with eight other officers outside the building, as well as one stationed in the kitchen. He had his gun in his pocket. The guests started arriving. Höglund was right. Many of them were quite young, as young as Isa Edengren. They were dressed up and the atmosphere was joyful. Laughter filled the lobby and dining room. Åke Larstam would have hated this display of happiness.

It was now 8 p.m. Wallander checked continually with the other officers, but no one saw anything suspicious. At 8.23 p.m. there was an alarm from Suprgränd, just south of the hotel. A man had stopped on the footpath and was looking up at the hotel windows. Wallander rushed to the spot but the man was gone before he arrived. One of the police officers identified him as the owner of an Ystad shoe shop. Wallander returned to the lobby, where he heard drinking songs coming from the dining room. Someone got up and made a toast.

Still nothing happened. Martinsson showed up at the entrance to the dining room. Wallander felt the constant grip of tension. It showed no sign of letting up. There were more drinking songs, more toasts. At 10.40 p.m., the party was beginning to come to a close. Larstam hadn't showed up. We were wrong, Wallander thought. He didn't show up. Or else he saw our men.

He felt a mixture of disappointment and relief. The ninth person, whoever he was, was still alive. Tomorrow they would go through the evening's guest list one by one and try to identify the intended victim. But Larstam was still on the loose somewhere.

At 11.30 p.m. the streets were deserted once more. The guests had gone home, all the officers were back at the station. Wallander made sure that the marina and the flat on Harmonigatan would be kept under surveillance all night. He returned to the station along with Martinsson and Höglund, but none of them had the energy to discuss what had happened. They decided to meet at 8 a.m. the next morning. Thurnberg and Holgersson agreed. They would have to figure out why Larstam hadn't shown up the next day.

"We've gained some time," Thurnberg said. "If nothing else, this manoeuvre gave us that."

Wallander went back to his office and locked his gun in one of the drawers. Then he drove back to Mariagatan. It was just before midnight when he started up the stairs to his flat.

CHAPTER THIRTY-SIX

Wallander put his key in the lock and turned it. From the back of his mind came Ebba's words about the lock having been stiff. The door was hard to open if it was locked from the other side with the key still in it, which only happened if someone was already there. Linda did this. When he came home and the lock was stiff, it was a reminder that she was staying with him.

His exhaustion was slowing down his thought processes. He unlocked the door, thinking about what Ebba had said, but now the lock was working smoothly. The reason for this dawned on him as he opened the door. He sensed more than saw the figure at the end of the hall. He threw himself to one side and felt a searing pain as something tore open his right cheek. He then flung himself down the stairs, thinking each moment was about to be his last.

Larstam.

This was not the situation Hansson and the Malmö officer had encountered earlier in the day. Nor was it the situation Ebba had been in, although Larstam must have been there when she entered the flat. I am the ninth victim, Wallander thought. He reached the bottom of the stairs, ripped open the front door, and ran. When he reached the end of the street he stopped and turned. There was no one there. The street was deserted. Blood gushed from the wound on his cheek. His whole head thudded with pain. He reached for the gun in his pocket, then remembered he had locked it in his desk. The whole time, he kept his eyes on the door to his building, waiting for Larstam to come out. He took cover in the shadows of another doorway. The only thing he could do when Larstam showed up was to keep running. Now he finally knew where he was, and this time there was no back door for Larstam to use for his escape. There was only one way out, and that was through the front door.

Wallander fumbled for his mobile phone with his bloody hands. Was it in his car? But then he remembered putting the phone down on his desk at work. He let out a stream of curses under his breath. No gun and no phone. He couldn't call anyone for help. His mind worked frantically to find a solution, but nothing came to him. How long he stood there in the shadows, his coat collar pressed against his bleeding cheek, he didn't know. He kept his eyes on the door the whole time. Every once in a while he cast a glance at the dark windows of his flat. Larstam is up there, he thought. He can see me down here, but he doesn't know I'm unarmed. After a while, when no police cars show up he'll get the picture. That's when he'll make his move.

He looked up at the sky. There was nearly a full moon, although clouds obscured it. What am I doing, he thought, and what is going through Larstam's mind? He looked at his watch. It was 12.07 a.m., on Thursday, 22 August. The fact that it was past midnight wasn't likely to help him now. Larstam had trapped him. Had he guessed Wallander and his colleagues would be distracted by the masquerade party at the hotel?

Wallander tried to work out how Larstam had broken into his flat. Suddenly he saw what must have happened, and it gave him a sense of how Larstam worked. He took advantage of opportunity. The day before, during

Svedberg's funeral, every police officer in town had been at the church. That would have given Larstam plenty of time to work on the lock. Once inside, he had probably found the spare keys.

Wallander's thoughts were racing, his cheek burned, and fear still throbbed in his body. The most important question was why Larstam had chosen him as his victim, but he pushed it aside for the time being.

I have to do something, he thought. Without merely attracting enough attention for someone to call the police. If they do, I won't have a chance to explain to the patrol officers the situation they're heading into. Chaos will result.

He heard footsteps. A man came around the corner and walked straight towards Wallander, who emerged from his shadowy doorway. He was youngish, probably in his 30s. His hands were pushed deep into the pockets of his suede jacket. When he saw Wallander, he pulled them out with a start and took a step back, looking frightened.

"I'm a police officer," Wallander said. "There's been an accident. I need your help."

The man looked at him, uncomprehending.

"Don't you understand what I'm saying? I'm a police officer and I need you to contact the station. Tell them Larstam is in Wallander's flat on Mariagatan. Tell them to be careful. Understood?"

The man shook his head, then said something in a foreign language. It sounded like Polish. Oh, hell, Wallander thought. That's just my luck. He tried his speech in English, but the man said only a few broken words in reply. Wallander, about to lose his patience, moved closer to the man and raised his voice, and the man fled.

Wallander was alone again. Larstam was still up there behind the dark windows, and soon, very soon, he would guess why no one was showing up. Then Wallander's only option would be to run. He tried to gather his thoughts. There had to be something he could do. He lifted his hand as if signalling to someone across the street. He pointed up to his flat and yelled a few words. Then he walked around the corner, out of sight of the dark windows where he presumed Larstam was standing. He can't know there's no one there, Wallander thought. Maybe it'll buy me some time, although there's also a chance he'll just take off.

Then something he hadn't even been hoping for happened. A car turned onto the street. Wallander jumped out in front of it, waving his arms. The driver seemed reluctant to have anything to do with him, especially after he saw Wallander's bloody face. But Wallander thrust his hand in through the half-open window and opened the door. A man in his 50s was driving the car, a much younger woman at his side. Wallander immediately had a bad feeling about them, but pushed these thoughts aside.

"I'm a police officer," he said. "There's been an accident and I need to use your phone." He managed to get his police badge out to show them.

"I don't have a phone."

Doesn't everybody have mobile phones these days? Wallander thought desperately. "What's happened?" the man asked anxiously.

"Never mind that. I need you to drive straight down to the police station. Do you know where that is?"

"No, I'm not from around here," the man said.

"I know where it is," the woman said.

"Just go there and tell them that Larstam is in Wallander's flat. Can you repeat that for me?"

The man nodded. "Larstam is in Wallgren's flat."

"It's Wallander, damn it."

"Larstam is in Wallander's flat."

"Tell them Wallander needs assistance, but that they must approach carefully."

The man repeated his words, then they drove off. Wallander hurried back to the corner of Mariagatan and surveyed the scene. He couldn't have been gone more than a minute, hardly enough time for Larstam to get away. Wallander looked down at his watch. It would take ten minutes at most for the first police car to arrive. How long was Larstam planning to wait?

A quarter of an hour went by with no sign of the police. Wallander finally realised the couple had lied. They had no intention of delivering his message. That put him back where he had started. He was trying to think of another solution when he heard a noise.

It was the sound of a car engine and it came from the back of the building. Without being able to explain why, he immediately knew it was Larstam. How had he escaped without being seen? He must have gone over the roof. There was a window leading to the roof in the stairwell just above his flat. Larstam must have seen it and climbed down to street level from the back of the house.

Wallander made it to the end of the street in time to see a red car flash by. He didn't catch a glimpse of the driver but he knew it was Larstam. Without a second thought, he jumped into his own car and took up the chase. He soon had Larstam's rear lights in view. He knows I'm after him, Wallander thought. But he doesn't know I'm unarmed.

They turned onto Highway 19 in the direction of Kristianstad. Larstam drove very fast. Wallander looked down at his fuel indicator and saw it was approaching the red strip just before "empty". He tried to think where

Larstam could be headed. He was probably simply driving aimlessly. They drove through Stora Herrestad. There was almost no traffic. Wallander had passed only two cars going in the opposite direction.

What do I do if Larstam suddenly stops his car? he thought. What if he gets out holding his gun? He had to be ready to stop if need be. Larstam suddenly increased his speed. They were at a section of the highway where there were a number of tight bends in the road. Wallander started losing sight of Larstam's car, and tried to steel himself for the possibility that Larstam was stopped around the next bend, ready to take aim at him as he appeared. He tried to think of what he should do. He was alone. No one knew where he was; he wasn't going to be able to tell anyone to send him the help he needed.

Then he caught sight of Larstam's car again. It was making the turn into Fyledalen, and Larstam had turned off his headlights. Wallander slammed on the brakes and approached the turn-off carefully. The moon appeared through the clouds from time to time, but otherwise it was pitch black outside. Wallander parked by the side of the road and turned off his own lights. There was no sound. Larstam must have parked his car as well. Wallander headed out into the darkness, tucking his white shirt collar inside his dark blue jacket. He brushed his cheek, which started bleeding again. Wallander clambered down through a ditch and reached a meadow. His foot came down on something that made a sudden crunching noise. He swore silently and crept away from the spot. I'm not the only one listening for sounds, he thought.

He continued carefully towards some bushes, where he paused. If he was right, he was now straight across from the road leading into the nature reserve. When he shifted his foot, he came up against another object. He put down his hand and realised it was a broken-off piece of timber. He picked it up.

I'm turning into a man from the Stone Age, he thought. The Swedish Police Force has started incorporating wooden planks in their armoury. Is this the truth about the way things are going in Sweden? A return to the age-old laws of revenge and retaliation that justify the taking of blood?

Now the moon emerged from behind the clouds. Wallander crouched down, smelling the earth and clay. He saw Larstam's car. It was parked just a little way in from the main highway. There was no movement around it. Wallander scoured the area, but the clouds came back and darkness returned.

Larstam must have left the car, he thought. But what is he planning? He knows that I'm still pursuing him. He probably still thinks I'm armed, but he must also know by now that I've failed to establish contact, and that we're completely alone out here in Fyledalen. Two armed men.

Wallander tried to work out what his options were, while straining to hear any sound. Several times he felt an unpleasant puff of chilly air on the back of his neck that made him think Larstam was right next to him, the gun pointed at his head. The gun that had already been fired once at his forehead. Wallander never heard the gun go off – all he had felt was the pain and something cutting open his cheek. Larstam had used a silencer.

How was his mind working right now? He couldn't have anticipated this chase, and so he couldn't have planned his escape route. Wallander sensed that Larstam was as confused as he was. He couldn't remain in the car, he didn't know whether he was staying close to it or whether he was proceeding deeper into the nature reserve. He can hardly see in this darkness either, Wallander thought. We're in the same boat.

Wallander decided to cross the street and approach the car from the side. The moon was still completely covered, so he ran in a crouched position across the road and plunged into some bushes on the other side. Larstam's car was now only 20 metres away. He listened, but there were no sounds. He held the plank firmly in his hands. That's when he heard it. A twig snapped somewhere in front of him. Wallander pressed closer into the bushes, then heard the sound again, fainter this time. Larstam was moving away from the car in the direction of the valley. Larstam must have been biding his time, just like Wallander. But now he had started moving. If Wallander hadn't crossed the road when he did, he would never have heard the faint sounds.

I finally have the advantage, he thought. I can hear you, but you have no idea I'm close by. There was another crunching noise. Larstam must have brushed up against a tree. The sounds were getting further and further away. Wallander slid out from behind the bushes and started walking along the road. He stayed in a crouch the whole time, and kept close to the undergrowth along the side of the road. After every fifth step he stopped and listened. When he had gone about 50 metres he stopped for 5 minutes or so. An owl hooted nearby. There was no further sound of Larstam moving. Had he stopped as well, or was he somewhere up ahead, out of earshot? Wallander's fear returned. Was he walking into a trap? Had Larstam snapped those branches knowingly, to attract Wallander's attention? His heart thudded loudly in his chest. Larstam and his gun must be somewhere close by.

Wallander glanced up at the sky. A break in the clouds

was approaching. Soon the moon would be out, and he couldn't stay where he was when that happened. If Larstam was springing a trap, he had to be somewhere just up ahead. Wallander crossed to the other side of the road and moved up a small incline. There he positioned himself behind a tree and waited.

The moon came out. Suddenly the landscape was awash in blue. Wallander stared at the road in front of him, but saw nothing. The bushes were thinning ahead, and he was approaching a rolling hillside. At the top of the hill was a single tree.

The moon was swallowed up by the clouds. Wallander thought about the tree at the crime scene in the nature reserve. He was sure Larstam had used it as his hiding place. He's like a cat, Wallander thought. He seeks out lofty and secluded places in order to maintain his sense of control.

He was convinced that Larstam was hidden behind that tree on the hill. There was no reason for him not to keep going until he killed Wallander, both to secure his escape and because he had singled him out as an intended victim. This was Wallander's only opportunity. Larstam's attention would be on the road. That's where he thought Wallander would be coming from.

Wallander knew what he had to do. He had to make a long detour down along the road, across to the left side of the hill and then up to some point right behind the tree from the back. What he would do then he didn't know, nor did he care to think about it just now.

He proceeded in three phases. First he walked back down along the road. Then he crept up the hillside, very slowly so he wouldn't attract any attention. Then he walked up, parallel to the road. He stopped. The clouds blocking the moon became thicker, and he had trouble seeing where he was. It was 2.06 a.m.

The moon didn't shine again until 2.27 a.m. It was enough to show Wallander that he was positioned some distance below the tree. He couldn't tell if there was a person behind it or not. He was too far away, and there was thick brush in the way. But he tried to memorise the terrain between him and the tree.

The moon disappeared. The owl hooted more distantly. Wallander tried to reason with himself. Larstam doesn't think I'll be creeping up on him from behind, he thought. But I can't underestimate him, either. Larstam will be ready for me wherever I come from.

Wallander started making his approach. He went very slowly, like a blind person fumbling in the darkness. Sweat poured from his body and his heart was beating so hard he thought it was loud enough for Larstam to hear. At last he reached an area of thick brush that he knew was 20 or 30 metres away from the tree.

It took almost 20 minutes for the moon to come out again, but when it did he finally saw him. Larstam. He was leaning up against the tree trunk, and seemed completely absorbed in watching the road. Wallander could see both his hands. The gun must be tucked in his pocket. It would take him a few seconds to get it out and turn around. That's all the time Wallander had. He tried to estimate the exact distance to the tree, searching out every possible obstacle in his path. He couldn't see one. He looked up at the sky and saw that the moon was about to go behind a cloud again. If he was to have any hope of reaching Larstam he would have to make his approach at the very moment the moon disappeared. He clenched the plank in his hands.

This is insanity, he thought. I'm doing something I know I shouldn't do. But I have to do it.

The moonlight was fading now. He slowly rose to his feet. Larstam hadn't moved. At the moment the light disappeared, he sprang up. Somewhere deep inside he felt the desire to utter a war cry. It would maybe give him a couple of extra seconds, if it scared Larstam. But no one knew how that man was likely to react. No one.

Wallander leaped forward and dashed at the tree. He was nearly there and Larstam hadn't turned around. There was almost no light. Then his foot hit a rock or root. He lost his balance and pitched forward at Larstam's feet just as he turned around. Wallander grabbed his leg, but Larstam grunted and pulled away. As he tried to get his gun out, Wallander rushed him again. With the first swing of his plank, he hit only the tree behind Larstam. There was a splintering sound. He aimed what remained of the plank at Larstam's chest, then threw a punch. He didn't even know where the sudden surge of strength came from, but with sheer luck he hit Larstam right on the jaw. It gave way with a wet, unpleasant sound and Larstam slumped down. Wallander threw himself on top of him and hit him again and again, before he realised that the man under him was unconscious. Then he reached for Larstam's gun, the one that had killed so many people. For a split second he wanted to place it against Larstam's forehead and pull the trigger. But he restrained himself.

He dragged Larstam down along the road. He was still unconscious, and it was only once they had reached Wallander's car that he started making low moans. Wallander got a length of rope out of the back of the car and tied his arms together behind his back, then tied him securely to the front seat. Wallander got in behind the wheel and looked over at Larstam.

Suddenly it seemed to him that the person in the other seat was Louise.

Wallander arrived at the station at 3.45 a.m. When he got out of the car, it was starting to rain. He let the drops run down his face before he went in to speak to the officer on duty. To his surprise he saw that it was Edmundsson. He was drinking a cup of coffee and eating a sandwich. Edmundsson flinched at the sight of Wallander's face. His clothes were muddy and covered with twigs and leaves.

"What's wrong?"

"No questions," Wallander said firmly. "There's a man tied to the front seat of my car. Get someone to go with you and bring him in. Make sure he's handcuffed."

"Who is it?"

"Åke Larstam."

Edmundsson stood up, his sandwich still in his hand. It looked like ham and cheese. Without thinking twice, Wallander took it out of his hand and started eating it. It made his cheek hurt, but his hunger won out.

"You mean to say the killer is tied up in your car?"

"You heard what I said. Put some handcuffs on him, take him to a room, and lock the door. What's Thurnberg's number?"

Edmundsson quickly brought it up on his computer and then left. Wallander finished the sandwich, chewing slowly. There was no reason to hurry any more. He dialled Thurnberg's number. After a long time a woman answered. Wallander told her who he was, and Thurnberg came on the line.

"It's Wallander. I think you should come down here."

"What for? What time is it?"

524

"I don't care what time it is, you have to come down here and make the formal arrest of Åke Larstam."

Wallander heard Thurnberg catch his breath. "Can you repeat that?"

"I have Larstam."

"How in God's name did you do that?"

It was the first time Wallander had heard Thurnberg caught completely off guard.

"I found him out in the woods."

Thurnberg seemed finally to have understood that he was in earnest. "I'll be right there."

Edmundsson and another officer walked by with Larstam between them. Wallander met his gaze. Neither of them spoke. Wallander walked to the conference room and laid Larstam's gun on the table.

Thurnberg arrived quickly. He too flinched at the sight of Wallander, who still hadn't been to the men's room to check his appearance, although he had managed to find some painkillers in a desk drawer. He also found his mobile phone, which he threw into the rubbish in a sudden rage.

Wallander told Thurnberg what had happened as succinctly as possible. He pointed to Larstam's gun. As if to mark the solemnity of the moment, Thurnberg fished a tie out of his pocket and put it on.

"So you got him. Not bad."

"Oh, it was bad all right," Wallander said. "But we can go into that another time."

"Maybe we should call the others and let them know," Thurnberg said.

"What for? Why not let them sleep for once?"

Thurnberg dropped the suggestion. He left to go and see Larstam. Wallander got heavily to his feet and walked to the men's room. The cut in his cheek was deep and probably needed stitches, but the thought of dragging himself to the hospital made him weak. It would have to wait. It was now 5.30 a.m. He went to his office and closed the door behind him.

Martinsson was the first to arrive the next morning. He had slept badly and anxiety had forced him to come into the station. Thurnberg was still there and told him the news. Martinsson then called Höglund, Nyberg and Hansson in quick succession. Shortly afterwards Holgersson arrived. It was only when they had all gathered at the station that someone asked where Wallander was. Thurnberg told them he had disappeared. They assumed he had gone to the hospital to have his cheek looked at.

At 8.30 a.m. Martinsson called Wallander at home but there was no answer. That was when Höglund wondered whether he was in his office. They went there together. The door was closed. Martinsson knocked gently. When there was no answer, they pushed open the door. Wallander was stretched out on the floor, the phone book and his jacket tucked under his head for a pillow. He was snoring.

Höglund and Martinsson looked at each other. Then they pulled the door shut and let him rest.

EPILOGUE

On Friday, 25 October, rain fell steadily over Ystad. When Wallander stepped out onto the footpath on Mariagatan shortly after 8 a.m., it was 7°C. Although he was trying to walk to work as often as possible, this time he took the car. He had been on sick leave for two weeks, and Dr Göransson had just ordered him to remain off duty for one more. His blood-sugar levels were much lower, but his blood pressure remained high.

He wasn't driving to the station this morning in order to work. He had an important meeting to attend, one that he had agreed to during those chaotic August days when they were still searching blindly for the man who had carried out the most appalling series of murders they had ever investigated.

Wallander could still recall the particular moment quite clearly. Martinsson had come to his office, and at the end of their conversation he had told him that his 11-year-old son was thinking of becoming a police officer. Martinsson had complained that he didn't know what to say to his son, and Wallander promised to speak to him once the investigation was over. Now the time had finally come. He had even promised to let the boy, David, try on his his policeman's cap, and had spent the entire evening looking for it.

Wallander parked the car and hurried into the building, hunching his shoulders against the rain and wind. Ebba had a cold. She warned him to keep his distance and blew her nose. Wallander thought about the fact that she wouldn't be working there in a little less than a year.

David was due at 8.45 a.m. While he was waiting, Wallander cleaned up his desk. In a few hours he was leaving Ystad. He still wasn't sure if this was the right decision or not, but he looked forward to the prospect of driving his car through the autumn landscape, listening to opera.

David was punctual. Ebba showed him to Wallander's office.

"You have a visitor," she said smiling.

"A VIP by the looks of it," Wallander said.

He looked like his father. There was something introverted about him, something that Wallander noticed in Martinsson as well. Wallander put his policeman's cap on the table.

"What should we start with?" he asked. "Your questions or the cap?"

"The questions."

David took a piece of paper out of his pocket. He was well prepared. "Why did you become a policeman?"

The simple question threw Wallander. He was forced to think for a minute, since he had already decided to take the meeting seriously. He wanted to make his answers honest and thoughtful.

"I think I believed I would make a good policeman."

"Aren't all policemen good?"

This was not a question written on the sheet.

"Most of them, but not all. In the way that not all teachers are good."

"What did your parents say about you becoming a policeman?"

"My mother didn't say anything. She died before I had made up my mind."

"What about your dad?"

"He was against it. He was so much against it, in fact, that we almost stopped talking to each other."

"Why?"

"I don't even really know. That may sound strange, but it's the way it was."

"You must have asked him why."

"I never got a good answer."

"Is he dead?"

"He died not so long ago. So now I can't ask him any more, even if I wanted to."

Wallander's answer seemed to worry David. He hesitated over his next question.

"Have you ever regretted becoming a policeman?"

"Many times. I think everyone does."

"Why?"

"Because you have to see so much suffering. You feel helpless, and you wonder how you're going to hold out until your retirement."

"Don't you ever feel that you're helping people?"

"Sometimes, but not always."

"Do you think I should become a policeman?"

"I think you should take your time to make a decision. I think you have to be 17 or 18 years old before you really know what you want to do."

"I'm going to be either a policeman or a road construction worker."

"Road construction?"

"Helping people get around is also good."

Wallander nodded. This was a thoughtful child.

"I only have one question left," David said. "Are you ever scared?"

"Yes."

"What do you do then?"

"I don't know. I end up sleeping badly. I try to think of other things, if I can."

The boy put the piece of paper back in his pocket and looked at the cap. Wallander pushed it towards him and he tried it on. Wallander gave him a mirror. The cap was so large it fell down over his ears.

Wallander accompanied him out to the reception area. "Feel free to come back and see me again if you have more questions."

He watched the boy walk out into the blustery cold. Then he returned to his office in order to finish cleaning it out, although his desire to leave the station was growing. Höglund appeared in the doorway.

"I thought you were on sick leave."

"I am."

"How was your meeting? Martinsson told me about it."

"David is a smart boy. I tried to answer his questions as honestly as possible, but I think his dad could have done as well."

"Do you have time to talk?"

"A little. I'm about to leave town for a couple of days."

She closed the door and sat down in the chair across from his desk.

"I don't know why I'm telling you this," she said. "I want you to keep it to yourself for the time being."

She's quitting, Wallander thought. She can't take it any more.

"Promise?"

"I promise."

"Sometimes it's such a relief just to tell one other person."

"I'm the same."

"I'm getting a divorce," she said. "We've finally agreed

on it, if you can call it that when there are two young children involved."

Wallander wasn't surprised. She had indicated that they were having serious problems early in the summer.

"I don't know what to say."

"You don't have to say anything. I just wanted you to know."

"I've gone through a divorce myself," he said. "Or was divorced. I know what hell it can be."

"But you've done so well."

"Have I? I would tend to say the opposite."

"In that case you hide it well."

The rain outside was falling harder.

"There was one other thing I wanted to tell you," she said. "Larstam is writing a book."

"A book?"

"About the murders. About what it felt like to do it."

"How do you know that?"

"I saw it in the papers."

Wallander was upset. "Who's paying him?"

"Some publishers. They're keeping the advance a secret, but I think we can safely assume it's quite large. I'm sure a mass murderer's memoirs will be a bestseller."

Wallander shook his head angrily. "It makes me sick."

She got to her feet. "I just wanted you to know."

She turned when she reached the doorway. "Have a nice trip," she said. "Wherever you're going."

She disappeared. Wallander thought about what she had told him, about her divorce and the book. They had caught Larstam before he had managed to kill his ninth victim. Afterwards everyone who came into contact with him was struck by his gentle and reserved manner. They were expecting a monster, but this wasn't someone Sture Björklund would have been able to copy for a horror film. Wallander sometimes thought Larstam seemed like the most normal person he had ever met.

He had spent many days interrogating him. It struck him repeatedly that Åke Larstam wasn't just an enigma to the world around him but also to himself. He seemed to answer Wallander's questions honestly, but his answers shed no light.

"Why did you kill the young people celebrating Midsummer in the nature reserve?" Wallander had asked him. "You opened their letters, you followed their preparations for the party, and you shot them. Why?"

"Is there a better way for life to end?"

"Was that why you killed them? Because you thought you were doing them a favour?"

"I think so."

"Think? You must know why you did it."

"It's possible to plan things and still not be sure why you do them."

"You travelled all around Europe and sent postcards in their names. You hid their cars and buried their bodies. Why?"

"I didn't want them to be found."

"But you buried them in a way that gave you the option of disinterring them again."

"I wanted to have that option, yes."

"Why?"

"I don't know, to make my presence known perhaps. I don't know."

"You took the trouble of following Isa Edengren to Bärnsö and killing her there. Why not let her live?"

"You should finish what you start."

Sometimes Wallander had to leave the room, knowing

he was in fact talking to a monster and not a human being, despite the smiling and gentle exterior. But he always returned, determined to cover all the aspects of the case, from the newly-weds whose joy Larstam had been unable to tolerate, to Svedberg.

Svedberg. They discussed their long and complicated love affair. Bror Sundelius hadn't known that Svedberg was betraying him with another man. Nils Stridh found out and threatened to talk. They talked about Svedberg's growing fears that the man he had loved in secret for ten years was somehow connected with the disappearance of the young people.

Wallander never felt satisfied with the answers he received. There was something absentminded about Larstam's way of speaking. He was always polite, always apologetic when he couldn't recall an event to his satisfaction. But there was a space within him that he never managed to penetrate. Wallander never fully understood the relationship between Larstam and Svedberg.

"What happened that morning?" he asked.

"Which morning?"

"When you shot Svedberg."

"I had to kill him."

"Why?"

"He accused me of being involved with the disappearance of those young people."

"They didn't just disappear, they were killed. How did Svedberg start to suspect your involvement in this?"

"I talked to him about it."

"You told him what you had done?"

"No, but I told him about my dreams."

"Which dreams?"

"That I got people to stop laughing."

"Why didn't you want people to laugh?"

"Happiness always turns into its opposite sooner or later. I wanted to spare him this fate. So I told him about my dreams."

"Your dreams of killing people who were happy?"

"Yes."

"So he started to suspect you?"

"I didn't realise it until a few days before."

"Before what?"

"Before I shot him."

"What happened?"

"He was starting to ask questions. It was almost like he was interrogating me. It made me nervous. I didn't like feeling nervous."

"So then you just went over to his place and shot him?"

"At first I was planning to ask him to stop making me so nervous, but he kept asking his questions. That's when I realised I had to do it. I went out into the hall and got my shotgun. I had brought it with me just in case. I got it out and I shot him."

Wallander didn't say anything for a long time. He tried to imagine what Svedberg's last moments had been like. Did he have time to see what was coming? Or did it all happen too fast?

"That must have been very hard for you," he said finally. "To be forced to kill the person you loved."

Larstam stared back at him without answering, devoid of any expression. Even when Wallander asked the question a second time, there was no answer. He finally brought up the evening when Larstam ambushed him in his flat on Mariagatan.

"Why did you choose me to be your ninth victim?"

"I didn't have anyone else."

"What do you mean?"

"I was going to wait, maybe a year, maybe longer. But then I felt the need to keep going since things had turned out so well."

"But I'm not a happy person. I don't laugh a lot."

"You had a job and a reason to get up every morning. I had seen pictures of you in the papers where you were smiling."

"But I wasn't dressed up. I wasn't even wearing my uniform that day."

Larstam's answer came as a surprise. "I was planning to give you one."

"Give me what?"

"A costume, a disguise. I was planning to put my wig on you and try to make your face look like Louise. I didn't need her any more. She could die. I had decided to make myself into another woman."

Larstam looked him right in the eye and Wallander returned his gaze. He was never sure afterwards what it was he had seen there. But he knew he would never forget it.

There came a time when he had no more questions. Wallander arrived at an understanding of a man who was crazy, who never fitted in anywhere, and who finally exploded in uncontrollable violence. The psychological examination corroborated this picture. Larstam had been constantly threatened and intimidated as a child and had concentrated on mastering the ability to hide and get away. He had lacked the resources to deal with his termination from the engineering firm and had come to believe that all smiling people were evil.

It occurred to Wallander that there was a frightening social dimension to all of this. More and more people were being judged useless and were being flung to the margins of society, where they were destined to look back enviously at the few who still had reasons to be happy. He was reminded of a conversation he and Höglund had once begun but never had the chance to finish. They were debating whether or not the decline of Swedish society was more advanced than people generally admitted. Irrational violence was almost an accepted part of daily life these days. It gave him the feeling that they were already one step behind, and for the very first time in his life Wallander wondered if a complete collapse of the Swedish state was a real possibility. Bosnia had always seemed so far away, he thought. But maybe it was closer than they realised. Thoughts like these kept returning to him during the long sessions with Larstam, who maybe wasn't as much of a riddle as he should have been. Maybe Larstam's breakdown could be tied to the breakdown of society itself. There was nothing more to say. Wallander declared himself finished; Larstam was taken away and that was that.

A few days later, Eva Hillström committed suicide. Höglund was the one who told Wallander. He listened to the news in silence, left the station, bought a bottle of whisky, and drank himself into a stupor. He never spoke about it afterwards, but he always thought of her as Larstam's ninth victim.

He turned into the roadside reataurant outside Västervik around 2 p.m. He knew it was closed in the winter, but he still hoped she would be there. That autumn there had been many times when he wanted to call her, but he never had. He didn't know what he wanted to say to her. He got out of the car. The blustery weather seemed to have followed him from Skåne. Autumn leaves clung damply to the ground. The building looked deserted. He walked around the back to the room where he had slept on his return from Bärnsö. It had been only a few months ago but it already felt unreal.

The sight of the deserted building made him feel uneasy. He returned to his car and continued his journey. In Valdemarsvik he stopped and bought a bottle of whisky, then had a cup of coffee and some sandwiches in a café. He told them not to butter the bread.

It was 5 p.m. and already dark when he started down the winding road along the Valdemarsvik bay towards Gryt and Fyrudden. Lennart Westin had called him out of the blue one afternoon at the beginning of September, after the Larstam case had ended. Wallander had been interviewing a young man who had assaulted his father. It was slow going and Wallander wasn't getting anywhere with him. Finally he gave up and handed the matter over to Hansson.

When he got back to his office, the phone rang. It was Westin. He asked him when Wallander was planning to come to see him. Wallander had forgotten all about the standing invitation and an earlier phone call when he had actually agreed to visit, thinking nothing would ever come of it. They decided on a date in October, Westin had called him a few weeks later to confirm it, and now here he was on his way.

They agreed to meet in Fyrudden at 6 p.m. Westin would pick him up in his boat. Wallander was going to stay until Sunday. Wallander was grateful for the invitation, of course, but it also made him nervous. He almost never socialised with people he didn't know. The autumn had been marred by health concerns. He constantly worried about having a stroke, although Dr Göransson tried to reassure him. His blood-sugar levels had stabilised and he was losing weight and had adopted a healthy diet. But Wallander felt it was already too late. Although he hadn't even turned 50 yet, he felt like he was living on borrowed time.

When he swung down towards Fyrudden harbour it was raining harder than before. He parked the car in the same spot he had used that summer, turned off the engine and heard the waves smack against the pier. Shortly before 6 p.m. he saw the lights from an approaching boat. It was Westin.

Wallander got out of his car, grabbed his bag, and headed over. Westin popped his head out of the wheelhouse. He smiled.

"Welcome!" Westin yelled, trying to make himself heard above the wind. "I'm taking you back right away. Dinner's ready."

He took Wallander's bag while Wallander climbed aboard unsteadily. He was freezing. It was rapidly getting much colder.

"So you finally made it up here," Westin said when Wallander entered the wheelhouse.

At that moment Wallander no longer felt hesitant. He was glad to be there. Westin swung the boat around and Wallander grabbed at the side to keep his balance. When they made their way out of the harbour, he felt the hold of the waves on the boat getting stronger.

"Do you get seasick or nervous in this kind of weather?" Westin asked.

He asked the question in a light-hearted manner but there was real concern in his voice.

"Probably," Wallander said.

Westin increased his speed and they sped out onto open water. Wallander suddenly realised he was enjoying himself. No one knew where he was, no one could reach him. For the first time in a long while, he could relax.